ARKHAM HORROR

It is the height of the Roaring Twenties – a fresh enthusiasm for the arts, science, and exploration of the past have opened doors to a wider world, and beyond...

And yet, in the shadows there are other powers at work. Mysterious members of a secret society known as the Red Coterie pursue objects of unearthly power across the world. Their motivations are uncertain, but the potential of their collection is colossal.

Against them stands the Foundation, a shadowy government agency with its own agenda, and a detective determined to uncover the truth.

But one single fact unites them: there are inhuman entities lurking in the emptiness beyond space and time, threatening to tear this world apart.

And secrets wrapped in scarlet may be our only hope of salvation.

ALSO AVAILABLE IN ARKHAM HORROR

ARKHAM HORROR™

SECRETS
in SCARLET

EDITED BY
CHARLOTTE LLEWELYN-WELLS

ACONYTE

First published by Aconyte Books in 2022

ISBN 978 1 83908 182 8

Ebook ISBN 978 1 83908 183 5

Cover art by Daniel Strange

Distributed in North America by Simon & Schuster Inc, New York, USA

Printed in the United States of America

9 8 7 6 5 4 3 2 1

ACONYTE BOOKS

An imprint of Asmodee Entertainment Ltd

Mercury House, Shipstones Business Centre

North Gate, Nottingham NG7 7FN, UK

aconytebooks.com // twitter.com/aconytebooks

CONTENTS

CONTENTS

THE MAN IN THE BUBBLE
David Annandale

"This is what a headache looks like."

Commissioner Qiana Taylor glared at the wreckage as her chauffeur maneuvered the black Rolls Royce through the devastation in the Chelsea warehouse district of Manhattan. Most of the block of West 19th Street between 10th and 11th Avenues was a disaster area. Building facades had been stripped away, gone as if taken by a wind sent by Hell itself. Floors had collapsed, spilling shattered timber and brickwork into the street. Cars lay crushed beneath rubble. Others, overturned and on their sides, rested like scattered leaves. A ruptured hydrant gushed water onto the pavement. Sunset bathed the ruins in red.

"A gas explosion story should stick, don't you think, commissioner?" Archibald Hudson asked. He rode in the back with Taylor, while her other field aide, Valeria Antonova, sat beside the chauffeur. The clean-shaven

Hudson had the creases of his suit sharp enough to draw blood. Antonova was tall, athletic, and coldly pale. The two agents worked as a synchronized unit, and they had sharply honed instincts for anticipating Taylor's orders before she gave them.

"If I didn't know better, I'd believe a gas explosion," Antonova put in.

"The story had better stick," Taylor said, still studying the blast zone. "The alternatives are too messy."

A bomb narrative would be almost as bad as the truth, whatever that turned out to be. Gas or bomb, either carried the price of the outraged public and the screaming headlines, but that much was a given anyway. No event this big could be swept out of sight in an instant. Investigations would happen, and fingers would point. A scapegoat would have to be found. The difference was a bomb story would linger in the public's mind. It would generate fear and unrest. It would refuse to go away. A gas explosion, on the other hand, could be replaced by the scandal of the day in fairly short order. The Foundation could ensure that it receded from the front pages, sinking into the procedural, political, administrative and bureaucratic quicksand that came, as surely as inertia, sooner or later to all matters of public urgency.

"There's a problem, though," said Taylor. "Can't you see it?"

Antonova did first. "Damn," she said. "No fires."

19th Street should have been choked with smoke. Nothing burned, nothing guttered. The blast had been as antiseptic as it had been destructive. Try as she might,

Taylor could not spot so much as a single scorched brick.

"Huh," Hudson said uneasily. "If not a gas explosion, then what do we use?"

"We go with the gas," Taylor said. "Until it doesn't work. It's the simplest explanation, and the one most people will think of first when they hear there's been an explosion. If we're lucky, the absence of fire will be ignored." The mind had a way of dismissing inconsistencies if they were too big and got in the way of what seemed normal. "We may have to see to it that there's a second explosion. One that has no unusual features."

Hudson nodded. "We'll watch for some promising gas mains."

The Rolls pulled up near the collapsed warehouse that marked the center of the blast. The police had cordoned off the area, and the firetrucks were in attendance, looking a bit forlorn in the absence of conflagration. Taylor put on her wide-brimmed hat and got out of the car. Flanked by her aides, she marched up to the barricade.

A police officer held up a hand as they approached. He looked a little unsure of himself, to be confronted by three people in identical black suits. Perhaps he sensed his authority was about to be put in its place. He wasn't going to let it go down without a fight, though.

"Sorry," he said. "No admittance."

"Stand aside, officer." Taylor flashed her badge, just long enough for it to register, not long enough for the officer to read it. "This scene is under my jurisdiction."

The officer's florid cheeks flushed a deeper red. It seemed he was not a man used to the fact, or even the concept, of being given orders by a Black woman. "Now just a minute…" he began.

"You will stand aside," Taylor said, her voice a whip that could crack stone. "Immediately."

The officer's partner stepped away smartly, wincing as if stung. The other man held his ground, anchoring himself with fury and humiliation. "The area isn't safe." He addressed Antonova, and then Hudson. "The investigation isn't complete."

The aides said nothing. Their faces, expressionless, turned as one to defer to Taylor.

"The area is not safe," Taylor agreed. "The investigation *is* ongoing. It is being conducted by *my* people. *You* and the Fire Department must wait for *my* OK to venture into the blast site. Is that clear enough?"

Cheeks shading into a deep violet, the officer slunk away.

Taylor marched past the barricade and through the rubble to the pit. About fifteen feet wide, it plunged diagonally into the ground, the slope steep but not too steep to be walked. One end of a rope had been tied around one of the warehouse posts that still stood, sheared in half. The rope's length disappeared into the darkness.

Lacey Osborne, the first of the Foundation's agents to have been on the scene, detached herself from a cluster of resentful firefighters she had been talking to and walked over to Taylor.

"Commissioner," she said. "Thank you for coming. I felt sure you would want to see this."

"By 'this', I take it you mean what's at the bottom of that shaft."

Osborne nodded.

"How much longer do you think we can keep the Fire Department at bay?" Taylor asked.

"They're growing restless," said Osborne. "I'm going to run out of convincing excuses soon."

Taylor thought the strategy through. She needed enough time for herself and her team to see what they needed to see, but without stretching things out so long that the fact of another investigating agency taking priority over Police and Fire became a story in itself. A combination of authorities had kept reporters away from West 19th altogether, but that wouldn't last much longer.

No perfect solutions. There never were. As ever, time to get the job done with what she had.

"Wait here," she said to Osborne and the aides. She strode over to the firefighters, flashed her badge again, and said, "One hour. Then, if it's safe, you can go down."

A man goggled at her. "If it's safe, *we* can go down?"

"Correct. Thank you for your cooperation." She turned on her heel and left them to their stunned objections.

Taylor took hold of the rope with one hand, a proffered flashlight with the other, and started down the slope behind her agent. Hudson and Antonova brought up the rear, each with their own torches.

Taylor played her beam around the walls of the shaft as they went descended. They were smooth as glass. Foundations, sewers and bedrock had all been cut away by a perfectly uniform, irresistible force. Taylor pictured it shooting up through the earth, compressed energy, and then exploding out in the sudden freedom of the air.

"What could have done this?" Antonova wondered.

"Whatever it was," said Taylor, "we're lucky it wasn't any stronger." She had a vision of the entire district vaporized, or all of Manhattan. What *had* happened here? And why? What was to blame?

No, not *what*, but *who*. In Taylor's experience, there was always a *who* to blame for a disaster like this.

Somebody had played with something they should have left alone.

She had no evidence to back up her gut feeling yet. Just years of hard experience.

The shaft continued straight down, heading west, for what Taylor judged to be at least half a mile. She had to hold tight to the rope to stay upright. They had to be a thousand feet or more beneath the surface when the shaft ended, opening up into a cavern hundreds of yards wide and high. Three other Foundation agents were here. They had set up a portable Kohler generator to power some lamps. They helped, but much of the scene still receded into an ancient, brooding gloom.

Taylor looked up at the structure that took up most of the space of the chamber. "We're going to need that second explosion," she said. There was no way she was going to allow any firefighter or police officer down here to see this.

She was standing at the base of a temple. Constructed from huge slabs of green-tinged black stone, its lower half rose in the shape of an octagonal pyramid. The top half formed a smooth dome, and its dark opening gave it the look of a skull emerging from the pyramid. A serpentine path wound up the near face of the temple to the gaping maw of the skull.

Taylor had seen a lot in her time with the Foundation. She had seen structures on this scale before, carved by inhuman hands. Seen enough of them that she had mastered the ability to conceal her emotions, to lock the fear away and get the job done. But the awe and the terror were always there, her blood always chilled by the vision of something tearing through the fragile, illusory veil of normality. Taylor was glad of this. It meant she was human. It meant she never forgot the danger.

"It doesn't look damaged," said Hudson.

"No, it doesn't," Osborne agreed.

They both did well in keeping their tones matter-of-fact, their terror on a tight leash. Taylor could barely detect the tremor in their voices. They knew their duty, and would follow it.

"It seems to be the origin of the blast, though," Osborne went on. "As if a focused beam of energy shot up from it."

It lashed out, Taylor thought. "Have you been up to the entrance yet?" she asked the other agents.

"We were just about ready to," said one. "We've checked all around the base, and it *seems* safe enough." He shrugged.

"Yes," said Taylor. "As safe as anything like this can be, you mean."

The man nodded.

"Let's go," Taylor said, and she started up.

She went carefully. The footing was slick. The stone oozed, like suppurating flesh, the substance grey, thick as petroleum jelly, and slippery. As the path wound up, Taylor felt as if she were making her way not towards the heart of some mystery, but towards its fangs. It would not do to go any further than was absolutely necessary.

At the top of the path, she said, "We aren't the first to come here." She aimed her light on three bodies lying at the temple's threshold. A cold wind blew from the darkness within. It wrapped around Taylor's exposed flesh with an insinuating whisper.

While the others held their beams on the corpses, Hudson and Osborne examined the dead. The force from the temple had killed them as it had cut through rock and concrete, shearing away half a head, a torso, arms at the elbows.

"Mid-twenties, at a guess," said Hudson. "Dressed for hiking, but nothing expensive."

"We need to know how they came to be here," Taylor said.

"Dumb luck?" Antonova ventured, sounding unconvinced.

"They went exploring in the sewers and stumbled upon this?" said Taylor. "A temple no one has seen before?"

"And that the Foundation has never heard of," Osborne added.

"Not necessarily," said Taylor. "We might have some hint of it, but one that we will only recognize with subsequent research." The Foundation's archives were extensive, and growing larger all the time. They were too huge for any one person to know fully, but this temple, in this location, would be something Taylor would have heard of, if there had been anything definite in the records. No, the temple would be a new entry in the vast catalogue of darkness.

Hudson was going through the backpacks that lay near the bodies. He unfolded a sheet of paper. "There's a map," he said, holding it up to the light.

Taylor looked at the diagram, drawn in pen, by someone with some drafting skills. "They were sent," she said grimly.

"Couldn't the map have been done by one of them?" Antonova asked.

"That's stationery," said Taylor. "Look at the address." Incredible, she thought. The map had been drawn with no concern for secrecy. Its creator had to be stupid, arrogant, or both.

"This is near the Flatiron," said Antonova, examining the letterhead. "Oh. The Davenport Tower."

"Ryan Davenport," said Taylor. It took some effort to hold back a growl of anger and frustration. Davenport had been hovering at the edge of the Foundation's attention for years. Always a person of interest, never quite interesting enough to be a concern. An acquisitive but indiscriminate collector of all things occult. He bought a lot, but hadn't seemed to do so with any real knowledge or agenda.

We were wrong, Taylor thought. She wondered if his wealth and political connections had played more of a role than she had thought in making him seem not worth doing anything about. If so, she was going to correct that past mistake.

Hudson dug up a battered notebook from deeper in

the knapsack. He flipped through the pages, then stopped dead. He stood up from his crouch and brought the book over to show Taylor what he had found.

The drawing was a crude attempt at capturing the essence of the relic's shape. Someone had tried to draw a triangle, then extend into a third dimension to form a complex knot. The effort looked like a nonsensical scribble, unless one had seen a more detailed, assured representation of the object. Taylor had. "The Coronal Prism", she said. One of the infernal Coterie's accursed Keys.

"Maybe they didn't find it," said Osborne. "Maybe they triggered a ward and it's still here."

"I would like that *maybe* to be true," said Taylor. "But I count four knapsacks and only three bodies."

"Could the fourth be inside?" Osborne asked.

"Possibly. But I think it's unlikely." She pointed at the bodies. "Look how they fell. They were on their way *out* of the temple, not in. I believe the blast was a response to the removal of the Prism. We have to assume it's gone, and we're almost out of time." She turned to Antonova. "Did you see anything we can use for another explosion?"

Antonova nodded. "About a hundred feet in from the shaft entrance. I saw the side of some piping, exposed but intact. Should do the trick."

"Good." Taylor started back down the side of the temple. "I want this sealed away until we have the time to examine it properly. Blow up the tunnel, then the police and fire departments can do whatever they like on the surface."

"And Davenport?" Hudson asked.

"Leave him to me."

The draft from the temple became more insistent, more probing. Searching for something that had been taken.

The Foundation had private facilities behind a nondescript door in the basement of the New York Public Library. The amenities were basic, just a couple of offices, empty except for furniture unless an operative needed to do some research there. Then, the Foundation had access to the entire holdings of the library, many uncatalogued as far as the public was concerned. Specific Foundation files would also be delivered to the offices as required.

Taylor required the complete dossier on Ryan Davenport. She spent the morning after the blast learning all she could about her foe. She had to look at him that way. He had, she was sure, the Coronal Prism. Possession made him the enemy, regardless of his intentions.

If Taylor could find any clues to what those intentions actually were, that would serve her well.

The dossier didn't point in any specific direction. Davenport collected occult objects, and did so very publicly. Sellers of every persuasion knew they had a ready market in him, whether their goods were genuine or not. Until now, the information about Davenport implied an enthusiastic dilettante, one with too much money and no discernment at all. His indiscriminate purchasing, often of certainly fake items at inflated prices, had been why he had not registered as a threat. He did not appear to know what he was doing.

Except he did, Taylor now saw. Knowledge about the Coronal Prism and its potential location did not fall into the lap of an amateur. The Foundation had been searching for that Key, and coming up against one dead end after another. The problem, Taylor now saw, was the same as it had so often been. Errors of interpretation around relevant clues, misplaced focus on irrelevant ones... It all came down to being able to see the right thing at the right time and knowing what to do about it. Davenport had succeeded in all three ways, and beaten the Foundation to the prize.

Did he know what he had? At some level, he must. But fully? she wondered. If Davenport really knew what he had, then would he risk owning it?

Maybe he didn't know. If not, that might give her some leverage. She wanted to secure the Prism with a minimum of conflict. How difficult things would become was up to Davenport.

In the early afternoon, the Rolls deposited her outside the Davenport Tower. She passed under the gothic arch over the main entrance, and into a lobby where more neo-gothic decor reigned. Gargoyles looked down from the vaulted ceiling to the gold-inlaid marble floor. The iron grille in front of the elevator looked more medieval than functional, and the operator's livery was worthy of a palace. Taylor noted the zodiac symbols embroidered in silver on the man's vest. Davenport's obsessions extended to every aspect of his little empire, then. The man believed in his right of absolute control. Not an encouraging sign, but also not unexpected.

Davenport's private offices were on the 20th floor. Taylor crossed the expanse of a huge reception area. The ceilings here were as high as in the downstairs lobby. The receptionist's desk, big as an ocean liner, blocked the way to high bronze doors. A lot of effort had gone into making the space one that would impress and intimidate.

The effort was wasted on Taylor. She saw the handiwork of a man who believed in himself too much or not enough. Both, she thought. The two flaws so often came together.

The receptionist, a young woman with a glare icier than her blonde hair, looked up at Taylor when she reached the desk. "May I help you?" the woman said, with the clear certainty that she would not.

"Commissioner Qiana Taylor to see Ryan Davenport." When the receptionist began to run a manicured finger down a column of the open book in front of her, Taylor said, "No, I do not have an appointment. What I have is the authority to see Mr Davenport. Now."

The receptionist's eyes twitched with a slight flutter of unease, but she maintained her pose of merciless decorum. "I'm sorry. Mr Davenport is unavailable."

Taylor lowered her head, so the shadow of her hat's brim fell over her face. "He would be well advised to make himself available."

Another twitch of an eyelid. "He is not available because he is not here."

"Then I'll wait."

This time, the receptionist's lower lip trembled. The thought of spending an indefinite period in Taylor's company clearly troubled her almost as much as Davenport's anger. "He really isn't here," the woman pleaded.

Taylor thought through her next step. She had no intention of waiting. That would be playing into

Davenport's hands, handing the power in this situation over to him, assuming he was in his office. Always the chance the receptionist was telling the truth.

Taylor could just walk past the receptionist and through the doors. But no, too public a display for the Foundation, and the exposure at the scene of the blast had already been excessive.

"Tell Mr Davenport he should expect to hear from me very soon," she said. "And tell him that nine tenths of the law are meaningless in his case."

Gabled, turreted, gaudy as a cardinal and ostentatiously brooding, Davenport's mansion dominated the 58th Street block of 5th Avenue. Its chimneys bracketed the full moon when Taylor looked up at the night sky. The moonglow fell on a skylight, turning the glass into a baleful eye. Another glow, from what had to be many large candles, wavered on the other side of the skylight.

Very forbidding. Very esoteric. Taylor imagined Davenport would be pleased by the first impression his home made.

She stood on the sidewalk before the porch with Hudson and Antonova. "Everything ready?" she asked Antonova.

"Yes, commissioner."

"Good. I'll speak with him alone first. If he has any sense, he'll make this easy, and that will be better for everyone."

One way or another, she would be leaving with the Coronal Prism in her custody. She couldn't let any more time go by. Even the few hours since her visit to his tower were a risk. The air felt taut, apprehensive. Beyond the glow of the streetlights, the shadows grew thick, dense with hidden muscle.

From the look on the face of the butler who answered Taylor's knock, the receptionist had passed on her message. The man looked like he might have been a boxer in a previous life, and his memories of that life were still fresh.

"Mr Davenport is not receiving," the butler said. He had learned formality and enunciation, but they were a thin veneer over the accent of the streets.

"You'll find that he is," said Taylor.

Hudson and Antonova stepped around her. They each took hold of the butler's arms. His eyes widened, the confidence born of his old skills draining away in the power of their grip.

"Wait for my signal," Taylor said.

She entered the house and made straight for the wide staircase leading up from the main hall. She didn't have to guess where Davenport might be. As soon as she had seen that skylight, and the flickering of candles beneath the moonglow, she had known where she would find him. Nowhere else would be suitable for him to gloat over his prize.

Taylor hurried to the top floor, and down a long corridor. She had always been a quick study when it came to a building's geography. There had been times when that skill had saved her life, and that had been in structures whose architecture defied the human sense of geometry. Locating Davenport's special retreat based on a quick scan of the exterior was child's play.

Taylor opened the middle door of the corridor and

stepped into a tasteless millionaire's conception of an alchemist's study. Symbols from a hundred different belief systems covered the black walls. The juxtaposition of the symbols made nonsense of them all. The arrangements were an open invitation to disaster.

He didn't know what he was doing after all.

Shelves groaned with ancient books and display cases. Taylor saw shrunken heads, saints' bones, ebony crucifixes, Elder signs of gold and iron, jewels forged from sculpted blood. Davenport had surrounded himself with a treasure trove of the precious and the deadly.

The man himself sat perched on his desk, turning the Coronal Prism over and over in his hands. The relic was as the doodle in the notebook had tried to suggest – a prism stretched out and then twisted into an unfathomably complex knot. Its texture made Taylor think of worms. Colors chased each other over its surface. Only a few of them had names.

Davenport had a high forehead, black, wavy hair, pockmarked cheeks and wide, self-satisfied lips. When he saw Taylor, he froze for a moment, then recovered his composure. "I think you're in the wrong house," he said. He spoke calmly, as befitted someone who had spent his life having people jump at his commands. He had inherited his father's railway line and wealth. He had expanded both, which would have been hard not to do given the ever-growing hunger of the nation's industry. He had thus acquired an unearned reputation as a genius. His cultivated image of eccentricity, though, was more than deserved.

"I'm where I need to be," Taylor said. "Let's not pretend

you don't know who I am. Give me the Prism and I'll be on my way."

"Why would I do that?"

"Because you don't have a choice. And because it's in your interest to do so."

Davenport shook his head. "You're right. I received your message, and I know who you are."

I doubt that, Taylor thought. He knew a name, and that was all.

"The thing is," Davenport continued, "I don't think you know who *I* am. You wouldn't dream of coming here, if you did."

"I know exactly who and what you are."

"Then you should go before I decide to make your life more miserable than I already will."

"You have a lot of money," said Taylor. "That means you also have a lot of political connections. You own a lot of powerful people in this city. I know who they are. That means things could be a bit stickier after I've dealt with you than I would find convenient. But that's all, and I can deal with inconvenience. As a courtesy, I'm giving you the chance to turn the Coronal Prism over, and I'm offering you the promise of protection."

"Protection?" Davenport sounded genuinely surprised.

He can't be that stupid. "Are you telling me that you can't feel it?" Just in the few minutes Taylor had been in the house, the tension in the air had grown. Something approached, drawing very close.

"If you think I need protection," Davenport said, "then you really are misled. I have all the protection I need."

Did he mean political protection? Or did he believe his nonsense agglomeration of symbols would save him from the consequences of his actions?

"You have no idea how wrong you are," said Taylor. She shifted tack. There were things she needed to know to get a sense of how much damage Davenport had caused, and that she would have to clean up. "Will you tell me how you found the Prism? We've never been able to get a good lead on it."

The appeal to his vanity worked. Davenport gave her a smug grin. "I cast my net very wide. I know a lot of what I collect is worthless. But that's the point. If people know you'll buy anything at all and pay well, they have an incentive to find and sell things to you. I got some books from an estate sale in Arkham. Manuscripts by a visionary poet. Except that her family thought she was delusional. They kept her locked away in the house, and buried her writings in the attic for a few generations. She knew about the Prism. It spoke to her in dreams." He looked down at the Key in his hands as if it were a materialized dream.

"And you sent a group of young people to do the hard part for you."

Davenport shrugged. "I paid them well. They were happy to do it. This was the kind of thing they lived for."

"They died for your collection."

"They knew there was risk. And not all of them." He spoke with the calm, untroubled tone of a man pointing out an accounting error. The deaths of his employees meant nothing to him at all.

"Of course," said Taylor. "The one who brought you the Prism."

"Right." Davenport frowned, irritated. "He was supposed to come by with some pictures of the temple today, after he developed them."

There we go. Taylor had the information she wanted. "And he hasn't responded to the telephone."

"No."

"Where does he live?" Taylor asked. Davenport gave her an address on the Lower East Side. She made a mental note of it. She would send some agents to investigate, but she knew they would be there far too late to do anything other than make a record of what had happened, and to make sure what remained would make sense to the police when they were finally drawn in.

"You realize he's dead," said Taylor. As she spoke, she noticed how tense her shoulders had become. The air crackled faintly when she breathed. The shifting colors of the Coronal Prism grew brighter. There wasn't much time left.

Davenport gave no sign of being aware that the atmosphere in his house was changing. "Why would he be dead?" he asked.

"Because the force that guards the Prism is tracking its thieves. It found him first, and now it is coming for you. I felt it stir at the temple, in the wake of the destruction caused by your useful idiots. It's almost here. Can't you sense it?"

Davenport looked at her as if she were speaking Latin. "What are you talking about?"

She saw him clearly now. She fully understood what he was, a man so completely insulated by his spheres of privilege that the idea that he could be under threat, from anyone or anything, was incomprehensible.

She tried one more time. "The Coronal Prism is dangerous," she said. "My organization has the means to keep it, and those who have come into contact with it, hidden from the hunter. Give me the Prism, and come with me, and we'll see to it that you're safe."

"You must think I'm stupid."

Taylor sighed. "As it happens, I do. So, you won't do as I ask?"

"Of course I won't."

"Then I'll leave you to the consequences of your decision."

She turned on her heel and walked out of the study. She'd left things as long as she dared. A faint hum, like the beating of a thousand moth wings, vibrated through the mansion.

Taylor looked down to the hall, to where Osborne and three other agents waited. Unlike at the temple, this time they wore sidearms. They had come prepared to deal with human opposition. "Do it," said Taylor.

The agents moved in, and they moved in fast. They felt the same urgency Taylor did, and they knew that the moment they seized the Coronal Prism, the hunter would be on their trail. They wore amulets that would provide them with some protection, and conceal the scent of their souls from the hunter long enough to get the Key to a Foundation vault.

Even so, it would not do to tarry.

Davenport started yelling when they entered the study. His threats of ruin and retribution followed Taylor as she made her way down the stairs.

The thrum and rustle of moth wings grew louder. At the point where the hall's chandelier met the ceiling, the plaster twisted back and forth like a bedsheet.

Taylor paused, eyeing the distortion. The chandelier began to swing. She cursed herself for having granted Davenport so much time.

She waited for her team, and they came pounding down the stairs a few moments later. Osborne and another agent carried a case between them, lead, and marked with an Elder sign.

Taylor stepped aside to let them pass, then hurried after them. The thrum of the wings grew deeper, louder, and a snarling moan reverberated up from the foundations. As Taylor reached the main hall, a tremor shook the mansion, and the chandelier crashed to the floor behind her. The ceiling ripped open, and she tore her eyes away before she glimpsed worse than a vortex of teeth and wings.

Davenport screamed. There were terrible layers of disbelief in his terror. As if he did not believe this could not be happening. Not to him.

Shortly after Taylor reached the street, and retreated across the way with her team, the screams became mindless. Then the mansion trembled hard, and began to collapse in on itself. Her skin prickling from the close brush with the hunter, Taylor made herself watch the destruction to the end, and worked just as hard not to imagine what was going on inside. There were so many things that her line of work forced her to know. She took the mercy of ignorance where she could find it.

"Another gas main?" Antonova asked, her voice strained.

"Yes," said Taylor. "And let's get some fire burning in there as soon as possible."

It helped to keep her mind on practical steps. That kept the thoughts of whirring darkness at bay.

CITY OF WAKING DREAMS
Davide Mana

I. China Steamer

True to its name, the Bell Buoy chimed, swaying idly on the river, and the engines slowed. Inspector Li Flint tapped his pipe on the balustrade, cleaning the bowl. The metal rang in response to the buoy bell, and ashes fell in the yellow water below, a spray of dying embers. A small motorboat approached the ship. A gangway was lowered, and the harbor pilot came on board, greeted briefly by an officer. They exchanged papers, and hastened to the wheelhouse. The iron and kerosene of the Blue Funnel Line steamship kept the marshy smell of the Huangpu River back, just as the churning noise of the engines seemed to drown any other sound.

Li Flint took off his glasses and massaged the bridge of his nose. In the misty light of the early afternoon, the buildings of the approaching Bund looked like ivory chess pieces, aligned along the edge of the board, waiting for the game to begin. The tall green pyramid of the Sassoon House roof was the queen's crown. Jardine Matheson House and the Russo-Chinese Bank were squat rooks protecting her flanks, and the slender Signal Tower at the north end of the Bund was the lean spear of a knight's jousting lance.

Inspector Li Flint had always thought of the city as a vast jungle of chessboards, over which multiple games were being played at the same time, by unseen players. Flint was reasonably good at chess. The game suited his personality. He cherished the planning ahead of the moves, the way in which the game expanded like a firework from a single point in the opening, how the possibilities multiplied with each move through the chaos of the midgame and then, as the endgame approached, everything inescapably collapsed back to a single point in the checkmate. Life, he sometimes mused, worked the same way.

Approaching the wharf, the steamer passed the line of barges anchored off the Bund. Mercantile pawns to the Bund's merchant chessmen, each one showed its three-digit identification number painted on the hull. The steamer passed a solitary boat, an old man standing at the poop, pushing on the single oar, his passenger a silhouette in a fedora under the domed canopy. A comprador, Li Flint thought, on his way back from an inspection of the wares awaiting delivery. Crossing the steamer's wake, the boat rocked dangerously. The old man at the back did not seem to mind, his rhythm unbroken. His passenger braced himself.

Li Flint's fellow passengers crowded the deck. Wealthy businessmen in Western suits, soldiers strutting like peacocks, a governess trying to herd a band of children. Calling their names, she pointed in wonder at the buildings, at the crowd milling along the Bund, the cars, the single-wheeled pushcarts, the rickshaws. The children were unimpressed and continued with their game of tag.

The International Settlement loomed larger as they approached their mooring. The Paris of the East, Gateway to China, the City of Never Night. Shanghai.

They filed down the gangplank.

The French officer at the customs desk took a perfunctory look at Li Flint's ICPC papers and waved him through with a nod of greeting. No routine questions. No need to check Flint's suitcase. The Kuomintang man at his side did not look pleased, but did not raise a fuss. Flint knew the type, and the man had many more people to harass. Some of the passengers in the customs line grumbled as he went through ahead of them, but Flint did not care.

Outside the customs house, the city was suspended in the twilight hours between business and leisure. Offices would soon close, and the commercial traffic was thinning. In an hour or two, the clubs and nightspots would fire up their neons, and the early birds of the Shanghai nightlife would take to the streets. Defiant of the traffic, Li Flint crossed the street, running a gauntlet with the speeding lorries, the drivers eager to end the last run of the day, and the cars with their honking horns. He joined the crowd of Chinese and Westerners on the busy pavement. He walked briskly, moving against the flow of pedestrians, while discreetly he scanned the crowd on the opposite side of the street. Men in black jackets, women in colorful silk dresses. Not the best place in the world to tail someone, Shanghai. Not the best place to spot a tail either.

In front of the brass lions of the Hong Kong & Shanghai Bank, two young women in rich red silk qipao came out of a taxi, adjusting their short golden capes, early for some teatime appointment. Flint caught the eye of the driver and got in after them, the passenger seats still smelling of tobacco and gardenias. The women looked at him as he pushed past them, sliding his suitcase on the floor of the cab. One said something in a low voice, the other laughed.

"One-eight-five, Foochow Road," he said.

The cabby gave him a look through the mirror. Flint looked back at him, then checked his watch. The taxi left the curbside. With a final look through the window, Li Flint sighed, and leaned against the back of the seat.

While officially assigned to Shanghai, the ICPC force was stretched so thin that Li Flint had spent most of his time abroad. Yet it was good being back home. He wondered briefly at what changes he would find.

II. London Planes

Two Sikhs in red turbans stood guard outside the gates of the Central Police Station in Foochow Road. Flint handed a silver Mexican dollar to the cabby, the metal cold in his fingers. The republican government was trying to drop the silver standard, but "Mexes" were still the preferred currency in China.

He walked in. A bewhiskered sergeant sat behind the reception desk, like a relic from the Victorian era. Flint showed his papers and was asked to wait. The sergeant spoke into a telephone. A tall man with ginger hair appeared a few minutes later.

"Inspector Li Flint? Superintendent Thrubshawe."

They shook hands, and then Thrubshawe led him through the maze of corridors and staircases, up to the third floor and a small office that smelled of tobacco and dust. Along the way, the superintendent made very British small talk about the weather and the busy roads, but he was all business as he sat behind his desk. "So, what can the Shanghai Municipal Police do for the International Criminal Police Commission?"

"We are looking for a woman," Flint said.

He had an envelope. In the envelope was a photograph. He placed the photo on the desk in front of the superintendent.

Thrubshawe studied it for a moment, turned it around looking for some note or detail, then looked up.

"Is this all you have?" he asked, his tone doubtful.

Flint nodded.

"Who is she? Why are you interested in her?"

"She is involved in a contraband ring. Stolen art exchanged for opium. We are conducting an international operation."

Not exactly true, but Flint knew his story sounded plausible. Thrubshawe nodded. "And you don't have a name?"

"Only a nickname, the Lady with the Red Parasol."

"Picturesque," the superintendent snorted, and handed back the photo. "No other details? About her associates, her base of operations?"

"Only that she is based in Shanghai."

"Just like three million other people. It's not like we can stop every woman with a parasol on the city streets."

"I was hoping your records might provide a lead." No need to lie about it. Accessing the police files would make his work easier. Faster.

Thrubshawe frowned. He picked up a pen.

"I can look into it," he said, "but it's a pretty weak lead." He scrawled a few words on a notepad. "Red Parasol. Art. Opium. Anything else?"

"She is probably moving in upper-class circles," Flint said.

Thrubshawe looked up from his notes. "Powerful friends?"

Flint nodded. The superintendent scrawled some more notes.

"Where are you staying?"

"I've yet to find a room."

"I can suggest a good hotel…"

"I have heard good things about the Sichuan Road establishment."

Thrubshawe frowned. "The YMCA?"

Flint nodded.

"I was expecting something more… glamorous, from the ICPC."

Flint shrugged. "I am afraid we currently don't have the budget for glamor."

The superintendent tapped his notebook with his pen. "I will get in touch at the YMCA as soon as something emerges from the archives."

"Thank you." Flint pushed back the photo. "You might need this."

Thrubshawe shook his head as he picked up the photo again. "It won't be easy."

"Is it ever?"

The YMCA on Sichuan Road greeted him with the rubbing alcohol smell of a gym and a young man in shirtsleeves, doing a crossword at the front desk. Li Flint got himself a room on the second floor. "There is a bathroom at the end of the corridor," the crossword man told him as he handed Flint the key.

Flint thanked him with a nod. He picked up his suitcase and ascended the stairs.

The room was small but reasonably clean, containing a single bed with an iron frame and a small bedside table. A niche in the wall served as a wardrobe, a wooden chair sat in a corner by the window. Flint pulled up the blind and opened the window to the sound and smell of the evening traffic. The place would do until he found a more permanent address, and possibly a second place as an off-the-record safe house.

A typed sheet thumb-tacked to the door gave the times of the laundry service, and the time of the religious services in the small adjacent chapel. Clean shirts and a clean conscience.

The single drawer in the nightstand contained a pristine copy of the Holy Bible, a folded map of the city, courtesy of the Shanghai Chamber of Commerce, and a bunch of blank postcards. A blunt pencil rolled against the side of the drawer when Flint pulled it open.

Flint checked his watch again, then he put his jacket on

a hanger in the niche. He ran his thumb under the strap of his shoulder holster, before deciding to keep the thing on.

He opened his suitcase, and took out the thin manila folder in the side pocket. He sat on the bed, and opened the folder.

Commissioner Taylor expected full collaboration, but she was decidedly tight-fisted when it came to sharing information. For the thousandth time since he had sort of joined Taylor's somewhat sketchy Foundation, Li Flint went through the frustratingly brief file on "Subject 46-Q".

The Lady with the Red Parasol.

She was in some way connected with the rest of the intricate skein in which Flint had been entangled since his partner had disappeared in London. A game of chess, in which reality itself seemed to shift and rearrange to the whims of some unseen, unknown players.

He suppressed a shudder, the room feeling suddenly cold.

The Lady with the Red Parasol was one of the players.

Average height, black hair, pale complexion. There were hints at connections with well-to-do patrons, but it was all pretty vague, and she was extremely elusive. Also, she was looking for something, maneuvering to acquire some kind of artifact.

And that's where Commissioner Taylor and her Foundation came into play. Where Flint came into play. The Lady was to be stopped. The artifact retrieved.

Easier said than done.

Li Flint snorted, and reached for his magnifying lens. Time to do the Sherlock Holmes thing. He had a single photo, a copy of which he had left with Thrubshawe. A grainy snapshot of a crowded Shanghai street. The Lady with the Red Parasol was standing among a bunch of other people, mostly Chinese. A man was carrying a bundle or a box on his shoulder, tied with a piece of string. Waiting to cross a road, probably. An old woman stared into the lens with faraway eyes. Behind her, the Lady's face was a blurry oval. Featureless like an egg. There was a hint of a high collar, a pale, straight-shouldered qipao dress. And a parasol, with a dragon motif. Red, he guessed, like a halo behind the nondescript face.

The shadows suggested the photo had been taken close to noon. Dismissing the sketchy faces of the bystanders, he moved to the background. Pulled the lens back, enlarging further the image. Trees.

Not a plate with an address, or a taxi-cab's registration number. Not a man with a billboard or a kid selling newspapers. Only trees, two neat rows of what looked like well-groomed plane trees. Common plane trees, also known as London planes.

Really not much to go on with. But everybody knew in Shanghai that tree, "le platane commun", meant the French Concession.

Time to go for a walk.

III. French Concession

One week of legwork and discreet inquiries led nowhere. The crowded streets of the French Concession were deserted of information, empty of sympathy. The Lady with the Red Parasol was like a ghost haunting Shanghai, one shrouded in silence, reticence and fear. People denied any knowledge, or were openly evasive. Questions were answered with questions.

Why was he looking for her?

Was this an official investigation?

When news finally came from Thrubshawe, the superintendent delivered it personally, early one morning. He came in and looked around the room with open curiosity, and accepted the only chair when Flint offered it.

"Your Parasol Lady is not in our archives," the red-haired man said, his expression somber. He took a deep breath. "I have also checked with my colleagues and…"

Li Flint frowned. "What?"

"I do not believe there is much future, for your investigation, here in this city."

"What does that mean?"

Thrubshawe shrugged. "The Parasol Lady does have some powerful friends. The sort of friends that do not like files and records. And they might not appreciate you asking questions."

"Is this intimidation we are talking about?"

The superintendent looked away. "Shanghai is a strange city, inspector. The rules here are more negotiable than, say, in London or Paris."

Li Flint was not surprised, but his anger flared all the same. "You mean corruption. Powerful people being above the law."

"Certain people are the law, in this city."

Li Flint looked at Thrubshawe for a long moment.

"And you serve the law," he said. Disappointment colored his voice.

The superintendent's cheeks burned, and he tightened his fists. Flint almost anticipated a physical reaction. Anger. Violence. But then the Englishman relaxed, and sighed. "And our involvement with the ICPC is amply discretionary."

Flint did not comment. Without support from the local police force, he had no way to apprehend and interrogate suspects, no power to arrest the criminals.

Thrubshawe sighed, shook his head, and stood. "Be careful, inspector," he said. "You will be alone on this one."

They did not shake hands as the superintendent left. The door clicked closed behind him.

Flint took a deep breath, and looked out of the window, at the city bathed in the morning light. Working without any support from the local law enforcement would make everything more complicated. He was playing too large a chessboard, and he was playing it alone.

The upper echelons of the city's society closed to him, Li Flint turned himself into a shadow, moving along shadow avenues, making shadow connections. He haunted the boulevards of the French Concession, walking in the shadows of the planes, hoping to catch a glimpse of the Lady, the red flash of her parasol. And he asked around, discreetly, in hotels and salons, where the powerful of the city assembled.

He talked to the invisible ones, the waiters and the flower girls, the drivers and the bartenders. Slowly, he made a little progress. An Irish guy called Cohan, who served as an in-house detective for the Majestic Hotel, gave him the name of a Frenchman who flew a charter plane service out of the Lunghwa airfield. For the price of two bottles of kao liang wine and a carton of imported Gauloise cigarettes, the Frenchman wrote down the address of a Russian who managed a flop-house off Avenue Foch. She had a young face, hidden under an older woman's makeup. She smoked black Sobranies and served him black tea in clear glasses. From her, Flint got a warning and an envelope.

The warning, delivered with an amused flirty attitude, was the same that strait-laced Thrubshawe had delivered earlier: the Lady with the Red Parasol enjoyed the friendship of powerful men, and it would be ill-advised to displease them. But if he was still trying to meet the Lady, there was an address on the envelope she handed him, and a letter of introduction.

A friend of a friend, who might help.

"Her name's Athena, despite being Chinese and Shanghai-born," the Russian woman said, pulling her purple kimono closed with a shudder. Her face was pale under the rouge. Her lips took a tart twist. "She deals in gossip, and might have some answers for you."

She squashed her cigarette in an ashtray. He thanked her, and she gave him a sad look as she saw him to the door. "You will have to tread carefully."

The letter was addressed to suite 809 in the Yangtze Hotel. Li Flint presented it at the front desk, and was asked to wait while a bell boy delivered the envelope and his calling card on a silver tray. He sat in a stuffed chair by one of the art deco columns in the lobby. He picked up a copy of the *Shanghai Times* and pretended to read it. Minutes dragged on. The hum of voices was like the thrumming of a motor. Hotel porters came in, pushing trolleys loaded with luggage. Men in fedoras and women in silk dresses came and went. Flint spotted a man in a pin-striped suit, hovering by the service staircase.

The bell boy was back, with a note folded in half. A careful feminine hand, in sharp blue ink, invited him for tea that afternoon. Flint tipped the boy, folded the newspaper, and walked out. The pin-stripe suit man followed him.

The sidewalks of Shanghai seemed to have a hierarchy, a stratification of sorts, that caused servants, laborers and loiterers to gravitate towards the edge of the pavement, while the well-to-do and the purposeful remained farther from the street, and closer to the shop windows and the building facades. One block away from the hotel, Li Flint paused by a pushcart that had been parked by the curbside in the shadow of a plane tree, a rich smell of onions lingering, and casually surveyed the river of faces walking by. There was a second man, in a long blue qingpao coat and a fedora, moving parallel to Pin-stripe on the other side of the street. It was a simple pursuing strategy, and when two minutes later Flint crossed the street, Fedora took point, and Pin-stripe fell behind.

Flint felt a familiar thrill. Finally, something was moving.

He wondered briefly who had set up his tail. The Lady was supposed to use less mundane methods. His chief suspect was Thrubshawe, possibly acting on behalf of the powerful men that kept this city in thrall. He led them in a leisurely chase along the sidewalks of the French Concession, for over one hour. Then they either realized they had been spotted, or lost their patience, and in a matter of moments were gone, swallowed by the bustle of the avenue.

IV. Darjeeling Tea

"So you are a friend of Helena's," the woman said by way of greeting. It was not a question. Li Flint shifted his weight from one foot to the other, feeling the burn of the woman's heavy-lidded stare.

"Merely an acquaintance," he said.

She picked his calling card from her nightstand and scanned it. "Inspector Li Flint, ICPC. Helena will never stop surprising me. The people she knows. You're aware she's not really Russian, aren't you? Of course you are."

Her voice was a husky tone that contrasted with her slender frame. The only splash of color in a white and cream bedroom, she was wearing an emerald green and purple dressing gown, and was busy attaching a cigarette to a long thin silver holder. Her black hair was fashionably styled in a short bob, and framed a triangular face with sharp cheekbones and thin, arched eyebrows.

On his way up he had tipped the lift boy, and learned the name of the occupant of suite 809. Athena Cai Chang, only daughter of one of the directors of the Bank of China. "The bees' knees," according to his earnest informer.

Now she gave Flint a look, expectant. He stepped forward and offered her a light. She hollowed her cheeks, the tip of the cigarette burning red. Her fingernails were long and sharp, painted the same maroon as her lips. She sat back on the unmade bed, and exhaled a thin stream of smoke.

"We did the town last night," she said. She gestured, brandishing her cigarette holder like a magic wand, and pointed at a chair. Flint sat down. "Dinner at the Cathai, then the Paramount for the Charleston, then the Del Monte for a breakfast of ham and eggs." Her voice had a posh British accent. She shook her head disapprovingly. "Nobody calls socially before noon in Shanghai. Not even to drop a calling card."

"I am sorry for my faux pas," he replied, wary. "I am afraid I am not overly familiar with the social rituals of this city."

"Quite obviously," she snorted. She looked him up and down. "You look the part but are not from around here. Helena's cryptic note says San Francisco. Is that where you caught that cowboy drawl of yours?"

Flint decided to offer some information, and see where it would lead. "I was born here," he said, "in Shanghai. But I was raised in San Francisco. My father worked for the China Light and Power Company Syndicate."

"The Kadoorie family," she said.

"Yes. My father was an engineer. He was sent to the United States, to work with the company's American partners."

"I met Laura Kadoorie once," she said. Flexing her social muscles, he thought. Establishing her authority. "A little before she died. She was a formidable woman."

"So I heard."

Aristocratic Laura Kadoorie had been a giant in Shanghai's social life, before the war. Either Athena had met her when she was a child, or she was older than she looked. Flint guessed the latter was true. There were thin lines around her mouth and eyes that makeup did not conceal.

The same maid that had greeted Flint at the door walked in carrying a large tray that she placed on the bed by her mistress, and then retreated again.

"And now you are back in Shanghai," Athena continued, "and part of the International Police Commission. A Chinese and English bilingual is certainly an asset for such a worldwide organization."

"I like to believe I'm valuable to the Commission for other reasons, too."

"Of course," she conceded. "And Helena tells me you are looking for Tzu San Niang. The Lady with the Red Parasol."

Flint made a mental note of the name. "You know her?"

"Everybody in Shanghai knows about her. Very few know her. Many want to. Some," she added, pouring the tea, "regret they do."

Flint shook his head when she offered him a cup.

"It's Darjeeling," she said.

Flint resisted the temptation to check his watch. He was not here for social pleasantries. "No, thanks. I'm more of a coffee sort of guy."

"How very American." She dropped a dollop of honey in her cup. "Why are you looking for Tzu San Niang?"

"What is the Lady with the Red Parasol to you?"

She smiled cruelly. "Having second thoughts?"

They were back at the old game everybody was playing. Questions answered with questions.

But she made a dismissive gesture, and sipped some tea. "I'm not her friend or her ally, her accomplice or accessory, if this is what worries you," she said then. "But this is a commercial city, you see, and everybody's got something to sell. I am my own agent. My trade is in gossip, one of the most rarefied commodities on the market. This is why you are here, after all. To sample some of my wares. And I did know her, once." She put down her empty cup, and picked up a biscuit. "Why are you looking for Tzu San Niang?"

"She is involved in illegal activities…"

Athena laughed. "Really? How surprising."

She nibbled at the biscuit, her eyes sparkling with amusement. Flint did not laugh. "We believe she is at the heart of an international drug-running operation. Something she is financing by smuggling stolen art."

It was a convenient cover story. Plausible.

The woman frowned. "Sounds sketchy," she said. She brushed the crumbs off her sleeve. "But I can see her involved in such a racket. Tzu San Niang craves power above all else. Power in every form or shape. It is like an addiction to her. She extracts an almost obscene pleasure from exercising power over others. She used to have a train of smitten hangers-on, following her around. Men and women. But even that was not enough. She now looks for power elsewhere. To get her fix, if you will."

"We believe she is trying to acquire some sort of ancient objet d'art," Flint said. "I am here to prevent that transaction."

But Athena was lost in her thoughts. "Yes," she whispered, almost to herself. "She's not above drug running."

He wondered at the nature of their acquaintance. "You seem to know her very well."

Athena started, and looked into his eyes. "And I have the scars to prove it."

Flint arched his eyebrows, questioningly. There was a hint of reticence there. The shadow of a mystery.

"There may have been a time," Athena said, drily, "when I too was part of that train of enthralled worshippers."

"But you are not anymore?"

"I am not."

And she would not say more.

"So far, Tzu San Niang has eluded us," Flint said, returning to business. He would trust this woman, as she was the only lead he had. "I need to track her movements. Know her associates. Learn about her plans, and thwart them. Can you provide me with details of her whereabouts?"

He tried not to sound too eager, but it was like there was finally a light at the end of the tunnel.

"I can give you much more than that, Inspector Flint," she said. "I can guide you into Tzu San Niang's hunting grounds. But you will need a dinner jacket to enter."

He frowned at her, surprised. Was she really suggesting a disguise?

"White, of course," she added.

V. RUSSIAN CHAMPAGNE

His room had been searched.

The slip of paper he had pushed between the door and the frame was on the corridor's floor when he paused to put the key to the lock. His first thought was Pin-stripe and Fedora.

Inside, nothing appeared to have been disturbed. But the window was ajar, and the blinds moved in the draft.

Flint placed the laundry bag with the dinner jacket in the wall niche with his other clothes, and then did a slow tour of the room. His suitcase was in order, the Bible was still in the drawer.

He went down to the front desk, and asked if anyone had left a message. He also inquired about the cleaning of the room. On Friday, he was told. It was Wednesday.

Back in his room, he checked the ventilation grille where he had placed the files and his other documents. The paper slip was still in position. His mysterious visitors had not thought about checking the pipes. Skilled, but lacking in imagination. Just like the men that had shadowed him in the street. Good, but not too good. He still suspected the local police.

He sat on the bed, smoking his pipe. He took his glasses off.

The pieces had been moved into position, the game was entering its mid-stretch. The hardest to predict, the more casually violent.

Flint spent the following three days, as he waited for Athena's call, roaming the city, and setting up a safe house in a cheap hotel in Huangpu Road, not far from the Japanese consulate.

He also found time to have his new jacket fitted.

•••

In a dinner jacket, and with Athena on his arm, Li Flint walked through the door of the Majestic Ballroom under the smoldering gaze of a colossal Russian with a pale scar on his cheek and a broken nose. Now they waded through the press, circling the dance floor.

"More champagne is consumed in Shanghai than in Paris," Athena said as she intercepted a passing tray and picked up a glass of bubbly wine. "Most of it imported from Russia."

Flint ran a finger around his collar. The frantic breathing of hundreds of dancers combined with the warmth and the humidity of the night to labor his breathing. There was an incongruous impression of Moorish Spain in the Majestic Ballroom. Slender columns supported the domed ceiling, and a white marble fountain sat in the middle of the dance floor. The night club was a-bustle with a kaleidoscope of women in extravagant evening dresses and men in what Athena called "Shanghai monkey suits": white dinner jackets over black trousers, with silk sashes as the only color allowed, the only sign of individuality.

"What would men be without uniforms," Athena mused, sipping her wine. She was wearing a long black dress. "About two years past its prime," she had explained. "But in Shanghai it is considered in poor taste to wear the latest Parisian fashion. The sort of ostentation that smells of new money. The mark of the parvenu."

Flint scanned the crowd. "Is she coming here?"

After all, this was his reason for attending the evening, not the champagne or the Filipino dance band playing jazz standards.

Athena arched her eyebrows. "Here? Of course not."

Flint had no time to protest. She placed the empty champagne glass on a passing tray, and picked another. "Upstairs," she said. And tightening her hold on his arm, she continued in her orbit of the dance floor, until they came to the short, wide fan of steps that led to a curtained passageway, and into the Majestic Hotel.

Past the curtains they went.

To avoid unwanted attention from the concierge, they strode across the lobby without haste to where the elevators waited in their iron cages. But before they reached the elevators, Athena turned sharply to her left, and pushed through an anonymous door. She dragged Flint along.

When the door closed behind her, she leaned with her shoulders on the wood, and gave Flint a piratical grin. She acted like this was some kind of caper, but Flint could perceive a hint of nerves underneath her playfulness.

"Welcome to the service stairs that will lead us to the hallowed corridors where people like us can't go," she said. She was still holding an empty champagne glass. She raised her eyes. "Two floors up," she said. "Tzu San Niang is holding court in the Red Suite, on the third floor."

"How–?"

Athena arched an eyebrow. "Gossip is my trade, remember?"

Flint looked up into the darkness of the service stairwell. "And was all this cloak and dagger necessary?"

"It's exciting," she replied. "And going through the main doors we would have attracted too much attention. In all likelihood they would have not let us in at all."

Flint detected a hint of bitterness in her voice. "This is absurd."

"This is the rotting carcass of the Empire, my boy," she replied, her humor failing to hide the anger. "My father can own a quota in this hotel, but he could never be a guest, and I could only on the arm of a Westerner. Which you are not. Come on, let's go. We are going to be in the next room, listening through the wall with a glass, or something."

"The next room?"

But she was already up the first ramp.

Flint followed her up the stairs and through an arch into a corridor illuminated by brass and crystal chandeliers. The silence was haunting, and it was hard to believe that two stories below a crowd of revelers was doing the foxtrot while a twelve-piece band played. The air was warm and still, the carpets soft. The light was liquid amber.

Flint let Athena lead, and focused on scanning the corridor as they went. They passed an alcove with a striped couch in it, and peeked around a tall silk screen. Behind a tall green potted plant, they spied two men standing in front of an unmarked door. Broad-shouldered and rough-featured, wearing cheap charcoal suits, they were as still as statues. Flint noticed their scarred knuckles. Russian hired muscle. The one closer to their hiding place had a bulge on his waist of the kind caused by a gun.

"Can you pick a lock?" Athena asked. Her breath tickled his ear.

"Of course."

"How fast?"

Flint gave another look at the two guardians.

"Fast enough," he said, slipping his lock-picks out of his inside pocket.

"Fine," she said, "because I am going to be disgracefully out of sorts as soon as you're ready."

The couple staggered down the corridor, being very loud. The man was holding the woman up as she sang "Baby Face" at the top of her lungs, and waved an empty champagne glass. She was wearing an expensive black dress, and walked on rubber legs. She was not a very good singer. Her voice was a nasal drone. "I'm up in heaven when I'm in your firm embrace…!"

The men at the door watched the couple go by, and traded a look. The larger of the two shook his head and rolled his eyes as the couple stopped in front of the door to the next suite. "Bogatyye idioty," he mumbled.

His pal chuckled. "Da."

The woman leaned against the lintel while her partner tried drunkenly to find the keyhole and then struggled with the lock. She fell silent as he worked his key with increasing difficulty. Her body almost completely blocked the line of sight, only the back of the man being visible. His key scratched on the metal of the lock as he tried to slip it in.

Another minute dragged on. The bulkier of the two guards frowned, his hand slipping inside his jacket. His partner caught his look and turned towards the couple.

"Hey–" he started, just as their door swung open and the man staggered inside, dragging the drunken woman along.

She gave a long, rattling laugh as the door slammed closed. The corridor was quiet again.

"Bogatyye debily," the guard snorted. His mate shook his head, and they went back to their duty. Just another wild night in Shanghai.

VI. Manchurian Rails

Athena pressed her shoulders against the door, and let out a deep sigh. Flint found the light switch. A Tiffany lamp came alive on a side table, casting a soft twilight into the suite's parlor. They checked the rooms. An archway led into a large, darkened bedroom. Past a door was an en-suite bathroom, all white marble and brass fittings. With a nod to his partner, Flint dragged a chair close to the wall, and stood on it.

"What if the suite had been occupied?" he asked.

"It's booked for the night," Athena replied, "by a friend of mine."

Flint looked at her, and she shrugged. "I've got lots of friends."

"I see."

"Is there a radio on somewhere?" she asked.

Flint listened, and then shook his head. He pulled the lever of the ventilation grille, and closed his eyes. There were voices, talking, in the next room. A tinkling of glasses.

"Five hundred thousand yuan is no laughing matter," a gruff man said. A faint accent, Dutch or German. The sound was so clear, it was like Flint was standing there by the man's side.

Flint turned to his companion, and nodded. "It's this," he whispered.

Athena shook her head. She pointed at her ear, and grimaced. She twirled her finger in the air. She was hearing something else. She put her empty glass on a table, and lit herself a cigarette. She sat on one of the couches, her foot tapping nervously a syncopated rhythm on the carpet.

"Are we to discuss this issue again?" a female voice asked. A rich, upper-class accent, and an icy edge. Flint held his breath. Was this the Lady with the Red Parasol?

"Well, of course not," the gruff one replied, "but…"

Flint glanced at Athena who was shifting on her chair. She had wrapped her arms around her body, and was rubbing her hands up and down her arms.

"This was a bad idea," she said in a low voice.

Flint frowned. It was like all her vitality had been drained from her. Her features were drawn and shrouded in cigarette smoke, and all the excitement for the adventure was gone. Her eyes kept darting around, and returning to the door.

He was about to ask what was up with her, when the female voice came to him through the ventilation pipe.

"You gentlemen asked for my help in closing the deal in Jinan," the woman said. "I closed the deal."

Different men started talking at the same time, in a jumble of accents and tones, and then were silent as the woman spoke again. "Moreover, these issues in Hong Kong and Kuala Lumpur are of a different nature, and can be solved swiftly, and much more cheaply. Something I am sure Mister Groteboer will appreciate."

The men mumbled and chuckled.

"I was just pointing out," the gruff man said, "if we had persevered some, the amount might have decreased a little."

Silence hung leaden for a whole minute.

"I do not deal in perseverance, Mister Groteboer," the woman said, then. "I deal in solutions."

"And your solutions are entirely satisfactory," a new voice said. "Let us not linger on the Jinan affair any longer. This labor strike thing is much more worrying than any warlord–"

"Then there is the railway business," a third man said. "We don't want Mantetsu to have full control–"

"And all of the profits," Groteboer added.

Flint jotted down some notes, more out of habit than from necessity. He was surprised at finding out this mercenary side of the mysterious Lady. He'd have to look into this Jinan affair.

On her couch, Athena was shifting nervously. She lit a new cigarette with the stub of the previous one. Her hands trembled. Flint squared his shoulder. Her fear was rubbing off on him.

"We will discuss the railway in due time," the woman said. "Right now, the matter at hand is the unions the workers in Hong Kong are setting up."

"This is costing us a pretty dollar," a new voice said, in an American drawl.

"We have the utmost faith in your skills, madame," said the third man.

"And we pay nicely for them," added Groteboer, a man clearly unable to let an issue rest.

"We need to go," Athena whispered behind him.

Flint half turned to watch her. She was peering into the shadows of the bedroom. All of her playfulness was gone and she was on the verge of panic. A creeping sense of foreboding came over Flint.

"I can guarantee," the ice-voiced woman replied, piqued, "that by the end of the month all the workers requests will be archived, and ..."

Her voice trailed off, and Flint felt a sudden chill, like an electric charge tickling his spine.

Athena was standing behind him. "We need to go now!" she hissed, a desperate urgency creeping into her hushed voice. She tugged at his sleeve.

The men in the other room were again talking over each other. Clapping hands silenced them.

"I am afraid there is something I will have to deal with first," the woman said.

It was like a pair of piercing eyes were staring at him through the wall. Flint pulled his hands off the wallpaper, like the wall was burning.

With a curse, Athena ran to the door, and threw it open.

Flint turned in time to see her go out. Breath escaped his lips in a wintry cloud of steam. The room was freezing.

In the corner of his eye he caught a ghostly shape as it took form in the middle of the room. It was vaguely human shaped, and as ragged and running as a wisp of smoke in the breeze. For a minute that lasted an eternity, he looked into the twirls and swirls of the ghostly apparition. Flint's throat tightened and dried, and he was caught in a swoop of vertigo.

Men shouted in the corridor. Flint saw the larger of the two guards run after Athena.

He jumped off his chair just as a pair of ghostly arms seeped through the wall and tried to make a grab for him.

The shape in the middle of the room threw back its head and screeched. There were evanescent chains wrapped around its form, and it seemed to carry a pickaxe.

Flint caught a drift of a sound, like a distant voice singing a lullaby. The song, insinuating and insistent, did what the ghostly shapes had as yet failed to achieve. A sudden surge of fear like he had not experienced since childhood swept over Flint. Blind, chilling, irrational. He had to get out of that place.

Flint ran to the door, slipped on the carpet, pushed himself into the corridor and collided with the second guard. They fell in a tangle of arms and legs. Flint caught a glimpse of a group of portly, middle-aged men crowding the doorway of the nearby suite.

In front of them, a Chinese woman in a pale qipao was staring at him. A perfect face, absolutely impassive. She lifted a red parasol in her gloved hands and opened it with a click that sounded like thunder in the corridor.

Flint smashed his elbow in the guard's face. The man rolled back, covering his face with his hands, and Flint scampered to his feet and shot through the nearest arch and through the service stairs door.

Steps echoed in the stairwell, and he spied Athena's black dress and pale face as she ran, the giant Russian bruiser behind her.

The lullaby still creeping on him, Flint ran down the stairs like hell itself was in pursuit.

VII. ITALIAN GARDENS

Going from the bright light of the Majestic lobby to the black night of the hotel gardens forced Flint to slow down. Gravel creaked underneath his feet. He squinted in the twilight of the distant neons of the city, trying to catch a glimpse of Athena, or of her pursuers. The dance hall band was an afterthought in the distance, but Flint's ears still rang with the melancholy wail of the ghostly lullaby. He shivered despite the hot, humid air of the night. Trees and ornamental shrubs were darker shadows in the blue evening, like squatting beasts waiting for their prey.

Flint cocked his gun, and strained to catch any movement. Russian voices called in the dark. There was no time to waste. He hastened towards the gates, confident in the fact that Athena would do the same.

A sudden movement, too close to evade. One of the Russian guards slammed into him. It was like being steamrolled by a truck. Flint hit the ground, breathless, the gun escaping his grip. A hand with scarred knuckles grabbed the front of his shirt and a fist smashed into his face, knocking off his glasses. Flint's head rang with the punch, the pain a further layer underneath the distant song still playing in his ears.

The man called his pals, and then loaded a second punch. Flint pulled up his arm, protecting his face. More voices called, coming closer. The Russian's eyes rolled into his head, and he let go of his hold and crashed on the ground.

Pin-stripe stood over Flint, holding a blackjack. He offered his hand to help Flint up.

"I'm Shaw," he said hurriedly. "From the Foundation. We need to go."

Still dazed, Flint got to his feet and followed the man Shaw towards the garden gates. "There's a woman–" he started.

"No time."

Mist-like shapes appeared among the edges of the Italian garden, faintly glowing with the same blue haze of the city lights.

Shaw cursed. "Run!"

The ghostly army of misshapen wraiths closed around them. They seemed to move like waves, advancing and retreating as they followed the rhythm of the song that now was the only thing Flint could hear.

The melody insinuated itself into his brain, shattering his resolve and scrambling his senses. He knew he needed to run, get out of the garden, but he no longer knew where the gate was. There was only the song, twisting and snaking. *Stop*, it said. *Relent. Abide.*

The song was the only reality, and the crowd of ghostly faces, drawing closer. Hungry. Desperately hungry.

Someone cried out in the dark. Shots were fired. The crying voice was suddenly silenced. The glowing shapes were upon them. Arms outstretched, fingers like claws, mouths gaping.

Shaw grabbed Flint by an arm and dragged him away,

jumping a perfectly trimmed hedge and running past a rose bush, onto a new gravelly lane. "Come!" he said, pushing Flint and pointing at the gates. Traffic streaks of red and white light ran past the iron bars. Flint shook his head, trying to clear his thoughts. He felt hungover.

Shaw's hand pressed between his shoulders. "Run, man. Run!"

Flint ran. Without looking back, without thought but for that gaping passage, and the lights beyond. His legs were leaden, breath came ragged in steamy bursts in the Arctic-cold air. Pale blue hands grabbed him but he tore away, screaming in panic.

He slammed into the hood of a black car.

The man in the fedora was at the wheel. He leaned to the side and opened the door.

"Get in, man! Get in!"

The seat creaked under his weight. He had lost his glasses and his gun. The engine started, and soon they joined the traffic of Bubbling Well Road.

"There was a man…" Flint said. He ran a hand over his face. His fingers burned as if from frostbite. "Shaw."

Fedora shook his head, shifting gears. "He's gone."

"And a woman," Flint said, Athena Cai Chang's pale sharp face flashing suddenly in his mind. "There was a woman, with me. In a black dress–"

"They're gone," Fedora repeated. "Nothing we can do about that."

Sichuan Road was blocked by fire engines, the sidewalks choked with the curious and the hangers-on. The night was painted orange by the flames consuming the top floors of the YMCA building, the smashed windows belching black smoke and embers.

The man in the fedora stopped the car and climbed out. Flint did the same.

"They're moving fast," Flint said. The sticky fingers of the Majestic nightmare were slowly retreating from his mind. He needed to tighten his hold on the little he had.

"Maybe you should leave," Fedora suggested.

Flint looked at him, squinting. "Leave?"

"New instructions from Commissioner Taylor," Fedora said. "And by the way, I'm Chen Guiying. From the Nanjing chapter."

Flint acknowledged him with a nod.

"I am sorry for our friend," Chen said.

Guilt twisted in Flint's gut. "What happened to her?" he asked. "To Shaw?"

Chen shrugged. "Dead, probably. Or soon to be. Nothing we can do about that."

Flint looked at the flames consuming the roof of the building. Police officers, Sikhs in red turbans and French Concession cops in their kepis were holding the people back. Beyond the line of officers, men in uniform and civilians were talking among themselves. One of them was Superintendent Thrubshawe.

"There's someone I need to see," Flint said. There was something he still could do.

"Wait." Chen handed him a massive Webley revolver. "Just in case."

•••

Thrubshawe looked at Flint like he was a ghost, and murmuring an excuse, left the other officers and came up to meet him.

"Are there any victims?" Flint asked. He was not going to allow the other man time to ask his own questions. He could not allow the superintendent to take control of the discussion.

"Only one, but–"

"Do we know the cause of the fire?"

"Someone smoking in bed," Thrubshawe said, glancing at the burning building. "But that's supposed to be you, so I think we'll have to revise that hypothesis, and the victim count."

Flint took a deep breath. "You know that even if the firemen are still at work?"

"Witnesses said the fire started in your room. Hence the smoking in bed hypothesis."

"I do not smoke."

"And you're patently not dead."

Flint felt the weight of the revolver in his pocket. "I'd like you to keep that last detail to yourself."

The policeman frowned. Again he looked back at the building, at his colleagues standing there. "You can't be asking me to hide evidence."

"Not really. Either there will be no body, or there will be a body that you will have to identify. I am asking you to delay the identification of my remains, to allow me time to solve a case."

"What case?"

"Please."

Thrubshawe sighed. "I can give you twenty-four hours. Then I will have to report in front of the magistrate, and–"

"Twenty-four hours should be enough." Flint stretched his hand. "Thank you."

The superintendent shook it. "Do not give me cause to regret an act of professional courtesy."

"I can't guarantee that. But I will try."

VIII. Shanghai Commercial

Flint retreated to his spare room in Huangpu Road, switching cabs twice to get there.

From the cheap hotel to the offices of the Shanghai Commercial and Savings Bank, it was just a short drive across the Garden Bridge to the Bund. Chen drove in silence, and stayed in the car when they got there. Once inside, Flint's ICPC badge carried him past the front desk, up four stories and into the bank's inner sanctum.

"I am here to see Mister Groteboer."

Finding the man had not been hard. There were not many Dutch bankers in Shanghai.

The young man at the desk stared at him.

Running on three hours of sleep and five cups of very bad coffee, Li Flint was a little worse for wear, but still reasonably presentable. He had bought a new pair of glasses from a man selling them off a tray on the Garden Bridge, and he was carrying Chen's Webley in his pocket.

The young man eyed his badge with open contempt. "Do you have an appointment?"

"I do not need an appointment to make an arrest," Flint said.

The young man's eyes goggled. His hand went to the phone, and Flint stopped him, putting his own hand over his. The physical contact shocked the young man, as Flint had hoped.

"What I suggest," he said, in a low, menacing voice, "is that you show me to Mister Groteboer's office, and then rush back here to call the bank's lawyers."

The young man glanced at one of the doors, and tried to articulate a protest.

"Thanks," Li Flint said, and moved on to the door. He did not knock, and went in.

A portly man in a stiff collar sat behind a massive mahogany desk, the two chairs in front of it occupied by a man and a woman in their fifties. Coffee had been served, and Flint's entrance clearly interrupted a friendly chat.

"What does this mean?" the big man bawled, his voice quite familiar to Flint. His jowly features lit up a bright red when he saw Flint coming in, his face suddenly so ruddy that his white whiskers seemed to glow. "Who are you? Berthelot, where are you?"

The young man ran by Flint's side. "I am sorry, director–"

The man and the woman in the client's chairs turned and stared at Flint, who showed his badge. "Inspector Li Flint, International Criminal Police Commission," he said, his tone level. "I am here in conjunction with the payment of half a million yuan to the Jinan warlord, and the disappearance of the daughter of one of the directors of the Bank of China, Miss Athena Cai Chang."

Groteboer opened his mouth and then closed it.

"I don't know what you are talking about," he finally said, but his voice had lost its edge, and his face was ashen. Nothing's worse than a bad conscience.

Flint saw a crack, and applied more pressure. "I am talking about money from the coffers of this and other companies, paid to a criminal to have one of your competitors intimidated, by having his daughter sequestered."

The two guests shifted in their chairs, clearly ill at ease. Flint suppressed a smile. Anything increasing the banker's panic was welcome.

"The daughter…? I know nothing about anyone's daughter!"

The woman in the chair stood, and placed a hand on the shoulder of the man by her side. "Charles, I believe we should leave."

"Yes, darling," he said. He looked at Groteboer. "We will call back when all of this has been resolved. Goodbye."

And they marched out of the room.

"Sir," the secretary said, "should I call Mister Dashwood?"

"Yes, Mister Berthelot," Flint said without turning. "Call the lawyers. Make sure they will be here before the journalists arrive."

"You can't do that!" Groteboer gasped.

"Go, Mister Berthelot," Flint said, his eyes on Groteboer's.

"No, wait!" The big man was sweating. He looked at Flint. "Let us talk like civilized people."

Flint made a show of checking his watch. "You have five minutes," he said.

"Go back to your desk," Groteboer ordered his secretary. He waited for the door to click closed. Then he took a deep breath. "You do not have the authority–"

"Really?"

This was the moment of truth. The banker was right. The ICPC did not have any authority to arrest the criminals it pursued. But Flint was betting on Groteboer not knowing. Again, he checked his watch.

"Four minutes. The gentlemen from the press will be here soon."

The banker's shoulders sagged.

"What do you want? I can pay…"

Flint kept his tone level. The banker's ego was working to his advantage. "Are you offering money to evade arrest?"

"Everyone has a price," Groteboer said, a shadow of his arrogance returning.

"In Shanghai, maybe. But I am not the Municipal Police, I am not the Kuomintang. As soon as you are in Foochow Road under lock and key, I will leave this city forever. And you have three minutes."

"You've got this affair all wrong," Groteboer tried to sound reasonable. "The money that was paid–"

"You admit to it."

"Yes. It was the ransom of our branch director in Jinan. He had been kidnapped by the local warlord and we–"

"What about Miss Athena Cai Chang?"

"I know nothing about this Cai Chang woman–"

"Wrong answer. We have proof she was abducted by your associate," he lied. "A comprador by the name of Tzu San Niang."

The bluff worked. Groteboer had got back some of his color, but now his face turned grey. "Not her!"

"Two minutes."

"You don't understand. Tzu San Niang is…" His voice broke. "I cannot."

Flint just arched his eyebrows, and looked at his watch again. There was a knock on the door.

"Things being so…" he said. As a chess player, he found this poker game both exhilarating and disquieting.

"No, wait. You don't understand. I cannot give you Tzu San Niang. She would know it's me–"

"Not if you remain off the record. Tell me where Miss Cai Chang was taken. Help me find her."

"I cannot. I don't know."

Again, someone knocked on the door.

This was the moment of truth. Flint felt like his only hold on the case was about to slip from his fingers. Groteboer read something in his face, and read it wrong.

"She's got a place in Bubbling Well Road," he said, and it was like he was deflating. He seemed to sink into his chair. "By the German Church."

He stared at Flint with haunted eyes. "That's all I know."

Without a word, Li Flint turned on his heels and went out, allowing himself a spark of hope.

Past the door, young Berthelot was about to knock one more time. Two men with a bellicose expression and impeccable suits were standing by, talking in hushed tones. The lawyers, Flint imagined. He nodded as he passed by them, and he was in the lift before they could react.

He put a hand in his pocket, caressing the rubber grip of the Webley.

Chen was waiting for him across the road. Next stop, Bubbling Well Road.

IX. German Church

The German School and Church in Bubbling Well Road rose just past the Bubbling Well cemetery. Past the border of the International Settlement, and outside of the laws of the West. Here the houses were as elegant as further down the road, but shops and stores were increasingly commonplace, as were machine workshops and warehouses. The general feeling, if not the actual fact, was that this side of the settlement's border laws were more lenient, easier to break, and such breaches more easily overlooked.

Which gave a modicum of consolation to Flint as he cracked the lock of a side door, and let himself in.

The bright light of noon did not enter this place, and even the skylights had been boarded up and blackened. There was in the air a smell of dust and dereliction, overlaid with the bitter smell of incense. His steps echoed in the vast, empty space. He pulled the gun from his pocket. He had asked Chen to stop along the way, so that Flint could post a note and buy a box of cartridges. Now the extra bullets clicked in his pocket with every step.

The vast space inside the warehouse was empty.

Not simply a physical emptiness, but also, Flint was certain, an emptiness of the spirit, a gaping moral void. It was hard to wrap his intelligence around what his instincts could not deny. The building was purposefully empty, like a space consecrated to Nothingness. It felt like the human warmth of the building had been stripped away, leaving a hole in its place.

And at the center of that hole, in the faint pool of light provided by two tapers, was Athena Cai Chang.

Flint kept scanning the shadows, but increased his pace. The woman was kneeling on the dirty concrete floor of the warehouse, her forehead resting on her hands.

When he was by her side, he called her name, in a low voice. She did not stir.

Squinting in the darkness, he placed a hand on her shoulder. He noticed the tears in her dress, and the broken fingernails. "We need to get out of this place," he said.

She seemed to wake up, and turned her face towards him. "She's gone," she said, an overwhelming anguish in her voice. She did not seem to recognize him.

"And we need to go, too." He nodded, and tried to pull her to her feet. He could not allow relief to distract him. They needed to get out. The car waiting outside felt like a million miles away.

"I bowed in front of her," she gasped, grabbing his arm, "but she did not stay..."

Her eyes were wild and unfocused, and Flint imagined she had been dosed with some sort of drug, to break her mind. He felt a stab of guilt. He put his arm around her waist to support her, and turned towards the door. They were halfway there when the minions of Tzu San Niang came for them.

•••

The first aggressor came for him with a knife. Flint side-stepped him, and kicked him in the knee. The articulation cracked like a broken twig and the man crumpled on the ground, screaming. Pushing Athena down, Flint shot the second incoming man in the chest, and the one after him in a leg. This put some caution into the survivors. None of them, apparently, carried a gun, and there were still four bullets in Flint's Webley; not enough to kill them all, but certainly enough to kill the first four that would come forward. No one felt like being one of those four.

Taking advantage of their hesitation, Flint pulled Athena up, and again started moving towards the door. His companion was regaining some lucidity. Her steps were steadier. She started talking.

"She can't forgive," she said. "No one leaves her court. Vengeful, she is. Jealous. Had me kneeling in front of her for… for close to forever."

The gun in Flint's hand weighed a ton. The men surrounding them were gathering their courage again. They would rush him en masse, gambling on the likelihood of being shot.

But before the men could make up their minds, with a roar of a revved-up engine, Chen's car crashed through the main gates of the warehouse, and came in with wheels screeching, undertaking a wide swerve. The radiator was smashed, steam escaping the hood, but the car scattered the minions, and came to a sudden stop where Flint and Athena were. A door swung open.

"What took you so long?" Flint asked. He pushed Athena in, and followed her.

"Traffic." Chen grinned.

The car started again, doing an ample curve and heading again towards the smashed entrance. One of the Lady's minions was not fast enough to jump out of the way. Another jumped on the running board, on the passenger's side. Flint shot him point-blank.

Drunkenly, Athena started singing "Baby Face."

Flint took it for a sign she was feeling better.

Then they hit Bubbling Well Road, avoided by a hair's-breadth a collision with a horse-drawn cart, and, trailing smoke, sped towards the International Settlement.

Athena stopped singing, slumped on her seat.

He had selected his hotel in Huangpu Road because it was the sort of place where no questions were asked, but when Flint came in carrying Athena, the old manager gasped and ran over. Like a fussing grandmother, she placed her hand on Athena's forehead to feel her temperature. She had a doctor they could call, she said. Flint just asked for his key.

Flint laid Athena on the bed, and checked her pulse. Her breathing was steady. Exhaustion, probably.

Later, Chen came in. He had ditched the damaged car, and acquired some provisions. He also had a copy of an evening paper. The fire at the YMCA was on page fifteen. No victims. The disturbance in Bubbling Well Road did not qualify for any coverage. At least not in the news. Flint was not surprised. It was like he had spent the last few days in a dream world. The place where the Lady with the Red Parasol moved was beyond the everyday life of Shanghai. What happened there did not make the news.

"I suggest you keep a low profile," Chen said.

Flint shook his head. "Tzu San Niang—"

"The Lady with the Red Parasol left the city last night, headed for Hong Kong." He caught Flint's frown. "The Foundation's got someone in the Customs House. And the Lady's gone."

"On a union-breaking mission for her rich patrons." Defeat and humiliation tasted bitter on his tongue.

"Whatever." Chen shrugged. "But her cut-throats are still out for your blood. And mine. And the girl's."

"Commissioner Taylor will not be pleased," Flint said. The chessboard had been overturned and the pieces scattered. A disaster for which he was the only one responsible.

Chen shrugged. "She is sending in fresh forces. People the Lady's minions do not know. You, in the meantime, should disappear. The girl too. I do not foresee a bright future for either of you in this city."

"Can you take care of her?" he asked. Athena had been his guide in the dream world of Shanghai, but she should not be trapped in this nightmare. He owed her that much.

Chen was cautious. "What do you have in mind?"

Flint shrugged. "Can you?"

A brief nod. "We have a safe house in Nanjing. You are both welcome—"

Flint cut him short. "Can you get me tickets on the next steamer to Hong Kong?"

The other man looked at him. "Are you sure it's a good idea?"

Flint lifted his hands, palms up, and shrugged. "I have some unfinished business."

BROTHER BOUND
Jason Fischer

"I do favors for friends," was all Javier would ever say, but Desiderio Delgado Alvarez did not believe his brother.

Javier worked in Uncle's cane field, but he owned his own car, a brand-new model T that he drove while the other cane-cutters walked to work. There were other signs. Late-night visitors, smoking cigars in the dark of the road while they spoke quietly. The newly installed telephone, jangling in the hallway at midnight, Javier rushing to answer it.

Mother watching all of this with wide eyes, and never saying a word, silently suffering a kiss on the cheek from her eldest son when he and a stranger filled the ice-box with pork. More cigars in the dark, but after the truck rumbled off into the night Desi blocked the front doorway against Javier. He was as stern as any nineteen year-old could manage to muster, and when he saw Javier fighting to hold in a smile, he scowled deeper.

"You have more questions than sense," Javier said. "Be grateful we eat."

"Is that pork from your honest labor?" Desi asked. "You must do the work of five men to afford it."

"Desi. Listen to me. Go back to your room. Read your new schoolbooks, and I promise you that you shall never have to cut the cane."

"Do you cut the cane?"

A pause, and then Javier placed his hands on Desi's shoulders, leaning in with a twinkle in his eye.

"I thought you wanted to become a doctor, little brother, but here you are playing at lawyer. Get out of my way before I make you regret it."

Desi stepped aside after a moment, still frowning as Javier patted him on the shoulder, lumbering up the hallway. A quiet enquiry from Mother, and more lies from Javier. Yes, I am to be the foreman soon. Uncle is paying me extra. Yes, the butcher is my friend, I helped fix his truck.

What wasn't said was we are comfortable for now, but there will be a knock on the door one day, or worse.

Everything will fall apart.

The cane fields made Desi's skin crawl. Their leaves rubbed and whispered slick in the breeze, stalks creaking as they drew up wealth from the soil. The syrup, sickly sweet whenever Uncle cut a cane for him to taste.

The cane had a disturbing hidden depth to it, and five steps into it you were lost under that rustling sea, pressed in on all sides, slipping between the rows like some hunted fish. He'd had more than one nightmare where thousands of canes would twine around him, dragging him down and away from the sunlight, underneath the loamy earth to break his flesh down into more sugar.

He feared the dense undergrowth of the cane, the biting insects and vermin that lurked there, but oddly enough Desi feared Uncle's cane cutters the most. They worked swiftly at the cane with their keen-edged machetes, hacking away at his nightmares one acre at a time. Cutting cane was backbreakingly hard work, and every stalk required a grown man to bend, hack at the root, stand again, hack at the grassy top, before reaching into the undergrowth for the next one.

Stoop. Chop. Straighten. Top.

Uncle paid them a pittance, just enough to keep them from torching his fields in protest. He fancied himself as a Henry Ford, but only so far as controlling the lives of his workers – prayers over meals, no liquor except on special occasions, and no women to the dormitories, no visits to the brothels.

The cane cutters were a hard lot, sunburnt and filthy, and they watched him with dead eyes as he passed on the driveway. The cutting gangs were paid by the cartload and rarely stopped work, but they drew up short as Desi approached, and he saw elbows to ribs, lips moving in smiles around soggy old cigar butts or clay pipes.

They watched him, hard eyes assessing him. Finding him wanting.

"I'm looking for my brother," he said.

"Ask at the house."

Desi nodded, and walked away as fast as he could, face flushed with red. He heard the chopping as they returned to the cutting though, blades rising and falling, stalks laying littered in their wake.

Desi ran to the house to find Uncle watching the cane cutters from a seat on his front porch, a mojito in one hand, the other ruffling the fur of his favorite dog. Uncle had ruined the vicious dog when he named him Blando, an irony considering the enormous dogo cubano breed was a slave catcher of old.

"You are not at your studies," Uncle observed. "Will you wander the streets of Havana when we send you there?"

Uncle's wealth was a finite thing, and in its decline. His wife had left him for an American. The big plantation house was in disrepair, and Desi imagined the cane creeping in to drag it down, removing all reference to man and his makings, until there was nothing but the green sea, rustling and clicking. All his uncle had to keep it at bay was a gang of surly men and falling sugar prices.

"I'm looking for Javier," Desi said. "An urgent message."

A year ago, he could have phoned Uncle from the post office with his question, and now from his own house, but there was no one that Uncle wished to speak to, and he had no money for the telephone company anyway.

Uncle sipped his drink, and then nudged over another chair with the tip of his boot, wood grinding against wood.

"Please, Uncle, I–"

"Indulge an old man for a moment," Uncle said, and so Desi sat.

"My abuelo told me a story about the old days, about our plantation. It's always been in our family, since we turned away from sailing to take up farming. Delgado hands cleared the jungle to plant this mighty weed!"

The buzz of a mosquito, and Desi resisted the urge to swat at it.

"Now each harvest I must pay these brutes more than they are worth. Every year I must go cap in hand to the bank manager. Money for lawyers. Money for bribes. Money to send nephews to school."

Desi had the grace to look at his hands.

"But my abuelo's story was before this," he said, vaguely gesturing at his crumbling house and the cane pressing in on all sides.

"He said, 'Everything you need to learn about violence and brutality, you can learn from sugar. We hack it from the earth. Burn it at the root. Drive men to their deaths for every sweet drop.'

"'Our family has seized upon learnings that are less than Catholic,' abuelo told me. 'Memories of the things that stalked the jungle before the Taino people, before us. We've heard of all of this through whispers and tall tales. It's all about blood, boy, which is a holy and most dangerous thing, but we have forgotten an older truth.'"

Here Uncle stared through his drink and his constant surveillance of the cane cutting. The glass shook, only a little, but Desi noticed.

"'For every animal slain over a god's stone, for every war fought in the name of a god or a king, there is blood, and there is sugar in that blood. So here came our people, with our guns and Bibles, and forced the Taino into the ecomienda, and then came the slaves from Africa, and so they bled for our sweet crop.'

"'This island, this world runs on blood, boy, and here we are, distilling it like fools, and every smiling child sticky with candy, every drunkard nursing his rum, they are all as bloated with blood as the old gods on their pyramids.'

"Abuelo told me the secret, Desiderio. When his time came, I followed my abuelo's coffin into the cemetery, but I knew the truth. It was packed full of rocks."

"He's out there," he said, pointing at the cane. "Burnt, turned into the earth, planted into the crop. Done in secret, and as it was with my father it will be with me."

Another shake of the hand holding the glass. The enormous dog yawned, offering a quick flash of its powerful jaws. Desi felt deeply disturbed at this revelation, the knowledge that his uncle's piety was a sham, worse, that his family practiced this dark magic.

"I know your future is not in the cane, Desiderio, and that is why you are allowed to chase your scholar's hopes, but Javier has no talent, save for being a scoundrel."

Mosquito buzz. The slosh of the shaking glass, a fat drop dripping onto the wooden boards. The shift and huff of a dog bred to terrorize and bring down escaped slaves.

"My wife bled me dry, but what is left of my plantation I offered to Javier. Drew up a new will," Uncle said. "I shared the family story. Our blood is out there, Desiderio, and so we remain here always, pushing up the cane, passing on that violent wealth to our family, paying that awful price."

Uncle raised the shaking glass to his lips, draining it in one pull, watching the cane. Desi wondered if he had the same types of dreams that he did.

"Javier put down his machete, and left the plantation. That was six months ago, Desiderio, and I have not seen him since."

Desi found Javier in the trainyard. Trains had always symbolized escape from Cienfuegos for young Desi. Even as the trains loaded with sugar cane sped towards the greedy mouths of the mills, there were passenger trains through to Havana.

Havana. A place away from family, from the quiet grind of obligations, and now from his family's blood curse, the thought of which shook him deeply. For years now he'd driven himself forwards on the promise of leaving for university, then he would get a good job, send money to Mother, and never set foot in Cienfuegos ever again.

The train yards were a little like the town itself. There was the new steam engine the Hershey Company had brought in for its mill, but everyone else made do with the older locomotives, the mill owners telling lies about the price of sugar, running their machines until they burst or seized up. Desi had seen a derailment once, an old sugar-cane engine not worth the trouble of rescuing, and the town carved it apart like piranha fish, taking everything down to the bones of the machine, which still lay rusting out in the tropical weather.

Desi knew that tough times bred tough people and

watched a parade of oxen delivering cart after cart of sugar cane, both beasts and their drivers exhausted, slaves in all but name. Ropes went around each bundle, and a crane made mockery of the muscles of the workers, easily hefting the sugar cane onto each car, sending on all of that pain to the mill to make rum, sweets, sticky chocolate to melt upon richer fingers.

Cane ruled all, but some of the trains were set aside for goods and passengers. Javier was in one of the seedier warehouses Desi knew about, where the storehands drank rum and played dominos for money. His older brother was losing, and was already in a foul mood when he spotted Desi.

"You should not be here," he said.

"You weren't at Uncle's farm," Desi countered, and Javier scowled, surrendering to his gleeful opponent with a slam of an open palm that scattered the dominos and set the gamblers to uproarious laughter. The brothers walked away, Javier seizing Desi by the elbow.

"Not a word to Mother," he said fiercely.

"Why did you lie?"

"I am the man of the house, and I make money the way I choose."

"Javier, there was trouble," Desi said.

"What kind?" he said, eyes narrowed warily.

"Your butcher friend. I saw him getting arrested in the main street. Six policemen came for him. Javier, what have you gotten yourself into?"

"Damnation," Javier muttered. "We'll have to go."

"You cannot run! They are the policia! Javier!"

Ignoring Desi's protests, he led him to his Model T, which he cranked into life, and then the brothers were in the cabin of the motor car, Javier driving at a dangerous speed. Rain struck then, the sudden furious kind, fat drops from nowhere that the windscreen wiper struggled to clear.

"You have to go to the police station," Desi said. "Whatever you have done, you may be forgiven if you are honest and penitent."

"Of course I'm going there," Javier said. "But not for the reasons you say."

The road to the train station was little more than a muddy track, and Desi felt every pothole as the Model T bounced and jolted, sliding around the corners, and then they were in the cobbled streets of the city, people running for the shelters of the pillared verandas, horses and mules left out to suffer in the sudden downpour. Javier slowed to a respectable speed when he got within sight of the police station, and pulled in next to a soggy horse on the hitching rail.

"Be silent," Javier warned. "I am now a lawyer, and you are my assistant."

"What? You cannot lie to them!"

"See? You have already failed at this."

Stepping out of the car and into the rain, Javier waved at the officer waiting under the portico, clicking his fingers at his brother as he held a newspaper over his head. Javier gave a curt nod to the policia, and just like that they were in the building.

Desi's heart was pounding. Whatever his brother was

up to, he was bearding the lion in its den. Everywhere he turned, he saw a lawman, and his imagination turned each casual glance into suspicion, and the handcuffs and pistola on each belt seemed heavy with significance.

Javier stepped up to the shining oak of the public desk, interrupting an old man who was arguing with the desk sergeant. He slammed his newspaper down and demanded immediate attention.

"You are holding my client Raoul Pérez in your cells!" he said, slamming the desk again. "He has been arrested unlawfully. I demand to see him at once."

"No," the desk sergeant said, unimpressed by the show.

"I shall have your badge for this, sir!" Javier thundered. "You will be carting dung by tomorrow!"

"You cannot see him, Mister Lawyer," the policia said, "because he has already been granted his bail."

"Oh."

"His friends paid for him. Americans, out of Tampa. When Mister Pérez saw them, he turned around. Fought to go back into his cell."

Face turning white, Javier turned from the desk sergeant's nasty smile, and walked briskly towards the exit, Desi in his wake. At any moment Desi expected a hand clapped on his shoulder, a baton in his ribs, but they were back out in the rain, Javier cranking on the starter.

"They got him," Javier said, and Desi knew enough of his brother to see the anguish, the tears that the rain hid. The car coughed into life and Javier drove them through the deluge, finally stopping at a butcher shop.

The door was open a crack, the bell tinkling merrily as the gusting wind waved it back and forth.

"Stay here," Javier warned, hauling a snub-nosed pistol out of a jacket pocket. Wide-eyed, Desi obeyed. He watched as his older brother nudged open the door, gun up and tracking.

A moment later he was back outside, retching in the gutter, gun forgotten.

Desiderio Delgado Alvarez stood on a razor of possibilities then. In one life, he waited for his brother to recover, and stayed in the car. Went into hiding with Mother. Then came Javier's disappearance, the cane farm failing, poverty and oblivion.

In this life, Desi came out of the car and into the rain. Comforted his brother. Took up the small pistol, scared witless but determined to protect Javier from whatever terrified him so.

Nothing but the gusting door, the merry tinkle inviting him in. Desi eased open the door, looking in on a neat butcher's shop. Carcasses on hooks. Dried meats festooning the walls.

On a counter was a neat stack of parcels wrapped up in butcher's paper, blood leaking through in the corners. It was a lot of meat, enough to feed Desi's entire street for a week. Puzzled, Desi stepped forward into the gloom of the shop, fumbling around until he found the dangling light string.

With a snap, the shop was flooded in light, and he realized the true horror. The butcher's severed head lay next to this pile of meat, frozen in a final scream of horror.

A moment later, Desi joined his brother's vomit with his own.

"What will we do?" Desi moaned over and over. Javier drove the car as fast as he dared, scattering livestock and setting off the klaxon whenever someone looked to wander over the road.

"You will do nothing," Javier said. "I am sending you and Mother to stay with Uncle. It is not safe for you at home."

"Let me help!" he said, as the new Desi who stepped into awful places and faced peril. "I am your brother!"

"This is beyond you, Desi. That is my final word on it."

"Javier, what is this you are mixed up in?"

"Nothing I cannot fix," he said, determined. As always Desi despised being brushed off, relegated to the role of the kid brother. To be protected, sheltered, and frequently lied to.

Next came the confusion from Mother, more lies as Javier followed her around her room filling up a carry-all with her things. Next the sudden appearance of a knife as Javier severed the cord for the telephone, and the hustle as he piled everyone back into his car.

"What is all this?" Mother said.

"We have an infestation," Javier said. "Italian cockroaches. I have friends who can deal with this."

"I did not see any cockroaches," she said.

"That's just the thing, Mother. You might run a clean house, but if one cockroach gets in, they all get in."

"Mother in heaven," she said, clutching her carry-all.

Javier deposited Desi and Mother at Uncle's house, rapidly unloading their things, and then he was back in the car, crunching the gears as he turned the vehicle around, finally launching back down the driveway in a spray of mud and small stones.

Uncle welcomed them into the crumbling manor with open arms and liquor on his breath, but the first moment he could make his excuses, Desi slipped out through the kitchen. Something important had flipped in his universe today, a binary point, and he'd stepped into some other life now, as if peeking around the curtains in a theatre and seeing all the things that the audience wasn't meant to.

Desi stole through the rain to the cane cutters' quarters, pressing his ear to the door. They were inside, sheltering from the downpour, and he heard them playing at cards and sharing bawdy jokes, safe from the dubious morality of Uncle. Desi found a bicycle underneath a lean-to, and he did not feel bad for stealing it from such rough and rude men. Let the man walk home tonight!

Desi rode through the rain till his clothes were plastered to his skin, and into a true tropical storm. He rode past the sea-wall as waves battered it, casting spray up onto the esplanada. Desi fought the strong gusts, felt like the bicycle might sprout wings at any second. When he came into the trainyards he saw Javier's Model T drawn up in front of the same warehouse he'd been gambling in, the engine still running.

Desi dropped the bicycle and ran inside, only to draw up short, arms wheeling as if he stood on the edge of a chasm.

The domino tables were overturned, the tiles scattered like broken teeth, and then he took in the turned over chairs, and saw where the corpses began, storemen riddled with bullet holes as they tried to flee.

Every instinct told Desi to turn and run, to fetch the policia, to save his brother even if it meant a life in a cell. Then he heard a distant cry of pain, and knew the author.

Javier!

Desi stole into the warehouse then, and immediately noticed the ransacking. Tea-chests had been torn apart, boxes smashed with hammers, sacks of coffee beans slashed open. A fast, brutal search, and deeper into the warehouse he heard the cracking of crowbars set to prying, a box being tipped. A question being asked, hard and brutal, and then a cry of pain.

Javier! I am coming!

Moving through the stacks of goods, he saw a swaying lamplight, and the shadows of people, perhaps a dozen or more.

"Where did you put it?" a nasally voice demanded in English.

"I do not have it," Javier replied with a pained gasp.

Desi pushed through the sacks of mail bound for Havana, and looked on in horror as his brother floated in the air itself, arms and legs stretched out painfully, some invisible grip pulling him this way and that.

Around him stood goons in suits, cradling crowbars and guns, but strangest was an older man dressed in the same snappy American style, holding an iron rod he tapped gently with a small hammer. Even as lightly as he brushed it, each strike gave a loud crack, and then Javier would move again.

Desi was looking upon dark magic, but he was attentive and did not ignore the man's companions.

He put together Americans from Tampa and Italian cockroaches and came up with the instant answer of mafia. He'd seen them before, visitors from America, swaggering around Cienfuegos, eyeing properties before traveling back to the casinos and partying in Havana. If there was anything he despised more than thieves and criminals, it was American thieves and criminals.

Once more the hammer to the iron, the unnatural crack that Desi could feel in his bones. His brother's cry.

"Tell me where the Key is. Now."

"I am dead anyway," Javier gasped. He named the man with the iron rod then, but something went wrong with the speaking of it, and Desi's ears could only phrase this sound as Magician.

"True," the Magician said. "But you can earn a neat little love tap between the eyes, instant lights out and goodnight. Or you can get what happened to your friends back there. Slow and awful."

Javier said nothing. The Magician and his goons were all looking at him, but Javier had noticed his brother hiding in the mail sacks, making the briefest of eye contact before looking away.

He then spat at the Magician, landing the spittle square on his forehead.

"You think this is funny?" the Magician shouted. "I can torture you for a thousand years!"

"I don't need to last a thousand years," Javier said. "I only need to last another day, maybe two. Because the Knight is coming for you."

The Magician snarled then, and struck the iron rod hard, shaking the warehouse with a thunderclap. That invisible grip broke Javier in a hundred places, and he fell to the ground. Desi cried out and one of the gangsters noticed him then, and the cry went up. Desi ran for the exit, bullets striking the cases and sacks all around him.

He ran through the warehouse and into his brother's Model T, trying his best to remember a handful of driving lessons, shouts and gunfire chasing him out of the trainyards and into a storm that matched how he felt.

Magic is real. It is a dark and awful thing, and my brother is dead.

Desi drove blindly through the streets of Cienfuegos. He could not return to Uncle's, and dared not go home. He'd witnessed his brother's murder, and the dark magic used to do it. Worse, they were mafia, led by a sorcerer. He was a spitting image of his older brother, and there was no mistaking who he was. Desiderio Delgado Alvarez would not be permitted to live.

Looking to the rearview mirror, certain that the gangsters had their own motor car and would come to chase him, Desi almost missed the wet dog that was running across the street. He jammed on the brakes sudden and hard, the Model T sliding to a halt.

Next to him, he heard something heavy bang against the front of the seat. Fearing a mechanical malfunction, he pulled over to the curbside, and that was when he saw a wooden panel, pushing slightly out from the bench seat.

A secret compartment!

Sliding the panel aside with shaking fingers, he found a hidden briefcase and yanked it free. It was made of expensive leather, and was heavy.

Grieving as he was, the need for answers forced his hand. Watching carefully for any other motor cars that might be prowling for him, Desi hid the Model T down a side street. He ran for the public library with the briefcase over his head as a makeshift umbrella.

The librarian scowled at his soggy clothing, but Desi was a regular and beloved by the staff. No one stopped him as he retreated to a reading desk, and he breathed a sigh of relief that the case was not locked.

He saw notebooks, a road map. A stack of letters and loose papers. Shuffling through the briefcase, he saw the bottom was lined with fat stacks of pesos and American greenbacks, the most wealth Desi had ever seen. Underneath it all, a revolver still in its case, and a box of bullets.

Eyes widened, he slammed the briefcase shut. After a long heart-thumping moment he eased it open, taking out the first notebook. It was filled with his brother's messy scrawl, evidence that would damn him in the hands of the policia. Stolen goods and their hiding places. Money owed to him by desperate men, and the atrocious interest he was charging them. A list of stores under his protection.

His dear, dead brother had not been dabbling in some

shady dealings. Desi realized he'd been a genuine criminal, a very bad man. A crime boss, with people who answered to him. For some time, Javier had been the picture of familial love, a giver of favors, but the hard truth was that he was truly despicable.

Desi felt a flush of strong anger against Javier. How dare he put them through this?

The accountings of Javier's nasty secret life ended abruptly some three months gone, as if he'd simply lost interest in the operation.

Pulling the road map out of the briefcase, he saw an X marking a site in the nearby Escambray Mountains, some distance into the bush from a lonely road. He'd visited the area with his school on a field trip, and knew the mountains were rugged and remote, a place of rainforests and brutal humidity. No place his city-loving brother would choose to linger.

Desi rapidly scanned the other papers and notes. Fearing the policia breathing down his neck, it appeared Javier needed a place to store money, stolen goods, rum for thirsty Americans. Somewhere to bury the bodies of his foes. Javier had heard a rumor from Uncle of all people, the site of an old cave in the mountains, a place remote enough to hide ill deeds. He knew he had his answer.

Then the sheaf of papers, complete with drawings. Javier had been a neat hand at sketching, and he had drawn the entrance to the cave, sealed up long ago, but with a recent mudslide revealing part of the entryway. Notes describing his gang breaking into an old cavern, and finding the biggest surprise of all.

People had lived in here in ancient times, and the system

was extensive, crudely tunneled into the mountain. Javier found ancient artifacts, and an archeologist who owed him money confirmed that these were incredibly old, predating even the original Taino and Guanahatabey peoples of the island.

There were Taino carvings on the walls though, a later addition. Petroglyphs captured in Javier's sketchbook, with more messy notes. His archeologist contact had never seen anything like it, and observed that they had been carved quickly, and only near the entrance to the cavern.

Desi's fingers shook as he looked over the drawings, the petroglyphs striking him at a primal level. There were the signs of people on their sides, and a sharp pointed shape, like a fang, and this was depicted over and over.

"A WARNING? KEEP OUT?" Javier had scrawled near these.

Then a rough chart of the cave system, as far as Javier had ventured, with notes describing where certain artifacts had been found, and then a final room, where Javier's explorations had finally faltered.

"BONES?" he'd noted here.

Desi moved onto the stack of letters, and saw Javier's next effort. To shift his debt to Javier, the archeologist had been helping him move and sell the pre-Taino artifacts to American collectors. He'd found a type of ceremonial seat, jars and pots, stone scrapers, and sculptures of spirits and ancestors, carved out of shell and bone, gold and precious stones.

Like the worst sort of grave robber, his dear brother

had been plundering the dead to feather his own nest. No wonder Javier had hidden the secret of his good fortune from his own family!

The money had come in thick and fast, but these unique new artifacts brought questions, and then there was a correspondence with a new friend, a wealthy collector who only referred to himself as the Claret Knight.

What this Knight wanted most of all was to explore the cave to its fullest, and he was willing to fund Javier and his crew an absolute fortune to do so, far more money than all of the artifacts he'd sold for thus far.

"Complete the mapping of the cavern," the Knight wrote. "But await my arrival before commencing the excavations. You must beware the Mirroring Blade at all costs."

There was a drawing on the letter, detailed painstakingly with colored ink. It was a sketch of what looked like a sharp jag of ice, as if the ancients had knapped a piece of flint from some dark and sinister glacier.

The second he looked upon the image, Desi felt his mind reel, and once more he felt that binary moment, that switch he could choose to flip one way, or the other. In one life, he took the suitcase into the policia, gun, money, and all, and told them everything he knew.

But in this life, he looked upon the image with hunger, and he had never wanted something so badly as he wanted this Mirroring Blade. Every shining edge called for him to run a loving thumb along it, and he knew it would draw deep, down to the bone if he pressed even lightly. Then there was the dark heart of the shard, and he knew there was a truth hidden in there, if only someone worthy of the Mirroring Blade were to look in here.

He made his choice. Desi took up his brother's suitcase of secrets for himself, and soon he was back in the clattering motor car. He had the map open on the seat next to him, and he drove the Model T towards the mountains and to that beautiful shining blade, as if the tip of it was already scratching at his heart, and he had but to throw himself upon it to know all things.

As night fell, Desi finally left Cienfuegos, but not in a way he'd ever hoped or planned for. Only yesterday he'd been ignorant of dark magic, fearing only the laws of man and his own disturbing dreams of the cane, and now he was climbing up into the mountains, where the prophets went to meet the gods, and the foolhardy went to defy them.

The road was empty, farmers and their wagons already home in ignorance and lamplight, and few owned motor cars this far away from town. He passed through a handful of sleepy villages and towns, but everything else was rough country road, bouncing and cracking across rut and pothole, steering wheel shaking in his hands as he climbed into the mountains.

Many bone-shaking hours later, Desi found the spot Javier had marked on the map. The rain had fallen back into a thick humidity, and as he climbed out of the car to shift some branches away from a hidden track, he realized his clothes were still soaking wet.

If he lived through this, was he likely to catch his death of the chill?

Then Desi felt it. A delicious tickle, a pull at his soul. The knowledge that he was meant for something here, and it belonged to him, he to it. He would not die here, not if he kept to his path and saw it through.

Then the roar of the engine, the sweep of headlights pushing through the switchback up the mountain behind him. Two motor cars, and they were getting closer now.

The Magician!

Fishing out a flashlight from the trunk of the car, Desi ran up a path made by many feet. In places someone had set a sleeper or piece of slate as a step, and in other places rocks and obstacles had been levered out of the way. He slid around in the mud as he scrambled up the mountain side, already sweating from the deep humidity of the rainforest around him.

Then he saw them below, two cars moving along the scar of the road, pulling up behind Javier's car. The shouts of several men, answered by the nasal voice of the Magician. Once more came the stroke of the hammer upon the iron rod, and the sound echoed against the mountain, rocks and mud sliding down the mountainside and threatening to drive Desi back down to the road.

He held the flashlight close, hoping to hide his position in the trees. Another peal of that unnatural magic, and this time Desi's footprints blazed for a brief moment with a bright magnesium arc of light, revealing his path to any who looked.

Desi froze in place like a terrified animal, betrayed by his own tracks. Again that moment where he'd peered around reality's curtain, he found himself afraid of this power that defied all explanation, put lie to all of the science and logic he'd ever crammed into his head.

Tempted as he was to dart away and hide in the brush, Desi felt the pull again, knew the Blade was near. Was his.

Wild gunshots came then, winging through the trees. Gasping wildly, Desi drew out the revolver and forged upwards, flinching as a close shot cracked against a tree just inches to his left. Then he came upon the stack of boulders, splintered from dynamite, and his flashlight made out the cleft of the cavern, the entrance widened and easy to slip into.

His flashlight danced across crates of supplies, picks and shovels, lanterns and helmets, everything Javier had bought with the Claret Knight's finances. The scale of the operation was impressive, considering this had all been ported in by hand. All of it was under the horrifying portico of the petroglyphs, and Desi immediately understood the intent of the message:

Great danger ahead. You should not be in here.

The shouts were getting closer, and the nearest of the gangsters let off a stutter of gunfire into the cave itself. A tommy gun in the hand of a killer, and here was untested Desi, never once having pulled a trigger. Casting about for succor, he found the answer as he fumbled through Javier's supplies.

A matchbook, and he applied the flame to the dangling fuse-cord of a stick of dynamite.

With the strong right arm that had made him the pitcher for his school baseball team, Desi hurled the sputtering stick of dynamite out and into the darkness, and a moment later he was rewarded with an explosion and a scream. Grimacing, he threw out another stick, but the next time he reached for the matchbook the entire pack flared up in his hands.

Fearing this to be the work of the Magician, he looked to the dynamite fuses for a worried moment, but they stayed unlit. Why would the Magician start a cave-in when he wanted the blade for himself? Desi felt a sudden flash of jealousy, and it was odd to observe his fear washing away in this emotion. Once more an American was coming for something that rightly belong in Cuban hands, and he was furious. More of a Javier than a Desi in that moment.

Desi ran into the caves, stepping ever deeper into the past, as if sliding down the brown throat of an ancient, buried beast. Echoing footsteps as the gangsters entered the cave itself, their shouts overlapping until they were one man with a dozen or more mouths. Nonsense and chaos, and through it all came the Magician, clanging his rod, the sound dogging Desi's every step.

A gangster lunged at him from the dark, and Desi pulled the trigger by instinct, dropping the man dead with a flash, the noise deafening within the tunnel. Instantly the clang of the rod, and Desi's revolver grew red hot, burning and blistering his skin, and he was forced to discard the molten weapon as it turned into slag.

He ran, breath catching, until his foot stepped on something with a crunch.

Desi swept the flashlight down to realize he was standing

on a carpet of human bones, hundreds of people thick, a pile of the dead, and he wasn't sure how far down it even went. The chamber above was a thick node, a cathedral that seemed shaped by some ill hand, as if in the shape of a bizarre heart that had no business beating.

Desi stood at one more junction in this strangest of days – here stood the boy who froze up in fear, waiting for a handful of moments to be torn apart by a secret mafiosi cult, one more body added to this mass grave. The nasally Magician emerging triumphant with the Mirroring Blade.

But in this life, Desiderio Delgado Alvarez refused to be that person, for now and ever again, and he stepped further into bone, wading through that sharp tide of calcium. He heard the call, the aching throb of an energy that had been pent-up for too long.

Burrowing underneath skulls and spines, Desi breathed in the dust of that unknown people, and he felt the weight of an ancient ritual, knew they'd come to their deaths willingly. Happy even. He understood their urge, felt the same call. The Blade had found this forgotten people all wanting in some way, but they'd served as sustenance, over and over until the last pair of hands had driven the blade in deep, and it had been a glory and a service to bleed out in this cave.

Then the Taino had come, and resisted, and buried the Blade for thousands of years.

He supposed his own family's ritual with the land was a cousin to this rite, but whereas the cane farmers had traded blood for something tangible, this was going to be a very different deal. Blood came to the Blade, and all it could return to the wielder was a sharp edge.

Desi accepted this trade, accepted this condition, and only then did he reach the bedrock underneath that weight of bone, closed his fingers around what he sought, felt that delicious sting and ache.

He emerged from that ancient grave with the Mirroring Blade in his bloody grip, and he stared at it in wonder. Just under a foot in length, the edges of the Blade were brilliant, sharp enough to shave steel, and it seemed to drink up his blood, thirsty for yet more. His flashlight could not penetrate the dark heart of the shard, but it served as a mirror with a black reflection. As he tilted the blade upwards, he recoiled in horror at what he saw.

His own face, twisted and malevolent, a grinning murderer ready to kill anyone and anything. He could not stare away from his reflection, and he knew this was the version of Desi that that Mirror knew, the secret self that lay deep below everything civilization could give him.

Faced with that dark reflection, Desi experienced a moment of the deepest clarity. He understood he was no better than the gangsters that hunted him, than Javier hurting others with his loansharking and other misery. Desi had reached for the books because he was simply too scared to project his will into the universe, to occupy a space and be known. Bound to the land by blood rite, true violence had always been his heritage – he'd just never had the chance to try it out.

He came out of the open grave and back into the tunnels. After a moment of thought, he smashed his flashlight against the wall, and slipped out of his shoes, skin now touching stone. The Blade knew this place of old, to the inch. He stalked through the honeycomb of caves and tunnels, creeping towards the footsteps and swaying flashlights of the gangsters.

There. A man with a pencil-thin mustache and a fedora, hesitating at a junction of tunnels. Desi darted forward, feet barely brushing stone, and he swung the blade down with all his might. He caught the gangster above the collarbone and tore through him on a diagonal, and met virtually no resistance.

The man fell to the ground in two pieces, but the Blade was not satisfied with that. It reached out and killed the same man in other places, other realities. Desi was a witness as he killed the man in a bath, stabbed him performing a baptism, murdered him as he piloted a zeppelin, and over and over he killed the man, finally leaving a ragged hole in reality where that person had once been.

And still, the Mirroring Blade was not satisfied. There were other realities where Desi also stood in the same spot, and drove the blade into his own heart there, waking with a gasp. He still lived, but felt a fraction lesser than he was, as if the Blade had shaved off a sliver of his soul for itself.

A mighty weapon, with a mighty cost.

Stalking the mafiosi cultists, Desi paid it gladly, again and again, and watched as he killed men in graveyards, in tea-rooms and train stations, even once on a ship that sailed between the stars, and again he slew himself, over and over, and still the Blade demanded more.

Then the tolling of the iron rod. Desi froze in place, every sinew and joint seizing up instantly.

A blood-soaked flashlight lay on the floor, and through its rosy light the Magician approached Desi, smiling widely. He circled him warily, watching as the Mirroring Blade continued to move and writhe, inch by inch.

"A conundrum," the man said. "This Key has claimed you. So you're an appointed champion, a guardian of this reality. All of that jazz."

The man clucked, rubbing the hammer along the iron rod with a slight rasp, and the sound penetrated Desi's teeth to the root.

"But you see, I don't think you deserve it. You certainly can't control it. That Mirroring Blade should be mine."

Desi lurched forward then, and face wide with surprise, the Magician once more cast the stilling spell, now keeping a wary distance.

"You're a strong one, even without the Blade. Makes sense why it picked you. Here, let's give you a bit of leeway. The eyelids. Blink once for yes, twice for no."

Another rasp of the rod. Desi blinked.

"Good. You're in that much control. Now, have you heard of Aesop and his fables?"

Blink.

"And have you heard of the dog in the manger? Couldn't have something others wanted, so stopped others from getting it?"

Desi wanted to kill him so badly. Ached for it. A universe of desire urged him to cut, and laugh, and take the life of this rotten American man over and over.

But all he could do was…

Blink.

"So here's how it's going to be. I'm going to work something now. Likely to turn you inside out. But I'll find a way to free the Blade from you, bind it to me, and become the champion, with all the fruits and laurels. Capisce?"

Blink.

"So if there's a way you can release control of the Blade, all voluntarily like, I won't need to do it the awful way. I'll give you a peaceful way out, and I can still wield the Blade for its intended purpose, as well as carving up anyone I disagree with. Will you let go of the Blade?"

Blink. Blink.

"All right, dog in the manger time. I'll kill you, hard. Here's another truth; might not be able to kill you proper, and you might cling to life a little. So, if the Blade won't take to me, I'll apply some sour grapes to this situation. Bring the whole place down on you."

Desi lurched, swung out with the Blade, coming within an inch of the Magician's throat. Once more the unnerving sound, as the stilling magic settled upon his muscles.

"You won't get that lucky, boy. Hand over the Blade, or you will spend a million years down here, dying in the dark."

"I cannot allow this," a voice said calmly. The Magician whirled around, rod and hammer raised. A man stepped into the flickering torchlight, and he stood in the ruddy glow, hands folded in front of him. The new arrival was a sophisticated gentleman, and he wore an old-fashioned set of formal clothing underneath a great coat.

"Stay back, Knight, or we all die!" the Magician said, and Desi thought he detected a quaver in his voice. Respect. Fear.

The Claret Knight! The hammer rasped against the rod, and the ceiling of the cave shivered in its own warning. The man nodded.

Desi thought about Javier's papers, about the way this stranger had dangled money over him, no doubt also hunting the hiding place of the Blade. This man of culture and poise walked calmly through a site of ancient evil, and this told Desi everything he needed to know.

This man was even more dangerous than the Magician, and not necessarily a friend.

"You are as foolish as this boy," the Knight said. He spoke English, but Desi detected an accent now. French, but with an odd archaic twang to it, as if the man was a provincial whose valley had been locked away from the world for a thousand years.

"The only fool in here is you, pal," the Magician said. "You're all alone, and a long way from all the places that protect you."

"I'm not alone."

Another stepped into the light, a Chinese woman who held herself like a ballerina, or a fencer. She held a closed parasol over her shoulders like a sword, and sneered at the Magician.

"Tzu San Niang!" the Magician gasped. "I'm warning you, stay back!"

"He means to bring the roof down with his little toy," the Claret Knight said. "Suggestions?"

"Use the magic of our enemies," the woman said. "Unname him."

The Claret Knight gave a sudden clap of his hands, his eyes flashing with a scarlet brightness. Eyes widened, the Magician struck his instrument hard, and Desi flinched. The rod clanged again, and again, but the ceiling remained in place.

Desi realized another truth then. He'd heard the Magician's name, many times. His own men had shouted it. His brother had named him in his notes. But he was a nameless person now, and it seemed that his own magic was failing him.

As did the spell which bound him in place. Freed, Desi fell upon the Magician, relishing in the glory as he slew the villain time and time again, and in each instance the man was more or less the villain that bled before him.

"Boy, you may stop," the Claret Knight said, and Desi turned to face them, Mirroring Blade raised. The Claret Knight merely stood in place, unafraid.

"Get out of my way," Desi snarled. "This is mine now."

"This is true," he said. "The Key has claimed you. You can go on your way and kill as you please, and the Coterie will not prevent this."

"Coterie?"

"We are the Red Coterie," the Claret Knight said. Desi could see now that the man's formal garb was of deep scarlet, the woman's parasol a brighter red.

"Young man, this secret world can destroy you," the Knight said. "Let us show you a wiser path."

"But you won't take it from me?" he said, clutching the glassy knife close to his chest.

"No," the woman with the red parasol said. "You are responsible for the Mirroring Blade now. You may entrust it to a new wielder, but even we would struggle to seize it from you."

The Blade wriggled in his palm, shaving away a little bit more of his soul, aching to taste directly from his heart. Desi's bond with the Blade felt like that of mother and child as much as it did predator and prey, and he despaired. He was as duped as any of the desperate gamblers that Javier had taken in, suddenly out of their depth and hand in hand with something dangerous.

Now these two had arrived, unfazed by this disturbing secret world, but they did not offer enticement or threat. Merely understanding, and the offer of knowledge, a currency he already respected.

He followed the other two sorcerers out of the cave, and watched in terror as they brought the entrance down with their magics, encasing the Magician and his cultists in that strangest of mausoleums.

In his chase for the Blade, Desi had neglected his family, and he returned to Uncle's farm with haste. Silence as he approached the house, where once Blando would have been out and snarling at strange visitors.

"Wait here," he told his new friends, and the Knight and his companion nodded, relaxing in the back of the Model T as if they were on a lovely driving tour.

No one answered his cries or his frenzied rapping at the

door, and he ran inside, the Blade held low by his side.

"Mother! Uncle!"

He found their bodies in Uncle's parlor, looked wide-eyed at an awful ending that showed the worst depths of human invention. The Magician and his mafia goons had visited mere hours ago, meaning that Desi had already avenged his family without realizing it.

His heart felt like a sharp, painful rock. With the Mirroring Blade, Desi had killed the thugs a thousand times over, and even this didn't feel like enough. He was the master of a strange sort of violence now, but it did nothing to stop his grief, his guilt. He took up the burden of his brother's sins, and added his own actions to the pile. He piled this weight upon his soul and decided he could never put it aside.

Over their bodies, Desi swore an oath, to anything that would listen. Never again would he allow this secret world of magicians and monsters to hurt those he loved. The thought of violence disturbed him, but now he had a way to protect people, and new friends to learn from. If ever this secret world brought harm to Cuba, he would give the Mirroring Blade something tasty to nibble on.

Desi gave his family the manor as a funeral pyre, and he set about torching the cane fields, once and for all ending the family connection to that ancient blood rite. He still had all of Javier's money in the suitcase, and Havana in his sights.

He found the workers still huddled in their quarters, where they'd hidden from the attack on the house. There they waited, gathering the courage to leave, afraid that Uncle's killers still lingered nearby.

Desi simply carved through their barricades with the Mirroring Blade, and stood before them, hard-eyed, grown into manhood in that one horrible day.

"You work for me now," he told them, and they nodded with fear. Respect.

Desiderio Delgado Alvarez decided he liked that.

HONOR AMONG THIEVES
Carrie Harris

Rosa Varela sipped her cocktail, watching the light of the early spring sun glint off the diamonds circling her wrist. She'd earned them. She'd earned *this* – a lazy afternoon spent on the terrace of one of the most exclusive yacht clubs in Buenos Aires. The wait staff wore pristine tuxedos as they glided through the packed patio full of movers and shakers just dying to be seen. Immaculate white tablecloths fluttered in the breeze off the Rio de la Plata. In the corner sat a man with mournful eyes, strumming quiet music on a gleaming guitar. Two tables away, a pair of men in fedoras exchanged glances with her in that age-old game of cat and mouse.

Rosa loved games. She always had.

Out of the corner of her eye, she saw her sister, Milagros, charging through the scattered patrons on the terrace with bulldog determination. Although they were twins, they couldn't have been more different. Rosa was petite and playful, with dexterous hands, a quick wit, and a daring sense of style. Milagros towered over everyone, dominating with her physical presence and her brushfire temper. By the looks of her, something had set it ablaze.

"I've been looking everywhere for you," Milagros snapped, kissing the air beside Rosa's cheeks. "Madre de Dios, Rosa. If you're drunk, I'll throw you into the river."

She spoke primarily in English, and that meant one thing: she wanted to discuss a new client. The foreign language reduced the chances that someone might overhear them discussing something illegal.

"Don't be such a spoilsport. I'm having a good time, and a well-deserved one, I might add. This is my first day off in months, and I'm going to enjoy it," said Rosa, sticking to Spanish out of sheer stubbornness. To drive her point home just a little further, she looked at the boys over Mila's shoulder and winked.

"Rosa! Please?"

Milagros rarely asked for anything. She ordered. Something had knocked her for a loop, and Rosa didn't like that one bit.

"What's wrong?" she demanded.

At that moment, the taller of the two fellows she'd been flirting with approached the table with his hat in hand. He sketched a little bow, meeting her eyes with the assurance of a man who had been fed everything he'd ever wanted with a silver spoon and expected the buffet to continue indefinitely. Although Rosa had spent an enjoyable afternoon exchanging glances with him, his appearance only annoyed her now. He couldn't have had worse timing if he'd tried.

"Señorita," he said, "would you and your friend care to join us?"

"No!" said the Varela twins in unison.

It must have been a word he didn't hear often, because he stood there for a moment, frozen in shock.

"But–"

"¡Volá, idiota!" Milagros snapped, waving him away. "We're talking. Go bother somebody else."

He opened his mouth and closed it again before slinking back to his table. Both women watched his defeated retreat before returning to their conversation.

"Mila, you're worrying me. What's going on?" asked Rosa, switching to English and leaning close to shield their conversation from listening ears.

"I've got a new client," said Milagros, drumming her fingers on the table in an uncharacteristic display of nerves. "I know you wanted a break, but like I said before, we've got to take what we can get until we make a name for ourselves. Then we can pick and choose."

Rosa looked down at her sister's tapping fingers with their sensibly short nails and sighed. She trusted Mila. Ever since their parents had died and the money ran out, it had been the two of them against the world, with only their quick hands and even quicker wits to sustain them. But something didn't add up here. Despite her dismissive attitude, Rosa was a professional, and she could read people like books. Something was off. She gestured, urging her sister to continue.

"It'll be easy," said Milagros. "The client wants us to acquire a few pieces from the Corregidor fashion collection. It'll be on display at the Palacio Errázuriz, and I've got a pair of tickets to tonight's costume ball. I create a distraction, you nick the rags, and we're done. Easy," she repeated, like she was trying to convince herself.

"Tonight? You must be kidding."

Rosa threw her head back and laughed, relief suffusing her limbs. For a moment, she'd bought into Mila's nervous act. But her sister would never take a job with no planning time. Rosa enjoyed the rush that came with improvising on the spot, but Mila didn't breathe without scheduling it first.

But Mila didn't laugh along with her, and Rosa's heart sank. For the first time, she found herself in the uncomfortable position of having to be the voice of reason.

"That's not enough time to plan, and you know it," she said. "That's why we haven't been caught. Do you *want* to get copped?"

"We won't." Dogged determination suffused Mila's voice. "It's just a hat and a coat. You could pinch that with one hand tied behind your back. It'll make us a pretty dime too. I asked for extra because of the short notice."

"If it's that easy, what's got you so rattled?"

"I'll admit it. The cat who hired us makes my skin crawl, but we don't have to play house with him. What do you say?"

Rosa sighed. "You really think we can't afford to say no?"

"Not if you want to keep coming here."

Milagros glanced around at their opulent surroundings pointedly.

"Fine," said Rosa, sighing. "But I don't like it."

The rest of the afternoon passed in a flurry of preparation. Mila had scored the tickets with barely any effort at all. Since they'd relocated to Buenos Aires a year ago, the pair of them had built up a reputation as flighty heiresses with nothing on their minds but the next party, a reputation they'd worked hard to maintain. It accounted for their frequent trips out of town on jobs throughout the Americas and Europe, as well as for the baubles that passed frequently through their possession. Besides, they'd learned that people spoke freely when they thought themselves in the company of a vapid floozy with nothing on her mind but the latest fashions and her next beau.

Over the past few years, they'd bounced into and out of high society often enough that when Milagros expressed interest in tickets to the costume ball, she got a pair without even having to ask. Now they needed a plan, and they walked through it over and over again, filling in the gaps. As they chatted, Milagros sat at the sewing machine, making adjustments to a vaudeville costume Rosa had worn in Vienna, when they'd swiped a priceless jewelry set from a steel baron with wandering hands and an overblown sense of entitlement. Thinking of that job made Rosa smile every time. He'd had it coming.

"Are you sure my trousers will fit under that thing?" she asked, eyeing the fabric on Mila's table with skepticism.

At every job, Milagros insisted that they wear black

trousers and a blouse beneath their clothes. A woman in such attire could be anything with the right props: a butler, a performer, even a man. She could flee unseen in the dark. The outfit provided a perfect blank canvas upon which to improvise. Rosa had to admit that it had come in handy, but she worried that it wouldn't all fit, even under the voluminous floor length skirt.

"You need to wear them," Mila ordered. "Our client wasn't as specific about the dimensions of our targets as I'd like. If they don't fit under your costume, you'll have to shuck the gown and wear the coat out. Tell people you're a pirate."

"I can do that," said Rosa. "But add another layer to that skirt, would you? I've got to hide a lot beneath it."

"I suppose you're right." The sewing machine whirred to life again. "Now describe the clothes for me again. Be specific."

Rosa swallowed a sigh. She knew this level of preparation was necessary, but it always rankled. Her fingers itched to get moving, eager for the rush of the game.

"A bright red coat. Long. Black piping on the sleeves and a row of black buttons down the front. It comes with a hat, black and wide brimmed, with a red band." She paused. "Can we hide a red feather somewhere in my costume? If I end up needing to go the pirata route, I can stick it in the cap."

"Good idea," Mila said around a set of pins clutched between her lips. "Go find one. Over there."

She gestured vaguely, but Rosa needed no instructions. The room was cluttered with disguises and cast-off clothes.

They'd posed as maids and singers, vaudeville dancers and beggars. Milagros haunted the fabric shops, maintaining a store of materials that could be used to whip up an outfit on the spot. She also sewed her own clothes, which had always impressed Rosa. She didn't have the patience for such things. Never would.

As she rummaged around in the feather bin for a suitable choice, she said, "The job does seem odd, doesn't it? I bet there are plenty of rich gowns worth much more than an old coat and hat."

"Probably," Milagros replied, distracted. "If I had to guess, there's something hidden in the lining. Jewels maybe?"

"Maybe it's a map to Coronado's gold," said Rosa, teasing. Mila had been obsessed with finding the treasure as a girl, and once she'd bought a map that hadn't even gotten the outlines of the continents right. Paid a pretty penny for it, too.

"I will shove these pins up your–"

"Sorry, sorry," Rosa interrupted hastily. She pulled out a feather and held it up for inspection. "This one looks good, yeah?"

"Sí," said Milagros. "Now hand it over. I'll make a garter and you can attach it to your thigh. You'll have the feather on one, and a cosh on the other. Just in case."

Rosa nodded. They made it a policy to avoid violence whenever possible, but sometimes there was no choice but to whack a bloke on the side of the head. She'd done it twice and still disliked it, but it was better than shooting someone.

"Speaking of that," she said cautiously. "Do you think I should accompany you for the drop off?"

Mila jerked, stabbing herself with a pin. "What? Ow!" She sucked on her finger for a moment. "We need to stick to the plan. One of us goes to the drop off. The other stays hidden as an insurance policy. Like we always do."

"Yes, but…" Rosa considered her words carefully, trying hard to articulate the growing sense of unease that overtook her every time she thought about this job. "This client is different. Every time he comes up, you stop sewing because your hands start shaking. And you still haven't told me his name."

Mila shrugged but didn't dispute it.

"What has you so worked up? I promise I won't make fun of you this time."

"I don't really know." Milagros caught Rosa's look of skepticism and crossed herself. "Honest. I can't put my finger on it. He wears red tinted glasses all the time, but we've worked with eccentrics before. Something about him just…" She shuddered, trailing off.

"All the more reason for me to come with you."

"All the more reason for you to stay away!" exclaimed Mila. "We need to be extra careful. Do things the way we always have. Take my notes; go to the safe house and wait for me."

"I've never seen you like this," said Rosa, frowning with worry. "I know you, Mila. If you're that scared, then there is something very wrong with this cabrón. There will be other jobs. Let's skip this one."

"We can't," blurted Mila. "He knows where we live. He

knows all our past jobs. I don't know who snitched, but whoever it is, they know *everything*. If we don't get him the clothes…" She trailed off, her expression bleak.

Rosa didn't need the details to know that it would be very bad indeed. Mila wouldn't lie about something like this, and Rosa trusted her sister's instincts.

"Okay," she said. "Then we do the job and scatter. Maybe set up shop in Paris for a while. We've been here too long anyway. He can't follow us if we disappear."

Mila nodded, taking in a shaky breath. "Yeah. Okay. Yeah."

"Will you at least tell me his name? That way if I run into him, I'll know to be careful."

"He calls himself the Sanguine Watcher."

Icy fingers ran up the back of Rosa's neck at the mention of the name. But that was ridiculous. The name was ridiculous. She forced a laugh that came out flat.

"That's unsettling," she admitted. "It shouldn't be, but it is."

"Yeah. We get the stuff, and then we run," said Mila, holding out the completed costume.

"Claro," said Rosa, nodding.

Bright lights illuminated the Palacio Errázuriz, striping its pillared exterior with shadows. A row of white banners flapped in the wind, lining the street where pristine Rolls Royces and Mercedes cars pulled up to disgorge their passengers, flouncing out in fluttery costumes and gem-encrusted masks. A fine lady rested her fingertips in the crook of her gentleman's elbow as they made their way up the stately walk to the front door, flanked by footmen in starched livery. They laughed and chattered gaily as they entered one of the most exclusive parties of the season.

Rosa had chosen to hoof it instead. They'd made an effort to disguise her, covering her dark hair with a reddish wig and crafting a mask that obscured all of her face save her mouth, so that if she was spotted taking the clothes, no one would link the theft to the Varela sisters. If asked, Mila would explain that her sister was taken ill with a headache and resting at home, and arriving together in the car would throw all that effort out the window. For a while, they'd debated having Mila drop her off around the block, but they'd ultimately decided it was too much of a risk.

So she'd gotten ready at one of their safe houses instead. They had a handful of them scattered around the continent, fully stocked with canned foods, medical supplies, clothing, and some ready cash. Every once in a while, one of them would live there for a few days, feeding the neighbors stories about sick relatives or university studies to justify their time away. So far, the system had worked, and at times like this, the advance preparation served them well.

Rosa made good time across town and arrived at the Palacio just in time to see Mila make her stately way up the steps to the door. Her sister had chosen to go as a queen, and the combination of crown and heels brought her to nearly six feet tall. Her gold lamé dress glittered in the floodlights as she disappeared through the doors without so much as a glance behind her.

Rosa took her time, ambling down the block with the many layers of her gown rustling around her. Mila had modified what had been a fluttery green confection into a magnificent peacock costume whose many layers could hide a lot of things. Like a coat and hat, for instance.

Considering their lack of time, the plan was a good one. Simple, as most successful plans were. When they'd started out, they'd made things too complicated, trying to account for every possible outcome, and only sheer luck and a well-placed bribe had kept them from being nipped. They'd gotten better since then. Rosa ought to have felt confident, but that couldn't have been further from the truth. Her palms prickled with sweat no matter how many times she wiped them on her skirt, and with each step, she had the uncomfortable feeling of being watched. But every time she whirled around to look, she saw no one.

Mila's vague warnings rattled around in her head no matter how hard she tried to settle her nerves. It was silly, really. After all, the Sanguine Watcher wasn't the first person to threaten them, and he wouldn't be the last. This business didn't exactly attract stand-up citizens. But Rosa hadn't survived for this long by ignoring her gut. It wouldn't hurt to be on high alert until they were on the ship and off the continent. She couldn't wait, even if it meant listening to her sister complain about her seasickness for weeks on end. Milagros didn't travel well at sea.

She climbed the steps to the front door, produced her invitation from an inner pocket, and held it out to one of the footmen for examination. He took it from her sweaty hand with only the barest flicker of his eyes. As she waited for his approval, she tried to talk herself down. No one would recognize her. She had the deftest fingers on the continent, and if she played her cards right, she'd never get caught.

It was time to play her favorite game, and she needed to get her head in it.

Rosa straightened her shoulders and accepted the invitation back from the footman, tucking it back into her costume before heading inside. Velvet ropes corralled the guests toward the party, although the guidance was unnecessary by this point. She could have located the shindig by sound alone.

The party was held in a long hall flanked by a row of pillars on either side. Footmen stood at parade rest all around the room, their keen eyes locked on the expensive fashion displays. Guards, more like. But the sisters had anticipated that.

She made an initial circuit around the room, snagging a glass of Malbec from a passing server to help her blend in. Ornate tapestries hung on the walls, lit by the subtle flicker of crystal chandeliers. The building was an interesting blend of old and new, Argentinian and European. The combination intrigued her, and under different circumstances, she would have loved to have a tour of the place. Perhaps in the future, when the Sanguine Watcher had forgotten all about the Varela sisters, they could return and attempt a visit.

The Corregidor collection was an eclectic one. Rosa hadn't had her customary time to research its contents, so she didn't know as much as she would have liked. But based on what Mila had said, it consisted of pieces owned by famous figures throughout history, so their provenance was just as interesting as the garments themselves. She saw plenty of glittering gowns laden with gems that could have financed her living expenses for at least the next ten years, but also pirate togs and flannel suits, conquistador uniforms and dressing gowns. Most were obviously expensive, but the greatest crowds seemed to cluster around the most everyday exhibits as the guests mused about what it would be like to spend a day in the shoes of a beloved figure or hated despot.

At first, that fact concerned her. If the hat and coat had been owned by someone sufficiently interesting, they might be more popular than anticipated. The plan hinged on the assumption that their targets wouldn't be one of the stars of the show. So she circled around the room, dodging clusters of chatting people dressed as cats and harlequins, until she finally saw the coat tucked in a back corner.

Like most of the displays, it hung on a blank-faced mannequin, with a little placard at the bottom explaining its significance. Rosa edged toward it, hoping that the information there would provide some illuminating bit of knowledge they could use against the Sanguine Watcher if he decided to double cross them. But the card simply read, "Wide-brimmed hat and matching overcoat. Owner unidentified."

They didn't belong in this impressive collection, and Rosa didn't like that one bit. The whole job stank. They'd been hired last minute by a mysterious figure who'd had plenty of time to dig up their past but waited to spring the job on them until it was too late for them to maneuver out of it. The target had questionable value, if any. With every passing moment, she became more convinced that the whole thing was a setup. She would have to play along long enough to find out who pulled the strings.

A flash of gold fabric in the crowd announced Mila's approach. Rosa turned, feigning interest in an elaborate dress of purportedly Mayan origin. She glanced at it this way and that, edging into a position just at the corner of the nearest guard's vision. Single attendees were in short supply, but she made it work by huffing every once in a while, and scanning the crowd as if searching for a wayward date. The guard didn't give her so much as a second glance.

Mila made her way through the crowd like a woman on a mission. As her wide skirts swept towards the corner where Rosa waited, she brushed up against a man in a gaucho costume, complete with a black mask and a camper hat. No one but Rosa noticed the quick flick of Mila's hand that deposited the diamond bracelet into the pocket of the gaucho's bombachas de campo. He continued chatting merrily to the pretty women on his arms, completely unaware of his surroundings.

But Mila paused, jerking away from him as if stung. She moved with such exaggeration that it attracted the attention of a few people nearby, including the guard. Then she held up her arm and shrieked in horror.

"My bracelet!" she exclaimed. "It's gone! You took my bracelet!"

The masked gaucho stopped midsentence, glaring at her in annoyance. After a moment, he seemed to realize that he was the center of attention. He threw his head back and laughed.

"Señora, rest assured that I stole nothing. I have no need to resort to such… antics," he said, sniffing in distaste.

"Then empty your pockets," Mila snapped. "If you're so innocent."

"Do you know who I am?" The gaucho's eyes glittered dangerously as he whipped off his mask to reveal a heavily mustached face. Mila had chosen her mark well. Rosa recognized him: a notoriously corrupt assistant to the mayor of Buenos Aires. If the rumors were true, he'd built his entire career on a tower of bribes. No one would have trouble believing that he'd nicked something, and he thought himself so untouchable as a result of his connections that he wouldn't hesitate to make a scene. "I am Benicio Fentanes, and I will not be so insulted!" he boomed.

"Then empty your pockets, and I will apologize," responded Mila, fluttering a hand in front of her face as if overcome by her emotions. "That bracelet was a gift from my dear departed mother, and I cannot bear the loss. Forgive me if it has driven me to rudeness."

By this time, everyone within earshot was glued to the spectacle. Rosa would get no better chance. She sank into an alcove in the back corner, unhooking the velvet rope that blocked the mannequin from reach and pulling it after her. She would have preferred to make the switch in a space with a door, but this was the closest option they could find with such short notice. At least no one would be able to see in unless they stood at exactly the right angle.

A quick tug released the coat from its moorings. The garment was heavier than she'd expected, the fabric thick-woven. A sickly sweet scent rose from it. Whoever had packed the thing should have used some mothballs.

Rosa eyed the clothing skeptically. Folded, the coat could be hidden among the many layers of her peacock gown, but the hat would pose a problem. They'd known it had a wide brim, but they'd been hoping for a flexible construction that could be tucked away. But this hat had a firm brim that wouldn't hold up to such treatment.

A change of plan, then. She shucked herself out of the peacock dress, pulled off the wig and tore off the mask, fishing out a plain black sequined one to go with her swashbuckler ensemble. As she swapped masks, she glanced out to make sure no one was watching. The guests were all still riveted by the confrontation before them as Fentanes pulled a diamond bracelet out of his pocket, to his immense surprise and her sister's fury. All was going to plan until Rosa made accidental eye contact with a familiar face in the crowd – the fellow from the club who had asked her for a drink. She lifted the new mask into place, but it was too late. His expression brightened as he spotted her, and he whispered a brief word to his companion before he began to push his way through the crowd in her direction.

Rosa murmured a curse beneath her breath, backing up into the alcove as far as she could. If he saw the discarded gown or the empty mannequin, she'd be a goner. For a moment, she considered slipping the peacock dress onto the mannequin instead, but its many layers lay in a hopelessly tangled mess on the floor. It would be impossible to straighten it out in time.

She would just have to hurry. She kicked the gown into the corner, stabbed the feather into the brim of the hat, and crammed it on her head. Fronds bobbed at the edges of her vision, dangling from the hopelessly cockeyed feather, but it would have to do. She shoved one arm into a coat sleeve, backing away into the shadows as she evaluated her options. They weren't good.

The fabric was cold, like it had been packed in an ice box and hadn't thawed out just yet. A shudder gripped her as chilly fingers ran up the back of her neck, sucking the life from her. She gulped in a deep breath of air, trying to stave off the sense of panic that rose up from deep within her. She had the strangest urge to get as far away from these clothes as possible. To throw them to the floor and sprint until she reached the ship that would carry them to Europe. Maybe once it left the port, the chill would ebb from her bones.

But she was a professional, and she'd stick to the plan, no matter how much it made her skin crawl. Teeth gritted, she thrust her other arm into the coat, her mind whirling with escape plans.

As her arm slid into place, her shadow stretched along the wall like taffy. At first, she assumed it was a trick of the light. But it deepened to a color that was beyond black, an infinite darkness that swallowed everything in its path. The empty dummy. The determined flirt from the bar. The guard. It gulped down the illumination from the chandeliers and devoured the heat from her skin. Rosa's heart skittered as it pulled her in – no, *through* – its frigid weave.

She emerged into some darkened chamber, her head whirling in disorientation. Deep red lights flickered at the edges of her vision, outlining the writhing forms of unspeakable creatures with shapes of such awful asymmetry that they made her recoil, shutting her eyes to block them out. But she could hear them still, their slithering, shrieking cacophony growing louder as they approached.

A fierce trembling seized her entire body, curling her in upon herself. She didn't want to see them when they fell upon her, as she knew they would. Poor Mila would wonder what had happened to her. She would never stop searching, if the Sanguine Watcher didn't make good on his threats and destroy her. Under these circumstances, the fear didn't feel unreasonable. If anything, Rosa hadn't been afraid enough.

They would come for Mila. Her sister needed her. Rosa wouldn't abandon the only person she cared about, and she damn well wouldn't give up without a fight.

"Screw you," she spat, turning to run.

She had no destination in mind, no concept of where she was or the details of how she'd gotten there. But she would go somewhere safe. Somewhere *away*.

As soon as the heel of her boot hit the unseen floor, the coat wrapped its freezing fingers around her once again. The shadows pulled her in. The ground disappeared from beneath her, leaving her falling through an unending void.

Her foot landed on a grassy slope with a jolt, her knee buckling with the unexpected impact. She somersaulted, tucking her arms in close to her body, coming back up to stand at the ready to defend herself from monstrous creatures, angry guards, or whatever else the night might throw at her.

But nothing happened. She stood in the grass before an ornate flowerbed dominated by a bush cut into the shape of a parrot, her heart thrumming like a jackrabbit. Recognition thrummed through her. This was the garden at the yacht club! She recognized that parrot, and over to her right stood the edge of the terrace she'd been drinking on just a few hours earlier. Astonishment, vertigo, and outright fear warred within her for dominance.

But how on earth had she ended up here? The exhibition was well over a mile from the club, and she'd crossed the space in seconds. It must have something to do with the clothing she still wore. And the horrific things she'd seen. Suddenly, she could barely breathe. She shrugged out of the coat, backing away from the heaped fabric on the ground like it might just bite or send her hurtling through space to an unfathomable hellscape. Again.

She couldn't dispose of it, though. The Sanguine Watcher wanted it, and now his vague threats felt even more sinister than before. Perhaps he was just as dangerous as the crimson coat. She needed to keep hold of it as a bargaining tool. But she had to get back, and quick. Mila would panic when she realized Rosa was nowhere to be found.

Very well then. The panic faded, replaced by a dogged determination. Rosa tucked the coat over one arm and dashed down the slope and over the wrought iron fencing. Although her fear lent her speed at first, a growing stitch in her side slowed her as she wove through the city streets and past the looming bulk of the cathedral. Although she'd never done much more than the minimum when it came to religion, she crossed herself. She needed all of the divine providence she could get.

While she'd always been naturally fit, and she put some effort into staying so, she wasn't used to extended sprints like this one. By the time she reached the Palacio Errázuriz, she was flagging badly. But she could see the white banners flapping in the wind, so she pressed on, squeezing her arm against her body to counteract the pain. She bit off the air in painful gulps, her lungs burning. But there! She could see the lights on the front of the building, and as luck would have it, a tall woman in gold making her stately way down the stairs.

The sight of her sister, safe and sound, made Rosa's knees weak. She stopped, leaning over with her elbows on her knees, to catch her breath. Sweat bathed her forehead, and without thinking, she used the sleeve of the red coat to wipe it away.

Nothing happened. She straightened, ignoring the pain of overtaxed muscles desperate for a break, and hurried down the street. She would meet Mila at the car. It didn't matter if anyone saw them now. Within a matter of hours, they would be at sea, with all of this behind them.

The loud crack of gunfire split the air. Rosa let out a squeak of surprise, crouching down instinctively as she scanned for the plug ugly with the gun. What she saw made her breathless with horror. Mila lay sprawled across the grand front steps of the Palacio as Benicio Fentanes stood over her, a smoking pistol in his hand. As she watched, he pulled the trigger a second time. Mila's body jerked. The footmen on either side of the door had fled for cover, and no one disturbed the killer as he ambled down the steps, stuffing his hands into his pockets as casual as you please.

Blood dripped down the stairs and dotted the walls in a red spray visible all the way across the street. Rosa wanted to shriek with grief and loss. To wail. To rush at him and beat him with her fists. She wanted to rush to her sister's side and beg forgiveness for not being here to help as she should have. But doing so would take her right past him, and who knew what he'd do? The only thing she could do was pray, and she did just that, with a fervor she hadn't felt since her parents' death.

Mila didn't move. As much as she wanted to deny it, Rosa knew her sister was dead. Tears spilled over her eyelids and tracked down her cheeks, and she sank to the ground, hugging herself tightly to keep the sobs from escaping.

One of the footmen stuck his head out the door to scan the area. Ever so cautiously, he crept toward the splash of crimson and gold on the steps, putting his hand down to check for any signs of life. He shook his head sadly as he crouched over the body.

What in the heck had happened? Part of Rosa wanted to stomp back to the costume party and demand the details, but what good would that do? Mila would still be dead. Fentanes untouchable, supported by cronies in high places. Besides, Rosa's sudden appearance in clothing that had once been a part of the exhibition would invite questions that could put her in the slammer. Then it would be a question of who got to her first, Fentanes or the Sanguine Watcher.

Mila wouldn't want that. She would tell Rosa to play it smart. She'd do just that. For her sister's sake.

A distant wail heralded the approach of the policía. She shoved herself to her feet, wiping her cheeks. There was nothing to do but back away and leave Mila cold on the stairs as a steady rain began to fall from the sky. She hated herself for it, but she did it.

Rosa didn't dare go back home. She didn't know what had happened with Fentanes – had he realized Mila had set him up? Lost his temper over being publicly accused? Or did the shooting indicate something else entirely; something more sinister? She had no idea, and therefore, their home wasn't safe. So she scurried down the street toward her safe house, trying to look over both shoulders at once, as she tried to decide on her next steps. She had to hide. Then and only then could she properly mourn her sister.

The wise thing to do would be to skip town. Dump the coat, and the hat too. Grab the rainy day money they'd set aside for a moment just like this. Set up shop in Paris. It would be more difficult without Mila to handle the business arrangements, but Rosa could manage. But something told her that wouldn't work, because the crimson coat was more than it seemed. The Sanguine Watcher wouldn't just let it slip through his fingers.

Besides, she had to know. Where had it taken her? What were those things that lurked there? The mere thought of them made shivers run up Rosa's spine, but a deeper part of her brain, the cold and calculating part, couldn't help but point out what an asset such clothing would be for someone in her business. It had carried her across town in a matter of seconds. If she could learn to control such an artifact, she could steal *anything*.

The thought brought her up short. She stopped in the doorway of a shuttered bakery and took a closer look at the coat. It bore no tailor's tags nor markings to designate its origins. The hat had no hatter's insignia that she could find. A quick pat down failed to alert her to anything hidden in the lining or beneath the brim. With enough time and the right tools, she could take it apart. She wasn't as good a seamstress as Mila, but she'd manage. But she had no way of knowing whether disassembling it would divest the garment of its strange powers.

If she could use it properly, she could stay one step ahead of anyone who came sniffing after her. Fentanes. The Sanguine Watcher. It wouldn't matter. But that would leave her uncomfortably low on information. The Watcher had known about the coat. He must have some insight into how it worked. For all she knew, his insight could mean the difference between life and death. Those creatures hadn't seemed friendly, after all.

That decided it, then. She would go and meet the Sanguine Watcher in Mila's stead. She would find out what she could from him. *Then* she would go to Paris. She'd become the best thief in the world, and she would do it all in Mila's memory.

•••

It didn't surprise Rosa that the Sanguine Watcher had chosen La Recoleta Cemetery as a meeting point. The melodramatic spot complimented the man's atrocious pseudonym. Unfortunately, after everything she'd seen, her efforts to scoff at it did nothing to quell her nerves.

She approached from the south, scanning the grounds through the thin bars of the metal fencing that surrounded the property. Night had fallen, the deep darkness broken by the light of a silvery three-quarter moon and the amber glow of the occasional gas lamp suspended along the cemetery pathways. Mist rose off the ground, clinging to marble mausoleums and intricately carved statues of angels, their hands pressed together in prayer. The stone glistened in the moonlight, almost seeming to glow from within. Nothing moved in this dead place.

Rosa clung to the bars, trying in vain to ignore her growing unease. This was a bad location for a handoff, and she couldn't believe that Mila had agreed to it. She'd always been a fan of public places and bright daylight, trusting that the presence of potential witnesses would keep their clients honest. Even if they tried something, at least she could see the double cross coming. The cemetery offered no such advantages. The Sanguine Watcher could have a hundred thugs lying in wait across those shadowed grounds. Every corner could contain an ambush.

These were reasonable worries, but Rosa's mind kept circling back to twisted monsters bathed in blood red light, and the harsh bark of the gun as Fentanes fired at her sister. Try as she might, she couldn't get them out of her head.

At times like these – when she'd frozen with fear of falling or at the sight of a bared weapon – the first step was the hardest part. Once she got moving, she could work through the fright. It didn't go away but instead honed her senses. Gave her an edge. She needed that now, especially without Mila's good sense to guide her. She never thought she'd say this, but she missed her sister's exacting ways.

Rosa crept down the length of the fencing to an unlocked gate on the back side of the cemetery. Although the grounds were heavily monitored to protect them from vandals and grave robbers, the Sanguine Watcher had promised safe passage through this gate. Perhaps he'd bribed the guards. Or done away with them entirely. Rosa didn't know.

The gate opened without the expected squeak of hinges, and Rosa inched inside, every sense alert for signs of trouble. Nothing happened. The grounds lay still and silent as she made her way into the shadows of the tombs, her heart thumping so loud that she thought it might burst.

Back pressed against the wall, she peeked around each corner, expecting all manner of creatures to come popping out at her. Time and again, nothing happened. But the lack of opposition only honed her anxiety. She clutched the fabric of the coat tighter, and for the first time, she took reassurance from its chilly folds. If things went badly, she would try to use it. She slipped one arm inside and draped the other side over her shoulder, hoping that this precaution would keep her from activating the thing by accident.

It seemed to work, and she made her way to the mausoleum described in Mila's notes. She'd pocketed them before they left, just in case the unthinkable happened. Now she wished she hadn't been right, but she kept her attention on her surroundings to distract herself from her grief and anger. The mausoleum was a sizable structure, its gate flanked by a pair of gargoyles, their mouths stretched in an eternal scream. Inside, a narrow set of stairs descended down into blackness.

The gate stood open.

Rosa took a deep breath, pushing the hat down more securely onto her head and tugging the coat back up onto her shoulder again. It had a tendency to slide.

She'd never been the superstitious type, but no one in their right mind would want to go down there. Nothing good happened in places like this late at night. Recent events suggested that at least some myths had an element of truth to them. Anything could be possible. Ghosts. Ghouls. Or something even worse. Something without a name, that people couldn't even begin to comprehend. She couldn't be sure they were there, but she couldn't be certain they weren't.

For a moment, she considered grabbing one of the lamps, but she knew better. A moving light would only draw potential attackers to her, and rob her of her night vision besides. It was safer to move about in the dark.

She edged past the gargoyles, watching them out of the corners of her eyes. It was silly to be afraid of stone statues, but their hunched figures reminded her uncomfortably of the creatures she'd seen, and the back of her neck prickled as she passed them by. Then she was in the staircase, her hand clapped to the top of her head to keep the hat on. Although there was little wind down here, she worried that it would get knocked off somehow, leaving her stuck and vulnerable. She placed each foot with deliberate care. First the toe, and then the ball, each movement choreographed like a silent ballet. She made no noise. After all, they didn't call her a master thief for nothing.

The staircase descended to a landing, and when she peered around the corner, she could see flickering lights down below where the stairway terminated in some kind of chamber.

Jackpot.

She approached carefully, not wanting to give away her presence before she could take the lay of the land. Her feet made no noise. Her breath was silent and steady. Although fear still gripped her, it had subsided to a low thrum in the background just as it always did. Rosa Varela was here to work.

"Miss Varela," said a voice from the unseen room beyond. "So kind of you to join us."

Despite her best efforts, she'd been made. That worried her. The voice concerned her even more. It creaked like an empty house, but dark amusement filled it nonetheless. It was the voice of a man who played a very different game than Rosa ever had. One that would be pleasant for no one but himself.

"The Sanguine Watcher?" she asked, freezing in place.

"The very same."

"You picked a dangerous spot for a rendezvous, señor. If

I didn't know better, I'd think you weren't going to hold up your end of the bargain."

"How astute. Very well. I will promise you safe passage until the completion of our business. Does that satisfy your nerves?"

She thought for a moment. "Until I leave La Recoleta," she countered. "Otherwise, you could give me the dough and then shoot me in the back."

"Agreed."

The promise failed to give her much in the way of reassurance, but the whole point of this expedition was to learn about the teleportation. She couldn't do that without talking to the man. So she grabbed onto the lapel of the coat, holding it at the ready, and turned the corner.

A sizable room opened up before her, its cavernous depths barely touched by the single gas lamp sitting on the metal table near the stairs. A chalky-pale white man stood next to the table, tall and gaunt, with a long face and a wide mouth stretched into a cruel grin. He was older than her by far, his skin creased with age. He wore a pair of curious, ruby-tinted spectacles the likes of which she'd never seen before. They were a strange hybrid of glasses and goggles, with glass sides that fit to his face, shielding his eyes completely from view. A black suit of fine old cut completed the ensemble.

He sketched a mocking little bow as she appeared.

"Miss Varela." He straightened, taking in her ready position, her arm poised to thrust into the sleeve at the first sign of danger. "Ah. I see that you have figured out the power of the crimson coat."

He knew what it did. The information sank in heavily, weighing her down with regret and a surprising flare of anger. He'd known all along. If he'd been more forthcoming, she and Mila would have planned differently. Rosa wouldn't have been teleported across town. She would have been there when things had gone wrong with Fentanes, and she could have done *something*. It didn't matter what. What mattered was that the Sanguine Watcher had manipulated them from the start. If not for him, Mila would still be alive.

"I have," she said, baring her teeth with sudden fierceness. "This was all a setup, wasn't it? Are you working with Fentanes, or was that just an unlucky break?"

"I don't know who that is. I need no partners."

The admission failed to reassure her. He could be lying.

"You aren't trying to con me, are you? If you don't play it straight with me, I'm going to poof right out of here, and then I'm going to burn this coat to cinders."

He froze, his manic grin fading.

"You wouldn't."

"Try me. My sister's gone now. I've got nothing else to lose."

"Just your mind."

The Sanguine Watcher delivered this line with a malicious glee, reaching out to turn up the gas lamp. The growing pool of light illuminated the room in a widening circle, glinting off stone shelves stocked with glass jars containing twisted and deformed creatures. One of them jerked as the light hit it, rattling the glass and making Rosa jump. The glow grew to encompass another shelf that held metal implements that looked like they belonged in a mad scientist's laboratory. With a jolt of shock, Rosa realized that this cavernous room was exactly that. She shuddered as she realized that what she'd been thinking of as a metal table looked more like a mortician's workspace, with groves built into it to collect bodily fluids and drain them away. There were even straps designed to hold the corpse's wrists and ankles.

But that didn't make sense. Why would anyone need to restrain a corpse? Only live victims struggled.

Rosa backed away from him, dropping the sleeve of the coat as horror grasped her tight. All of her plans vanished from her mind, washed away by her growing fear. Did the Sanguine Watcher intend to put *her* on the table? To use those cruelly bladed devices on her?

Her throat went dry as she contemplated the possibilities, and she stumbled as she retreated. The Sanguine Watcher laughed when she fell, ripping the leg of her trousers and skinning her knee. She scrambled backwards towards the steps with nothing on her mind but escape.

She ran into something – or *someone* – that hadn't been there just a moment ago. She looked up to see a young man in a black suit very much like the Sanguine Watcher's. He reached for her, long, delicate fingers spreading as he offered his assistance to draw her to her feet. Moments before she slipped her hand into his, he looked down at her.

He had no face.

There was nothing there but blank, featureless skin. Flat, like a drawing that hadn't been filled in yet. But she could feel him watching her nonetheless. Another one joined him, stepping up alongside. It wore the same clothes, wore its hair the same way. Its face too was a blank circle of nothing.

They were twins. Just like her and Mila.

The thought of Mila broke her frozen fear. Rosa shrieked, and the faceless twins recoiled from the noise. She took advantage of that to scramble to her feet, ignoring the sting of palms abraded by the rough surface of the ground and the wet trickle of blood down her leg. But this brought her face to face once again with the Sanguine Watcher.

"Give me what I want, and I will let you live," he said, holding out his hand. "The hat. The coat. Give them to me."

He'd promised her safe passage, but she couldn't trust that. She couldn't trust anything. She whipped her head around, searching for some way out, barely able to think. Her heart thumped like a frightened rabbit, and her eyes welled with tears as she backed up against the horrid table, the icy cold of the metal sinking into her skin.

"Come now," said the Sanguine Watcher. "You must see that there's no escape, just as I do."

To punctuate his words, he whipped off his glasses. Rosa stared up at him, barely able to believe what she was seeing despite everything that had happened already. His eye sockets were empty pits, caverns of black that swallowed all light. The gas lamp failed to illuminate their depths. Perhaps they went on forever.

But he still saw her somehow, and his cruel smile promised something beyond pain.

"Yes, I can make something of you," he said, confirming her worst suspicions. "Put her on the table."

The faceless twins moved in perfect unison, reaching down to take her by the arms. Their touch made her skin crawl, and she kicked and scratched like an angry cat, drawing blood. She reached for the cosh, her fingers grazing the handle before knocking it uselessly to the ground. Her attackers didn't give her the time to recover it. They were implacable. One of them pinned her legs in a vise-like grip, while the other struggled to restrain her arms.

For the second time that night, she prayed aloud, tears running down her face, panic lending a hoarseness to her words. The words came in halting, barely remembered spurts, but she could remember her parents saying them with her. Mila, holding her hand as they lit candles on the altar.

Her family was still with her. She would never be alone.

Mila would want her to fight.

They began to drag her toward the awful table as she kicked and screamed. The coat thrashed with her movement, the empty sleeve arcing up to hit her in the face. She shrank from the blow as her mind cleared. The coat! In all of the chaos and fear, she'd forgotten it. She tore her arm free from the faceless minion. He clutched at her again as she pawed at the sleeve, his hand wrapping around her forearm.

"Don't let her put it on!" shouted the Sanguine Watcher, his voice sharp with concern.

Rosa tugged at her arm but couldn't dislodge her attacker. He leaned closer, his grip tightening. Pain flared in her arm; her hand immediately began to go numb. But he'd come too close.

She head-butted him right in his featureless face.

He released her so quickly that she fell to the ground, driving all of her air out in a pained gasp. Then he arched his back, hands pressed to his nothing of a face, body language clearly communicating his pain. Rosa could hear faint screams hovering at the absolute edges of her hearing, but that made no sense. He didn't have a mouth. But there was no time to dwell on such impossibilities.

She thrust her hand into the coat and threw herself towards the door despite the faceless man still clinging to her legs. The past two times she'd used it, she'd been moving, and she'd been thinking of a destination. Maybe it had been a coincidence, but she'd repeat the steps exactly until she could determine precisely how it worked.

Home, she thought. Please take me home.

As the room dissolved into darkness, she heard the garbled, furious cry of the Sanguine Watcher.

"You can't escape me!" he shouted. "I'll see that you pay!"

Despite her immense relief at the ease with which she'd teleported to safety, Rosa didn't stay at home long. The Watcher would be searching for her, and he would look here first. In fact, she wasn't too sure about the boat either. If he tracked her there, she might find herself at sea in a vessel full of his faceless servants. There would be no escaping then.

A change of plan made sense. She'd go to the safe house for her bag and then travel by land. There were plenty of cities in Central America that offered riches for the taking. If she ran out of funds, they'd be easily replaced.

She grabbed the bag and the boat tickets she'd left at the ready and hurried across town to the shabby safe house, looking over her shoulder the entire time. The streets were deserted at this time of night save a lone drunk who stepped out of a darkened doorway, took one look at her face, and let her pass without a word.

The safe house was quiet and dark, but the evening had been so eventful that she remained on high alert. Rather than waltz in through the front door and into a possible trap, she leaped the wall that led to the small backyard garden. The place was coated in shadow, and she kept the crimson coat at the ready just in case she needed to teleport out of harm's way once again since she'd lost the cosh.

She crept toward the back door, put her face to the glass, and peered inside. The sparsely decorated back room sat still and silent. She turned to get the key and only then did she notice the shadowy figure seated at the wrought iron café set tucked in the corner.

"Miss Varela," the man said.

She paused with her hand halfway down the coat sleeve. That wasn't the Sanguine Watcher. Not even close. This voice sounded much warmer. More reassuring. It was probably a trap, but if he knew her name, she needed to find out what she was dealing with.

"Who wants to know?" she asked.

He leaned into the light, revealing an urbane visage of indeterminate age, eyes shaded by a wide-brimmed hat. Red leather gloves peeked out from the sleeves of his grey double-breasted jacket. He offered her a faint smile.

"My colleagues call me the Red-Gloved Man. I'm sure that you of all people understand the wisdom of using a pseudonym."

"Your colleagues?" Suddenly, it all clicked into place. The crimson coat that led to that red-tinted hellscape. The Sanguine Watcher with his red-tinted glasses. And now the Red-Gloved Man. All those red things had to be connected. If this gent was friends with the Watcher, she wanted nothing to do with him no matter how good his manners were. "I think this conversation is over. One of your colleagues tried to kill me tonight, and if you make the same mistake, I'm leaving."

The Red-Gloved Man glanced down towards the coat, his brow creasing.

"You can put it on," he suggested. "It won't transport you unless you are in motion and putting intent into a destination."

"Yeah?" She thawed the slightest bit. "I thought as much, but I haven't used it enough times to be certain."

"Please sit with me for a moment. I promise not to try and kill you. I do not subscribe to the Watcher's methods, and there are things you should know."

It was the kind of offer Rosa couldn't afford to refuse, and she resented that. She pulled out the other chair and sat far back from the table, where she would have plenty of time to get away if things went poorly. Then, her belly fluttering with nerves, she slid the coat on the rest of the way.

Nothing happened. He'd been telling the truth.

"I am sure you have put much of this together on your

own," said the Red-Gloved Man. "But I represent a special interest group, a Coterie if you will, that collects items of mystical significance."

"Why are they all red?" she asked, unable to restrain herself.

"I have my theories, but I cannot say for certain. It is an intelligent query though. But what I do know is that not many people have the ability to pick one up and use it so easily. They require a certain... knack, shall we say? It takes an immense amount of willpower to activate one and retain some semblance of sanity."

"Yeah." She shuddered, remembering all of the things she'd seen that night. "I understand that."

"With that in mind, I would like to offer you options. I am sure I do not need to tell you that the Sanguine Watcher will pursue you as long as you have the crimson coat." He paused, waiting for her nod of acknowledgment. "If you like, I can take it away from here. I cannot guarantee that he will stop in his pursuit of you, because he can be a vindictive sort, but with your skills, I'm sure you can stay two steps ahead of him. He will eventually give up once he realizes you are no longer in possession of the coat."

As offers went, it wasn't a bad one. Most people would have been desperate to get back to their normal lives, free of faceless thugs and shadowy monsters. But Rosa could never go back. Not without Mila.

"What's option two?" she asked.

He smiled, drumming his gloved fingers on the table to punctuate his words.

"You join us. A woman of your skill with control of the

crimson coat could help us acquire the artifacts we seek. They are dangerous in the wrong hands. You would be doing the world a service."

"And the Sanguine Watcher is a part of your little club too? No, señor. I cannot. I will not play nice with him."

"You don't need to. This is not a social club."

She frowned. "This is a big decision, and I must think it through. Meet me in a few days. I must see my sister safely buried, and then I will give you my answer."

"The Watcher will be searching for you," he cautioned.

"I'm sure he will." She flipped up the collar of the crimson coat and smiled bitterly. "Let him try."

The next few days were incredibly busy. The police left her messages at the house, but she couldn't risk staying there. She called in and made arrangements to pick up Mila's body in private. Then she arranged a church funeral where she played Mila's favorite hymns on the pipe organ. She would have played and cried all night if the padre hadn't made her stop.

The Sanguine Watcher's minions had dogged her steps after the funeral, but she'd become increasingly adept at evading them thanks to the crimson coat. She'd become reliant on it in the short time it had been in her possession. With the aid of the coat, she'd planted stolen goods in the office of Benicio Fentanes. She couldn't let him get away with what he'd done, and no one at the party had been willing to speak up. So she'd nicked a few things from the private collections of men who would not take such theft lightly and put them in his office where he couldn't cover them up. Within twenty-four hours, Fentanes had disappeared.

It wouldn't bring Mila back, but at least both sisters could rest easy knowing that justice had been served. Rosa stood next to the freshly piled earth of Mila's grave as the wind tried to carry the hat away. She clapped a hand to her head to hold it in place as she waited.

It didn't take long.

The Red-Gloved Man approached with a bouquet of red roses, placing them gently against the headstone. The gesture touched Rosa despite her efforts at impartiality. Either he was a good man or a good actor. She hoped it was the former.

"If I join you," she said, "you must promise me that none of the artifacts I personally acquire will go to the Sanguine Watcher."

"And you will work extra hard to bring them in before he finds them?"

"Something like that."

"I acquiesce. As I said, I don't agree with many of his methods myself."

Rosa took a deep breath, overcome by a wave of excited nerves. All of her training had prepared her for this moment. This would be the game of her life. Her fear had faded away, replaced with a deep-seated well of determination. Mila would be so proud of her.

"I accept," she said.

He clapped his gloved hands in satisfaction.

"Excellent. Then from this day forward, the name Rosa Varela will be lost to history. You will be the Girl in the

Crimson Coat from now on. Leave your old life behind. I am sorry to ask it, but it is safer for those you love."

She looked down at the gravestone. "Everyone I love is gone. There is nothing left for me but the game, and I intend to win it."

"It will be my pleasure to witness it."

He offered a hand, and she hesitated for a moment before she took it. Whatever secrets the red gloves held, they didn't reveal themselves during their handshake.

"Welcome, Girl…" he stumbled. "That title doesn't exactly trip off the tongue, does it? We may need to rethink."

"Let me try," she said, sweeping the hat off into a bow of introduction after a moment's thought. "La Chica Roja, at your service."

A FORTY GRAIN WEIGHT OF NEPHRITE

Steven Philip Jones

I. Who

Kymani Jones gazed through the scissor gate covering a French window overlooking San Francisco at night, captivated by the sparkling parcels of house lights and streetlamps tumbling down to the bay where the water was as black and flat as a display cloth. Spanning the horizon was a nearly flawless cluster of shimmering stars momentarily marred by twin streaks of one meteor chasing another's tail across the moonless sky.

"Beautiful sight," a man said from behind.

Kymani turned.

The watchman who had been acting as their chaperone was gone, replaced by a comfortable-looking, keen-eyed, ruddy-cheeked gentleman. "A Nob Hill view still gives me a thrill. Maybe it's because I'm not allowed in places like this too often." He extended a hand to Kymani. "I'm Barlow

Pointer, the adjuster assigned to the Xiamen Bi theft. The owner will be along in a moment. Lieutenant Justin Beahm from Robbery Division wanted to meet you, too, but he's out on a call right now."

Kymani smiled and shook Pointer's hand, determined to make a good impression. "I appreciate Professor Vayner agreeing to see me. I hope I didn't step on anyone's toes writing to him, but I thought he should know an attempt might be made on the Bi."

"And you were right. All that matters right now is the Bi is a priceless insured object and Professor Vayner is one of Hellman's most important clients." Pointer lowered his voice. "And Hellman isn't anxious to pay out on a large claim like this unless they have to, but right now the police and I are stymied." Speaking normally he continued, "Besides, it's not like Hellman has a liability consultant on the payroll who happens to be a leading authority on security and objets de art, although we would gladly remedy that if you ever want to give up the independent life."

Kymani could not have felt more complimented. Hellman Occidental was one of the country's most respected insurance companies and Pointer its most respected claims adjuster.

"Thank you, but for now it's best I remain my own boss. Besides, there is plenty of action elsewhere to keep me busy." Kymani did not mention this action included preventing powerful magical objects known as Keys from falling into the wrong hands, be they human, unearthly or somewhere in between, nor that they believed the stolen Bi was a Key.

"Is this your first time in San Francisco?"

"It is, but I read up on it during my train journey." Kymani always learned as much as possible about any new place they went to, especially those where they were working. It did not pay for someone in their professions to be a stranger in a strange land, and Kymani – a cosmopolitan who had traveled everywhere from the Abu Simbel temples to the ruins of Wat Phra Sri Samphet – was finding San Francisco to be a beguiling amalgam of frontier America and urbane New England. Pointing out the window they asked, "That is Russian Hill and Fisherman's Wharf, correct?"

"You got it. Think of it as a topographical sliding scale from high society to seafaring proletariat."

"Sounds a little like the East End of London, although this looks far more inviting. Over there are Union Square, Civic Center and the Tenderloin? Basically parks, government and downtown?"

"Yes, and then there's the Financial District – the name pretty much tells the story – and of course there's Chinatown. You can't come to San Francisco without visiting Chinatown. You have a flat near Boston, don't you? It has a Chinatown, doesn't it?"

"I do and it does. I'd be glad to show you around it if you ever get out that way."

"Thanks. I suspect San Francisco's is more veritable. I think that's the right word. We're close enough to China that our Chinatown tends to be quite the gateway between the two countries."

A third person interrupted: "And what does that have to do with what happened to the Bi?"

Kymani watched a tall, eagle-nosed, white-haired Caucasian man in his sixties with a waxed moustache and carefully pointed beard stride into the room. Keeping pace a step behind him was a clean-shaven Asian man of average appearance, height and weight who could have been thirty or fifty or any age in between.

Pointer said, "Kymani Jones, this is Professor Aron Vayner."

"It's a genuine honor, sir." Kymani hoped they did not to sound too wonderstruck by the renowned archaeologist and explorer.

Vayner looked Kymani up and down with the practiced eye of someone with a lifetime of experience appraising people. "So you're the art historian who predicted the Bi would be stolen?"

"I was very careful to say it 'might' be stolen."

"Would you mind telling me how you came to suspect this might happen?"

"I'm also a security expert."

Pointer interjected, "Jones has been enlisted by insurance companies, art dealers and law enforcement agencies around the world to locate and recover stolen and looted works of art."

"Yes, yes, but that doesn't answer my question."

Kymani said, "The three star symbols engraved in the Bi tipped me off to the possibility."

Vayner looked somewhat discouraged. "It's purely conjecture that those symbols represent anything astrological."

"Academically, yes, but not to the thief." Kymani cleared

their throat, feeling the same way they had during their dissertation defense. "You are probably aware that one of the symbols is believed to represent the Celestial Wine Cup, part of the Chinese constellation known as the Well, and a second symbol is believed to represent the June Böotids of Comet Pons-Winnecke. What the third and last symbol represents has been a bone of contention for centuries, but there is a growing theory – supported by work taking place at Lowell Observatory – that it represents the relative position of an unverified celestial body orbiting the edge of our solar system to the ecliptic. The late astronomer Percival Lowell named this celestial body Planet X. If that theory is correct, then the alignment of the star symbols on the Bi now matches the current alignment of the Wine Cup, the Böotids and Planet X, which only occurs every two million years."

"But why should that prompt someone to steal the Bi?"

"If someone believed there is a significance to this rare alignment that that person might gain by, then they could be motivated to steal the Bi."

Vayner shook his head. "It all sounds like H. Rider Haggard to me."

"Nevertheless, the Bi is missing," Pointer said.

"Yes." Vayner turned to his manservant. "You may return to your duties, Shibing. I'll ring if you're needed."

A valuable and revealing skill in Kymani's work was observing people and things, so they paid attention to Shibing as he departed. The man's carriage was blanketed under the classic cut of his black buttoned-down suit, but his skilled manner of walking and lightness of step suggested that he was as much minder as manservant to the professor, which suggested to Kymani that Shibing was someone who warranted future attention.

Vayner looked at Kymani. "Pardon my effrontery, but you seem rather young to have carved out your reputation."

"No offense taken, sir, but you weren't much older when you led your first expedition to Fujian Province, which was a highlight of my senior year Asian Art classes."

"They're teaching that in school now? Where did you study?"

"I was an undergraduate at Straight College and studied for my doctorate at the École du Louvre."

"I was unaware Straight offered an Art degree. Where did you learn about security matters?"

"Mostly from a patron who supported me after my father died."

"I see." Vayner kept his own counsel for several seconds and then asked, "Do you think you can recover the Bi?"

"I'll do everything I can to return it where it belongs."

"Recover it and you can name your fee. What do you need to begin?"

"I actually started before I left Arkham, and I took the liberty of examining this room while I was waiting." For Kymani it was a grand room, and not because it was thirty feet by twenty feet with a twelve foot ceiling or because it had Italian painted and parcel gilt Chinoiserie boiserie wall panels. Its furnishings, dragon fur curtains, hanging scrolls, silk art, pottery, ritual bronzes and Buddhist sculptures were an inspiration to the glories of the Yangtze. "I noticed that all the windows have both scissor gates and solid steel shields that can slide out from the wall. I presume the shields are always closed at night."

"Yes, from ten to six, during which time a watchman is also posted here."

"How long has the guard that was on duty last Saturday been with you?"

"Two years. I can vouch for his trustworthiness if you're thinking he assisted the robbery in any way."

"Thank you." Making a mental note to ask Pointer later if he had independently checked the guard's background yet, Kymani said, "During my train ride I read everything I could find about the history of this mansion, including how you donated it to the Rovers Club last year."

"Except for this wing," Vayner corrected. "Most of the house was going unlived in since I retired. I never married and have no living relatives. I was spending most of my days at the club anyway, so I offered to donate it on condition I continue to reside and store my collection here."

"I see." Kymani felt a little sorry for Vayner. They could sympathize with having no one close in their life.

"That doesn't mean the club has access to this area. It does not nor will it until I die."

"All right. Now this mansion is the only house on Nob Hill to have survived the earthquake and fire in 1906?"

"It is." Vayner's puzzled expression suggested he found this an odd question. "Our neighbors built timber mansions that resembled stone, but my father insisted on the real thing."

"However, the interior was gutted. Who reconstructed it?"

Vayner started to answer but faltered. Clearing his throat he deflected, "I fail to see what that has to do with what happened to the Bi."

Kymani was not surprised Vayner appeared unable to answer the question. The only records about the reconstruction Kymani had been able to locate before leaving for San Francisco were in the athenaeum, safeguarded by a furtive government agency called the Foundation that helped from time to time with locating Keys. Not even the elite design firm of Bachelard and Corner that performed the reconstruction had any recollection or receipts of the job.

Instead of pressing this question Kymani said, "I have a theory about that. At least about how it was stolen. But I will need to see where you kept the Bi."

"That is no problem." Vayner removed a key from a vest pocket and walked towards one of the wall panels. He pressed a spot on the panel and a jib door sprang lightly open to reveal an inset 1912 Rosengrens heavy valuables cabinet.

Kymani requested, "I know the police have examined the vault door, but I'd like to give it my own onceover."

"Go ahead."

Kymani moved within an inch of the vault and after about a half minute commented, "You could not have selected a better safe. It's crackerjack." The front of the door was a one hundred millimeter sheet of steel while the whole surface in front of the Sjölander mutator lock was secured and the keyway shafts were reinforced with grains of carborundum. After verifying that the casing trim was undisturbed, Kymani said, "There are definitely no unusual scratch marks to indicate any sort of pick was used to enter the safe. That makes sense. The best yeggman I know would need an uninterrupted hour to crack this box." Kymani thought it prudent not to mention that they were this yeggman. "Would you please open the vault now, professor?"

Vayner unlocked and pulled open the safe door.

Kymani leaned into the vault.

The treasure chest was an airtight compartment fashioned from polished steel and large enough to hold two average adult men. Drawers lined its rear wall and the bottom half of its side walls, while shelves monopolized the top half. Its contents included over two hundred ancient cloisonné, ornaments and jewelry, including half a dozen Lungshanoid jade animal pendants.

Kymani pointed to an empty spot on one shelf. "Is that where the Bi was the last time you saw it, professor?"

"It is."

"May I step in and look around?"

"As you wish."

As Kymani entered the vault compartment, they heard Pointer mutter how he would give a week's pay to know how the thief was able to grab the Bi. "If my theory pans out, I might take you up on that. I could use the money." Kymani searched for any welding marks to indicate a forced entry, but as they expected there were none. "All right, professor, would you shut the door and lock it?"

This request did not sit well with either man as Vayner said, "I'm not about to entomb you in there!"

"You have the key. Wait five minutes, then open the door. There's enough air in here for that long."

"But there's no light. You won't be able to see."

Kymani pulled a baby flashlight from a jacket pocket and thumbed it on to show that it worked. "I promise I'll be fine."

A perplexed Vayner did as asked. "But I shall not be held responsible if anything goes awry."

Kymani took a deep breath as the door shut and the tumblers locked into place. Being trapped in a sepulcher or a facsimile thereof was nothing new, but that did not mean they liked it.

"I hope I'm right about this."

One minute passed.

Then two.

Three.

Four.

A few seconds later Shibing entered the grand room and announced, "Kymani Jones."

Kymani entered the room as Shibing exited, the two exchanging side glances as they passed while Pointer practically shouted, "How did you do that?"

Vayner somewhat stuttered, "Was I sold a safe or a magician's cabinet?"

Kymani, feeling rather pleased to have flabbergasted two such accomplished men, told Vayner, "You're on the right track. Open the safe and I'll show you."

Vayner unlocked the door but to his horror there was no vault compartment. "Everything is gone!"

"Look over to the right."

Vayner did and gasped. "There it is!" And more than that, "There's a tunnel in here!"

"Which leads outside the mansion to a spot between the buckeye tree and the surrounding wall. You might want to have someone trim that tree or maybe you should just cut it down."

"How in Heaven's name did the thief accomplish all this?"

Kymani sidestepped the question by saying, "I'm still working on that."

Pointer said, "I'll notify Beahm. After the police hear about this, I'm afraid they will insist on talking to you."

Kymani's expression softened with resignation as they thought, *if I had a penny for every time I heard that.*

II. What

Two hours later Kymani and Pointer were grabbing a late supper at Coffee Dan's on Mason Street, an all-night ham-and-egg emporium as well as a favorite Tenderloin speakeasy.

Kymani was enjoying a chicken salad sandwich, Postum, and listening to the pianist and MC Tiny Epperson perform "Hesitation Blues" while Pointer broodily consumed a grilled cheese with bacon and glass of buttermilk, when a good-looking lanky man in his thirties entered the eatery and zeroed in on them.

He snatched a chair from an empty table and patted Pointer on the shoulders. "My condolences, pal. Looks like Hellman might have to pay through the nose on this claim."

"Don't go blowing taps just yet. Maybe the law is giving up on recovering the Bi, but not us." Pointer told Kymani, "This is Beahm from Robbery."

Kymani shook Beahm's hand. "Thanks for talking with me here instead of the Hall of Justice. I haven't eaten since breakfast."

"Hey, I like to get out as much as the next guy." Beahm's eyes lingered on Kymani a second longer than necessary before he told Pointer, "And who said we're throwing in the sponge? But you know the recovery rate on these cases is around ten percent, so even if we're hitting on all eight we're going to need to get lucky, too." Looking at Kymani, "Which brings me to my first question for you. How did you know someone was going to pinch the Xiamen Bi?"

"'Might' pinch the Bi," Pointer corrected.

"Whatever." Beahm listened to Kymani repeat what they had told Vayner and Pointer about the Bi's star symbols and then asked, "You really spend your time studying that stuff?"

"Someone has to. Besides, there's more where that came from."

"Like what?"

Kymani swallowed the last bite of their sandwich and crossed their arms. "Like, for instance, a thirteen hundred year-old anecdote believed to have been excised from China's *Book of Documents* that talks about 'a sky disc of forbidden colors'. All ancient bi can be considered sky discs because they were buried with the dead as a symbol of the afterlife or 'sky', but because the Xiamen Bi is blacker than any other jade known on Earth, there is a theory the gemstone it was carved from came from a meteor or sky stone. In any case, starting with this anecdote, nearly every possible ancient and historical account of the Xiamen Bi includes some mention of it bringing dismay and destruction wherever it's taken. Examples include the Great Flood of Gun-Ya during the third millennium BC, the fire that destroyed the city of Jiankang during the Northern and Southern dynasties, a great famine that started in 875 AD and the San Francisco earthquake."

Beahm was caught off guard by the last disaster. "Excuse me?"

"Vayner brought the Bi home with him from Fujian Province on April 17 1906, the day before the earthquake."

"You can't believe some piece of jewelry was responsible for that."

Kymani thought it very likely, but told Beahm, "It doesn't matter what I believe. It only matters what the thief believes."

Pointer asked, "But why would anyone who believed that want any part of the Bi?"

"Because that anecdote goes on to describe the sky disc as not only having star symbols like the ones I've already mentioned, but also strange hieroglyphs representing 'unknown yauoguai from beyond the Way' who predate the Three August Ones. The inference seems to be that these unknown beings imbued the sky disc with its cataclysmic power, creating a volatile talisman that is best left alone… except when the stars represented by the symbols match the alignment on the sky disc. During that time anyone possessing it can harness and control its power."

"Do you really think the thief believes the Xiamen Bi is this sky disc?"

"Why not? It is engraved with what may be star symbols as well as with pictographs that correlate with no known writing system. If it's not the sky disc, it sure could be."

There was more Kymani could have told the men. Doing so would have been less frustrating than dancing around the truth, but Kymani doubted Pointer and Beahm would believe them. How could Kymani convince the men that the Bi might be a Key? And even if Kymani had been permitted to talk about the Foundation, how could they explain the agency's mission included collecting Keys to use in the defense of humanity against entities known as the Outsiders, beings that preyed on humans and reality by ingurgitating the actual existence of their victims? Or that the Foundation suspected the Outsiders were gearing up for something big, that might involve Keys like the Bi, and had asked Kymani to forewarn Professor Vayner someone might try to steal it.

Kymani had agreed even though they did not completely trust the Foundation. Actually Kymani did not completely trust anybody. To complicate matters further, according to the Foundation there was another organization known as the Red Coterie that also ostensibly collected Keys to use in defense of humanity against the Outsiders, but some of its members were not above using Keys for their own benefit.

Beahm asked Kymani, "How did you figure out Vayner's box had a back door?"

"That wasn't difficult. Just a logical process of eliminating everything that was impossible." Kymani leaned forward out of habit and did not mind when Beahm reciprocated. "The safe hadn't been accessed from the front; ergo it had to have been opened from the top, bottom or posterior. I found no cutting scars anywhere inside the vault, so there had to be a way to detach the compartment from the front of the safe. To do that there had to be a way to reach the vault compartment through the mansion's wall cavity."

"Oh, come on. There had to be more to it than that."

Kymani smirked. "Nope."

Pointer snapped his fingers. "That's why you asked Vayner about the reconstruction of the mansion's interior. You think that's when the tunnel was built."

"It would have been the perfect opportunity."

Beahm disagreed. "Any reconstruction must have been completed in 1907 or 1908. Why wait over a decade to pull off the heist?"

"Because back then the Bi was volatile since the stars were not aligned. Again, it doesn't matter what is or isn't real about the Bi, but what the thief thinks is real."

"You keep saying thief, but a gang must have worked this job. There had to be one or more persons in on it at Rosengrens and ditto the interior design company. By the way, did either of you ask Vayner what contractor he hired?"

"Kymani did but Vayner never answered," Pointer said. "I got the feeling he couldn't recall."

"Really? You'd think he'd remember about a big job like that. I'll ask him tomorrow and if he still doesn't recall I'll see if the morgues at the *Chronicle and Examiner* can dig up an article that lists the company."

"If you do, would you pass it on?" Kymani knew no one would find or remember anything, but it looked better to ask. "In the meantime, I wouldn't mind hearing what you two know about the professor's valet."

"Shibing? You think maybe he was in on this, too?"

"Just dotting my t's and crossing my i's."

Pointer pulled out a pad. Imprinted in tiny gold letters in the lower right corner of its black leather cover was *Hellman Occidental Insurance Company*. Pointer flipped pages until he located his notes on Shibing. "He has been working for Vayner since September 1905. According to the professor he was one of several laborers hired during the excavation in Xiamen where the Bi was found. One night their camp was set upon by bandits and in the conflict Vayner's batman, Arthur Charpentier, was killed and Shibing saved Vayner from joining him."

"So the professor hired Shibing out of gratitude?"

"He seems like a handy guy to have around."

Which further validated Kymani's earlier suspicions that Shibing's skills extended beyond butlering. "What did he do before Vayner hired him?"

"No records about him exist before then. That is not out of the ordinary in China, but Vayner must have greased some wheels at the Bureau of Naturalization to wrangle Shibing a visa in spite of the Chinese Exclusion Act."

Kymani did some ruminating. "Was Shibing hired after the Bi was discovered?"

"Yes. Are you blaming the Bi for what happened to Charpentier?"

Kymani shrugged. "Not exactly." Considering how

things played out it seemed more likely to Kymani that human agents were responsible for the bandit attack.

Epperson finished "Tonight You Belong to Me" as Beahm glanced at the watch on his wrist. "This has been dandy, but I think I'll call it a day." To Kymani, "If you need a guide to your hotel, I'd be happy to oblige."

Kymani did not mind the offer, but had learned the hard way not to mix pleasure with business. "Thanks, but I know how to flag down a hack."

"Another time maybe?"

Kymani smiled with their eyes. "No harm asking."

III. WHEN

It was almost midnight when Kymani returned to the Hotel Sutter. Almost instantly they realized their room had been searched and by someone who knew how. A suspect leapt to mind and the next morning this presumption was upgraded to an educated guess after Kymani checked in with Pointer.

"I can't shake the feeling that someone has been in my office and went through my files on the Vayner case," Pointer said. Soon after this the educated guess graduated into near certainty thanks to Coil Biaggi, the eponymous owner of a dive on Pacific Street where Chinatown fringed into San Francisco's Latin Quarter.

Kymani had no contacts in the San Francisco underworld, but a connection of theirs in the New England Mob suggested that Kymani talk with Biaggi if they needed information. Biaggi was unpretentious though, so Kymani did not mince words. "I need a lead on who stole the Xiamen Bi. Can you help me?"

Biaggi asked, "Who was it again gave you my name?"

"Dart Viczko in Eastie. He says you mind your own business, but if you told me anything it would more than likely be right."

Biaggi might have nodded. "Viczko told me you might come here. He also mentioned you find things but don't always give them back after you find them."

"Are you sure Dart didn't say that I return what I find to its original owner?"

"He might have put it that way."

Biaggi might have nodded again. "All right. Viczko is the Real McCoy, so I figure you're on the square, even if someone flashing an international cop's badge is asking around about you."

Kymani thought, I knew it! Then asked, "A tall man with a crewcut? Red hair and round glasses?"

"That's the Joe. So who is he?"

"His name is Cyrus Fletcher and he is an agent with the International Criminal Police Commission." Fletcher was also associated with the Red Coterie, but it was unclear if he was a member or just helped them the same way Kymani assisted the Foundation. "The ICPC can't prove I do what I do with the things that I find, but they suspect it and don't approve." Even so, Fletcher seemed almost obsessed with exposing Kymani's activities.

Why? So far Kymani had been unable to find out, but Fletcher's presence in San Francisco strongly suggested the Red Coterie had a hand in the theft. Even if they hadn't,

Fletcher would certainly try to catch Kymani in the act of returning the Bi to China.

Biaggi silently sized things up. He was in no hurry. Finally, "No guarantees. I only pass along what I've heard. And only if it goes no further."

"Dart told me that, too."

"Okay. There's a new bunch in Chinatown. Very nasty types. They took your bauble."

"Who are they?"

"No one knows. No one wants anything to do with them. That includes the Chinatown Squad. Nobody will even say where they hole up, except it's somewhere in Chinatown. The only thing I can tell you for sure is you best be careful if you stir up this hornet's nest."

Biaggi had nothing more to add so Kymani headed to Chinatown, keeping one eye peeled for Fletcher all the way. The agent was more than a nuisance, he was becoming a Javert. But Fletcher was good, so if Kymani was going to avoid apprehension they needed to be doubly careful.

San Francisco's Chinatown turned out to be more populated but less diverse than its Boston counterpart, encompassing an area six blocks in latitude and two blocks in longitude. Its prime meridian was Grant Avenue, a safe haven that bedazzled tourists with dragon streetlamps, xieshan roofs and sprightly painted shops and chop suey houses. American jazz was more the order of the day here than the Chinese flute, so Kymani ventured into the aromatic side streets and alleys where residents, store owners and associations comingled with highbinders and gambling houses, which seemed a more preferable locale for the cabal that Biaggi described. It was also more preferable to Kymani, who was most contented when searching the dark corners of the world for interesting things average people might not like.

On Waverly Place Kymani was passing a temple where some boys were playing marbles in the street when they noticed a truck up ahead making a delivery of green vegetables to a grocery. To Kymani's surprise the carriage of the man stacking the crates seemed familiar even though it was blanketed under a dark blue tang suit shirt and black pants.

Kymani cautiously approached and greeted Shibing, "Xiàwǔhǎo."

Shibing casually replied, "Hāi."

"So are you moonlighting or were you waiting for me?"

Shibing continued in Southern Min: "Neither, but since you are here I think we should speak. Preferably in private. There is an arts store around the corner with stairs leading to a cellar. If you like you can descend a few steps until you are out of sight from the street. I will join you soon."

"That sounds like a fine way to get waylaid or worse."

"I suspect you can take care of yourself, but what you do is up to you." Shibing went on unpacking.

Kymani had accepted worse invitations, but their instincts tingled like exposed nerve ends while they waited for Shibing and did not subside even after he arrived a few minutes later and told them, "Thank you for your patience and your trust."

"I wouldn't be reading too much of the latter into this."

"Then what should I read into an art historian who was raised by the finest art thief in Paris?"

For the second time Shibing surprised them. The identity of the patron who brought up Kymani after their father died was known to an extremely select few. Although taken aback, Kymani nonchalantly said, "Sounds like a well-rounded person to me."

Shibing bowed his head slightly as if to say this made perfect sense. "If I was so well-rounded and I located the Bi, I might not be inclined to return it to Professor Vayner."

Kymani decided to return serve. "And if I was a valet who walks like someone adept at shinobi stealth techniques and I didn't consider myself well-rounded, I think I would be doing myself a disservice."

Shibing's face was a tabula rasa. "Perhaps it is time that we be frank."

"Okay. You first."

Shibing bowed his head slightly again. "You are familiar with the Bi's history?"

"Yes."

"Including the calamitous legends surrounding it?"

"Yes."

"I am pledged to a secret Fujian order that knows many untold things, such as who might have raised a particular art historian or that the legends about the Bi are true. Our order arose centuries ago in opposition to a cabal that is determined to possess the Bi. They will do anything to acquire it, and to protect civilization we will do anything to forestall them."

"Like murdering Arthur Charpentier?"

Shibing appeared unaffected by the accusation. "Would you prefer we had killed everyone in the camp? We knew the Bi would be safe with Vayner. He is admirable… in spite of himself… and there were advantages to hiding the Bi in the open, so long as one of our order remained close by as a vigilant guardian. Except I turned out to be neither." For the first time Shibing showed emotion as he glared into himself. "There is a doctrine in war not to assume your enemy is going to come, but to always be ready to meet him. I failed to see the cabal's machinations, which permitted them to obtain the Bi."

Kymani appraised Shibing as he spoke and decided he was being honest. Kymani could also sympathize with Shibing's contrition, but advised him, "Maybe you should hold off on the sackcloth and ashes." Without revealing their source Kymani repeated the information they got from Biaggi. "So is this bunch your cabal? You're here looking for them to get back the Bi, right?"

"Things are more complicated than that. In recent years the cabal has fallen under the sway of a mysterious and dangerous woman. Somehow she manipulated the mansion's reconstruction and the safe's alterations without anyone in our order being aware and erased all evidence of it. Then when the stars were nearly aligned with the Bi she dispatched acolytes here from Shanghai to steal it."

"Any idea who this woman is and how she muscled in?"

"No. All we know about her is that she is never seen without a red parasol."

The blood drained to Kymani's feet. "Isn't that just swell?"

"You know this woman?"

"It's more like I know of her." Kymani almost sighed. It was against their better judgment but after everything Shibing had confided it seemed as if the time had come to finally tell someone the whole truth. "Have you ever heard of the Red Coterie?"

"Yes. And the Foundation, the Outsiders and Keys."

Kymani felt like they had been ambushed. "Oh. Okay." Paused. "You really do know a lot of untold things, don't you?"

Shibing said nothing, his face a blank slate again.

"Well, in case you don't know this, Coterie members wear a red piece of clothing or own a red object that connects them with one or more Keys, which in turn provide them with supernatural powers. That would explain how this woman subjugated the cabal, but some Coterie members may be in league with the Outsiders, which would explain how all evidence and maybe even memories of the reconstruction and safe's alteration were eliminated."

"And I have been notified that the woman with the red parasol will be arriving soon from Shanghai to claim the Bi."

"Great."

"Whatever powers this woman has, I intend to retrieve the Bi."

"And return it to Vayner?"

"No. I shall return it to Fujian and a place where it can harm no one."

Kymani was all for returning the Bi to China, but was not

sold on the idea of Shibing being the one to take it there. Keeping this to themself for now, Kymani warned, "If the Coterie wants the Bi they'll track you down."

"Let them try. Fujian is the realm of the Bi and only a son of the province may return the sky disc to its cradle. It is a perilous journey. The valley I go to has its demons and no man who goes there has ever returned."

Kymani had not heard this legend before so could not vouch for its authenticity, but just told Shibing, "A one-way ticket sounds drastic."

"It is a fitting penance. I should have protected the Bi in this world. I shall see that it is protected forever in another." A steely gaze settled in Shibing's eyes.

It was obvious that Shibing was not going to be dissuaded, so instead of arguing Kymani told him, "Good intentions aren't going to get the Bi back, so how about this? We call a temporary truce and search Chinatown together but separately. You take the west side of Grant Avenue and I'll take the east side, and if one of us finds the hideout we come get the other so we can go in together. Defendit numerus. Tóngyì?"

"Tóngyì. May I also propose that if you fail to find the lair in two hours that you come to the Grand Chinese Theatre? If I do not meet you under the building's left bay then presume you will have to continue the search alone. I shall presume the same if you fail to arrive."

Kymani felt sure Shibing did not trust them any more than they trusted him, but the suggestion made practical sense, so Kymani agreed and the pair of them split up.

Waverly ended a half block further on. Kymani turned

north onto Washington, walking casually while discreetly keeping both eyes peeled, and did not walk far before they caught a reflection in a barber shop window of a tall man with cropped red hair and high-set round frame glasses adroitly following across the street.

IV. WHERE

Kymani turned at the nearest corner and entered Ross Alley, where they stepped up the pace once safely out of Fletcher's line of sight.

Abutting buildings lined the street like the walls of a gorge, and after a pawn shop, two gambling houses and a general store the row on Kymani's side abruptly set back six feet further from the road. Parking behind the protracted section of wall that adjoined the general store with a row house, Kymani glanced at the residence, then took a second glance and thought, "Eureka!" Kymani then waited to see if Fletcher would get wise that he had been made and break off the chase or if he continued down Ross Alley.

Seconds passed.

A few more.

Too many.

"Are you playing cat and mouse with me?" Kymani peeked around the wall, but instead of seeing Fletcher they found Shibing standing in front of the general store, his right cheek bruised and a cut over his left eyebrow.

"Why didn't you tell me you were being shadowed?" Shibing asked.

Confounded, Kymani snatched one of Shibing's wrists

and tugged him around the wall. "What happened to you taking the west side?"

"Would you prefer I did nothing after noticing a stranger following you? Now why didn't you tell me?"

"I thought you knew everything. Are you all right?"

"I am unharmed."

"Where's Fletcher?"

"You know his name?"

"Did you kill him?" For a moment Kymani was unsure if they would prefer to hear yes or no.

Shibing presented Fletcher's ICPC identification. "No. He is merely indisposed. Are there more like him I should be on the lookout for?"

"Not that I know about." Kymani slipped the ID into a pocket.

"Does he belong to the Red Coterie? He was wearing a red tie."

"He might but I'm not certain. In any case, I think I just hit paydirt." Kymani jerked a thumb at the row house. "Look at those red painted steps and front door. They could be signposts for the Coterie."

"Perhaps." Shibing gazed at the shabby two-story structure, its windows securely boarded over with thick planking. "But such decorations are not uncommon in Chinatown."

"But how common are purely residential buildings like this? This is the first row house I've spotted in Chinatown that doesn't have a business on the street level floor."

Shibing gazed at the structure again. "You are most observant."

"Just a tool of the trade."

"If this is the cabal's hideout, they must have watchmen posted. If so, they know we are here."

"Maybe they do. Maybe they don't. Wait here a minute." Kymani visually examined the steps and saw nothing untoward beyond their color, but it was a different story with the front door. "Whoever lives here is protecting their privacy. Come up here and see, but try to act like we're checking the house number."

Shibing joined Kymani.

"There's a rubber insulated wire tucked around the door frame and blended into the paint. It looks like opening the door will close an electrical circuit that will set off an alarm somewhere inside. The wire also extends into the wall behind the entablature. There's probably a switch spring up there that keeps the alarm going off after the door is closed and the circuit is broken."

"So we must find another way to gain entry."

"Patience, please." Kymani loudly commented they had a rock in their shoe and lowered themself to one knee. "Stand in front of me and look concerned. We don't need passersby watching what I'm doing, although I wonder if anybody in this part of Chinatown would care."

As Shibing moved in front of Kymani he said, "Ross Alley might surprise you. More than anywhere else in San Francisco the souls of the dead can most easily visit the living here, as evil spirits are forbidden to exercise their powers."

"I sincerely hope you're right." Kymani grasped the heel of their left shoe and twisted it, exposing a hollow center packed with burglary implements the size of doll house tools. "My proctor called this his 'ever ready buster.'" Kymani unfolded a pair of scissors. "Electricity is the Achilles heel to these electromagnetic alarms. Eliminate its source and the circuit can't be completed." Kymani cut the wire where it came up through the steps near the sill, then exchanged the scissors for a pick to unlock the door. "However, if it's hooked to a backup battery we're going to be jimmy-jacked. You can move out of the way now." Kymani replaced the pick and then the heel, stood up and opened the door. "But what's life without a little risk?"

"You sound like you enjoy this."

Kymani had not been brought up just to survive. Most people were content with that, but Kymani wanted more and taking the occasional risk was one of the sweetest ways to feel alive. Smirking, they said, "'Enter freely and of your own will.'"

On the other side of the door the pair found a dim front room sparsely decorated with pieces of cheap and battered furniture. A stairway led to the second floor and Kymani found alarms fitted to the second and third steps and the handrail. "I can avoid these. You search the first floor. I'll scrounge up here."

"What if there is a cellar?"

"Oh, there's always a cellar. How about we search that together after we finish with the upstairs?"

Both wanted to locate some proof that they had discovered the cabal's lair, but on the second floor Kymani found only an empty bathroom and three bedrooms with more of the cheap and battered furniture, while on the first floor Shibing uncovered nothing helpful in the front room, its coat closet, the adjoining sitting room or the kitchen at the rear of the house. If not for the alarms there would have been no evidence that anyone was using the house.

Kymani returned to the first floor feeling frustrated as Shibing pointed to a narrow door in the cramped hallway between the kitchen and the front room. "I think that leads to the cellar. Perhaps better fortune awaits us there."

That would be a first, Kymani thought, but said, "Lead on, Macduff."

Shibing opened the cellar door, but instead of serendipity they found seven cabal acolytes brandishing jian swords.

Not good! Kymani thought, as Shibing yelled, "Get back!" But Kymani had already retreated a few steps to the somewhat more spacious confines of the front room and pulled a silk bandana from one pocket. One corner was weighted with three square bullets from a 1718 Puckle gun and Kymani wrapped it around one hand, wrapped another corner around the other hand and girded their mind for battle.

Kymani also watched Shibing withdraw a dao knife concealed under his tang shirt just in time to parry a thrust to his heart. A follow through nearly decapitated Shibing's opponent, but during the riposte an acolyte slipped past Shibing to charge Kymani.

Too bad for him.

Kymani took a breath to calm themself and in one smooth motion snared the jian in the slack between their hands, spun, twisted the sword from their opponent's grasp and used the man's own momentum to hurl him into the nearest wall.

The acolyte crumpled.

Kymani took another breath as they sensed a subtle buckling in the wooden floor slats.

Another acolyte was coming from behind.

Releasing the jian, Kymani twirled the weighted corner of the bandana overhead. A half pirouette and Kymani whipped the advancing acolyte's face but missed the target, cracking his skull crown and dazing the man instead of breaking the bridge of his nose to incapacitate him. A swift second swing remedied the error.

Suddenly a rumpus and a death wail erupted under the house and Kymani dashed to lend Shibing a hand.

They needn't have bothered.

The top of the stairs turned out to be a ringside seat to a one-sided skirmish. Shibing was surrounded front and side by the three surviving acolytes, but to Kymani's amazement Shibing's dao and a commandeered jian whirled like the blades of an oscillating fan as he sliced his adversaries down to two, one and then none. Tossing the jian into a corner he asked, "Are you still enjoying yourself?"

Killing was something rarely to be relished, but in light of what Shibing had just gone through Kymani let the comment pass. "Are you okay?"

"I am unharmed."

"So what was that you said about evil spirits?"

"Evil or not, these minions are not spirits. They bleed."

"So I see," Kymani said as they descended the stairs.

"You eliminated the two who evaded me?"

"They're tucked in for long winter naps." Kymani curiously perused the four bodies. "Why do you think they waited here to jump us?"

"It makes no sense. The upstairs provides many advantages, but this basement only obstacles."

Kymani surveyed the low-ceilinged cellar. The fusty earthen floor was churned like a plowed field and muddy with gore but otherwise appeared normal. Not so the walls, particularly the rear wall. Something within the organization of its graywacke stones suggested a curious artifice. Kymani inched closer until – bit by bit – the hint of an archway materialized. "Now I get it. These minions weren't hiding down here so they could ambush us. They were passing through here to meet us and when they heard us approaching the cellar, they did their best under the circumstances."

"If that is so, where did they come from?"

Kymani pointed. "Through there."

Shibing stared at the assemblage of stones splotched with niter and moss. "I see nothing." He tried tapping the wall and listening until there was a change in pitch. "There! This might lead us to where they took the Bi."

"Let's hope so." Kymani felt along the perimeter of the archway for any interstice that would give away the presence of a latch, but the door fit too exactly. "When did you say that lady from Shanghai is arriving again?"

"Very shortly, if she is not already here."

"Terrific." Kymani slapped the wall. Failure was not

something they ever accepted gracefully. "Whoever built the pyramids must have worked on this wall. If there is a bolt or a spring that opens this door it's going to take me more time than we have to find it. It'd be faster to dig under the door."

Shibing gave these words some consideration, then knelt down and with the blade of his dao started scraping away dirt.

"Hey, I was being facetious."

"You underestimate yourself as a teacher."

"And how's that?"

"What is the strength of this door? Concealment."

"That and unparalleled craftsmanship."

"Then unearthing the door should be its Achilles heel. Would anyone even consider excavating here unless they knew about it?"

Shibing made an excellent point. How often did workmen in Arkham, Boston and other New England burgs dismiss the bricked-up arches and wells leading to nowhere that they frequently found while demolishing old houses and buildings? Kymani retrieved the jian from the corner and told Shibing to "Move over."

The pair did not need long to reach the bottom of the footing beneath the wall and from there burrow like moles until they were in a passage on the other side of the secreted door.

The pathway was dark, so Kymani turned on the flashlight to check out their surroundings, which offered all the charm of a grave. The passage was maybe seven feet high and certainly no more than three feet wide with a hardpacked dirt floor that kept the air musty. "I don't see any traps."

"We can't rule out an ambush, although I see no nooks or crannies for an attacker to hide."

The pair brushed off dirt and wiped off loam from their clothes, skin and weapons and then moved on. To mark their trail Kymani used their pocket watch to track the passing of time while Shibing carved notches in the shoring at regular intervals. The tomblike atmosphere improved not quite imperceptibly when the floor inexplicably changed to cement, and soon after that they came to a flight of unhewn timber steps that descended to another passage with its own assortment of left turns, right turns and forks that led to another set of stairs. This pattern was repeated again and again with some variations but always one frustrating and increasingly claustrophobic constant: the tunnel always headed downward.

"If we were Beowulf and Wiglaf hunting the Worm of Eeananæs," Kymani whispered, "I'd say we might be heading in the right direction, but since we're not, your guess is as good as mine."

Eventually their trek reached a lengthy, narrow, ill-lit hallway. Standing close together on either side was a series of heavy, brass-laden, dun-colored doors, and waiting at the far end was a soapstone Chinese moon gate framing a red door. Kymani put away the flashlight as Shibing took point, and as they neared the gate an inscription became legible in its tiles: "With red we are bound. Through red we are one".

Shibing asked, "What does that mean?"

"Probably something like 'Abandon all hope. Sincerely, The Red Coterie.'" Flippancy could usually lighten Kymani's spirits but not this time. The hallway was as inviting as a rabbit gum and Kymani doubted the Coterie's warning was mere window dressing.

Reaching the gate, Shibing took the jian from Kymani to watch the way they had come as Kymani crossed their arms and scrutinized the door. Broad and tall with no handles or hinges, it appeared to be cobbled together from twelve wooden blocks all painted the exact same sanguine color. "This is different. I'd call it a puzzle door."

"Which is what?"

"You know what a puzzle box is?" Kymani asked. At first the blocks looked to be wooden and featureless, but upon extremely close examination four different intaglios became noticeable: a tortoise, a dragon, a phoenix and a tiger. In China these represented the guardians of the cardinal directions.

"Yes. Professor Vayner was given one when he was a student in England. He keeps it in a drawer with his socks."

"This door is like a puzzle box. You move blocks into a certain position and if you solve the puzzle you unlock the door," Kymani said.

Further examination revealed that each guardian appeared on three blocks, but the blocks with the dragon intaglio were not wooden but slatestone. Kymani grinned, remembering that the dragon is associated with the element of wood. Thinking this was not meant just to be ironic but a clue, Kymani shifted the dragon blocks around until they were in the same positions within the door frame as the star symbols were on the Bi.

Almost instantly all twelve blocks clattered to the floor to reveal an ashlar dungeon barely big enough to hold one person. "End of the road."

Shibing glanced over a shoulder. "Do you see the Bi?"

"I'm going to have to search." But as Kymani started inspecting the cramped chamber the hallway's faint illumination dimmed further. Kymani turned to see the hallway's ingress being swathed by a preternatural gloom as a woman's calm and taunting voice saturated the air.

"Looking for something? Lose your way, perhaps?"

A subtle laugh that dropped the temperature ten degrees gave way to an abhorrent growl that emanated from the gloom.

"'Abandon all hope'," Kymani mumbled. Rattled by the voice and revulsed by whatever might be prowling in the darkness, they asked Shibing, "What was that again about evil spirits?"

Shibing raised his swords and shouted to Kymani to keep searching the dungeon as he bolted down the hallway into the gloom.

At first nothing happened, then came savage sounds of fighting.

Kymani never liked being told what to do, but finding the Bi was the only way they knew that might help Shibing. Finishing the inspection and turning up nothing, Kymani desperately withdrew into the corridor to perceive the dungeon from a different perspective.

"Think. You were taught by the best. What would Mörkrets do?"

But a terrible thought shivered Kymani's soul. What if something like this had happened to their proctor when he disappeared?

Kymani felt on the verge of panicking.

Taking a breath, they focused on the dungeon.

From this angle it struck Kymani that they had seen bigger caskets, and then they realized the ashlar chamber's dimensions were its primary safeguard, since most people were repelled by such compact spaces. Ignoring the vicious sounds as best they could, Kymani carefully reexamined the dungeon, disregarding its confines as they ran their fingers over every crack, crevice and surface until they discerned an etching on only one floor slate. It was a qilin, the guardian of the Earth.

Anxiety transfigured to expectation as Kymani pulled out their Swiss soldier knife, unfolded a reamer and pried up the slate. Beneath it was a deep safehold and inside the safehold was the Xiamen Bi.

Kymani grabbed the black sky disc and a luxurious tingle instantly radiated throughout their purpose and being. Twice the size of a Brasher Doubloon, the disc nestled sumptuously in their palm and in spite of its Stygian color glistened like a pearl, the gleams highlighting the intricate otherworldly ideograms ringing the hollow nucleus. Giving this beauty up was not going to be easy, but Kymani forced themself to jump up, tamp down their fears and sprint into the gloom.

They were enveloped at once by a darkness that

expanded in all directions, permeated by a viler reek than the bowels of the Cloaca Maxima. Kymani also sensed the essence of something abysmal that was more powerful than the churning plunge pool of Angel Falls. The glistening of the Bi intensified even as it seemed like the gloom constricted, as if the sky disc was consuming the blackness and transforming it. The stars were aligned and the Bi was reacting to Kymani's desire to rescue Shibing from this netherworld.

Kymani spotted Shibing and saw he was stunned by the shadow-shrouded sight of what he had been fighting, an ill-formed and gargantuan something slurping and shifting amongst the gloom. Kymani ran to Shibing and as they grabbed him heard a familiar voice in the collapsing murk. A voice once warm and caring, but now clammy and ravenous as it pleaded for Kymani to come save him.

"Mörkrets?"

Kymani heard the subtle laugh again, and shrieking with grief and rage they wished the Bi would finish the job.

There was a woman's wail, and a moment later Kymani and Shibing found themselves in the hallway as a paradimensional eruption rattled the ground like an earthquake. Ignoring their traumas the pair hurriedly followed Shibing's notches through the quaking pathways back to the cellar and once they were back in the house the pair rushed to the front door. Kymani was about to open the door when the shaking ceased. Using the reprieve to think, Kymani decided to crack the door and peek outside first.

Sure enough, glaring at them from across the street was a beautiful Asian woman clutching the handle of a red parasol.

"She's here."

Horrified at first, Kymani realized the woman looked pale and poorly, and recalling the wail surmised the Bi's blast must have sideswiped her. Spying a trickle of hope, Kymani tamped down their predisposition against trusting anyone completely and placed the Bi in Shibing's hand. "Go out the back. You're on your own if you run into any minions. I am going to stall the woman as long as I can, but I'm counting on you returning the Bi where it belongs like you said."

Shibing vigorously shook his head. "No. We will both try escaping out the back."

"That won't work. The Coterie knows me and can always find me if they think I have the Bi. It's possible they don't know you, so you have the better chance of returning the Bi." Shibing started to argue again but Kymani shouted, "Good luck," and sprinted outside.

Across the street, the woman was gone.

V. Why

Later that evening Kymani answered a knock on their hotel door.

"Lieutenant Beahm. Good to see you again."

"You too." Accompanying Beahm was Fletcher, who was sporting a black eye, some contusions and skinned knuckles.

"I see you brought along a friend."

"I thought he was your friend. Mind if we come in?"

"Please." As Fletcher entered Kymani commented, "You've been here before, haven't you?" Then, indulging a guilty pleasure, Kymani retrieved the ICPC identification. "Here, Agent Fletcher. I think you lost this."

Fletcher took his ID without comment.

Beahm asked, "Where did you find that?"

"In Chinatown. Agent Fletcher and I must have almost crossed paths there this afternoon."

Beahm pointed to Kymani's suitcases, which were packed and beside the door. "You weren't going to check out without saying goodbye?"

"My job's finished. Time to return to Arkham."

"You found the Bi?"

"No," Kymani lied.

"Do you know who took it?"

"The only solid suspect I have is Shibing, but he's disappeared."

"Lieutenant," Fletcher said, "wouldn't it be prudent to search Jones and their luggage?"

Beahm gave Kymani a reticent look. "We really should. Agent Fletcher says he spotted you and Shibing conspiring on Waverly this afternoon."

"Did he?" Kymani smiled coyly at Fletcher. "Go ahead. I'm not hiding anything." Being frisked by Beahm was hardly the worst part of Kymani's day and watching Fletcher come a cropper with their luggage was well worth the repacking Kymani would have to do. "I've talked with Professor Vayner already, but I have a typed compte rendu

for Hellman Occidental that you're welcome to read."
Kymani pointed to a file folder on the nightstand.

"Thanks." Beahm scanned the report. "This says how you
suspected Shibing and followed him to Chinatown, where
you decided to confront him. Shibing told you he was there
helping a relative and you couldn't break his story."

Fletcher asked, "So why did you two go the art store's
stairs to talk in private?"

Kymani replied, "That was Shibing's idea. He said it is
considered suspicious if occidentals who aren't part of a
tour group are seen talking very long with locals."

"But apparently," Beahm said, "Shibing didn't consider
you a threat, unlike Fletcher."

"Is that what happened? Did he jump you, Agent
Fletcher?" Kymani did not even try to sound surprised or
concerned.

Fletcher sneered and walked to a window overlooking
Kearny Street, his back to Kymani and the detective, while
Beahm asked, "Any idea where Shibing is?"

"No." That was true. Kymani could only assume the Bi's
blast had incapacitated the woman enough to force her to
retreat and fight another day. They had no idea if Shibing
had gotten away or where he was now.

Beahm handed the file to Kymani. "Here you go."

"Thanks. I need to drop this off to Pointer on my way out
of town."

"Who's Pointer?"

Kymani did not comprehend Beahm's question at first,
then answered, "Barton Pointer. You know. The claims
adjuster Hellman assigned to the theft."

Beahm shrugged. "I'm afraid I don't know him."

Kymani's heart seized. Not again, they thought as they glanced at Fletcher.

The agent's posture had been ramrod straight with irritation, but now it was relaxed and the man appeared almost gleeful.

Kymani walked beside Fletcher and spoke in a low enough voice that Beahm could not hear. "She sent you, didn't she?"

"Whatever do you mean?" Fletcher asked coyly.

"The woman with the red parasol. She wants to be sure I know about Pointer."

"I don't know who you're talking about." Fletcher told Beahm, "I'm satisfied here." Then, "Until next time, Kymani Jones."

Furious and mournful, Kymani soberly promised, "Be seeing you, Agent Fletcher."

STRANGE THINGS DONE
Lisa Smedman

Rex Murphy walked down the pier, suitcase in one hand and portable typewriter, secure in its leather carry case, in the other. His roving reporter's eye took in the passengers bustling along the wooden planks of Seattle's Pier 2, noting details for the story he planned to write. Those bound for Alaska included miners in hobnailed work boots and flannel shirts; cannery workers with duffel bags slung over their shoulders and wool caps on their heads; and the occasional tourist.

Rex's gaze picked out the unusual: a thin man in an expensive-looking suit, with a bright red cravat knotted at his throat – his snappy clothing a sharp contrast to that of the rough and ready workers – and an orthodox priest wearing a black cape and fur hat, his long black beard covering his chest, a reminder that Alaska had once been part of the former Russian empire. The priest strode along the pier, an elaborately carved staff thumping the boards with each heavy step. Closer to the end of the pier, a man in a frayed woollen sweater watched as a shipboard crane lifted wooden crates, each containing a barking dog. Sailors shouted to each other over the din, and the smell of seaweed, creosote and coal smoke hung in the air.

Rex checked his ticket. The ship the dogs were being loaded onto was the one: the *SS Martha*. When he'd booked passage north with the Alaska Steamship Line, he'd expected something a bit bigger, a bit grander. A modern liner with staterooms and smoking parlor. The *Martha* looked more like a sailing ship, wooden hulled and only about a hundred feet long, with tall masts fore and aft. Smoke rose from her single funnel as the crew got up steam preparatory to departure. Her hull was scraped and her paint flaking; Rex imagined the antiquated ship had seen a few decades of service, grinding her way through drift ice to the remote ports she served.

The *Martha* looked old enough for Robert Service to have sailed aboard her. Rex was following the route the poet had taken north in 1904, first by ship to Skagway, then by train to Whitehorse, capital of the Yukon. Rex hoped his usual bad luck didn't manifest on this trip; it was late in the season, and an avalanche had closed the White Pass & Yukon Route tracks just last week. Not that he'd mind a few extra days in Skagway, with the *Advertiser* footing the bill. The journey would certainly be more colorful, judging by the mix of characters he saw boarding the *Martha*.

Rex approached the man with the dogs, who was kneeling beside one of the crates, talking softly to the animal inside it. The dog had one brown eye and one blue, and thick gray-white fur.

"That's a fine looking dog," Rex said. "What breed is it?"

"Siberian Husky," the man answered, not looking up. He poked fingers inside the wire mesh at the front of the crate, scratching the dog's cheek. "Samu here is my lead dog, from the same litter as Balto." The man glanced over his shoulder. "But I expect you've never heard of him."

Rex concealed a smile; his research on sled dogs had turned up that very name. "In fact, I have. Balto was the lead dog in the team that hauled diphtheria antitoxin from Anchorage to Nome in 1925. They staged a parade for him in Cleveland, earlier this year. Although some say it was Togo that should have gotten the credit, since he led the team on the longest and most dangerous stretch of the run."

The man turned his full attention to Rex, eyebrows raised. "You a breeder?"

Rex shook his head. "Reporter." He held out a hand. "Rex Murphy, from the *Arkham Advertiser*."

The man stood and shook hands with a firm, calloused grip. The tips of the last two fingers on his right hand were missing. Rex guessed there was a story behind that. "Morris Persky," the dog breeder said, introducing himself. "Where's Arkham?"

"Massachusetts."

"You're a long way from home."

"I'm on assignment. I'm headed to the Yukon, by way of Skagway, to do a story on Robert Service."

Morris' brow furrowed. "Never heard of him."

"He's a poet – as famous as Kipling, in his way.

Service wrote *The Shooting of Dan McGrew, The Ballad of Blasphemous Bill…*"

Morris shrugged.

Rex quoted Service's most famous poem:

"'There are strange things done in the midnight sun

"By the men who moil for gold;

"The Arctic trails have their secret tales

"That would make your blood run cold.'"

"Oh yeah," Morris said, nodding at last. "The poem about the prospector that burns the body of his dead pal in a furnace. That one, I've heard. Kinda creepy, when the dead guy comes back to life at the end."

"Where are you bound for?" Rex asked.

"I'm taking these dogs to Nome. It ain't much these days, compared to when the placer mines were operating, but there's always a market there for sled dogs."

"Can I interview you during the voyage?" Rex asked, pulling out his reporter's notebook and pencil to scribble down Morris' name and that of his dog. "I'd like to learn more about sled dogs and 'mushing', as they call it."

Morris watched fretfully as the crane lifted Samu's crate, the dog inside it barking furiously as the crate was swung up into the air, over the gunwale and down into the hold. Only then did he answer. "Sure. I guess."

"Looking forward to it." Rex made his way up the gangplank behind the other passengers. Just ahead of him was the priest. The man checking tickets butchered the man's name as he read it aloud.

"Father No Nob?" He laughed. "That right, Grandpa?"

Rex sighed. When the priest didn't speak up – he

probably didn't understand English – Rex glanced over his shoulder at the ticket. The letters were in the Cyrillic alphabet. "It's Popov," Rex said, sounding it out. He printed the name in his notebook, and held it up for the benefit of the ticket taker. "Popov. Like this."

Then it was Rex's turn; the ticket taker barely glanced at his ticket. "Proper American name," he said. "Not like them foreigners."

"Actually, Murphy's an Irish name."

"Whatever you say, Mack."

"And the first name's Rex, not Mack." Rex took his ticket back and lowered his voice to a theatrical whisper. "You want to be more careful about who you let on board. For all you know, the priest might be a Bolshevik in disguise!"

The man gave him a sour look. "There's always a wise guy."

Rex followed the black-robed priest, who was thumping his way toward a door further along the deck. They entered a narrow corridor lined with passenger cabins. The priest seemed to be having trouble figuring out which cabin was his. Rex motioned for his ticket, glanced at the number on it, then pointed the man toward Cabin 6. Rex's room was the next one along.

The cabin turned out to be small, with two bunks opposite the door, their privacy curtains pulled open. Rex had been hoping for a cabin to himself, so he could write undisturbed, but the *Martha* only offered shared accommodation. Rex sighed, wondering who he'd wind up sharing the cabin with. With his luck, it would be some tiresome old biddy who snored.

The top bunk had a small porthole, dogged shut. There was a small wooden side table against one wall, and two wicker chairs with sagging cushions. Rex slung his typewriter onto the table and hung his heavy winter coat on one of the hooks just inside the door. He placed his suitcase on the upper bunk.

"I see you have staked your claim," said a voice from the doorway.

Rex turned and saw the thin man with the red cravat he'd noticed on the pier earlier. The fellow was fair haired and clean shaven, with narrow, almost effeminate features and a willowy frame. The voice, however, was a firm baritone, with a trace of what might be an English accent.

"Were you hoping for the top bunk?" Rex asked.

The man waved a gloved hand. "No matter."

Rex stuck out his hand. "Rex Murphy, from Arkham." He expected the query that typically followed, but the man surprised him.

"An interesting town."

"You know it?" Rex was only partially surprised. Arkham was a small town, but the strange events that occurred all too frequently there had often made it the subject of national headlines.

"I am well-traveled." The man gave a slight incline of the head Rex took for an old-world bow. "I am Thorne."

Rex lowered his hand. "I'm a reporter. What line of work are you in?"

Thorne motioned in a sailor, who dragged in a heavy looking trunk. Thorne gestured for the sailor to place it against the wall. "I am in the business of locating and acquiring art and antiquities for private collectors."

"What sort of antiquities?"

Thorne hesitated. "Native art. Carvings, masks, that sort of thing."

"Sounds interesting. Do you have a card? Could I interview you some time?"

"Those I work for prefer not to advertise their collections, lest by doing so they attract unwanted attention."

"I see." Rex glanced at Thorne's trunk, which was secured by a lock. He wondered what was inside it – what was so valuable that Thorne didn't want it stowed in the hold. "I'm going as far as Skagway. How about you?"

Thorne squeezed past his case and began removing his coat and gloves. "I will be disembarking somewhat further north."

"Uh-huh." Rex sighed. This guy was better at evading questions than a politician. "Well, I think I'll start chatting to the other passengers, see who has a story to tell. I'm going to start with the… the man in the cabin next to ours. The man who…"

Rex stopped, unable to assemble his thoughts. An odd feeling gripped him: like when you walked into a room to look for something, and forgot what you were looking for. He took out his notebook and flipped through it. He saw the words "Morris Persky, dog breeder, Nome," and "Samu, same litter as Balto." Those, he remembered writing. But a few lines further down were the words, "Orthodox priest" and "Popov".

He had no idea who that was. No memory of writing that. Yet it was his handwriting.

"Did you see an Orthodox priest come on board?" he asked.

Thorne shook his head. "Why do you ask?"

Rex stroked his moustache: a nervous habit. He folded his notebook shut and shoved it into his pocket. "Excuse me."

Stepping into the corridor, he rapped on the door of the cabin next to his. It opened, revealing a middle-aged woman in a raccoon-skin coat. "Can I help you?" she asked.

"I'm looking for someone. The man who shares your cabin."

"I think you're mistaken," she said. "I'm traveling alone."

Rex's eyebrows rose. "They gave you a cabin all to yourself?"

"Of course. There are no other women on board – they can hardly expect me to share with a man." She tilted her head and gave him a coquettish smile. "But I am open to sharing a dinner table, if the conversation is engaging. I'm Gladys Federov, by the way." She held out her hand.

"Gladys… Federov?" Rex fumbled out his notebook. "Shouldn't it be… Popov?"

"What an odd thing to say."

Ignoring her outstretched hand, Rex peered past her into the cabin, trying to damp down a creeping feeling of dread. "This is wrong," he whispered to himself. "There should be a man in here."

Gladys' cheeks flushed. "I'll thank you to keep your opinions to yourself!" she snapped, closing the door in his face.

Rex rubbed his forehead as he returned to his own cabin.

He'd been through his share of scrapes in his career as an investigative reporter, taken more than one hard knock to the head. The docs had warned him a concussion could mess up his memory, even years down the road. That had to be it. He was far from Arkham, in a part of the world where only everyday, mundane things happened. Here, there were no antediluvian monsters with multiple eyes and puckered tentacles. No chanting cultists holding sacrificial daggers that dripped red. No towns filled with people with unblinking eyes, croaking through slit-throat gills.

Thorne stared at Rex as he entered their cabin. "Are you unwell?"

With an effort, Rex forced the haunted expression from his face and grabbed his coat. "Just feeling a little claustrophobic," he lied. "Think I'll go up on deck and get some air."

The *Martha* entered Canadian waters later that morning. She steamed north up the Inside Passage, with mainland British Columbia on the right, and Vancouver Island on the left. Rex had decided to start with general impressions of the voyage, and move on later to interviewing the passengers. Alone on the upper deck, he recorded every detail of what he saw in his notebook. The landscape was uniformly wild: thick forests of dark evergreens and rocky bluffs, gray skies above and gray-green water below. They passed the occasional town or sawmill, smokestacks emitting plumes of black into the overcast sky, but otherwise the landscape was empty. At one point Rex spotted the leaning totem poles and moss-covered longhouses of an abandoned native village. Despair clung to the place like fog. Gulls wheeled behind the ship, shrieking madly.

Rex wondered when they'd start to see the glaciers the northern coast was so famous for, and icebergs. He sighed. With his luck, the *Martha* would probably run smack into one. All his life, Rex had been dogged with bad luck. That old woman in Romania who'd told him he was cursed had probably been right.

Eventually a thin snow started to fall, dampening the pages of Rex's notebook and forcing him inside. It was late in the season for a journey north, almost winter. When he'd first pitched a feature piece on Robert Service, Rex had been hoping for an all-expenses-paid trip to sunny France, which the poet had made his home after leaving the Yukon. Instead, the editor had decided Rex needed to "pack a parka and go to the source" – Whitehorse and Dawson City, two gold rush era towns Rex had never dreamed he'd one day visit.

He made his way along the corridor leading to the cabins. Hearing a muffled barking, he decided to head below to see how Morris and his dogs were faring. He clattered down a narrow metal stairway to the hold, and wove his way between the stacks of cargo: crates of clothing and tools; barrels of gasoline; sheets of tinplate for the canneries; cast-iron stoves and stove pipes – all held in place with netting. There was even an upright piano, its strings vibrating with the chugging of the ship.

The dozen dog crates stood in the middle of a clear space. Morris kneeled beside one of them, mucking out the straw that lined the bottom of the crate. A black-and-gray husky sat next to him. The dog looked nervous, ears back and tail between its legs. It let out a low growl.

"What's gotten into you, girl?" Morris asked the dog. He started to pat her, but she shied away from his hand. She kept glancing at one of the other crates.

The rest of the dogs began barking. "All right!" Morris shouted. "You'll get your supper. Keep quiet!"

"Need some help?" Rex offered.

"Sure. Grab that bucket. Ladle some chow into each of the bowls."

Rex rolled up his sleeves and did as instructed. The bucket held a soupy mess of organs and fish guts, meat that smelled like it was on the verge of spoiling. He spooned some into each of the dozen tin bowls, and handed one bowl to Morris. The breeder offered it to the dog, but she only sniffed at it, never taking her eyes off the one crate whose occupant was silent.

"What's up with the dogs?" Rex asked.

"Beats me. The sea is calm, and they're used to being crated." Morris gestured. "You can let Samu out to eat, if you like. He seems to be the only one behaving himself."

Rex moved to the crate and peered inside. The husky stared up at him with ice-blue eyes. "You sure this is Samu? This dog has two eyes the same color."

"Of course it's him. You saying I don't know my own dogs?"

Rex shrugged. Maybe he'd made a mistake earlier, confused Samu with another dog. In any case, Samu was utterly silent, watching Rex with an intensity that was almost human. Rex had the strange sensation that the dog had been listening to their conversation. He noticed that Samu's hackles were raised, the fur along his spine standing up.

"Does he bite?"

Morris laughed. "He wouldn't be much use as a sled dog if he did."

Crouching, Rex held the bowl where the dog could see it as he unfastened the latch. "Nice dog, nice boy," he said in a soft voice. "Here's your–"

Samu exploded out of the crate, bowling Rex over backwards and spilling the bowl's soupy contents all over his shirt. In a flash the animal was across the cargo hold, tearing into the dog beside Morris. The smaller dog yiped and flailed back, her ear half ripped off and blood staining her fur a bright red.

"Grab his hind legs!" Morris yelled. "We've got to pull them apart!"

Rex clambered to his feet and moved warily forward. The dogs tangled together, Samu biting furiously while the female cowered and tried to avoid his fangs. Rex saw his chance and grabbed Samu's hind legs, down near the hock, as Morris did the same to the female.

"Lift his legs up!" Morris shouted. "Like a wheelbarrow, then spin! That way he can't bite you."

Rex yanked the dog's legs high into the air, turning rapidly as the powerful male snarled and twisted. Samu's teeth grazed the back of Rex's forearm, scoring a red line. The situation was terrifying and ridiculous at the same time, like some sort of strange dance.

Rex was wondering what the hell to do next, when all at

once the dog he was twirling suddenly grew lighter, rising from the ground and growing visibly thinner. Suddenly, the dog wrenched itself from Rex's grip. It flew through the air as if launched from a cannon, rebounding off the piano with a discordant clash of keys. Then, in a fluid, unnatural *twisting* motion, it disappeared into the loose tangle of netting where the piano had been.

Where the…?

Where had what been?

Rex looked down at his empty hands, then at Morris, who was squatting next to a black-and-gray dog, scratching her ear as she gobbled up the food Rex had just slopped into her bowl. The dog wagged her tail. The hold was silent, just the occasional anxious bark from the dogs still awaiting their turn to be fed.

Rex strained to think. There had been blood. A fight of some kind.

Hadn't there?

He glanced down at his forearm, then wondered why he was looking at it. He felt the front of his shirt, wondering why he expected it to be damp. He held up the bowl he'd just filled, and felt a strange sense of deja vu as Morris gestured for him to take it to the next crate.

"You can feed my lead dog next," Morris instructed. "I don't want him thinking I don't appreciate him."

"Your lead dog?"

"Yeah. The brown one in the crate over there."

Rex moved toward that crate, feeling off kilter. His legs felt rubbery, and he nearly stumbled. Odd – the ship wasn't rocking any more than usual. Gradually, however, the dizzy sensation he was feeling began to ebb. He let the brown husky out of his crate and set down its bowl, then flipped open his notebook while the dog ate. He picked up the thread of the conversation where it had left off earlier, on the pier. "So, you're a dog breeder, headed for Nome."

"That's right."

"And your lead dog, Samu, is from the same litter as Balto."

Morris laughed as he moved to the next crate. "I wish! That animal would really be worth something. But no, you got the name wrong. Mishka's the name of my lead dog."

"Mishka. Got it." Rex made the correction in his notebook, drawing a line through the word Samu; he wondered what had possessed him to write that down in the first place. "Tell me what dog sledding is like."

"It's beautiful. The silence, the panting of the dogs, sparkling white snow all the way to the horizon. And cold – so cold your breath freezes and there's icicles in your beard. If you aren't careful, frostbite will take your nose and ears."

Rex pointed with his pencil. "Is that how you lost your fingers? To frostbite?"

"Yeah. During a trip by sled to my cabin, near Nome. Stupid of me: I lost a glove. My fingers turned black, and I had to cut them off." He rubbed his injured hand, and grimaced. "When it's thirty below, a man can freeze solid in ten minutes, if he doesn't have the right gear. Sometimes even when he does. That's what happened to a guy I knew: Polish Mike, a musher from Anchorage."

"Did he get caught in a storm?"

"Nope. He let the fire in his cabin go out, one cold midwinter night. They didn't find his body until spring. He'd froze to death sitting at the table, his dinner still on his plate." Morris looked up, a twinkle in his eye. "I suppose he didn't eat it because it had gone cold."

Rex smiled. "Good one." He scribbled furiously in his notebook as Morris told story after story about the far north. He imagined Robert Service doing the same: listening to the tales of the prospectors, jotting them down as fodder for his poems. He was thankful to have met Morris; this was going to add some great color to his story.

Rex spent the rest of the afternoon typing up the stories Morris had shared with him. When he was done, he made his way to the dining saloon, a room as wide as the ship, its walls hung with faded tapestries. Dinner was surprisingly good: a choice of poached salmon or roast beef and boiled potatoes, with celery soup to start and oranges and vanilla wafers for dessert, followed by coffee and cigarettes. No wine or whisky – it was Prohibition, after all. Rex wondered if there were speakeasies up north.

He made a point of sitting at the captain's table. Gladys, the woman from the cabin next to his, was also seated there. She pointedly ignored Rex as she explained she was heading north to live with her brother in Valdez. "I'm a music teacher. A pianist. How I wish I could have brought my piano with me, but the expense of shipping such a bulky object north was completely beyond my reach. Now that I'm a widow, I have to be careful with my money."

That struck an odd chord with Rex; he couldn't shake the feeling that something about her story was just... wrong. But now Captain Joseph LeBlanc was talking, and Rex was caught up in the scramble to faithfully capture his words in his notebook.

"I've been aboard the *Martha* since she launched in 1880," he told them. "Worked my way up from deckhand to captain over the nearly fifty years since. And oh, the things I've seen!"

Rex had already gotten all the pertinent data on the *Martha* from the chief engineer during a hot, noisy tour of the boiler and engine rooms. The ship had a gross tonnage of 320, and burned 3,000 pounds of coal a day. At a top speed of seven and a half knots, her run from Seattle to Skagway normally took six days. All the way to Nome, her last port of call, was fifteen days.

As well as being a steamship, the *Martha* was also rigged as a two-masted brigantine, for times when the engine failed or couldn't be used. Captain LeBlanc was telling the tale of one such voyage now, living up to his "Laughing Joe" nickname with a wide smile that split his long gray beard.

"It was the winter of 1900, and a heavy southeast gale blew us nearly three hundred miles out to sea. A heavy wave broke over the deck, and the boiler shook right off its mount and the steam pipe burst. Lucky for the stokers, none of them was scalded. We were dead in the water, and sent up a flare, but no ships were around to see it. We raised sail, but the ice formed so fast the rigging sagged and the sails tore. We wound up drifting for sixty-three days, our rations gone, trying to keep our spirits up by joking about which of us would be eaten first. Only by the grace of God did the currents carry us in to shore. The angels themselves were watching over us that trip."

He crossed himself theatrically as those seated at his table listened with wide eyes. Rex jotted it all down in his notebook, even though he suspected the tale had been embellished a touch by repeated telling.

"Then there was the time we struck an iceberg," LeBlanc added. "Stove in our hull, and the water came in so fast it was up to the carpenters' waists, even with all pumps going full bore, before they could put in a temporary patch. We put in to shore and sheltered under tents of driftwood and canvas for a week while the carpenters repaired the hole. The company thought we were lost – but we proved them wrong."

LeBlanc took a sip of black coffee, which smelled of rum. He scanned his audience, clearly savoring their anticipation. "We even sailed through a volcano, once."

"Now you're having us on," one man said, shaking his head in disbelief. "A volcano?"

LeBlanc laughed and raised calloused palms. "It's true, or may God himself strike me dead as a nail. It was back in 1912, when Mount Katmai erupted. The smoke went up two, maybe three thousand feet into the sky, then flattened out across the sea. It was so dark you couldn't see a lantern in front of your face. Birds fell dead from the sky, and the ash piled up on deck so thick it was up to our knees. All was thunder and brimstone. I ordered full speed ahead; we sailed by dead reckoning for hours, coughing and blinded all the while. I never was so glad to see Kodiak hove into view as when we finally found our way out of that terrible black cloud."

"Sounds like the *Martha* has the misfortune to be in the wrong place at the wrong time, on more than one occasion," Rex commented. "She gets into – and out of – more scrapes than even I do."

LeBlanc threw back his head and laughed. "You got that right, son. The *Martha*'s got more lives than a black cat."

"I've heard the Alaska coast is dangerous – is that true?" The man who asked the question, Robert Middleton, held a cigarette that burned, forgotten, between his fingers. Rex had interviewed him earlier. Middleton was going up to clerk at a bank, the very job that had taken Robert Service north, back in 1904.

The captain answered the question in a low voice. "Dangerous, indeed. Sometimes ships just disappear. Like the *Stikine Chief*, back in 1898. She sailed from Fort Wrangel and was never heard from again. We were the ones to find what little remained: just a few broken boards, and a little white dog, balanced on a life preserver. Forty-three souls were lost that day."

"Was the dog saved?" Gladys asked.

"I brought the poor little creature on board myself, and named her Lucky Lady," LeBlanc assured her. "That dog was our mascot for many years, and was honored with a proper burial at sea, when she finally passed."

LeBlanc held an imaginary hat over his heart a moment, then drained the last of his coffee. "Now if you'll excuse me, ladies and gents, I should return to the wheelhouse."

The men at the table politely rose as the captain did, then broke out cards as stewards cleared away their dishes. Gladys insisted they deal her in. Rex declined to join them, instead taking a longer route back to his cabin. He went out on deck and shuffled through the snow that had fallen, savoring an ink-black sky filled with thousands of twinkling stars, his head buzzing with the stories he'd just heard. The *Martha* and her captain had been through a lot over the years. Enough to make Rex wonder if the ship was as much of a magnet for disaster as he was.

With a shiver, Rex headed inside to his cabin.

The next morning, Rex awoke to the familiar *zzzip* of paper being pulled from a typewriter. He yanked open his privacy curtain and saw Thorne holding the manuscript Rex had been working on yesterday.

"What are you doing?" Rex demanded, taken aback. "Put that down!"

Thorne ignored his protest. "Is this fiction?"

"No. It's part of a feature story for the *Arkham Advertiser*." Rex climbed down from his bunk. "The piece I'm writing about Robert Service. Hand it over."

Thorne ignored him. "But you are embellishing, is that not so?"

"Embellishing?"

Thorne touched a finger to the page. "Here, you write about sled dogs being loaded aboard the ship by crane, as if you had witnessed that. And here, you write about feeding the dogs in the hold."

Rex felt momentarily dizzy, as though he'd been drinking.

The sea felt rougher today, the ship rising and falling as it plowed steadily north through an increasing swell. Yeah, that must have been it. He was feeling seasick. Nothing weird was happening, he told himself firmly. "I never wrote about sled dogs."

"You did." Thorne finally handed him the sheet of paper. "Observe."

Rex took the typewritten page and read, in open-mouthed disbelief, whole paragraphs he'd never seen before. "I don't remember writing any of this."

Thorne gestured. "And yet it was in your typewriter."

"I remember the name Morris Persky," Rex said. "I talked to him on the pier, when he was…" He paused, searching for the words, but there was a hole where the memory should have been. It was like trying to use your tongue to touch a tooth that had recently been pulled, leaving only a raw wound. "No, that's not right. I talked to him in the hold, when he was feeding his…"

"Feeding his sled dogs, according to what you wrote. Yet there are no dogs aboard this ship."

"But there is a Morris Persky," Rex said. He was certain of that, at least.

"Is there?" Thorne gave him a penetrating look. "Or is the man you spoke to yesterday now an imposter?"

"I'm not sure I follow you."

Thorne tensed slightly as someone walked down the corridor, then relaxed after the footsteps receded. "They can change anything," he said. "Except abstract symbols. Language is difficult for them, and the written word, impossible."

Rex set the paper down. This was sounding all too familiar. "They?"

"You have a keen eye and a quick hand," Thorne said. "I would encourage you to record everything you see and hear – to keep notes on everyone you meet. I will pay handsomely for the opportunity to read the results." Thorne took out his money clip, removed a twenty-dollar bill, and offered it to Rex. "It will be helpful, should something else… change."

Rex took the twenty. He tried to be glib. "You want to pay me a week's salary to proofread my first drafts? Sure. Why not?"

But doubt gnawed at him as he stared at the words he'd never written. Had something terrible followed him from Arkham? Had the horrors he'd encountered there reached out across three thousand miles to this desolate coast?

And who was this Thorne guy? He was starting to remind Rex of Professor Walters, with his talk of language and symbols.

"You've had experience with the occult?" Rex asked. His eyes strayed to Thorne's trunk; once more he wondered what it contained.

"It is best we end this conversation here," Thorne said. "We can speak again once you have learned more." He turned and began tidying his bunk, a clear indication the interview was over.

Rex decided to seek out Morris Persky instead. He scooped up his clothes and hurried to the bathroom down the hall. He splashed water onto his face and changed out of his pajamas. He put his spectacles on and stared at his narrow face in the mirror. His eyes had dark circles under them, even though he'd slept well. His thick brown hair was uncombed and his cheeks stubbled, but he didn't waste time shaving. He had to find out what was going on.

Morris Persky wasn't in the dining salon, where the other passengers were having breakfast. Nor was he inside any of the cabins whose doors Rex knocked on. Rex made his way down to the cargo hold, confirming that there were, indeed, no dogs on board. He climbed back up to the main deck and ventured outside. Snow was falling heavily this morning, turning the deck white and slippery. The sky was a sullen gray.

Rex spotted his quarry standing near the lifeboat on the starboard side of the ship. The man wore a suit and tie – somehow, that felt wrong – and stood with one hand on the gunwale of the lifeboat. He was shivering and snow dusted his hair and shoulders; it looked as though he'd been standing there awhile. He looked familiar, and yet...

"Morris Persky?" Rex asked.

The man startled. "That's me."

"Rex Murphy," Rex said, introducing himself. The hand that shook his was cold as an icebox. And it was missing the tips of two fingers. But it was soft, not a working man's hand.

"Do I know you?" Morris asked.

"We met yesterday, on the..." No, that wasn't right. "Down in the cargo hold, we..." Rex took a deep breath, struggling to call to mind the typewritten text he'd read not so many minutes ago. The words were slippery as ice. He'd faced many dangers in his career as a reporter, but they'd all been physical. The prospect of losing an eye or an arm was far less frightening than losing his memories. He had the terrifying sense of something invisible reaching into his brain, slicing away with a cold, sharp blade at his mind.

Rex shook his head, forcing himself to focus on the interview. "Why are you standing out here in the cold?" he asked.

"I don't know." Morris blinked, looking like a man who'd just been wakened from a dream. "Everything just feels... wrong, somehow. Like I shouldn't be here. Or like I should be here, but not... here." His eyes strayed to the lifeboat, his fingers picking nervously at the ties that held in place its canvas cover.

"I think we should go inside," Rex gently suggested.

"Yes." Morris nodded, eyes still fixed on a distant point on the horizon. "Yes, we should."

In the dining salon, Rex plied Morris with questions amidst the clatter of stewards clearing away breakfast plates. Morris grew increasingly animated as the hot coffee warmed him. His face had assumed a normal color, and his eyes no longer had a haunted look.

"I'm with the Spratt's dog food company," he said. "I'm taking crates of biscuits north, to hand out as samples to 'mushers' to feed them to their sled dogs." He fished an object out of his suit pocket and laid it on the table: a thick brown biscuit that looked like hardtack. "Spratt's is hoping to expand into Alaska. Maybe cut a deal with one of the canneries to process their waste into dog food."

"Is this your first trip north?"

"No, I..." Morris looked confused a moment, then

shook his head. "Yes. First trip to Alaska. I'm excited to see the 'land of the midnight sun.'"

"Strange things done..." Rex murmured.

"Excuse me?"

"Nothing. I'm curious about something. What happened to your fingers?" It was a blunt question, but Rex had learned long ago to take a direct approach. If you started by asking an interviewee if they minded being asked a personal question, they usually clammed up.

Morris held up his hand and laughed. "Oh that. Not much of a story, I'm afraid. Before I became a salesman, I worked the factory floor at Spratt's. My hand strayed a little too close to one of the cutting machines, and that was that. Hurt like hell – but there was a silver lining. It pushed me into the job I have today."

"I see," Rex said. But he didn't. Not really. Belatedly, he realized he hadn't even taken notes. He remedied that by excusing himself and moving to another table, where he hurriedly jotted down what he'd just been told. It all felt wrong, somehow, like a story that had been made up. But Rex recorded it anyway. For all he knew, these memories were going to disappear, too. Better to have a written record.

His next stop was the purser's office. It was a cramped space on the upper deck, home to a wireless radio set and a desk strewn with papers. The radio operator was bareheaded and in shirt sleeves, but the purser wore a proper uniform, his cap emblazoned with the Alaska Steamship Company's trademark red flag with its white "A" on a black circle. His jacket buttons were neatly polished – a fastidious man. Good. He'd probably keep accurate records.

It took some convincing to get the purser to show him the passenger manifest. Convincing, and a pair of dollar bills. Scanning the list of names, Rex saw that there was no Popov – either in Latin letters or Cyrillic.

Rex frowned. Why had he just thought that?

Reporter's habit, he decided, closing the manifest and sliding it back to the purser. Always check the spelling.

Over the next two days Rex feverishly collected notes on as many of his fellow passengers as he could. He interviewed the bank clerk, talked to some prospectors returning north, and listened from a nearby table as Captain LeBlanc laughed and gesticulated his way through another round of tall tales of the dangers of the sea. Rex shook his head, wondering what the steamship company thought of that. Such dire tales couldn't have been good for business.

Rex shared his notes with Thorne, who read them in silence.

"Do you notice any discrepancies?" Rex asked nervously. "Has anything else changed?"

Thorne shook his head. "All is quiet, for the moment." He handed back the notebook. "Please continue your investigation."

"But what if–"

"We will talk later. Not now."

Throughout the fourth day of the voyage the wind and waves picked up. That night, as Rex lay in his bunk, the bow of the ship rose and fell as it cut through the swells. Every now and then they'd crest a bigger wave, and the bunk would drop out from under Rex: an unsettling feeling.

He glanced out the tiny porthole and at first saw nothing but the darkness of the sea – but then the *Martha* rolled slightly and he saw streaks of green across the sky. The northern lights! He hadn't expected to see them until he was much further north.

Clambering down from his bunk, Rex steadied himself with a hand on the wall as he pulled on his clothes and coat. When he opened the cabin door, lantern light from the corridor revealed that Thorne's bunk was empty.

Rex hesitated, one hand gripping the door frame as the ship rose and fell beneath his feet. Had Thorne disappeared?

No, the man's trunk was still on the floor beside the bunk, sliding back and forth across the floor as the ship rolled.

Rex found his cabin mate out on deck. Thorne's gloved hands clasped the rail as he stared up at the sky. Rex joined him, looking up at the ripples of bright green light. The sight took his breath away. Ghostly shimmers in a thousand shades of green swirled through the sky as if stirred by an invisible hand. Rex completely forgot the heaving of the ship beneath his feet, the slipperiness of the deck and the terrible chill of the black sea below.

"They're beautiful," he breathed, his breath fogging in the cold air.

The sky was alive with light. Gauzy curtains of green rippled across the blackness of the northern sky, hiding and then revealing the puny stars.

"They are so vast," Thorne said. "They make one feel insignificant."

Rex had almost forgotten that Thorne was beside him. "You got that right."

"It was the Romans who coined the term 'aurora borealis'," Thorne continued. "Literally, 'dawn wind'. They imagined Aurora, goddess of dawn, racing across the sky in her chariot, leaving light that swirled like dust in her wake.

"The Laplanders say the northern lights are caused by a fox that runs so swiftly across the ice, its tail throws up sparks. The Inuit believe they're the spirits of the dead, playing ball with a walrus head, of all things. But it is the Vikings whose legends come closest to the mark. They believed the northern lights to be glints off the shields of the Valkyries." Thorne gestured up. "In their sagas, these lights are the Bifrost Bridge that leads to Valhalla."

"You're well versed in mythology," Rex said. "But I suppose you'd have to be, in your line of work."

Thorne continued to stare upward, his expression sharp as the cold. "Not mythology," he said, "but fact. There are indeed places where the curtains between worlds are thin – rents in the fabric of reality. The aurora borealis is one such manifestation; another was the strange lightning storm in Seattle the evening before our departure. The Outsiders use them to enter our world."

"Outsiders?" Rex prompted. He was shivering now. The night air was cold and sea spray chilled his bare hands where they gripped the icy rail.

"Paradimensional entities." Thorne turned at last to stare at Rex. "I have the feeling that you know what I am speaking about – is that correct?"

Rex nodded. Here we go again, he thought. It's starting. Just like it did in Arkham.

"One is aboard this ship, having assumed a form that will allow it to pass undetected. It knows I am aboard and what I am looking for, and seeks to stop me from finding it. So far, I have been fortunate; the Outsider has not isolated me. There is too much noise obscuring the signal." He waved a hand. "Too many souls aboard the ship."

"What do we do?" Rex asked. "What *can* we do?"

"Nothing, until we can identify the form it has taken. We can only watch. And wait."

"Can it be stopped?" Rex asked.

"That remains to be seen. Perhaps if we lure it out…" Thorne shivered, then drew his coat closer around his neck, tucking his cravat inside it. Then he gestured at the notebook poking out of Rex's coat pocket. "For now, please continue your interviews. And pay close attention to the captain and crew. I have a feeling that may be vital."

With that, Thorne turned to stare back out at the horizon. Once again, Rex had the feeling he'd been dismissed.

"Well," Rex said at last. "It's too cold out here for me – think I'll turn in. Good night."

As he headed back to the cabin, he took one last glance over his shoulder.

Thorne remained at the rail, his thin body silhouetted against the twisted canvas of the glowing green sky.

Rex wondered if he could trust Thorne. What was the fellow actually up to – why was he headed north?

The answer, Rex suspected, was inside that trunk.

•••

The next day, the weather was even worse. Rex had been unable to sleep much the night before; what sleep he'd managed had been troubled by dreams of green-limned doorways leading to horrific landscapes filled with the howling of dogs and the screams of men.

He clambered down from his bunk – nearly tumbling from the ladder due to the pitching of the ship. His typewriter had slid off the table some time in the night; he picked the case up and opened it to ensure the machine hadn't been damaged. As the ship rolled, Thorne's trunk slid across the floor, bumping into Rex and nearly knocking his legs out from under him.

Rex glanced at Thorne's bunk – it was empty – then down at the trunk. The lock didn't look all that complicated...

Rex got to work with his pocket knife. After a few minutes, he jimmied the lock and the latch of the trunk sprang open.

The trunk was filled with books and maps. Rex scanned the titles of the former, and saw they were mostly about early explorations of Alaska. Some were in Spanish or Russian, with cracked leather covers and loose pages that looked very old. Rex wondered if Thorne spoke those languages.

He unrolled one of the maps: it turned out to be of Kodiak Island and was titled "Alaska Ice Inc. Mining Operations". Rex remembered the name from his research; apparently there had been a lucrative trade, back in the 1850s and 60s, of hauling ice down to San Francisco, where it was used for food preservation. It was a long way to haul ice – but the ships bringing supplies north needed something to use as ballast on the return voyage.

Words were scrawled at the bottom of the map: "The source?"

Source of what? Rex wondered.

A yellowed newspaper was tucked under the books: a copy of the *Anchorage Times*, dated 1918. Rex unfolded it, expecting to see news of the Great War. Instead, the page-wide headlines read: "Anchorage Stricken by Massive Quake – Townsite Flattened – Hundreds Feared Killed".

Rex felt a prickle of fear. That earthquake had… never happened. It would have come up in his research if it had. And yet here was a story about it, filling several columns of type.

Something had caused a shift in reality. The world had changed – all that remained of the earthquake that had never happened was this echo in ink.

Rex put everything back in the trunk and closed the lid. He wondered what else in the world had changed without anyone realizing it. How much of this current reality was true, and how much had been removed and rewritten? He took off his spectacles and rubbed his eyes. How much of his *own* life was real?

Did Thorne know? Rex was determined to find out. This time, he'd force Thorne to give him some answers.

Exiting the cabin, Rex made his way aft to the dining salon. One glance out its windows told the story of how much the temperature had dropped overnight: the entire deck was coated in glittering white ice. It hung from every rail and roofline in long icicles; each smash of spray over the bows slicked on yet more water that instantly froze. The *Martha* was lower in the water than she'd been previously, weighed down by thousands of pounds of ice.

A man's voice came from behind as Rex stared out the windows. "Do you think they'll be serving breakfast?"

Rex turned and saw the bank clerk bracing himself with a hand on either side of the door.

"I think the crew has more pressing things to worry about."

The clerk nodded nervously.

Where the hell was Thorne? Rex descended to the cargo hold, but saw no sign of the man there, or in any of the public areas of the ship. Could Thorne perhaps have gone up to the wheelhouse?

Rex made his way back to the door leading out on deck. He had to bang it open with his shoulder; the ice had frozen it shut.

An icy wind buffeted him as he made his way outside. He had a moment of panic as he slipped and fell while climbing the stairs to the wheelhouse; he grabbed the handrail just in time as the ship rolled hard to port. This is ridiculous, he thought. If he fell, he'd slide right over the edge into the sea. But he continued upward, driven as much by a desire to learn if the ship was in danger as by his quest to find Thorne.

Five men occupied the wheelhouse. One grappled with the wheel, while a second looked out the ice-crazed windows with binoculars. A third man was bent over charts spread across a desk at the back of the wheelhouse, frantically plotting their course with dividers and pencil, while the fourth shouted orders into a voice tube next to the ship's telegraph. The fifth man was LeBlanc. He stood with arms folded across his chest, his body swaying easily in time with the wild plunges and rolls of the deck beneath his feet. Above him, the ship's bell clanged with each movement, adding further confusion to the scene. No sign of Thorne.

"What the hell are you doing here?" the helmsman barked over his shoulder. "Passengers aren't allowed in the wheelhouse."

"I arranged an interview with Captain LeBlanc," Rex lied.

"We're fighting a heavy southeaster. Get back to your cabin!"

"Is the ship in danger?"

LeBlanc slowly turned to stare at Rex. He had the same grizzled beard and stocky frame, but the laugh lines were gone. Ice-blue eyes stared out from under the brim of his captain's cap: a long stare that caused the hairs on the back of Rex's neck to rise. All sound and color drained from the world, and the air became still. Rex had a powerful sensation of standing on a brink that was about to drop out from under him.

Then LeBlanc turned away, and the sounds of the storm returned.

"Captain," the lookout with the binoculars said. "Lighthouse, bearing zero zero three."

"It must be Point Arden," said the sailor bent over the charts. He looked up, a worried expression on his face. "Sir, I make us less than a mile offshore."

"Captain, our speed is full ahead," the sailor at the telegraph chimed in. "Should we reduce speed?"

"Captain!" the helmsman shouted urgently. "Your orders? How shall I steer?"

LeBlanc swayed gently as the ship pitched and rolled. Slowly, he raised a hand and pointed slightly to the left. He spoke in a hollow voice: "Turn."

"Turn?" the helmsman sputtered. "To what bearing?"

The navigator abruptly stood. "Captain LeBlanc, I relieve you of command." Then, to the helmsman: "Starboard fifteen. Engines, half ahead."

"Starboard fifteen," the helmsman repeated, looking relieved. He started to spin the wheel – but then LeBlanc was suddenly at his side, one hand tightly gripping a spoke of the wheel.

"No," LeBlanc said.

The two men fought for control of the wheel as the ship plunged frantically through the heaving waves. The helmsman gurgled as one of LeBlanc's hands wrapped around his throat.

The Outsider! Rex thought. The creature Thorne had warned him about. It was LeBlanc! Rex started to move forward, intending to grab LeBlanc and wrestle him to the deck. But before he could, time seemed to falter, then jump ahead. Suddenly, the coast was much closer than it had been an instant before. A wave-lashed bluff topped by the white spire of a lighthouse loomed large in the windows of the wheelhouse. A loud grinding shuddered up through the *Martha* as she struck the rocks, and the ship listed hard to port. Rex was hurled against the wall of the wheelhouse in a tangle with another man. A window shattered, letting in the mournful dirge of the lighthouse horn.

"We've run aground!" the lookout shouted, blood trickling from a gash in his pale cheek.

Rex heaved himself up and looked around. The inside of the wheelhouse was now a shambles, sea spraying through the broken window as waves crashed against the side of the ship. The *Martha* groaned and shuddered, rolling and settling, rolling and settling, as her hull sawed itself against the rocks.

Shipwrecked! he thought. He shook his head. Why did disaster seem to follow him, everywhere he went?

The man lying next to him groaned. He wore a captain's uniform, gold bars on the sleeves of his black coat. Rex rolled him over, and stared down at a face he didn't recognize: the narrow features of a man in his thirties, with thick auburn hair and clean-shaven cheeks. It was Captain…

The name was gone. Rex had come to the wheelhouse to interview this man, but now he couldn't remember the captain's name, or anything about him. They'd had supper together the first night on board, and the captain had said… he'd told Rex… Yes, that was it: the captain had laughed and said… something about nine lives. And a black cat. Or maybe a white dog.

No, that wasn't right either.

"Should I send up a flare?" the young lookout shouted.

The navigator heaved himself to his feet. He took one look at the unconscious captain, and took charge. "No use – no one's going to see it in this gale." He fired off orders: "Hubbard, tell the wireless operator to send out an SOS. Caldwell, call down to the engine room for a status report. Muller, go tell the stewards to get the passengers into their life jackets and mustered on deck. We're abandoning ship."

There was a chorus of nervous, "Aye, sirs," as the crew scrambled to their tasks. In the middle of it, the navigator noticed Rex. "What the hell are you still doing here? Get down to your cabin and grab a life jacket!"

Rex gulped. He climbed out the wheelhouse door and ran, slipping and sliding his way down the ice-coated stairs as the ship rocked precariously. Wind-blown snowflakes and salt spray stung his eyes, and his winter coat grew heavy. Even in gloves, his hands felt like blocks of ice. He was trying to fumble open the door leading to the passenger cabins when it crashed open, forcing him back. A welter of passengers burst out on deck, some screaming, some crying, others shoving as they fought their way toward the lifeboats. Sailors roared instructions that fell on deaf ears. The bank clerk was struggling to keep his feet when yet another towering wave smashed into the ship; he slid on the icy, tilting deck and tumbled over the rail and into the sea.

Terrified that he'd be the next one overboard – that was how his luck usually went – Rex fought his way along the corridor. He needed to get his life jacket, his mind screamed. And his manuscript.

He was surprised to find Thorne in their cabin. The man was bent over his open trunk, grabbing maps and stuffing them into his pockets. Rex scooped up the pages of his manuscript. He picked up his typewriter case – the portable Remington was brand new, and had cost him fifty bucks – but then sanity prevailed and he let it drop.

There was something he needed to tell Thorne. Something about the captain…

There was that hollow feeling again. Something had been torn from Rex's mind, leaving only a raw ache and dizziness behind. The horror of it almost dampened Rex's fear of what would happen next, now that the ship was on the rocks and possibly sinking. Almost.

"They've given orders to abandon ship," he told Thorne. "Where are our life jackets?"

Thorne gestured at the far wall. "Under the bottom bunk."

Rex staggered across the cabin. He hauled out one life jacket, tossed it in Thorne's direction, then dragged the second one over his head. It was nearly impossible to tie the straps with his cold-numbed fingers. The jacket fit awkwardly over his heavy winter coat, but somehow Rex managed it.

Rex started to make his way back to the door, but Thorne blocked his path. "I require your help."

"Help?" Rex echoed. "Help with what?"

"The Outsider will stop at nothing to eliminate me. It couldn't locate me, due to my… protections. But it intends to eliminate me, so it has wrecked this ship. It will only continue to follow me, wreaking havoc, unless I can stop it."

"That's your problem, not mine." Rex tried to move past Thorne and out the door, but the other man shoved him back into the cabin. For a skinny guy, Thorne was surprisingly strong.

"The Outsider has marked you as a threat, as well – I can smell its spoor on you. Unless you help me destroy it, nothing will remain of you but a hole in the fabric of the cosmos." He snapped gloved fingers. "Rex Murphy will simply cease to exist." Rex had a jagged flash of memory: icy eyes that seemed to bore a hole into the very fabric of his soul. He shivered.

"It is entirely possible it has already changed you," Thorne continued grimly. "You may no longer be the same Rex Murphy who boarded this vessel. I've noticed subtle changes."

"Changes?" Rex echoed.

"Read your notebook."

Rex plucked it from his pocket, flipping it open to the last page. On it were two words: "TRUST THORNE".

He had no memory of writing that.

Rex took a shuddering breath. "What do we need to do?"

"We'll lay a trap," Thorne said. "One that will destroy the Outsider. Follow me."

Rex followed Thorne out of the cabin and down the tilted stairs to the cargo hold. Sailors shoved their way past the two men, shouting at them that they were going the wrong way. Thorne ignored them.

The hold was a shambles, cargo ripped from its netting and crashing about as the ship rolled. Thorne dodged his way into the chaos, and Rex somehow managed to follow him without getting crushed.

At the far end of the cargo hold, a door slammed open. The chief engineer Rex had interviewed earlier scrambled out, spotted them, and shouted as he ran past: "She's taking on water fast. If it reaches the boiler, she'll blow." Then he was gone, scrambling like a rat up the stairs to the deck above.

"This is crazy," Rex shouted at Thorne.

Thorne had picked up an axe from somewhere during their frantic foray into the hold. One foot braced against a wall, he chopped at a barrel like a cop from the dry squad going at a keg of whisky. Gasoline sprayed into the air, filling the hold with a pungent, eye-watering smell.

"Another axe is on the wall near the door," Thorne shouted. "Grab it and help."

Rex did as he was told. He remembered the pale blue eyes of... of the man in the captain's uniform. How terrifying being pierced by their icy gaze had felt. Awkward in his life jacket, he swung the axe overhead – again and again, smashing open barrels. All the while, the ship rolled and groaned.

Frigid water began pouring into the hold. The gasoline floated atop it, lending it an oily blue-green sheen. Rex was reminded of the aurora borealis.

The gateway between worlds...

"Enough," Thorne said, tossing aside his axe. "Back to the stairs!"

Rex sloshed through the water swirling around his ankles. He had barely reached the stairs when the ship's electric lighting went out. Blackness surrounded him as the movements of the dying ship buffeted him back and forth in the narrow stairwell; from above came the sounds of crashing waves, and the muffled screams of the passengers. Rex swallowed his fear. The possibility of drowning paled compared to the prospect of being erased from reality.

Behind him, light blossomed. He turned and saw Thorne holding a match. Thorne's other hand was at his throat, stroking his cravat. Then he began to chant: "Come, O thing that be not of this world. Here I stand! Food for ye to sup upon. Come!"

Beyond him, something rose, dripping, from the water in the hold. It had a vaguely humanoid shape, but was only a twisted mockery of a man, its limbs misshapen and elongated, its face shifting from man to woman to dog to slavering beast – and finally settling on a replica of Thorne. Ice-blue eyes locked on the spot where they stood. Then the creature began to slosh through the gasoline-fouled water toward them.

Rex felt his mouth go dry. He raised his axe, even though his gut told him it was a futile gesture. But if he was about to be edited out of this world, he'd go down fighting, damn it.

"No," Thorne said, thrusting out an arm to block Rex. "We can't fight it that way." He dropped the match. Flames licked across the water toward the Outsider.

"Run!" Thorne shouted.

Rex's animal instincts took over. Without conscious thought, he dropped the axe and scrambled up the tilting stairs, not bothering to check if Thorne was behind him. He reached the corridor above and half ran, half crawled down it, sometimes moving along the carpeted floor, and sometimes along the wall that tilted crazily underfoot. He forced open the door at the far end as a loud *whumph* sounded behind him; a boil of black smoke followed him outside. Coughing, eyes stinging, he slipped on the ice and fell, and found himself sliding, out of control, down the deck. Then came a splash, and water so cold it nearly stopped his heart when it enveloped him.

Somehow, he fought his way to the surface. Somehow, he clawed his way to shore through the breakers. The ship behind him provided a breakwater, calming the sea just enough for him to swim without being pounded under. He scrambled out onto rocks to which other exhausted and shivering passengers were clinging, then fumbled his way to the top of the bluffs where the lighthouse stood.

Once there, he turned, panting, and stared out to sea, doing his best not to look down at the bodies being tossed by the waves: killed either by the terrible cold, or by being dashed against the rocks. Instead, he focused his attention on the ship.

The *Martha* rolled back and forth in the swells, grinding against the rocks and burning fiercely. Flames shot as high as her masts and thick black smoke billowed into the sky above. Snow fell thickly, drawing a white veil across the hellish scene.

As Rex stared, teeth chattering uncontrollably, unable to feel his hands or his feet, he spotted something through the snow and smoke. A figure – possibly a man, possibly something else – balancing effortlessly on the rolling deck, its arms wide and its head thrown back.

Laughing.

The figure glided to what remained of the rail and surveyed the storm-chopped water, staring down at a man who was swimming frantically away from the ship. Then the Outsider's head rose, and it locked eyes with Rex.

Rex felt a cold beyond any he had ever experienced take his gut and start to *twist*...

And then, with a roar that shook the rocks under Rex's feet, the *Martha* exploded as her boiler finally blew.

Shivering uncontrollably, Rex staggered toward the lighthouse with the dozen or so others who had survived the wreck. He dimly noted that Gladys was among them, her life preserver strapped tight over a bedraggled raccoon-skin coat. The two keepers took everyone in, dolling out blankets and hot black coffee. For several fitful hours, Rex and the other survivors huddled around the lighthouse's small woodstove, drawing restoring warmth from its cheery red glow, while the keepers used their wireless to relay news of the sinking.

Later, once the storm had passed, the keepers helped what remained of the *Martha*'s crew recover the bodies that washed ashore.

Thorne was not among them.

What had happened to the man? Had Thorne been the one desperately swimming away from the ship when it exploded? If he had made it to shore, where had he gone? Rex had noticed a sled and some huskies tied up outside the lighthouse as he'd staggered toward it immediately after the wreck, and now the sled and dogs were gone. Had Thorne taken them and slipped away, during all the confusion? And if he had, why?

Rex hoped that was what had happened. Thorne had

been secretive and aloof during the voyage, but in the end he'd made himself a target, deliberately drawing the Outsider to him. That took guts.

More guts than Rex had demonstrated by leaving Thorne behind in the hold, and only worrying about his own hide.

The next day, the *SS Alaska* – several times the size of the *Martha* and all spit and polish – arrived and anchored offshore. Her sailors launched lifeboats and rowed the survivors, a few at a time, out to their ship, past the black shadow that lay just under the waves; the *Martha* had burned to the waterline.

The *Alaska* was on the return leg of her journey, headed south to Seattle. But her captain agreed to detour to Juneau, which turned out to be little more than an hour away. The *Martha* had almost made it.

Rex spent that hour in the dining salon, reading over the manuscript he'd salvaged in his fateful scramble from the *Martha*. The typewritten words were barely legible, thanks to his plunge into the sea. But he could make out a few phrases here and there.

He spotted names he didn't remember, and fragmented descriptions of events that had never happened.

At least, not in this version of reality.

His notebook was in slightly better shape. He flipped through its pages. At the bottom of the last page, Rex spotted the word "TRUST" in capital letters, followed by a name that had been reduced to a smear of ink.

Had he written that? *Trust who?*

He couldn't remember.

Slowly, Rex folded the notebook shut, and tucked it back in his pocket.

"Strange things," he said to himself. "Strange things done."

IN ART, TRUTH
James Fadeley

The woman paused, her hand slightly trembling, before drawing the aging book away from the shelf. She swallowed as she opened the back flap, giving the air the taste of dust, and read the names written there.

The bottom of the checkout card held two entries. The first was her own, Ece Şahin, with a return date of June 9, 1924. Beneath it, the same date was entered in the checkout column, under the name "Ali Veli".

Ece scoffed, shaking her head. It was a ludicrously common name, not unlike what the English might call a "Tom, Dick and Harry". Yet that fact only fueled her unease. She knelt, setting the book on the carpeted floor beside a copy of the *Chronographia* by Michael Psellos, also opened to its card. Like the former book, her return date back in May coincided with the next borrower, one "Murad Osman".

She glanced up, scanning the bookshelves before discovering another familiar title. *L'art Byzantin* by the Frenchman Charles Bayet. Setting it beside the prior two, she opened the back. Returned by Ece Şahin on June 2. Checked out that same day... by Mehmet Ağaoğlu.

Ece's brow rose in surprise. Ağaoğlu was a fellow art historian and a very respected one at that. Yet an inkling pestered Ece, her stomach fluttering faintly not with butterflies but moths. Something didn't add up, but she couldn't remember exactly what. Perhaps her assistant, Haluk, knew.

She narrowed her eyes, comparing the three signatures beneath each of her own.

The elifba alphabet did not make it easy. Read right-to-left, the cursive of individual characters changed based on their position. She focused on the simple alif characters that all three possessed, and only looked elsewhere when she was sure their slants were nigh identical. Although not the same letters, the ğayn in Ağaoğlu used a "hook" like the opening ain of both Ali and Osman, names of Arabic spelling. Then she concentrated on the opening mims, the M's, that began both Murad and Mehmet. Again, alike right down to a slight descender dipping below the cell's bottom line. She considered factors to suggest discrepancies but found little – the cards were of the same factory quality. The stroke width and ink color suggested the writer had used the checkout desk pen.

Most damning was how all three signatures curved downward after completion, lightly smudging the final letter. As if aborting a paraph, an underlined flourish to finish their work. Perhaps the signer was more accustomed to writing checks than borrowing books.

Ece swallowed, her pulse racing. She was almost certain that the signatures were from the same person. Someone who clearly did not want to be identified.

Someone who was trailing her research.

Her skin crawled. Instantly, she looked over her shoulder. No one was there, neither behind her nor beyond the library's backless bookshelves. She stood, stepped out of the aisle, and surveyed the room. A few students sat quietly at round tables, reading intensely and scribbling notes. The librarian glanced up from her desk for only a moment, before returning to her own book.

It might not be anything so sinister, Ece assured herself as she collected the three books from the floor. Perhaps it was a colleague who saw her as competition on a research paper.

If what she sought was not so dangerous, she might have even believed that…

The librarian grimaced as Ece set the trio of books on the checkout desk instead of the return cart before she swiftly departed. Once in the hall, she tucked a strand of hair beneath her vermillion hijab, then crossed her arms over her chest. It was defensive gesture, but Ece couldn't help herself. Someone was following her scholarly footsteps, but who? A fame-hungry colleague from the university was an inconvenience, but there were other interested parties. Members of esoteric societies, "cults" as outsiders would call them… or perhaps even her own, the Coterie.

The idea sent a shiver down her spine. Would her own

group have sent someone to track her? Might they no longer trust her? If so, how long did she have before they decided to trail her physically as well?

She checked over her shoulder again, relaxing only a little when no one was there.

The walk to the Süleymaniye Complex took more than ten minutes. A more direct path through the university campus might have been quicker, but Ece preferred the more densely populated route. Residents hung about, talking with one another, or shouting up to people watching from second story windows. Groups of students flocked around a few street vendors, haggling over prices for pencils and notary.

Despite the noise, Ece took solace in the crowds. It was not just the security, but the sights and sounds of change sweeping through the newfound Republic of Turkey. A country not even a year old, born of the Treaty of Lausanne and rebuilding itself atop the remains of the Ottoman Empire.

Yet President Kemal Atatürk's progress came to the chagrin of many, visible even on the streets. A man argued with a phone serviceman trying to drill a hole in a wall. A mother publicly scolded her embarrassed daughter for wearing chic European heels with a more form-fitting black çarşaf. An aging Renault putted behind an ox-drawn cart, and the drivers of each soon engaged in a shouting match for right-of-way. Yet perhaps the most promising hint of progress rested on a newspaper a clerk read beside his stall.

"Dr Safiye Ali Hanım receives female and pediatric

patients every day and in the afternoon, except Friday and Sunday, at her clinic number 52 on Nuruosmaniye Street in Istanbul," an advertisement read.

"Another who earned her place," Ece whispered to herself, walking a little taller. It was the first time she'd heard of a woman becoming a licensed doctor. She smiled faintly, daring to think it would not be the last. After all, Ece herself had recently been appointed a curator to the Museum of Turkish and Islamic Arts. The 1920s were proving to be an age of enlightenment.

Yet even this little progress will not matter if a mere handful of people exploit the signs of the stars.

The grim reminder set her on edge, and she hurried along to her office.

The Süleymaniye Complex was a gorgeous sight. A symmetrical arrangement of arches under many domes. The grandest and highest was that of the mosque in the center, although even that was dwarfed by the four minarets presiding over each corner of the courtyard. The sight of the beautiful building rekindled a spark of faith in Ece. A comfort that the Ever-Merciful still watched over them.

Ece's office was in one of the extra madrasa buildings, some distance from the medical school. She remained quiet as she slipped through the patio, where students bowed in study over copies of the Quran. She passed through the halls and up the stairs, wondering if she would miss this commute when the time came to relocate to the museum.

Her assistant looked up from his newspaper as she entered, perking a brow as he adjusted his spectacles. "You didn't get the books, Ms Şahin?"

"No." She stood in front of the office door, both hands behind her back. "Haluk, do you know where Mehmet Ağaoğlu is right now? Is he still in Istanbul?"

"Ağaoğlu?" Haluk closed his newspaper. "No, he... last I heard, he was at the University of Vienna. I think he's still there. What's wrong?"

Ece chewed her lip. Haluk believed they were researching artwork of the post-Byzantine era, an effort the directors hoped would win prestige with Western academics. He didn't know the whole truth, for it was too much to burden her assistant with. Pieces and facts might be fine, but Ece could only hope it did not lead to him being initiated into the... other side. She drew a sharp breath before speaking, "I think we're being followed. Academically."

Haluk stood, his eyes wide in alarm. "How?"

"At the library, I checked a book I once borrowed. Someone had checked it out the same day I had returned it. I looked at two other recent books. Same date pattern. Same handwriting but different names."

Haluk's face paled faintly. "Fake names? Someone is trying to poach your work!"

If only it were that simple. Ece walked to her desk with a scowl. "It's possible."

"Did you make translations for that book at least?" Haluk snapped his fingers, trying to recall. "The one by the Frenchman? Could it be published, create a paper trail of your efforts?"

"*L'art Byzantin*, yes." She frowned. "I only translated the parts that I felt were important. To put forward just those for publication–"

"Would give away our true goal." He sank into his seat, rubbing his temples as he spoke quietly. "Since when has Mavropoulos drawn so much academic competition?"

Ece's smile was as gentle as it was sardonic.

"Haluk," she leaned on her desk, looking her assistant in the eye, "can you go to the university library and check out a few titles I need? They're watching for me, but I doubt they'll be on the lookout for you."

"Yes, ma'am!"

Ece drew a slip of paper and a fountain pen from her desk and began drafting a list of titles and authors. "If they limit how many you can take, prioritize the ones on top."

"Yes, Ms Şahin. I'll be back as soon as I can."

A tapestry next to the exit swung as Haluk almost slammed the door in his haste to obey. Ece watched the piece settle before sitting down. She drew a heavy breath, held it for a long moment before exhaling slowly. Her eyes fell on her candlestick phone, and she knew she was not going to get a better chance today to make that call.

Ece found herself playing with the cord nervously as the operator picked up. "How may I direct your call?"

"I need to place a collect call to Professor Tuwile Masai in Nairobi. This is the curator for the Museum of Turkish and Islamic Arts."

"It may take a while to connect," the operator warned.

"I understand."

"Hold please."

The wait proved lengthy indeed. In her boredom, Ece found herself staring at *J'ai baisé ta bouche Iokanaan* and *The Climax*, two versions of the same illustration, each side-by-side on her wall. Both were Art Nouveau drawings by Aubrey Beardsley for Oscar Wilde's play *Salome*, portraying grotesque scenes of a pleased woman holding the severed head of John the Baptist. Yet it was the background that drew Ece's eye, with circular shapes suggestive of growths or perhaps even fish eggs. She gazed at them for so long, she swore they became strange, fuzzy tumors.

Or perhaps even eyes. Eyes that stared back…

"E-sey?"

She blinked, realizing how painfully dry her cornea had become, yet broke into a chuckle. "It's pronounced *Ed-jey*, Professor Tuwile."

He coughed out of embarrassment. "Apologies, Ece. I'm unfamiliar with Turkish names. However, it's wonderful to hear your voice for the first time."

"It certainly beats writing letters and waiting weeks." She smiled sympathetically. "I know a call is costly but, I may have an urgent matter. Someone's trailing my checkouts."

"Are you all right?"

"Yes, I'm fine. Nervous though. I've sent my assistant for the next batch, although I may have to purchase books from now on. Less conspicuous, harder to trace."

"Hm. A prudent decision. Any idea who it may be?"

"I don't. It might be another scholar looking into Mavropoulos as well. Although…" Ece swallowed and squeezed the phone line in her palm. It took an act of willpower to overcome her reluctance. "Tuwile, I hate to ask… do you think I've done anything to earn the Coterie's ire?"

"Not to my knowledge. I don't deny that some of us are brutes, but even they know we cannot locate the artifacts with mere sadism."

She sighed with relief, the knot in her stomach becoming uncorded. "Thank you, Tuwile. I know we're all on the same side but… it's difficult to trust them."

"Ece, you are not wrong to do so. There is conceit in some of them, and cruelty in others. But you and I know that as long as knowledge guides us to wisdom, there is hope yet. Speaking of, your timing is good."

"Oh?"

"Two things. First, I sent you a parcel of old journals this morning, some primary sources that reference strange sightings and trade deals. I can't guarantee their value, but they could be worth checking. Arrival could take a week."

"I'll keep an eye out for it."

"And second, as luck would have it, I transcribed something new perhaps half an hour ago. Just a moment." Ece could hear pages being flipped. "Let's see… yes, here. Pardon my rusty Arabic.

"'For reasons unknown to me, my partner had accepted the one-sided deal. I could not allow it to pass and sought the trader. The man of Mavros intended to set sail that night, but when I approached him, I found him deep in prayer. He whispered, rubbing something in his hands, then he blew out his lone candle. When he did, something conjured against the backdrop of the cloudy, black night. A great shadow with massive wings, like the stories my Assyrian grandfather told me of the "djinn". I was so fearful that I turned and crept away, abandoning my misgivings.

Arkham Horror

The next day, the man of Mavros departed, returning to Constantinople.'"

Ece's stomach had turned to ice as she struggled to come to terms with the last of that passage.

"Ece?"

"Yes, sorry." She drew a deep breath and sighed away her discomfort. It was only a story, after all. The writer could have been drunk or drugged and might have misunderstood what he had seen. Not all primary sources were totally reliable. She reached for her notes, biting her lip as she looked over her scribblings. "You said 'Mavros', not Mavropoulos?"

"That confused me. Mavros is a tiny islet around Greece, no one lives there."

"Yet the suffix 'poulos' means 'son of' in Greek."

"Interesting."

"Where did you find this passage?" Ece dipped her pen in the well, prepared to add to her notes.

"A collection of old scrolls I had delivered from Cairo. Now, here's the intriguing part. Shortly after this, the writer detailed the fall of Sultan al-Mansur Uthman, which happened in March of 1453."

Ece's eyes went wide as she jotted this down, the ink splotching in her eager haste. "And Mehmed the Conqueror's siege of Constantinople began in April that same year."

"So, if our 'man of Mavros' was in your city then, he would have had great difficulty escaping." Ece heard Tuwile's seat creak from the other end. "But does that necessarily mean the artifact is still there?"

"No. After the Turks' victory, Mehmed was forced to let his men loot the city for three days. The artifact, this 'talisman', may have very well changed hands in that time. Nevertheless, all I can do is follow the trail and see where it leads me."

"You are wise not to get your hopes up. I should warn you that I will be busier with my tasks down here, but I'll still help whenever I can."

"Thank you, Tuwile. I appreciate it," Ece replied as her office door opened, and Haluk slipped inside with a few books under his arm. "I should get going. My assistant has returned."

"Good luck, Ece."

"You too." She slipped the phone back on the receiver.

"Who was that?" Haluk asked as he set the titles on her desk.

Ece wished she could explain. Up until that moment, she and Tuwile only knew each other through regular letters. Although they had never met, she had become fond of the professor, and grew to trust him as fellow scholar. Certainly, more than any other member of the Coterie.

"A colleague of mine. I'll introduce you if he should ever come to Istanbul." Ece stood and examined the books. Instantly her attention was drawn to the cryptically titled *Lamentations of the Muses*. "This isn't one I requested."

"I know. I found it in the same sections and thought it might interest you."

She picked up the thin, crimson book and opened it. There was no frontispiece, just a title page with no author, no publisher, and no preface. Ece sighed doubtfully, yet her opinion flipped with the pages, and she quickly understood Haluk's decision.

Illustrations. Not a mere few either, but dozens. Perhaps a hundred. The most she had ever seen in a single book. Painstakingly constructed diagrams of buildings and architecture as well as drawings of paintings, rendered dark with fastidious hatching. Some of the pieces were of familiar subjects, but several were not. Ece kept turning pages until she discovered a sight that froze both her hand and heart.

In the center was a handsome, calm-looking man holding a bag in his arms. The details of his clothing suggested fine embroidering, opulence in the style of the Eastern Romans. Behind him stood a dark figure, almost black. Briefly Ece thought it was the man's shadow until she studied the protrusions on both sides, recognizing a pair of magnificent wings. An angelic figure, without the characteristic Byzantine halo.

Her eyes widened, something stirring in her chest. Images of demons, including winged ones, were not unheard of in Byzantine portraits, although usually portrayed in dramatic, biblical fashion. Seldom did artists try to hide or leave them as merely suggestions.

"Is it useful?" Haluk asked hopefully.

His innocent question shook Ece from her catatonic state. His brow rose in surprise when she showed him the drawing.

"This isn't the work of a historian but an artist," Ece said, perusing the French text beside the illustration. "'They were going to cover it up again later that day and left me alone in the meantime. However, a senior official told me to leave around noon and I couldn't finish this piece'. I think this is a journal someone tried to publish. I've never seen this painting before, but something about the style seems familiar… this is quite promising, Haluk."

"So where was this drawn? And who made it?"

Very good questions. The drawing sported no signature, and without the raw details of the paint and techniques, Ece couldn't be sure who created the original painting. No way to guarantee it was another by Mavropoulos. She reread the text, then flipped to the prior and former pages. There were no hints in the text. However, there was a diagram of a floorplan, with a hall to the south and two parallel lobbies on the west side of a large center chamber. She tapped it as she showed Haluk. "Does that look familiar to you?"

He squinted through his spectacles as he examined it. "Not really."

"Cover it up again later that day," Ece repeated as she peered at the diagram. Thinking about a location from a bird's eye view was quite a feat, but something about that layout was familiar. "Chora?"

"Chora?" Haluk echoed.

"Kariye Mosque. I believe it was once a church before the Ottomans' siege."

"They would have covered up the frescos." Haluk wagged a finger excitedly. "Ma'am, I think you're right!"

"Call the imam and see if you can schedule an appointment. Don't mention anything about uncovering Christian art though. I'd rather request that face-to-face."

As Haluk picked up the phone, Ece studied the illustration

again. She didn't dare get her hopes up, having suffered red herrings before. Then again, Chora Church was an angle she had never considered. A new approach, bound by red tape thick enough to obstruct her scholarly tail.

With luck, she would find the "djinn" of Istanbul first.

"Ma'am, isn't it strange to you that the imam could meet us so quickly?" Haluk asked as they walked up the street towards Kariye Mosque. The air was mildly warm that June morning, and the rising sun promised greater temperatures to come.

"Honestly, no." Ece tucked a strand of hair under her hijab. "After you went home yesterday, I called a connected friend for some useful gossip. It turns out that Imam Gökhan Çoban made the mistake of condemning President Atatürk's views on Caliph Abdulmejid. Then the Law of Unification of Instruction was passed the very day the caliphate was abolished."

"A real one-two punch against his career." Her assistant scratched his scalp. "Will our good imam be replaced soon then?"

"Although the Ministry of National Education is still training replacements, Çoban's retirement is no doubt forthcoming."

Haluk stirred uncomfortably, his next question unasked. Ece sympathized. In her satchel was a hefty wad of lira. She prayed such a bribe would not be required, but given the gravity of what they sought, Ece was prepared to get dirty. The need was simply too important.

As they approach the Kariye Mosque, a bearded man in

a long tunic and a taqiyah swept the path. He smiled as the pair approached. "Asalamu alaykum."

"Wa alaykum salaam," Ece responded. "Do you know where I can find Imam Çoban?"

"You need not look far, child. How may I help you?"

Ece startled. She had imagined a pompous man dressed in finery, leaving such mundane tasks to volunteers while he handled more important issues. Instead, here he was, tending his own mosque and dressed modestly. "My name is Ece Şahin, and this is my assistant, Haluk Duman. We're here from the Museum of Turkish and Islamic Arts."

"Ah yes, you called yesterday." Çoban reached for the door. "Please come in."

They passed through the outer and inner narthexes, the walls of both plastered to mask the frescoes and mosaics. Rather than guide them into the main chamber, the imam turned left, down the hall before a taking a right. He turned while they walked. "Can I offer you both some coffee?"

"No, thank you," Ece responded with a smile. "We actually have a delicate matter to discuss."

"You wish to unveil some of the Christian art?"

She nodded. Given their agency, it was no surprise that Çoban knew. But did that mean he was amenable? Could he want something from them? Or worse, was he thumbing his nose at the new administration before departing? Ece's heart sank, hoping she wouldn't be involved in such pettiness.

"I should warn you that earthquakes have taken their toll on the underlying work," the imam said as he took a left and began to climb the stairs.

"As we cannot permit such images in a mosque," Haluk quipped, "wouldn't it be easier to remove them? Cut them out and send them elsewhere?"

The imam laughed as he opened a door at the top, leading to his study. "There are so many, you'd have to build a whole new mosque. And besides the iconoclasts, we have tombs to consider as well."

"Seems the Christians left quite a mark," Ece said as she stepped into the small room, taking a seat in front of a desk. Haluk took the one beside her.

The imam said nothing, but his countenance bore troubles at mention of the Christians themselves. Haluk opened his mouth to speak, but Ece put a hand upon his, silencing him. It was not the time for such discussions.

Çoban sighed as he took his seat. "So, do you have an idea of which pieces you want to examine?"

"We're hoping you could help with that." Ece drew the crimson journal from her satchel and turned to the image of the shadowy angel. She showed the imam. "The passage suggested this was drawn here. Have you seen a piece like this?"

The imam leaned forward, squinting as he studied the book. "I don't recognize it. Although I do remember an artist, a Frenchman I believe, who visited perhaps a year ago. We had suffered a tremor the day before and entire chunks of the walls had fallen away, revealing the art. Apparently, the last fellows to work on it had done a poor job, so we had to tear off the plaster and start afresh. The artist politely sought permission to draw while we were on break, so I allowed him an hour."

Ece closed the journal, scowling at these perplexing details. So, only a year ago, an artist had been in Kariye Mosque and had drawn the hidden images. That didn't mean these drawings were the work of that very artist, but it was unlikely to have been anyone else. Yet hadn't Ece scoured over those bookshelves of the university library, trying to find something, anything of value? How could she possibly have missed this small, crimson and title-less book? Unless...

"Do you remember his name, by chance?" Haluk tried. Ece's eyes went to her assistant, and not just because he was speaking. "Or which particular fresco it was?"

Çoban shook his head.

Ece blinked, letting the thought go, and turned to their host. "May we have permission to unveil some of the artwork?"

The imam rocked back in his chair. "If it were just one piece, I wouldn't mind. But you don't know how many it could be, do you?"

It was Ece's turn to shake her head. "It could take a few days. Perhaps even a week or two."

"I'm not going to oversee Kariye much longer, and I doubt they'll be sending me to the Hagia Sophia next." Çoban smiled sadly. "I would rather not give the Ministry more reason to be cross with me."

Haluk coughed uncomfortably while Ece sighed. "Imam Çoban, I really doubt you would be arrested or anything, certainly not with the recent court reforms President Atatürk enacted."

"I know, I know." He opened his hands earnestly.

"Although I don't agree with Atatürk's vision for our people, I made rash statements publicly that I shouldn't have about his decisions. I am trying to show respect for our new and fragile republic and have no wish to do anything that could be misconstrued as spiteful. We've been through so much as it is."

Ece realized he was testing them.

Haluk's brows dropped, and he leaned forward, preparing to debate.

Ece put a hand on her assistant's shoulder and drew him back into his seat. Haluk's features rose in surprise, as she turned her attention to their host.

"We are all Turks in a new country, Imam Çoban, doing our best to serve our people. Despite your circumstances, you still show respect for the Ministry of National Education. Just as we respect our directors at the museum, and those who appointed them as well. Having met you in person, I understand your prudence in the face of uncertain times. And no matter what, we don't doubt your patriotism."

The imam settled back again, pursing his lips in thought, and slowly began to nod in acquiescence. "I have two requests. The first is that you replaster the artwork as you go. Only unveil one at a time."

"Simple enough," Ece said. "And the second?"

Çoban paused. His hesitation caused a sharp pang in Ece's chest, and she struggled to calm the dozens of untoward things he could possibly request.

"Is your museum hiring?"

"I…" Flabbergasted, Ece struggled for words. "We do

not have any positions, but we regularly seek consultations with religious scholars."

"But you have your state-sanctioned imams, do you not?"

"We do," Haluk intruded. Ece almost rounded on him, but her assistant continued. "However, their studies focus on more current teachings. They often lack the historic wisdom that more experienced scholars would provide."

"Exactly," Ece said, regaining control of the conversation. "If you find yourself with time, we would appreciate and compensate your services."

Çoban sighed in relief, his body visibly relaxing. "It's good to know that even an old man like me can have a place in this new world. You can use our tools and plaster, but you may need to get more later."

Ece nodded and stood as the imam did the same. As he guided them downstairs, her face flushed warmly from embarrassment. She felt like a fool, having expected Gökhan Çoban to be egotistical or perhaps even corrupt. Instead, she recognized an elderly man seeking purpose for his faith, just as an artist sought meaning for their talents. Different mediums that were no less spiritual, and somehow Ece had failed to fathom such a simple human need.

When had she become so distrustful?

Her cheeks cooled by the time they reached what was once the church's parekklesion. Çoban wagged a finger at a few canisters and tools in the corner. "I forgot there was one piece that needed replastering. Why not start there?"

"We'll happily cover it for you," Haluk said, his tone sincere.

"I would appreciate that. Oh, and please, work quietly. We have prayer within the hour."

As Çoban sauntered away, Haluk knelt to pick up a claw hammer from the set of tools. "We can do this more quickly if we keep our holes small. But we'd need light to see what's inside."

Ece stared at him, her lips drawn into a flat line and her jaw flexed. So far, she had kept her temper in check. Yet Haluk had crossed a line, injecting himself like that into the conversation with the imam. He was her assistant and would do well to remember that.

Whatever face she wore caused Haluk to lean back, hands raised defensively. "Umm, Ms Şahin?"

"We'll discuss it later. Not in a mosque," Ece said with a controlled tone and drew a flashlight from her satchel. Her anger could wait. Haluk nodded and took the hammer's curved edge into the cracked wall nearby. Wedging off a few pieces, a hole was left large enough for her to shine through. Inside was the image of a saintly man in robes standing in front of a dark blue background. His head was encircled by a holy nimbus. Twisting the beam of light, Ece looked around, only to discover more figures wearing different colored robes.

"Any luck?"

Ece sighed. "No. It's a shame they can't reveal these. The artwork is much more interesting than drab stucco."

Haluk groaned and picked up the plaster tin, taking the hammer claw to the lid. "One down, dozens to go…"

●●●

The work stretched into the afternoon. Their labor was quick when Haluk could keep the cracks small, covering their fresh holes with just a dab of plaster. Sometimes, however, he took too large a chunk. It cost them time to set sticks in the opening, forming wooden frames to hold the putty.

Ece's doubts vexed her when they were halfway finished with the hall. The uncovered works had been pieces of piety, beautiful and devout. Nothing like the image within the crimson journal. Every unveiled piece of art left her wondering if they had been led astray.

"We'll need a ladder to check the ceiling," Haluk insisted.

Ece shook her head. "No... I think we're doing this wrong."

"What do you mean?"

"We're looking for a dark image, not exactly in keeping with Christian... well, anyone's holy traditions. If it's here, it wouldn't be somewhere immediately visible, would it?"

Haluk scratched his chin, leaving a smear of beige putty on his countenance. "You make it sound like graffiti."

Graffiti... Ece pondered that, surveying not the walls or ceiling, but the floors. The sun came through the parekklesion's eastern window, creating a shadow in a corner. It was an alcove doorway that led to one of the two small domed chambers. Sooner or later, a priest would have noticed any work on the walls, but there were places where it might not have been seen for a while. At least not immediately...

"Haluk, give me the hammer." He offered it without question, and Ece walked toward the door and knelt. She resisted the urge to peel back the covered walls, taking only a sliver out and using the flashlight.

Darkness, and not from the shadows.

She removed a larger chunk, her eyes widening. Setting the hammer down, she began to pull entire pieces away with her bare hands. Haluk approached, eyes wide. "Is that? No, but–"

"But close enough," Ece finished, turning the flashlight's beam on their discovery.

It was the image of a man, dressed in finery, with his face turned to the right and head bowed in piety. Behind him a woman wept, her head raised to him though he did not notice. As though pleading, trying to pull him away from something. Looming over the man was a dark patch, a blot without definition. Ece stepped back, and realized it was a massive figure, with a pair of magnificent, leathery wings extending from its frame.

Not merely two, but three eyes were embedded in the angel's forehead.

It was wrong. Ece's mind flashed through every piece of Byzantine craftmanship she could think of no matter how esoteric and strange. Every demon, every monster and yet she had *never* seen anything like this. She bit her lip to suppress a mad giggle, almost daring to believe this painting was fake. It wouldn't be the first time the museum had dealt with forgeries.

"What," Haluk asked incredulously, "in the Protector's name is that? Why would a painting like that be in a mosque or… or a church?"

Ece coughed to clear her morbid mirth and stepped

closer, shining the light on the edges. The line work was like the other pieces. The strokes and techniques were crafted in haste, but there was no denying their familiarity. Sure enough, she found the large M that started the signature, and her heart sank, her amusement fading. There had never been a work like it, yet there was no denying the authenticity. "That's to be Mavropoulos' mark."

"I don't understand." Haluk shook his head, huddling close. "Every other piece by him seemed so divine, so gracious. A worldly man, traveler, trader, and artist… now here he is, desecrating a church too?"

Ece stared into the dark corner, but her mind was elsewhere, dwelling on Haluk's words. Little by little, a new idea formed, and her eyes widened even as they became so dry. "That's been our standing theory, yes? We assumed that Mavropoulos was a polymath like da Vinci, ibn Khaldun or Baha al-Din al-Amili, because the name was prolific."

"We got it wrong?" her assistant asked, as she blinked, her stinging eyes appeased by fresh moisture.

"Sometimes the truth isn't so complicated." The melancholy wore heavily on Ece as she studied the details. She shined the light on the man. "Look at him. Beautiful, isn't he? So detailed, so… painstakingly made. The robes, the facial expressions. This was crafted by the hands of someone who loved their subject."

"You mean…"

"Yes." Ece turned the circle of light to the woman. "Look at her. The lack of details, just an idea of who she is. The man is practiced, a subject well known to the artist. But her? No. It's not bad, but it's a simple abstract. Incomplete, not fleshed out. Mavropoulos invested in every piece of work, except this one. Because I don't think she ever did a self-portrait."

"She?" Haluk's voice rose a few octaves.

"As you said, he was a merchant, traveling often. When would he have had time and calm to develop these skills? On a horse drawn cart? On the seas? No, he couldn't have, but his dutiful and homebound wife would. So committed to her husband, she'd even sign with their shared surname."

Haluk was stunned into silence. Ece leaned towards the image of the woman, noting the ruinous streaks in the paint. Could the artist's very tears have found their way into her work?

"Then-then why would the church let her do this?" Haluk stammered. "Was Chora a pagan church or something?"

"A good question," she admitted, looking around for more details. The light fell on what could have been letters, and she tore away a little more plaster, finding shaky Greek writing that somehow survived the ages. "Look, here. I believe these read… 'The invaders come. Our city has fallen. There is no time left. My sin was in letting my love be taken by the black angel. Lost in a dark faith I could not share. May God forgive us.'"

Haluk took a deep breath and released a shuddering sigh. "A last-minute confession."

"Trying to save the soul of her husband."

"But why is this black angel so significant?"

Because it wasn't an angel. Ece swallowed and put a hand against the doorjamb to keep from swaying. Her skin chilled and her stomach threatened her with nausea.

Everything until now had been a mere guess based on recorded rantings and inconclusive, psychological analysis of ancient mosaics. This was new. More damning than anything since the Coterie let her imbue her hijab with the vermillion gift.

"Are you all right?" Haluk asked.

"Yes," she snapped a little too quickly and stood up, forcing the fear back. She couldn't let on, not now. Every step of their investigation brought her assistant closer to being initiated with the truth, a truth he could not be ready for. "We can't dally. We need to take pictures of this and cover it quickly. If Çoban sees this, he may decide to have it removed."

"Yes, ma'am." Dutifully her assistant drew a No 1A Autographic Kodak Junior from his bag and began snapping photos. Ece helped by holding up her light, then illuminating from the side rather than directly. "I don't have much roll left."

"Use the rest. I'd rather not need to return."

A few snaps later and the camera was spent. After folding the lens bellow back inside the film container, Haluk reached for the putty and *tsked*. "We're out."

"Get some more. I'll take a few quick notes, then ready the plaster frame."

"I'll be back soon," Haluk said, almost running out.

Alone, Ece pulled a notebook from her satchel and a pencil. She had to pinch the flashlight between her cheek and neck as she jotted down the words exactly as they were written. Her Greek was decent, but it wouldn't hurt to have another set of eyes transla–

"Poor selfless wretch."

Ece spun, the flashlight clattering against the floor. Quickly she looked both ways, trying to find the source of the speaker. She saw no one. "Who's there? Who is speaking? Please…"

"All that talent, wasted…" It was a man's voice, his accent English. Ece couldn't be sure, but it seemed to come from the walls. "Trapped in a prison of love. Do you worry, Ms Şahin, that it could someday be the same for you?"

"Who are you?" Somehow, she kept from trembling, and narrowed her eyes as she studied the alcove across from her, one of the tombs.

"Oh, I'm not that interesting…" he feigned meekness. "Just a man who lives in interesting times. Interesting if a little repetitive."

"Repetitive?" Ece asked. She focused on a dark hole in the wall that she hadn't noticed before.

"Of course, as history is wont to be. Take a good look at her."

Ece remained still.

"Go on. I won't bite." He chuckled. "Not today."

She gave in, facing the painting. At the kneeling Mavropoulos, at her tears.

"The women of the Byzantine had little power over their lives. They married, birthed, and raised children. Spun, cooked, washed clothes. Masters of home and hospitality but little else. Do you know what Mavropoulos was truly guilty of? Just what her sin was?"

Ece glanced back to the tomb's hole. Straining her eyes, she thought she spotted a light inside. The man in the wall continued.

"She was *free,* woman. Unlike thousands of others, she was free to be an artist. A creator. Still, she spent her last days begging God to spare her husband's soul. Wasting all that time she could have spent seeking prestige to call her own. Tell me, where was her Magnum Opus, Şahin? Where was the great work that would have made her a truly celebrated name in your field?"

"What are you getting at?" Ece snarled, anger dawning over her fear. She knew the speaker's words were designed to inflame, to incite her. A skilled orator, this one, especially given how much of what he said was historically true.

"Do you really think tomorrow will be brighter, child?" The voice dripped with acid, and the light in the hole grew closer. "Do you really think the master of this country will share meaningful power with his subjects? Let them just... do as they will? He waged a war to drive the Greeks out. He took away your sultanate and banished the caliph. Then he threw out the courts and judges, the cornerstone of the law. Now he preaches for a modern republic but, well, who are we kidding?"

A glowing glyph appeared in the black hole. Ece squinted, realizing it was a painted eye, turned vertical.

"Do you really think Atatürk intends to share power with everyone? And after all this time, all these traditions, why would he grant it freely to women? At this very moment, he and his lackeys dally on choosing a new civil code. I suspect he'd rather the law not constrict his power too badly..."

The voice was closer than ever, almost echoing in the parekklesion. The cold sensation spread over Ece's skin again. Yet she found the strength to reach for the flashlight, holding it like a club.

"There is only one sin, Ece Şahin," his voice eased into a welcoming tone. "And it is in not using the power and gifts we possess to seek greatness in our chosen mediums. To aspire to more."

"That's not true…" Ece said, barely louder than her breathing. "Men who think that way are wolves who prey on others."

"You too are sinning. Even now, you squander the boon you wear upon your head."

Her eyes shot wide. She defensively grabbed her hijab. How could he know?

"Oh, I know you, Şahin. I know of the other circles you travel, your brutal and untrusted 'colleagues' of the Coterie. They know these lessons well, and I applaud them for applying themselves as they do. Meanwhile, you prove a slow learner despite your scholarly disposition, obstinately standing apart from their vision. From a very simple truth. History will repeat itself, but only if you let it."

The light of the glyph began to fade into the shadows. "Use it. Use your power while you can. Seize what you can. Claim what is yours. Because if you do not, then tomorrow you will walk the path of another powerful man's shattered promises… the oldest pavers on history's road."

The hole was black with darkness again. Ece waited, unsure if she was alone, but his voice did not return. Scared as she was, she couldn't keep his words out of her psyche, deeply buried splinters that needled at hope. Her fingers curled into fists, her nails biting into her palm. What upset her most was how right the voice was. She had made a career of studying art and history, the former a haven for the creative and new. Yet the latter was an old wheel that turned, leaving the same tracks in the dust. How long would it be before Atatürk bent to the conservative views of the day? How long until the Coterie's cruelest members grew tired of their agency's shadow games?

"Ma'am? Are you all right?"

She spun, eyes wide. It was Haluk, freshly returned with a can of plaster.

"Ece?" he tried again.

"Yes," she managed, blinking. "Yes, I'm sorry. I got caught up… taking notes. Let's patch this up and go home."

Ece fidgeted as she walked back with Haluk, studying every passerby for any hint of suspicious behavior. Was that man in the shop gazing at her a little too long? Had that sweeping woman averted her eyes to avoid Ece's? They even passed a blue-clad policeman, nonchalant about those around him. His complacency angered Ece, until she wondered if the lawman was too comfortable. Could the speaker's people have infiltrated the police as well?

"Ece? Are you listening?"

"What?" she snapped irritably. What was he babbling on about now?

"I asked if we should unseal other frescos. You seemed awfully quick to call it a day."

"We know who we should be researching now," Ece said, glancing over her shoulder again. No one followed them down the city streets, yet she held the back of her arm, protecting her chest. "We can always return later."

"But who knows how long Çoban will be in charge. I admit he's more reasonable than I thought, but President Atatürk is right to replace him."

Atatürk, Atatürk, Atatürk. Ece scowled bitterly. Why was the president all people prattled on about lately? A man reading a newspaper caught her attention, the frontpage reading "Commission Still Considering Civil Code Options", followed by the subtitle, "Scholars Unsure How Long Process Could Take".

Of course. Why would those above freely grant anyone power? How long would it be before Atatürk broke his word and settled, just to keep the new country unified and himself in power? She was a student of history, so how could she have let herself be fooled by him?

"Do you always pin your hopes on others?" Ece demanded of her assistant. "The president? The Grand National Assembly? Me?"

"What?" Haluk's brow rose.

"You're always waiting for someone else to elicit change or improve the world, fawning over those in power. It's exhausting." Honesty flowed from her lips like water from a jug, frustrations Ece did not realize were bottled up until then. She was tired of weak people yearning for heroes instead of saving themselves.

"How could you say that?" her assistant scoffed. "There are brilliant men at work, men daring enough to try new things for us and for the Islamic world! We are moving swiftly and improving even now."

Ece cursed, wondering how she could have been so blind. Whether it was the Grand National Assembly or the Coterie, the story was always the same. History's ceaseless pattern of the champions du jour becoming corrupt, accepting responsibility before twisting it for their own ends.

"Do you really think Atatürk intends to share power with everyone?"

Ece froze. For a moment, she almost looked about for the voice again. Except the familiar words had come from her own mouth.

"I do," Haluk asserted defiantly, stopping to look her in the eye. "Turkey is an early draft of the work to come. As art historians, it's difficult for us to judge until the labor is finished, until it is in the past. How often are we asked to wait for something new?"

Ece's jugular throbbed, her vision turning red. Haluk's intrusive statements during the meeting at the mosque flashed before her eyes, enlivening embers that might have otherwise gone out. "Oh really? So you know better than me now?"

Haluk began to shrink before her fury. "Ms Şahin, I didn't mean to–"

"Didn't mean to what? Didn't mean to interrupt my discussion with Imam Çoban? Didn't mean to suggest I don't know current events? Didn't mean to think you knew better than me?"

Haluk's eyes were huge, his lips twitching worthlessly.

"Enough, child!" Ece reached into her satchel and peeled a few bills from the wad of lira. She held them out, arm trembling from her fury. "Go to the Grand Bazaar. Browse the used bookstores and see if you can find something about Mavropoulos. Antique trade journals, charts, maps, I don't care. Make yourself useful and bring back words by people *who knew what they were talking about.*"

His quivering fingers took the lira and he turned to leave with his head bowed low. Ece's anger silenced her instinct to apologize. Instead, she stormed off, without wondering why pedestrians were gawking at her.

Her choler endured, even after a few hours of research in her office. It only ended when she accidentally ripped a page and felt a pang of remorse for the damage. Both the physical and emotional kind. Yes, Haluk could be a know-it-all. He didn't act that way around her often, but with others he sometimes transformed into an academic giving a lecture. Still he was knowledgeable and helpful and respectful. A good student and good assistant.

Ece shut her eyes to pull back a remorseful tear as she settled into her chair. She had let the voice of the "aspiring" one get to her. She had even repeated his very question at Haluk. Word for word.

It was not the first time Ece had encountered a cult. A rival society, calling themselves the "Readers of the Elder Word", had once tried to recruit her. Charmed, Ece had considered switching allegiances until they proved overly persistent. Eventually, she spoke of their attempts to the Claret Knight, the Coterie's representative. He told her the matter would be dealt with.

And Ece learned how brutal the Coterie could truly be.

The last she saw of the Readers was when one of their members came to her office. Mercifully, Haluk had not been there, for the sight of the bandaged and bruised man would have been impossible to explain. The Reader had apologized profusely, swearing that he and his colleagues would never disturb her again.

Departing, he had donned his hat with a hand of only three fingers, where last there had been five.

Ece shuddered at the memory yet reflected on how the Readers had almost wooed her. Many cults used such manipulative orators, and no one was completely immune. Even intelligent, rational people such as attorneys, scientists or scholars were fallible. All it took was gentle nibbling at fears, anxieties, and doubts until their victims started asking questions. Questions that guided brilliant minds down the roads of knowledge. Solving puzzles that opened doors that should have remained shut. Mistaking "truth" for knowledge, and "knowledge" for truth.

Just as Beardsley must have. Ece gazed at the artist's work again. This time she relaxed her sight, and the "eyes" in the background of *The Climax* began to dance. The follicles and lines of *J'ai baisé ta bouche Iokanaan* began to quiver and shake with excitement.

Ece shut her eyes until the stinging went away, and sighed. It was late. Haluk would show up in the morning and she would apologize then. As she reached to turn off her lamp, the phone suddenly rang.

Reluctantly, she answered. "Hello?"

"Ece?" The voice was high, laced with panic. "It's me! I need help!"

"Haluk, what's wrong?" she stood, her skin cold.

"Some men are stalking me. I bought some books like you asked and they followed me from the store. I ran into a coffee shop to see if they'd go away. But they're still out there and the shop is closing soon!"

"Which coffee house? Did you call the police?" Ece fetched her notepad.

"Twice! At first, they laughed and said it wasn't their job to escort me home. Then they insisted they were too busy."

"Where are you?"

"Old Pasha's Café. The one that we–"

"I know it. Stay put, Haluk, I'm coming." She hung up. Swallowing, she reached for the bottom drawer and opened it. There, a sheathed khanjar knife rested atop some books. It was nothing elegant, just a simple weapon with few details. Ece picked it up and slipped it into her satchel, then killed the lamp before running out the door.

Ece clutched the dagger inside her satchel as she neared the café. She did not rush inside, taking a moment to survey the surroundings. There were only a few lingering shoppers. Most of the hallway's stalls and stores were closed or closing. No one noticed or cared about the aging coffee shop.

Still, her pulse was up, and the hairs of her arms raised on end. She could feel eyes on her, and the sensation kept her vigilant.

After some hesitation, she opened the door to a small room with a handful of tables. An exasperated huff came from the host. "Ma'am, I am sorry, but we are closing."

"Ece!" Haluk stood from his seat, rushing over.

"This is the person you were waiting on?" the host asked.

"Y-yes." Haluk blushed and offered the man some lira. "Thank you for letting me stay here."

The host kindly waved away the payment. When he spoke, his voice was softer. "Be safe out there, you two."

To the café host's credit, he watched as Ece and Haluk slipped out. The pair headed down the arched hallways of the Grand Bazaar and looked back before their next turn. The host waved them luck, and only then shut the door.

"That was kind of him," Ece said as they walked with haste.

"And brave. One of my stalkers tried to enter, and he sent them away. A good man but I couldn't ask him to fight my battles for me," Haluk bemoaned. "Why is this happening, Ms Şahin? What do these people want?"

"Because…" she drew a sharp breath. There was no more room for lies, but the entire truth was also too much. "Haluk, this is happening because I accidentally pulled you into my battles."

"What?"

They paused before the next turn to peek around the corner. The hallways were filled with cloaked carts. The colorful mosaics and tiles gradually turned grayscale as a boy turned off lanterns one by one to save fuel.

How should she explain this? Ece chewed her lip ragged, until she noticed the art store where she had procured her copies of Aubrey Beardsley's work. She realized she had to start small, with what he could understand, and work up to the truth.

"Haluk, do you remember when I got those Art Nouveau pieces?"

"*The Climax*? That was uncharacteristic of you, yes." He shook his head, scowling. "What does tha–"

"It reminds me of the awful things I'm fighting," she turned to him, her voice a heated whisper. "Do you know how Beardsley died?"

"No…"

After checking behind them, she took her assistant's arm and led him down the hall. "He was only twenty-five. Tuberculous, they say. A skilled artist who started a new movement. Yet in his last days he converted to Catholicism, and begged his publisher to destroy his art."

"Why?" Haluk asked with a countenance of worry. "Because of the debauchery in his work?"

"The debauchery in his art and his life was an effect, Haluk. He didn't understand until the end, but he was subconsciously drawing the cause as well. It's there in his art, in the details that aren't human."

"I don't understand," her assistant said. The two grew quiet as they walked by another corner. A man walked towards them, though elderly and bearing a cane. He paid them no mind as they carried on.

"Art is the gateway to truth. And the truth is that not all history was written by human hands."

"As taught by the Quran, yes…" Haluk said before they stopped. The rest of the hall before them was unusually black. A cold sensation ran up Ece's spine, and she turned away, towards another path that still had some distant lights.

"Then you understand the impact of the All Compassionate, and His angels loyal or fallen. The djinn, peri and divs. All of this is maktub, it is written." Ece swallowed. This moment was the crucible upon which everything depended. "But there are also the unwritten ones."

Haluk's sudden stop jerked Ece around. Releasing his arm, Ece instinctively corrected her hijab as her assistant stammered. "W-what do you mean 'unwritten ones?'"

"I can show you more later, Haluk. What matters right now is that there are those that believe in them. Believe enough to pursue you and I, to trail my wor–"

Sturdy footsteps echoed from the halls behind them.

Ece snapped around. Two figures approached, figures wearing long black cloaks, with faces masked by the shadows of their hoods. Their billowing, oversized sleeves ended with the tips of daggers.

"Ece?" Haluk's voice was high with fear.

"Run!"

They bolted. Behind, Ece heard the rustle of thick garments and the *thump* of boots upon tiled floors. She snatched the khanjar from her satchel as she moved, but prayed they could elude their pursuers. She doubted these were the only two.

She turned left, Haluk staying with her. Neither of them was in peak form, but terror gave the pair enough steam to keep sprinting. To her surprise, Haluk veered to the right and grabbed a cart, ripping it towards him. The tarp gave way as beautiful, colorful dishes crashed, unleashing sonorous thunder throughout the marketplace.

"Help!" Haluk screamed desperately as he took off running again. "Police! Help!"

"Help! Anyone!" Ece joined in as they fled. She looked over her shoulder, watching worriedly as the cultists vaulted over the crashed cart. Still in pursuit, despite the alarm the pair gave.

They pushed harder. Into the darkened and deserted halls. Where was everyone? Surely there must have been a few shopkeepers still amid their closings. Or a custodian to sweep the floors. Then Ece spotted a man, his face frozen with terror, watching from a door.

She moved to speak, to plead for aid.

He slammed the door shut, the *thunk* of the bolt punctuating his answer.

There was no time to dwell on it. With the cultists hot on their heels, they pressed on through the hall. Turned left. Then right. Ece grabbed Haluk's arm to keep them together. Where were the police? Security? There! Ahead lay the exit. Surely someone outside would help.

Haluk dashed ahead, reaching his arms out. Stiffly he slammed the door open, leading them into the safety of the night.

He stopped bodily. Hunched over. A shape was before him.

"*Haluk!*" Ece screamed, almost dropping her khanjar. She got there in time to catch her assistant falling backward, his weight bowling her over. A pool of crimson expanded from his white shirt. Panicking, Ece crawled away from the door, pulling him towards a wall with one arm.

The shape stepped inside the Bazaar. It was another cloaked figure, blood dripping from a held blade. The other two pursuers paused some distance away, content to allow their accomplice to finish the job.

"If only you had listened to me," the familiar, English voice of the Aspirant came from the hood of Haluk's murderer. "He might have even seen another dawn."

"Haluk," Ece tried, her throat painfully constricting. She held a hand on his chest, trying futilely to stem the flow. She wanted to use two hands, but didn't dare relinquish the khanjar.

"If you had just used your gift, you could have avoided this. You knew we would come for you eventually."

Ece snarled at him, holding her blade up. Before the Aspirant could advance, the sound of whistles and running could be heard outside. The police at last.

The Aspirant's brow began to glow. The glyph of the vertical eye appeared, pulsing with its terrible light, growing brighter and brighter. It cast everything around Ece into the pitch.

"The Haunter watches you, Ece Şahin. Its next lesson will not be so merciful…"

The light of the glyph faded, and the world appeared from the black again. The Aspirant was gone. Ece looked to her left. The other cultists had disappeared as well. She was alone with only Haluk. The khanjar clattered on the floor as Ece put both hands against her assistant's wound, his chest growing cold.

"Ms Şahin," Haluk whispered, his eyes fluttering closed. "I'm sorry… about what I sa…"

He was gone.

The police had questions and doubts. After all, her hands were still covered in Haluk's blood, making her arrest almost a certainty. Then the café host was found and spoke on their behalf, as did the shopkeeper who had shut the door in her face. Hat in hand, he apologized to her for not doing more, for being cowardly.

"You call yourself a man?" The police chastised him. "A woman comes to you, terrified and in need of help, and you slam the door in her face?"

Ece bit her tongue at first, until it was too much. "Haluk called you."

"Pardon?" The policeman turned, alarmed.

"My assistant. He called the station. *Twice*. Asking for help. But you called him a coward yourselves or were too busy."

She shook from anger but said nothing more. The policeman coughed and looked to his superior officer, who bowed his head. "Ma'am, I will speak to our operators personally and ensure that such behavior never happens again. Rest assured, we will see these muggers brought to justice."

Muggers. The lie was bitter, but it was the best she could come up with. Against the nature of the evil she fought, justice could not be served by the law.

"Sir?" A policeman approached. "We found boot prints."

The officer pointed to Ece's feet. "Like hers? Or the victims?"

The policeman took one glance at Ece's flats and the

shoes protruding from the white sheet over the body, before shaking his head.

"Coming," the officer said, before looking back at her. "One of my men will escort you home."

She knew they could not truly protect her, but Ece did not object. It would not serve to utter such thoughts aloud.

Weeks passed. The police had little evidence, no names, and no leads. With the headlines occupied by politics, there was little pressure on them to pursue the murderer of one Haluk Duman. Ece hated it, but it was for the best. Otherwise, they would poke and prod. They might even ask about Mavropoulos and the black angel.

They would ponder motives best left in the dark, answers that came with the cost of blood, and worse…

Ece went through the motions. She kept her distance during Haluk's funeral, and mercifully his parents left her be. The rest of the time was spent in a cycle of going to her office, pretending to work, eating little, and sleeping when she could. Even the arrival of Tuwile's parcel, and the return of the camera and books the police had confiscated from Haluk's body, did not shake her from this shadow of a life.

It was all her fault. He'd be alive if she'd either kept him out of this, or perhaps told him sooner. At least then he could have prepared better.

She had taken that lesson to heart. The police never returned her khanjar, so she bought another, and always kept it at her side. Ece told herself it was for protection,

but there were days she stared at it just a little too long…
pondering for whom she truly intended the blade.

Until that day in August 1924. She was walking to
the office when her eyes fell upon a few agitated people,
gathered about a newspaper cart. A boy was holding the
paper up, shouting to the gathered men, "Read it here!
Ministry of Education gives girls permission to enroll in
boy's high school in Tekirdağ! Says coeducation in primary
schools to be new norm!"

Eyes wide, Ece pushed her way past a few of the men.
"I'll take a copy, please!"

She dug into her satchel and handed him a bill worth
more than twice the price, not even waiting for her change
before wandering away. Ece leaned against a street wall,
her eyes poring over the articles from beginning to end.
Her heart skipped a beat as she read points made by the
Republican People's Party that this "was another step in the
many changes to come".

"Maybe you were right, Haluk." A tear caught in Ece's
eye, and she wiped it away. In all the studies Ece had read,
coeducation was touted as a small but important step
towards gender equality. It was by no means a guarantee
of equality. But maybe, just maybe, it was the start of
something after all…

"And maybe even people in power can be trusted," Ece
dared to muse aloud.

What good would that do when tomorrow it will all
be wiped out? She heard the thought in the voice of the
Aspirant. History itself is just a blink of the stars…

Yet the voice failed. Ece's despair was gone. All that was

left was more important, a steely resolve that straightened her back and squared her shoulders. She folded the newspaper neatly.

"I'll never again involve those who haven't dealt with the dark before," she swore to herself as she started walking towards her office. Still, she knew she couldn't fight the cultists by herself, nor could she trust the Coterie.

Perhaps the time had come to ask for outside help...

CROSSING STARS
MJ Newman

Power is the ability to forsake cowardice. To look fate in the eyes and force it to yield to your will. To face the roar of a lion, plant your feet, and roar back. Or so Haresah was taught. The weak serve the strong or perish; their only life, their one chance to defy their fate, wasted. Father had made that much clear over the course of many bloody lessons.

Haresah Izem would not waste her one chance.

Beside her, Khalid snarled, weary. For a beast who slept twelve or more hours at a time, he could be truly impudent when pressed. And pressed they were, for their party had endured many miles of harsh Sahara to reach their destination, and if the reports were true, this would be the easiest leg of their journey. She placed her hand, golden-brown in the sun, upon Khalid's back and ran her fingers through the lion's thick, golden mane. "Soon, my beautiful," she cooed. A low grumble of begrudging approval emanated from the beast. Khalid was not used to walking such long distances at a time.

"Your pet grows impatient," said a voice over the howling, dusty wind. Haresah tasted venom in her mouth and swallowed hard. Siddiq ibn Yasin might be her beloved's most treasured advisor, but to Haresah, he was nothing but a thorn in her side. Were he to come to an unfortunate end on this journey, she would surely rejoice. The man wore a gandura of gold-wrapped silk, with a white turban over his tunic to shield his warm, russet brown skin from the wind and sand. Attached to the girdle at his waist was a variety of pouches and satchels – just a few of the materials he had brought along with him, the rest strapped to the camel he guided next to him. His eyes, the color of a ruddy topaz, were set keenly upon Haresah.

"Khalid is not my pet," she corrected. The lion sensed the bitterness of her tongue and growled, though he made no move from Haresah's side and merely glanced in Siddiq's direction. His tail swished hard once or twice in annoyance. In truth, the creature was more like family. Father had gifted the noble creature to Haresah as a cub and told her one of two things would happen: she would either tame it, or it would grow to maim her.

"No ill was meant," the advisor replied. "I am merely wondering if perhaps we should not have brought such a wild beast on this endeavor."

Her eyes narrowed. Even with her veil obscuring much of her face, she noticed the man recoiling at her glare. No one else would dare speak to her in such a manner. Were it

not for her love of Razin, she might have had Siddiq's head
long ago.

"Khalid goes where I go," she stated plainly. "Be happy
I am here to keep him *patient*." She stroked the beast's
fur again, wordlessly reassuring him. Khalid had never
disobeyed her. If he were to lash out at Siddiq, it would
be at her command. Perhaps then, she alone would have
Razin's ear. Her lips curled at the thought.

They crested a sandy outcropping overlooking forsaken
lands. They had ventured east for many days, past
Sijilmassa and into the uncharted wastes of the desert, to
reach their destination. In the distance, the dunes caved
inward, a great maelstrom of sand and dirt and vine, not
unlike a sinkhole.

"We have arrived," her beloved called from the front of
the small caravan. Her heart swelled at the mere sound of
his voice, deep, melodic, beguiling. Razin Farhi was nothing
if not commanding, the gravitas of his presence impressing
upon all of them the importance of their task. He wore an
ornate tunic, embroidered with red, and covered in a red
silken mantle. Upon his head, he held his scarlet red ghifara
with one hand to prevent it from flying off from the wind.
Haresah silently thanked him for keeping his handsome
face and his chiseled features exposed. "The entrance is too
small for beasts of burden. We shall have to part with them
here."

"Would that we could part with other unnecessary
pests, as well," Haresah uttered under her breath, just loud
enough for Siddiq and her companion Zoeya to hear,
earning her a stifled giggle from the veiled woman. Siddiq

bristled and hurried to Razin's side, where his presence was more welcome.

"I see your patience for one another has reached its limit," Zoeya remarked once the man was out of earshot, which did not take long considering the wind. Indeed, Haresah could scarcely hear her companion's voice over her own mantle and veil, obscuring Zoeya's rich ebony-black skin aside from the intricate pattern of red henna across her arms.

"He is callow and weak-minded," Haresah said.

Zoeya glanced in the direction of Razin. "And he does not approve of your... partnership." To the point, as ever. But she was right. Siddiq had whispered to Razin for many years and had his trust. Many times had he advised Razin to stay away from Haresah and warned him of the dangers of emotional attachment. But even he could not separate them or defy their love. Haresah would sooner feed that fool to Khalid than allow that to happen.

"He matters not," Haresah snapped back. "A hound barking at a snake."

"Hounds may still yet bite."

Haresah and Zoeya shared a brief smile despite themselves. The woman had been at her side for nearly as long as Khalid – first her servant, then retainer, now steadfast companion. The two were raised together, ate together, learned together, grew together. When she was not with Razin, she was with Zoeya. The two were practically kin, and they shared more secrets between the two of them than they dared share with anyone else. But Zoeya had always been overprotective of her. "You worry too much. The day I fear the word of Siddiq ibn Yasin is the day the sun rises in the west and sets in the east."

Even obscured as Zoeya was by her dark veil, Haresah knew her smile by only the shape of her eyes. But it was brief and replaced thereafter by a foreboding pause. She looked out over the strange pit and let out a heavy breath. "Given what we know of this place, that day may soon be approaching."

What they knew was very little, and what little they knew was disturbing. They had sent scouts far and wide seeking signs of what they called the *kisra*, mysterious relics left behind by *those who came before*. Razin Farhi was already a man of great influence, but this was only the tip of the spear that was his ambition. Razin's inner circle was composed of enigmatic people from across the world, people who sought true power – not just the ability to command others, but the power to command reality itself. He had traveled far and wide, across many lands and many tongues, and came to her bearing just a few of the trinkets he and his scarlet-bound cabal sought. "With these, *ya amar*," he had told her, "our legacy shall be as stone."

He'd promised her a glorious future together, a future in which the two of them would rule side by side for centuries to come; in which their love would never waver, never diminish, never fade into memory; in which none would stand to oppose them or tear them down.

With the *kisra* at their command, she would never hurt again. Ever.

So they were elated when one such scout returned, bloody, exhausted, and alone. He spoke tales of a place to the east where the land had been corrupted. Warped. He spoke of black vines, of red thorns, yellow eyes, and a stone door. He spoke of death and blood and evil. Then he expired upon the floor of Razin's chamber, and her beloved grinned. To them, disturbing was promising. A sign of the *kisra*.

Siddiq had, of course, cautioned Razin against venturing to such a place. He might have even listened, had Haresah not insisted. It was, after all, as her father always stated: Submit, cub, and perish; or roar, lion, and rule. This was what they had waited so long for, she had convinced him. This was their chance. Their one chance.

And so they had set forth at once. Their entourage numbered seven in total: Razin and Haresah, his advisor Siddiq, her companion Zoeya, two of their most trusted guards, and of course her loyal Khalid. Together they would pierce the heart of this strange, forsaken pit where so-called black vines tore the earth asunder and rendered flesh from bone.

But Haresah was not afraid, for father had wrung the fear from her long ago.

"An interesting tale," Luciana Diallo finally declared. "But I still do not understand what this has to do with me."

Her patron smiled with all the elegance of a countess and the authenticity of a salesperson. It had been several weeks since the woman had come to Professor Diallo's office in the University of Barcelona. This was not a common affair, as Luci's studies usually kept her out of the hands of beautiful, wealthy aristocrats. Indeed, she looked much the unassuming sort in comparison to the woman's refined elegance – Luci had packed only the typical blouses and long skirts she might wear at home, while her patron wore a sequined black dress hemmed above her knees, with a narrow waistline and just enough of a low neckline to draw the eyes of about everyone on their train, Luci included. The only thing that made her stand out more was the flower that sat in her short, curly black hair, its long crimson petals contrasting with her dark outfit and pale skin.

Amaranth was all she called herself. Several others in black suits and red cufflinks followed her at a distance everywhere she went, and she carried with her an alluring air of mystery, danger, and money. Crime, probably, or perhaps old money. It mattered not. Luci had hit a rough spot in her career. Her research in what she called "metaphysical history" had been quite predictably difficult to authenticate. Her thesis regarding the unseen and the unwritten might have the potential to explain all of Earth's mysteries… if only anyone was willing to listen.

When Amaranth came to Luci offering to fund her research for the remainder of her career in exchange for her professional opinion, it had been her first stroke of luck in a long while. Even without the offer of patronage on the table, Luci might have agreed just to get away for a short while.

Her new patron had given her no explanation, no details – just an invitation. They were to head to Algiers by boat, then take the train to Morocco for some unknown purpose. Presumably, there, Amaranth would have some use for Luci's expertise, earning the woman's patronage and possibly saving her career. The Algerian Western Railway was recently built and a smooth, if slow, ride. Near the Moroccan border they switched to a private line, a reconstruction of an old military route. How Amaranth and her escorts were able to secure the train for themselves, Luci hadn't the slightest clue. At a laborious fifteen miles per hour, the journey would be a tedious one.

Hours passed before Amaranth finally summoned Luci to the parlor car for a chat. She'd spun her tale without a hint as to its greater meaning – if one even existed.

"What do you make of them? Haresah and the others," Amaranth asked, idly twirling a spoon through her cup of espresso. Luci could not help but notice the slow, steady swirl upon the surface of the dark roast. Every motion was purposeful, deliberate.

Luci cleared the stammer out of her throat. "There are many records of explorers who went willingly into dangerous or uncharted places. For fame, money, perhaps the favor of a ruler," she said. "There are also the tall tales of those in search of places or objects of great power. Juan Ponce de León's supposed search for the 'Fountain of Youth', for example. But those are all either myths or cover stories for the cruel truth. For many who went on such expeditions, the journey turned out to be a fool's errand, and those arrogant few who returned did so either scarred or rich off the exploitation of others."

Amaranth smiled a devil's smile. Luci cringed, hoping she had not somehow insulted her new patron. But the woman sighed. "It is as you say. They were young and unafraid. They believed themselves to be masters of the *kisra* they sought. That it would bend to their will. That they would conquer it." Her gaze meandered to the window of the train as it chugged along the northern coast of Morocco. To the south, the Atlas Mountains loomed in the distance, ruling over an expanse of arid plains.

"Are you looking to verify this tale's authenticity?" Luciana Diallo asked. She had taken out a small pad and was jotting down notes in her own shorthand. "This must have been during the time of the al-Murabitun dynasty, yes? Late 11th century, perhaps? There is no way such a place as you describe would have gone undisturbed for so long, if it ever existed."

"No, my dear," her patron drawled, "the veracity of this story is not in question. Our goal is far more valuable than that."

"How did you hear all this, anyway?" Luci asked, her curiosity getting the better of her. "I have never heard this tale before."

"In due time," Amaranth replied. "I still have much more to tell." She sipped again, and Luci did the same. The espresso was bitter, hot, intense.

The pit was a churning maelstrom of sand obscuring an underlayer of creeping black vine, extending in all directions like a thousand outstretched arms. It was as wide across as the main hall of Razin's estate, and none living knew how deep its caverns stretched. At the core of the sunken crater of shifting sand a gaping chasm, like the jaws of a terrible creature, yearned for them to enter. Haresah was restless. She had waited years for this day. Years of worry and doubt and hunger. She craved the life the *kisra* would give her. She could almost taste it.

As their beasts of burden could not navigate the ravenous sands, they immediately set to work unloading any necessary equipment for their venture and made their way toward the pit. Zoeya was well trained in the art of archery, and a short bow of yew was slung over her shoulder, with the bowstring digging into her ebony skin. Her quiver lay strapped to her waist, and she carried a long coil of rope wrapped around her other shoulder.

Siddiq and Haresah were armed with curved blades, each engraved with a crimson pattern that marked their allegiance. While Siddiq did not consider himself a swordfighter, Haresah had ample skill with the blade, having been taught by her father personally. Plus, she had Khalid for defense – the creature was trained to tear apart any who dared to harm her.

For Siddiq's part, he claimed to be more of a scholar than a soldier, and so his other trappings consisted mostly of satchels containing supplies they might require along the way: poultices, chalk, dressings, and the like. An excuse for his frailty, Haresah surmised.

Razin's two bodyguards took the vanguard, wearing armor of banded leather and chain below their headscarves. They each bore simple iron blades and wooden shields slung over their backs. Though Haresah loathed to let anyone close to her beloved but herself, even she had to admit the two guards had always served Razin well and true.

As for Razin himself, he had no need for such trifling

things. Whispers of the mysterious Razin Farhi's many talents went far and wide but died on the tongues of those who would tell them. They called him words such as philosopher, poet, tactician, advisor, but none of these struck upon the marvelous truth of Haresah's beloved. For Razin was an artificer – a sorcerer, able to manipulate the very winds of change with but a thought and the implementation of various esoteric componentry. Haresah had once seen him draw the venom out of a living cobra's fangs like it were water from a spout, then shape it into a hardened needle that could kill any of his adversaries with but a prick of their skin. He could manipulate the flickering flames of candelabras within his estate, alter the flow of rivers, and imbue artifacts with mystical power. His power enchanted and enthralled all who entered his orbit, Haresah most of all.

They gathered at the edge of the sinkhole, and Haresah's cheeks flushed as Razin's fingers intertwined with hers. He gestured at the black vines that crept, almost as if intelligent, through the sand and dirt.

"My dearest." Her beloved's voice was very much like a purr as he addressed her. "You were right to convince me to come here. Just look at this place. It is as if the ground is alive. I can *feel* the power emanating from this pit like blood through my veins."

"Master, if I may," Siddiq said, his impudence grating on Haresah's nerves as always, "I would be remiss in my duties if I did not suggest we send others in your stead. Now that we have confirmed the site's location and its power with our own eyes, the safe course of action would be to–"

"Safe," Haresah interrupted. "That is why you are weak. You would have the great Razin Farhi take the path of a coward. To send another is to allow them to claim the glory that should be ours." Khalid rumbled as if in approval, topaz eyes turning on Siddiq and measuring him as one might a meal.

It had not been the first time Siddiq had been threatened in such a manner. To his credit, he did not flinch or back away. He instead kept his eyes trained firmly on Razin, who seemed to be considering his words, despite her plea.

"Razin, my dear," Haresah said, draping her slender arm across his shoulder. "If you wish to claim power – if all that you have promised me, the world that you desire for us, is true – you have but to take it. Fate has given us this boon. Do not turn away from it."

Razin stroked his beard and chewed on her words. Then, with resolve, he declared his decision. "Siddiq. You speak wisdom. But you underestimate the influence of the *kisra*." He withdrew from underneath his neckwrap an amulet of brilliant Mozambique ruby, cut imperfectly into the shape of a scorpion's stinger, hanging on a cord of leather around his neck. Such a show might have been discreet were it not for the many stories of its power. The scarlet implement – the source of Razin's artificing knowledge, said to be bound to one of the *kisra*, hidden away for the safety of all. "I have seen them with my own eyes. None who survive contact with the *kisra* walk away unchanged. My beloved flower is right. If we sent another, they would likely either perish or claim it for themselves." He gazed directly into Haresah's eyes as he named her.

Her cheeks flushed. To have her beloved's trust filled her heart with pride.

With the decision made, they descended into the pit, one by one. Haresah and her beloved Razin were the last, taking advantage of the momentary solitude to swim in one another's eyes. Razin brushed a calloused hand against Haresah's cheek, and she exulted at the mere touch of him. She kissed him, lips dry and hot and wanting so much more. Soon, the world would be theirs. She could wait no longer.

Amaranth paused to take a final sip of her espresso. For the first time since their meeting, Luciana noticed the slightest hesitation in her voice. She decided to earn her keep and fill the silence with her own observations.

"I must say, I am intrigued by these two you speak of, this 'Razin Farhi' and 'Haresah Izem'. They seem to have eschewed many of the customs of their time." Indeed, the idea of a political power couple in that day and age was very interesting to her. And evidence of a secret cabal of influential people from around the world was precisely the kind of discovery she needed for her thesis. Still, she had to be sure. "But even I must admit, it sounds quite like fantasy."

"Much of reality must appear as fantasy to the ignorant, professor."

The implication bristled Luci's feathers. Patron or no patron, she had not immersed herself in decades of rigorous study to be questioned by a haughty rich girl. "What is that supposed to mean?"

"We once thought a myriad of falsehoods about the

world, until we were shown the evidence that proved otherwise. Is this not the pursuit of all who claim to be academics?" Amaranth said.

And more to the point, it was Luciana's entire thesis. Her career rode on the idea that the many unsolved mysteries of Earth's history were merely discoveries not yet made. But Amaranth did not offer evidence. Just a story. "Right, I understand. You are saying I should throw away years of education and expertise just to believe the imaginings of – no offense meant, but – a stranger?"

"Not entirely. I am merely asking you to open your mind to the likelihood that there are hundreds – perhaps thousands – of events and people you do not, could not, know about."

"You mean 'we', not 'you', yes?" Luci interjected. "As in, humanity, collectively?"

"Yes," Amaranth chuckled, "of course," and she resumed her tale.

Below the surface, sand and dirt coalesced into sheer, blackened rock, interspersed with dark, pulsating vine that dripped of ichor. Unnatural moss, covered in a deep violet gleam, ran along the rough cavern floor. The vines were everywhere, a tangled nest of quivering, slithering tendrils. Above, grains of sand fell like gentle droplets of rain around the rim of the pit's entrance, around a column of sunlight that pierced the center of the chamber. Deeper still, the cavern continued into dark places where the sunlight could not touch, webs of tunnels like rivulets through the earth.

They secured a line of rope to the only piece of stable rock they could find at the edge of the sinkhole and traveled into the depths, one at a time. Zoeya was first, being the swiftest and most agile of the party. She lit a torch upon reaching the bottom, and Haresah was pleased to see that the descent was barely more than a dozen feet – an easy enough drop for most of them, and even Khalid need not be left behind with their pack animals. Zoeya set her torch along the stone floor and helped Haresah down from the surface. Khalid obediently followed, letting out a lazy yawn and taking a brief respite in the sunbeam.

Haresah's skin crawled. It was warm, *too* warm, and strangely wet. The air was thick and pungent with a scent like rot. She felt as though she was inside a fresh corpse. Even as the rest of her company climbed down into the pit, a sense of isolation overtook her. It reminded her of the cellar of her childhood estate, where Father would lock her whenever she was insubordinate. She blocked out the bitter memory. She was her own master now. She would go where she desired and take what was hers, and none would oppose her.

Upon reaching the bottom himself, Siddiq studied the strange moss along the ground, careful not to touch it with his bare hands. A glance upward, and his brows contorted with suspicion. "It grows where this loathsome mucus drips," he said. His words were directed at Razin alone, as if Haresah and her companion were not present. She found herself suddenly wishing one of the vines might come alive and strangle him, but she was not so lucky, at least, not yet.

"Then we follow the vines," Razin declared. "They seem to be the source of this… disturbance."

"Or they extend from it," Siddiq agreed.

The group, spurred onward by Razin's urgency and Siddiq's curiosity, began to venture into the dim tunnel nearest to them, where the vines were thickest and densest. Zoeya, however, stood frozen at the rear, as though the patch of sunlight was a sanctuary she dare not leave.

"No sign of the other scouts," she said, retrieving her torch to examine the chamber more thoroughly. In the pale torchlight, the ceiling seemed to undulate with the twisting and sinking of the sandy crater above. "A strange foundation for a cavern. What is keeping the entire thing from collapsing?"

"The flora, I suspect," replied Siddiq. "See how it digs and churns? Its thorns run deep. The earth clings to it. Like the roots of a great tree."

Haresah approached her companion and tugged on her arm to spur her from her troubles. "Come, Zoeya," she whispered, not wishing her beloved – or, goodness forbid, Siddiq – to hear. She could not show any weakness, not now, not even for Zoeya. Not when she was so close. "It is time to move."

Zoeya turned on Haresah with deep, umber eyes that gleamed in the last remnant of sunlight. "I do not believe we should be here." She glanced in Razin's direction, her lips a stiff line. Zoeya had long been wary of Haresah's relationship with Razin. Zoeya was wary of anything that might bring Haresah harm.

But that was not her place. "I know… how you feel,"

Haresah said. Her voice was suddenly distant, taut. This was not a subject she wished to get into, not ever, certainly not here, not now.

"This is dangerous," she hissed. "He is dangerous."

"*He* is the love of my life," Haresah snapped back, barely a whisper, but with enough bite to give Zoeya a startle. "And this is my opportunity to cement my position at his side. As an equal. I want this, Zoeya. I want the power to take what I desire. I want *him*."

"That is the problem. You want too much. Sooner or later, you will want something you cannot have, something you do not need."

"Want, need," Haresah said, following the rest of the party and snapping her fingers for Khalid to follow. "To me, there is no difference." The lion yawned and lumbered after her, and Zoeya's soft footfalls confirmed that she, too, abandoned her worries to follow behind, as she always did.

Deeper and darker, the descent continued. Minutes passed. The tunnel grew narrower and narrower until they were forced to walk in pairs, with Razin's two guards in front. After her exchange with Zoeya, Haresah had wrestled her way to Razin's side, giving Siddiq a look that could freeze his blood, would that she had that capacity.

She snuck a glance at the rearguard to see Zoeya alert as ever, her bow strung and at the ready, eyes darting with every strange sound, every drop of ichor upon the floor and every *shlick* of oily vines shifting in the shadows. As the descent led them into gloomier passageways, one of the guards lit a second torch, slinging his wooden shield over his shoulder.

Haresah almost wished he hadn't. Ahead, the pit was...
different. The change had been gradual, but now the
sheer evil of this place was unmistakable. The black vines
and their red, jagged thorns were everywhere, obscuring
the cavern walls, quivering with unnatural energy. It was
as though the burrow was alive, undulating, *breathing*.
Haresah could not shake the feeling of eyes watching her in
the dark. Something observed them. Stalked them.

And the worst part was, whatever it was, she got the
feeling it wanted them there.

Luciana Diallo set her espresso down, shuddering at
Amaranth's detailed descriptions of the vile pit and its
foul entrails. *Almost too detailed.* "Sounds like a tale for
one of those magazines – *Strange Accounts!* or *Tales from
Nevermore* or some such drivel. I daresay you would make
for a chilling author. But as you know, I am a historian, not
a publisher."

"I take it then you do not believe the possibility that this
may be a true account?" Amaranth asked, her blood-red
eyes never wavering from Luci's.

Luci tore her gaze away. She wished it were that simple.
It would be so easy to be swept up in Amaranth's tale, to
believe in such things as sorcery and *kisra* and accursed
pits. Was this what her colleagues thought of her research?
That it was all esoteric nonsense? Luci was starting to think
that perhaps she was being mocked. "Believe you? No.
Well, it is not a mere matter of belief. I have studied this
region's history extensively, as you no doubt know. I am
the foremost expert on events political, cultural, and even

pertaining to the earthen sciences with regards to the era during which you claim this tale transpired. And I have not yet heard a shred of evidence that these people or this place ever existed."

Amaranth narrowed her eyes. "Yes, that much is true. You would not find this tale or its players in any historical record. But that does not mean it did not happen."

"And how might you know this to be true?" Luci took another sip of her drink to hide the frustration in her voice. "Surely you do not claim to be a primary source?"

At that, Amaranth grinned a toothy grin. "Why, of course not. But perhaps any record of such matters – of Razin Farhi and the fate of his expedition – were, for whatever reason, expunged from history."

Luci leaned in, her eyebrows raised. Now the woman had her attention. Luci had no doubt that this *kisra* they sought was nothing more than a tall tale, and the whole thing about Razin being a sorcerer certainly reeked of exaggeration. However, if perhaps elements of this account were true – and that was a big *if* – it could mean the existence of a socio-political cabal operating within the Almoravid with enough power to erase any record of their existence. And that alone could be the thing that drove her thesis from impossible to credible. It would be the discovery of her life.

"So… in other words, you claim to possess the only known record of this expedition?" Luci confirmed.

Amaranth nodded. The blossom in her hair unfurled half an inch or so, but she snapped her hand up to shift it back into place without so much as batting an eye.

Luci looked out the window for a while, biting her

thumbnail. While she pondered a great many possibilities, Amaranth ordered a bottle of wine and two glasses from one of the train's servers, then leaned back and studied the professor's meandering thoughts. "If what you say is true, that information could indeed be valuable," Luci finally replied once her teeth had reached the quick of her thumb. "From an academic standpoint, of course."

"Of course," Amaranth echoed.

"In any event, I suppose I have nothing better to do to pass the time. So, tell me: what did they find down there?"

Down, down, down, they drowned in the deep. The air was thick and pungent with a moldy scent, dark mites of dust and pockets of miasmic vapor. The walls contorted, gnarled, and tangled with vine. It felt like Haresah was being choked, or perhaps devoured. Here, in this garden of evil, the scouts had met their end. The expedition found them implanted in the cavern's breathing walls, swathed in sticky vine, red thorns digging several inches into their flesh like iron maidens.

Grim silence permeated the group as they examined what remained of their former agents. None wished to speak first. Haresah wondered how many of them worried this might soon become their own fate. She studied Razin's expression more than she did even the corpses, noting the narrowing of his eyes, the twitch of his lower lip, the rapid intake of breath. He would never admit doubt or fear. It was one of the things she admired in him, for she too had been taught to keep such emotions at bay. *To show weakness is to expose yourself to attack.* Her father's lessons were branded into her from youth. Like her, Razin would never show weakness… but if Siddiq insisted they retreat, he might concur. She would have to keep her doubts at bay if she wished to convince Razin to press onward. She could show no weakness, no fear. She tore them from her mind as one tore a leech from flesh.

"It is a… cocoon of sorts." Siddiq finally broke the silence. He had ventured closer to the nearest of the encased corpses, though he dared not step within arm's reach. "But who placed them here?"

"Or what," Zoeya uttered under her breath.

Do not show your belly. Haresah did not shy away from the cocooned corpses. She passed by Siddiq and approached the nearest one, tracing the tip of a finger along a length of vine and smudging the black tar-like substance across her fingers. "It must be related to the *kisra*. This, all of this, stems from the cavern's core." She met Razin's gaze with a smile. "It is here, my dear. This is the power we seek."

"Power?" Zoeya was incredulous. "This isn't power. It is death. It is foolishness to think otherwise."

Haresah turned on her companion, furious. Zoeya would not dare to stand in her way, would she? Razin's advisor and many of his agents, perhaps. Those who aided Haresah often did so only out of fear. Even without her connection to Razin, she was not one to be taken lightly. With Razin at her side, to raise her ire would be to court death. But Zoeya was different, or so she thought. She might have had words for her friend right then and there, had Siddiq not interrupted.

"I am not so sure." He had walked closer and was now

examining one of the bodies. The rest of the company hung on his words, waiting for an explanation. His eyes were wide, his fear exposed. "That this power leads only to death, I mean. Look." He gestured to the corpse's neck. Tendrils of vine slithered around the throat, constricting and retracting in a steady rhythm, covering flesh with its sickening, syrupy excretion. In, then out. In. Out. In. Out.

It was breathing.

Razin took command at once. "Get them out of there," he instructed his guards. The two drew their steel, dropped their shields, and rushed to the vine-wrapped bodies. Gripping patches of oil-slick creeper with one hand, they hacked with their blades, trying to separate the victims from the cavern walls. One of the two guards instantly reeled back with a painful yelp, his hand riddled with bloody wounds. Red thorns, long as fingernails and sharp as needles, bore into his palm.

"Careful, you fools," Razin hissed, and he gestured to Zoeya to aid them. She went at once, stripping tangled wreaths of vine from the wall, careful not to touch any patches of thorn lest she suffer the same fate. Haresah was unable to simply stand idle and watch. She too joined in the tiresome work, shoving her blade between wriggling cords of red and black and tearing them apart with little care to avoid wounding the scout trapped within.

Finally, the cocoon gave way. Gravity tore the mound of flesh and vine from the soil. It collapsed in a writhing clump between them. Where it had adhered to the wall, strange flowers bloomed along its length – gangly and sickly, with spindly scarlet-hued petals dripping in that very same thick tar. The caverns bled with ichor in the cocoon's absence. Haresah's stomach turned. The stench was nauseating. She held her breath to keep herself from retching.

"Siddiq," Razin barked, "what manner of flora is that?"

His advisor stepped forward and knelt before the tangled heap, studying the blossoms while the rest of them set to work tearing their companion free from its grasp. Siddiq withdrew a small knife from his belt and clipped off a single stem of flower, bottling it in a glass jar. He covered the lid with a strip of heavy cloth, tied it shut with a length of cord, and held it up to his eyes. "I have never before seen its like. How fascinating..."

By blade, knife, and nail, the party tore the scout free. The last vine encasing the body shriveled as it was ripped apart, and before they knew it, the whole of the cocoon had shrunk to a bed of flattened black weeds. Inside was indeed a man, or what remained of one. His skin was bruised and blistered from head to toe. His eyes were gone. His muscles and stomach were gaunt from atrophy and malnourishment, and he scarcely moved but to twitch now and again. And yet, breath still escaped his lips.

One of Razin's soldiers lowered himself to check the man's vitals and attempt to shake him out of his stupor. They tried names, but it was no use. The body's countenance was nigh unrecognizable, and even if he did hear his own name, he did not speak, *could* not speak. The only sound that escaped his lips was a terrible, gurgling croak, something between the final throes of agonizing death and the first cry of a newborn. Haresah swallowed her revulsion and spoke not a word that would give her away. Sweat dripped down her forehead, but it was just the heat, or so she convinced herself.

"It is no use," the guard said. "He will not wake, and yet he looks to be in agony."

Razin's attention turned from Siddiq's flora sample to the body of the tormented scout. "Then put him out of his misery," he ordered.

The guard nodded, lifted his blade high over his head, and uttered a solemn prayer. He paused for only a moment, as though seeking permission from some unseen arbiter.

Then a black vine lashed around the soldier's neck and yanked him to the flowerbed. He let out the shortest of grunts before more of the withered flora wrapped itself around his mouth, muffling his cries. The scout shot to his feet – no, it was not the scout moving, it was the *vines* lifting him up – and it was dragging the guard along the floor with its writhing tendrils as it stood.

Chaos erupted at once. There was much screaming, their words all indistinguishable in the sudden ruckus. Haresah rocked on her heels, lifting her blade in a defensive stance. Zoeya leaped back and pulled her bow off her shoulder, fumbling for an arrow. Siddiq, coward as he was, fled to the side of Razin's remaining guard, who kept his shield raised and his sword at the ready.

Flump, flump, flump. More cocooned bodies detached from the walls and fell in messy nests of vine, lashing wildly as they came alive, one by one. Haresah heard her beloved call her name, but nothing would deter her. She would not give Razin any cause to fear the path forward. She would rather die than suffer that mockery.

The tangle of leaf and vine that had encased the scout stepped forward with thorny appendages that rooted to the cavern floor. Behind it, the captive guard wriggled in vain. It was no longer human, no longer the scout they had sent to seek signs of the *kisra*. It had been consumed. Changed. There was no end to the husk that was once the man and no beginning to the blossom – they were one and the same.

Haresah was at the head of the fray. The thing lashed at her with several swipes of vine, one latching onto the forearm of her sword arm, another her left thigh. It squeezed her limbs tight, tight, tighter still, so tight no blood could flow through them. Her head spun, lighter than air. Panic threatened to take her mind. Anger and zeal pushed the pain away. *Plant your feet and roar back.* She snapped her other hand up and pried her blade out of her numb fingers, then hacked at the tendrils until she was free. Life once again returned to her arm and leg, agonizing tingles crawling through them. Another vine wrapped around her blade to try and yank it from her grasp, but it cut itself in twain upon the sword's sharpened edge.

Yet none of it mattered. For each coil severed, another grew to take its place. It was upon her now, a tangle of thorns and lashing creepers covering the once-living husk of a man. She swung to sever the husk's head from its body, but her wrist was intercepted with surprising strength, her blade inches from its neck. Uncanny strength wrenched her arm aside. Its dead, empty eyes somehow glared into hers as it approached. It reeked of mold and death.

She dug her heels in and screamed, and a lion's roar joined with hers.

Khalid was upon the thing – five hundred pounds of fur and tooth and claw. He latched his jaw onto the husk's neck and tackled it to the ground. The lion tore at its jugular, but no blood flowed. Instead, something dark and slimy oozed from its wound like sewage. Haresah did not flinch at the telltale sound of snapping bone, nor Khalid's feral growl. Even with its neck snapped and its throat open, its arm still twitched. It was still fighting. Still trying to kill. But it was just creepers manipulating dead flesh.

"Focus on the corpses!" Haresah shouted. "The vines are merely the puppet strings." She ran past her loyal partner and drove her blade into the chest of the next walking corpse, thorny tendrils whipping all around her. Neither fear of death nor pain would cease her advance. Blood trailed down her arms from wounds she could neither see nor feel. She roared and plunged the blade deeper with all her strength, until it pierced the husk's back and drove it to the cavern floor.

That was two; eight was the number they had sent. An arrow whistled by Haresah's ear and found its mark in the head of a third. "Stay low!" Zoeya yelled. Haresah tugged her blade out from the corpse's ribcage and hunched over it as several more shots whizzed over her head. The moment she spotted her opening, she advanced through a gauntlet of jagged thorns. Khalid followed close behind, mirroring her movements as though they were two lions on the prowl.

Three more of the husks fell around her, arrows piercing their skulls. She and Khalid charged the last of the things at the same time, striking as one. A swift and sure blow with her blade was all she needed to sever its head clean from its body. A wet *shlick* sounded as it fell, headless, to the ground. Khalid was tearing the other apart with vicious disdain.

They had only a moment of respite before the dreadful croaking of lifeless husks and the whipping of tendrils resumed. There were more of them ahead, so many more, shapes that twisted and flitted in the dark.

"But there were only eight scouts," Siddiq said, panic in his voice. Yet Haresah grinned. For over the din of battle, over the cracking of vine and the scratching of thorn, Razin was chanting. Bellowing. His voice echoed through the cavern, the words alien to Haresah's ears, and yet familiar. Her beloved's power was indeed a marvel to behold. Razin stepped forward and joined Haresah's side as his mystic bidding reached a crescendo. Then, palm outstretched, he summoned forth a ball of fire. Names were uttered – Cthugha, The Living Flame, Kathigu-Ra; Fthaggua, Seeker of Fire; Aphoom-Zhah, burning progeny. And then Haresah closed her eyes and bent over to cover Khalid's eyes, for she knew what came next.

The light was that of the sun, or an entity even grander. It spiraled into the distance, illuminating a horde of walking dead puppeted by blackened vine, and when it reached its destination, Razin snapped his fingers.

The explosion rocked the Earth. Siddiq fell to his knees. Zoeya struggled to keep her balance. Razin's remaining guard lifted his shield to block the wall of flame that erupted forth. Haresah merely cackled in acknowledgment of her beloved's power. Power she might soon hold in her own grasp, if Razin's promise to her remained true.

They shielded themselves, but nothing could stop the wave of intense heat that washed over them. When the dust settled, all that lay before them was burnt to a crisp. The vines along the walls were seared and shriveled, the husks charred, smoking. The odor was nearly unbearable. But it had not been the first time Haresah had smelled burnt flesh, and surely it would not be the last.

In the distant darkness, the last of them jerked to life, then collapsed once more in silence. It was done.

Haresah, Zoeya and Razin's escort were panting and sweating from the blast of heat. Blood trickled down Haresah's arms and her sides from countless lacerations, more than she cared to count, and more than her body cared to disclose. Pain was a luxury she could not afford. Siddiq, of course, had not moved from his craven post at the rear of the party.

As for Razin himself, the spell had taken its toll on him. His fingertips were singed and convulsing with pain. Cold sweat caked upon his forehead. Calling forth such power always had a terrible price. Even so, Haresah had never seen him make a single sound of discomfort. He wielded his power with the grace of a king and the wisdom of a sage. A smile spread across her lips as she admired her lover.

It was only then they heard the continued muffled cries of their other escort, who was still bound by lifeless vine. Haresah tore him free with the tip of her curved blade and pulled him to the ground. He was shuddering from head to toe and covered in bruises like the rest, though his skin had not yet withered. In other words, he was alive – unlike the other unfortunate victims.

"Talk to me," she commanded. Only stuttered cries and gasps for air emerged from the man's lips.

"Haresah! Step aside," Siddiq said with all the impudence of an untrained hound as he approached. He was holding a length of cloth and a poultice made from a decoction of r'tam and several other medicinal plants. The scholar knelt over the wounded man and applied the buttery mixture to his wounds, then covered each one in cloth wrapping. By the time he was done, nearly a quarter of the man's body was bandaged, but the twitching and much of his pain had eased. "Hush. Rest now."

"There is no time for rest," Haresah said. They were so close now, and the path lay bare before them. Soon they would find the source. Soon, she and her beloved would hold this power in their hands. Then none would question them. None would stand in their way.

"Surely you do not mean to press on?" Siddiq asked. "It is too dangerous to continue. We must return to the surface and study what we have discovered. Perhaps we may return when we understand more of what we are dealing with."

"I did not know you spoke for my beloved," she threatened, and turned her gaze to Razin. Such impudence deserved to be punished. Her beloved was their leader, not this wretched worm. But Razin merely stroked his beard in thought. Was he truly considering the words of this coward? No, she could not let that happen. Siddiq would have them return to safety, to secrecy, to mediocrity. Siddiq would wrest her power from her hands and succeed Razin if he had the chance. A bitter taste fell onto her tongue. She fell into Razin's arms, a practiced gesture.

"Razin, *ya amar*, my dearest. Can you not feel the pull of the *kisra*? Can you not taste how close we are to achieving our goal?" She dragged a finger along his neck, teasing his skin. Then, under her breath, she struck the final nail: "Did you not *promise*?"

Razin's hesitation felt eternal. His eyes glinted in the torchlight. He scanned hers, then looked beyond to the rest of their party. "I did, *ya amar*," Razin said, and she drank of the sound of his voice, deep and dark and dangerous. "And I do not break my promises. We shall have the power we seek."

The bandaged soldier was brought to his feet, his blade and shield returned to him. Like Razin, he endured his pain with grim resolve. He would serve, loyally, to any end. Haresah was prepared to send him to that end herself if it meant claiming the *kisra* for themselves. Each other such artifact discovered by Razin's cohorts was bound to a mortal. She was worthy. A noble scion of an old family, a broken family, but noble nonetheless. She would use its magic to protect the life she had forged for herself in the crucible that was this cold, brutal world.

As the company prepared to advance deeper into the cavern, Zoeya silently dressed Haresah's wounds, the two removing thorns from her skin and applying the last of Siddiq's poultice to her many bleeding cuts. "Haresah, you almost died," she finally uttered under her breath. "We all could have. Do you not see the danger in this?"

"I am not blind," Haresah said. "But only by facing this danger can we claim the power we seek. The power we *need*. Power to guide the weak and keep our loved ones safe. The power to change the future. Only a coward would look fate in the eyes and avert their gaze when danger gets in their way."

"I know. 'Stand and roar'. You know I will follow you anywhere," Zoeya said, although the slight tremor in her voice suggested otherwise. "And I am sure you know I am no coward. I just want to make sure… I just want to know we are doing this for the right reasons."

Haresah met her friend's gaze. A slight shimmer in Zoeya's eyes wove a tale of worry, fear, regret. A quiet part of Haresah wished to take her away from this place, to return to a life of simple pleasures and honest work. But that life had never been an option for her. Her upbringing saw to that. Father's lessons saw to that. She clenched her jaw and looked away. If she and her beloved were to be together – if their rule was to change the world – she could not cower now.

"There is no reason more right than to defy fate," she answered.

Zoeya grimaced, but nodded along. It was the answer she expected. But perhaps not the answer she wanted. Silence lingered between them as she finished dressing Haresah's wounds. With each thorn removed, the stinging pain subsided, but in her mind, turmoil raged; a whirlpool of doubt and love and worry and ambition she covered in a mask of stone.

"Just permit me to ask one question." Zoeya pierced the silence once her work was done. She lowered her voice and motioned in secret to the guard who had been swallowed by the vines. The man's arms, chest and left leg were covered in bandages, and he scarcely had strength remaining to wield his blade and shield. He tried his best to hide his grunts of pain, to not show any sign of weakness as Haresah had commanded, but the truth was plain to see: if they met with more danger, he would likely never return to the surface. "Were that me – had I been the one so severely wounded in his stead – would you still wish to advance without delay?"

Haresah's hesitation was only a flash. Just a fleeting moment, no longer than the beating of a heart. But in that weighty pause, a world of truths lay bare before the two of them. She cared for Zoeya, that much was true, would always be true. She could not imagine a world in which Zoeya was not at her side. But she could not let anything stand in the way of the future she desired.

She was made for more. She deserved the life she sought. To be free and never under anyone else's thumb ever again. To be with her beloved forevermore. There was no sacrifice she would not make to fulfill her desired destiny.

"I see," Zoeya said. She hefted her bow over her shoulder and walked away before Haresah's maelstrom of emotions could stand in the way of her fate.

Amaranth paused to sip her Malbec, leaving Luci to incredulous thoughts. Between the bizarre description of the pit, the grotesque fate of those they had sent to scout the region ahead of them, and their implausible battle with what can only be described as the living dead, the professor was feeling somewhat out of her element. As an objective historian, Luciana Diallo was only concerned with proven evidence and the authenticity of historical accounts. She spent many years vigorously vetting her own speculation, comparing contradicting records of historical events, and debunking rumors with political purpose. The idea that she should take a fanciful tale such as this at face value grated on her nerves.

And yet, she could not dismiss it out of hand, either. Being a historian meant weighing all evidence. Dismissing an account without even considering its validity would be just as problematic as outright assuming it was legitimate. Preposterous though it may have seemed, there were hundreds, perhaps thousands of tales of similar exploits – profane evils, strange sorcery, and the like – and though most were pure nonsense, nuggets of truth often lay buried within.

Still, Luci could not help herself. "This story is somewhat embellished, but I am guessing that what you are after has something to do with this secret organization Razin and Haresah were a part of. Am I correct?"

"Very astute of you," Amaranth drawled with a smirk. Her lipstick, dark and red, shared its hue with that of her drink. Luci could not help the shudder that ran through her. She felt like prey.

Luci could not tell if this was genuine praise or sarcasm. She decided to trust her instincts and continue. "I have never heard of a Razin Farhi, nor any of these others, but the idea of a hidden power attempting to run things behind the scenes is intriguing – and relevant to my own research. In every era, there are conspiracy theories regarding those in 'true' control of society, the masterminds making puppets of us all. The 'Illuminati', or what have you. It's mostly baloney, of course, but powerful people have risen in secret before. If this Razin did exist, it could change everything about our knowledge of historical events."

Her patron nodded, her eyes narrowed, her smirk widening. "It could indeed. And should somebody – let's say, a prominent historian with the backing of her eccentric patron – acquire firsthand access to such knowledge and proof of its veracity…"

"… it would be the find of a lifetime," Luci finished, rolling her eyes. "I know where you are going with this."

"Then please, allow me to finish telling you what happened," Amaranth said. "I promise, by the end you will be certain of the account's veracity, and from there we can determine where to go next. At worst, you are entertained by a silly tale. As you yourself said, you have nothing better to do to pass the time." Then she leaned in close, her devilish smile enticing and somehow menacing all at once. Her perfume, a floral scent not unlike her namesake, washed over Luci. "Or, you help me uncover something truly priceless."

Luci shakily brought her glass to her lips. The train leapt in its tracks, and she fumbled the wine, causing a gentle splatter on the pristine tablecloth. She dabbed her lips with her napkin and forced herself to stay calm. It was just a story, after all. Just like Amaranth said – at best, something that happened many centuries ago; more likely, a work of fiction. But if so, what was this feeling of dread that crept along her shoulders?

•••

The descent was long and arduous. The further the party traveled from the surface, the more hostile and alien the burrow became. The tunnels twisted in upon themselves like tangled intestines, with more routes joining theirs, funneling them toward some ultimate nexus deep below. Black vines now covered the cavern walls from top to bottom, creeping and slithering with wet, oily *shlicks*.

At times, the passage became narrow and cramped, and they were forced to travel in single file. They squeezed through tight spaces with only the vaguest certainty that there would be room to breathe on the other side. Jagged crimson thorns caught on their clothes and bit into their skin as they tiptoed through narrow crevices and crawled through low passageways. Haresah gave almost no thought whatsoever to how they might return to the surface. It did not matter. Forward was the only way to go. Fate lay ahead, Haresah's ambitions laid bare. They were so close now. They would claim it soon.

Hours passed. The silence between them was thundering. None dared to question the undertaking. They were damned either way. Fatigue and doubt tormented Haresah plenty, but it was the terrible sense of otherness in this sinister pit that was her worst enemy. The pressure of the deep; the stale, moldy air; the undulating creepers that grasped for her as she passed; the nauseating sounds of oily things sliding and squirming all around her; if this was still Earth, there was almost no sign of it left.

The caverns were alive. They *breathed* like the inside of a gullet. The walls wept with black ichor. Angry vines roiled along the floor, clutching and biting at their ankles. Siddiq had begun praying under his breath, just loud enough for Haresah to notice, but certainly not loud enough for any entity with the capacity to rescue them to hear.

More cocooned victims populated the tunnels as they ventured deeper and deeper. There must have been dozens of others who ventured here before them, or who were brought here for some terrible purpose or another. It was not lost on Haresah that the only tale of this *kisra's* existence was the lone scout who had barely survived the trip back to Razin's manor and succumbed to his wounds shortly after.

The odds of their survival were looking grim. But she was unafraid, *had* to be unafraid. They were too close to turn back now. *Stand, lion, and roar.* She pushed on, making sure to not disturb the cocoons latched to the walls. There was no saving these unfortunate souls. Their fate had already been decided. Hers lay ahead.

Finally, after much toil, they reached a place where the various serpentine tunnels met, the vines culminating in a bizarre gateway of sinuous tendrils. The path was barred by thick black flora and a bed of thorns. There was no sign of soil, stone, or sand in sight – only the thing that lay beyond; the source of this corruption, whatever it may be.

Haresah did not hesitate. She drew her blade and set to work, hacking at the vines with abandon. Nothing would stand in her way now. She could feel it, beyond. Calling her. It wanted her to find it. Zoeya called her name, but she only grunted in response. Each swing of her crimson blade brought her closer. Closer. Closer.

Khalid growled at invisible predators. Siddiq tried in vain

to grab her elbow and pull her away. Zoeya was pleading now. Their bodyguards were in a panic. Their reason had fled long before they reached this terrible place. Only Razin stayed silent through the struggle. Sweat and blood caked to Haresah's skin. When she finally pierced through the curtain of vines, her beloved was the only one who approached her side. Beyond, something pounded and milled through the malefic flora.

Razin took her hand in his and held her close. She gazed into his eyes and saw a glistening clash of love and doubt. "Worry not, *ya amar*," she whispered. "Soon, we will have everything we have ever desired. Power over life and death. We will be together in eternity. And never will we ever have to cower to anyone anymore."

"Everything I have ever desired is right here," he said, gripping her hand tighter. Even in this awful place, lit only by the barest of torchlight, with evil nesting in every crevice, both of them exhausted beyond repair, he had never looked more beautiful.

Haresah advanced, still holding her lover's hand. She parted the hewn vines and crossed the threshold. She was surprised to see rich, warm light gleaming through the gateway. It bathed them in its sanguine glow, forcing their eyes to adjust momentarily before they could behold the fruit of their labors.

The chamber on the other side was the beating heart of the pit itself. Pulsating black vines covered the hollow's walls. A tangle of thorny tendrils hung from the ceiling in swaying coils. The ground was a bed of flora that oozed oily nectar. At its center, propped up like some kind of altar, the tangle of vines ascended along the stem of a fist-sized flower, with long, crimson petals that steadily furled and unfurled with life. It glowed with unnatural crimson light, casting terrible writhing shadows along the walls.

"*Jahannam*," Siddiq intoned.

"Perhaps for you," Haresah said. For her, this was destiny. She could hide her smirk no longer. They did it. They found one of the *kisra*.

For a moment, they merely stared in awe – and perhaps, for some, in dread – at the simple blossom that seemed to be the source of all this corruption. Under her skin, Haresah felt it yearn to be touched. Images of living corpses encased in vine flashed through her mind, their jaws agape in horror, their flesh corroded into lumps of decaying meat. She shuddered and took a single step forward, her left hand still intertwined with Razin's. She would not submit. *Stand, lion, and roar.* This power was theirs to claim.

"Let us not stay here any longer than we need to," Zoeya said under her breath, as though the noise might disturb the thing. She followed Haresah and Razin close behind, an arrow nocked and ready to fly. Their guards crept along the perimeter of the chamber, scanning the vines along the walls for any activity.

Together, Haresah and Razin trudged through the bed of vines toward the core of the verdant lair. Khalid trailed behind with a low snarl of discontent, his back arched and his tail curled up above his back. *Even you, my loyal Khalid?* She let go of Razin's hand and approached the blossom with as much care as a mother checking on her sleeping child. Despite the nightmarish ordeal they had gone through to get here, it looked tranquil, serene, like a lone, beautiful rose in a meadow of dry grass.

Siddiq took up the party's rear, studying the burrow and its otherworldly flora. "I could spend years studying this... phenomenon," he whispered. "Provided it were under control, of course."

"Can anybody truly control something like this?" Zoeya said, her eyes darting to every shifting shadow and uncoiling creeper.

"Soon, we will," Haresah promised. She peered over at Razin, who stood just beside her. He gave her the slightest of nods, a bead of sweat inching down his forehead. *Worry not, my love.* She held the words at the tip of her tongue. It was Razin's fearless drive and his endless ambition that caused Haresah to fell in love with him. The caution in his eyes pained her to witness. "Are you ready, *ya amar*?"

"I..." Razin stammered, eyes fixed on the eldritch blossom. He observed it with all the demeanor of a man staring at his own gallows. A thousand possibilities seemed to be dancing across his thoughts. "Perhaps, if Siddiq were able to verify..."

"*Siddiq*," she spat. Siddiq would have her torn from Razin's arms and sent back to her father's estate with Zoeya. Siddiq wished to have the same power she did, but was too scared to *take it*. "This is our fate. You dare turn away from fate?"

Their eyes met. For the very first time in her life, she saw Razin Farhi's uncertainty. She knew the doubt that had crept into his mind. The tenacious spirit that she fell in love with was at war with its own shadow. But she would not let him succumb to his weakness. If he was afraid, she would have to roar twice as loud. Haresah stepped forward, clutched the stem of the blossom, and pulled.

Tendrils of vine abruptly shot up all around her. The heart of the chamber pounded, thundered. The walls were alive, stretching, grasping for them. There was shouting at the entrance. Razin called for her. Worry strained his voice. Vines wrapped around Haresah's ankles. Somewhere behind her, blades swung and hacked through leaf and vine. There was a scream of agony to her right, just far enough away to know it was not Razin or Zoeya. But she dared not turn away. This was her fate. To show weakness now would be her true doom. There was only one path forward.

However, plucking the blossom from its lair was a more tremendous feat than she'd imagined. She pulled at its stem with care at first, but it didn't budge. She dug her heels into the shifting ground and tugged with a grunt of effort. Tendrils scaled her legs and lashed all around her. Thorns sliced across her thighs, her back, her shoulders, her arm. Warm trickles of blood ran down her body and soaked her clothes. Still, she did not yield.

Beside her, Razin was chanting with a fervor, gesturing, calling forth once more to some terrible power from beyond to aid them. But the vines were everywhere. They snapped at her beloved's arms and shoved themselves around and into his mouth, trying to smother his words. *Does it know? How does it know?*

"Haresah! Above you!" Zoeya's voice cried. Haresah could feel something sliding down her neck, but it didn't matter. The blossom was becoming dislodged. She groaned and yanked with all her might. An arrow flew into one of the black tendrils that had swung down from the ceiling to lasso her. Another did the deed. It noosed itself around her neck, pulled her throat taut, and hauled her off the floor to hang her. She held onto the petals for dear life. Panic swelled in her chest. Her heart thundered. It was trying to quarter her.

Khalid ran to her side and snapped his jaws at the vines around her ankles, attempting to free her. It was a vain effort. The spongy bed of vines was far deeper than they'd guessed. More of them emerged in a deafening fountain of ichor, like the spraying of a roiling sea. The conglomeration was an unstoppable mass. No array of blades could cut her down.

Her vantage point from on high was a curse from which there was no escape. No nightmare could outhaunt the grisly display she witnessed. She had not noticed the demise of the wounded guard – he had been first to go. The other stepped before Razin to shield a long vine laced with jagged thorns from striking him, but his shield was not enough to stop it. The wood splintered in half with a simple swat, and he was next. A look of sheer terror remained upon his countenance as the thorns encased him.

Zoeya was drawing arrow after arrow and sending them at the vines holding Haresah, but it was no use. Eventually, she dropped her bow and ran to Khalid's side to try to pull her down with but her bare hands. *I'm sorry.* Haresah's voice strained to escape her. *I should have told you – I should have listened –*

She tried to tell her to go. To flee. To live. The words only wheezed from her dry lips. Then the bed of vines exploded once again. The rolling mass of black and crimson crashed into all that lay below her, and she heard only screaming.

But she still had her grip. Thorns bore into her hands as she yanked and wrenched at the damned thing. Her palms were slippery with blood. Almost, she could feel it wrenching from the Earth. It was almost hers. Almost, almost!

Siddiq had turned to flee and was met only with a wall of thorns barring the entrance. There was no escape, not for him, not for any of them. Razin was tearing vine after vine from his body, desperately trying to finish his spell. But a blast of fire would cause the whole entity to recoil, perhaps have it retract suddenly out of her ailing grasp. *No, no, no!* She desperately tried to shake her head with the last of her strength. *I almost have it, my dear, please! Trust me!*

Her wish was granted. Razin's spell would never finish. A single lance of vine tore through his back, through his heart and out the other side. His jaw hung open in eternal shock, his chant cut short.

Haresah screamed a silent scream. As much as she could let out. Her throat rasped for air. Tears mingled with the blood running down her cheeks. This could not be their fate. It could not be. She dug her nails into the accursed blossom and tore and raked and wrenched at it with every last gasp of life she had left. *You are mine! Mine!* she roared. *Mine!*

And just like that, the blossom finally slipped free. Haresah held the crimson petals in her grasp and watched its roots quiver to and fro in anticipation. The vines around her neck loosened their grip as she held it aloft. Its stem reached for her. Calling to her. Like it had been this whole time. *I am yours*, it seemed to say. The roots crept along her shoulders.

Yes, she replied.

Together, it crooned, together at last.

Yes. The power she was promised, it was finally hers. She felt the roots nestling into her tangled hair. Something sharp pierced her skull, but it did not matter. From her hammock of vine, the remains of her entourage looked small and insignificant.

Only Siddiq stood, trembling before her, still trapped. "Foolish woman!" he declared at her from below. He had grabbed Haresah's own blade and brandished it at her as the vines lowered her safely to the ground. "You've killed us all!"

Her body was faint, sluggish, but the vines propped her up like a floral throne. She did not care to respond to the plea of an insect. Her gaze snapped to the small length of plant fiber Siddiq had encased in a vial along his sash. She pointed at it with her finger, and it stretched through its confines, piercing the glass of the vial. Thorns erupted along its surface. With a wave of her hand, it coiled around Siddiq until his screams were stifled. Then, her body was lowered into the bed of vines, and for a long time, there was only darkness.

Luci had not drunk from her glass of wine in some time. Sweat beaded on her forehead. Her throat was dry.

"You…" she sputtered. It was only then she realized

there were very few others in the dining car with her. Just a handful of Amaranth's so-called retinue, all in suits and formal dresswear, adorned with red cufflinks and ruby bracelets. None of them were observing her directly, but their subtle glances and hushed conversation was evidence enough. She was being watched. "You cannot mean that…" Her eyes snapped to the crimson-petaled flower sitting idly in Amaranth's hair. "But that is…"

"Impossible?" Amaranth rolled her eyes. "Always the same with you skeptic types. You use words like 'cannot', 'never', 'impossible.' How arrogant of you to think you know everything that is possible."

The professor was agape. "So you mean to tell me you *are* a primary source? That you are… *Haresah*?"

The woman blinked and gave a slight shrug, as if it wasn't the most outrageous tale ever told. "In a manner of speaking."

No. This was a con. A grift. It had to be. Luci snapped alert, studying everything about her patron and the others who observed her. "You do not even look like how you described her."

"Ah, yes, that," Amaranth said. "The blossom did not preserve Haresah's body. That body was its food, I imagine, for a long time." Luci shuddered, the woman's description of the living corpses they had found still fresh in her mind. "But her memories – *my* memories, my consciousness, my life, that it kept. Until one day, a small bud of scarlet flower grew, solitary and beautiful, in the Sahara. And it was found. And that day, I claimed a new body. And so I have done ever since, whenever mine becomes… frail."

Luci swallowed this information like a lump of coal, then cleared her throat. "Let's say I believed you... *if* I believed you..." she began, then shook her head. No, there was not a chance. Amaranth's request for Luci had been strange ever since the day they met, and her mannerisms, too, were uncanny; but this, this was too much to take. And yet, her mind could not stop from inquiring further. "Why string me along with you like this? What use could you possibly have for me? You already have the thing you were after, right? Where are we even *going*?" She gulped. Her fingers were trembling. "You do not mean to... we are not headed..."

At that, the woman only chuckled, her laughter dripping with derision. "No, of course not. I tried looking myself, after my return. But it was gone, the pit, the vines, all of it gone. However, years later, I learned of a paleontological dig. The University of Barcelona was searching for prehistoric creatures in the middle of the Sahara. Strange place to go, but what do I know, I am only eight-hundred and something." She gestured off-handedly.

Realization sparked in Luci's mind. *Oh. Oh, no.* "I did hear about this. They did not find what they were searching for, but instead stumbled across a pit of desiccated human remains. A few odd creatures, as well. They theorized that it must have once been a lake or a basin of some kind, and the bodies of those who perhaps drowned there. Then, after it dried up, it was buried by the sand."

Amaranth grinned. "Ah, Professor Diallo." She placed a soft hand over Luci's. Hers was still trembling. "I knew I was right to come to you."

"But it wasn't a lakebed, was it? It was that *place*."

Amaranth nodded. "And now you come to the crux of it."

It is the key to power over both life and death. Luci was standing now, her knees shaking. But she still did not understand. "The bodies would have been taken for study. By the university. But I had nothing to do with it, I swear."

"Those I have already recovered," she said, her eyes narrowing. The quality of her voice had shifted from coy to threatening. "And the fools I spoke to at the university knew nothing of the others. But you, my dear, might. So tell me."

"I do not know," Luci stammered. Amaranth had gone to the wrong person. Luciana knew nothing of any of this. She had to find a way off this train. Her imagination was filled with the terrible, gruesome descriptions of the blossom's power. Her eyes darted for an escape and found that all of Amaranth's escorts were staring directly at her. One stood nearby, a hand in the coat of his suit. "*I do not know.*"

"Ah, but I think you do." Amaranth rose to her feet, towering over Luci. The blossom in her hair furled and unfurled again, like a pet waking from its slumber. There was nowhere to run. "Where is he?" she repeated, louder.

Luci shook her head. "I am telling you everything." She began inching away from Amaranth instinctively, but it was no use. The moment she reached the aisle, something slipped around her wrist and tugged her back onto her seat. She glanced down in horror to see a slithering black vine gripping her tight.

Amaranth rounded the table and slammed her palm into Luci's throat, lifting her into the window. The rumbling of the moving train rippled through Luci's spine. More vines emerged from the blossom in Amaranth's skull, coiling about the aisle of the train car. The others stood back, but did not dare interfere.

"Where. Is. My. Razin?" the woman snarled.

Luci's fingers clawed for something, anything, she could use to escape. She was going to die. She was going to die here and forgotten, lost to history just like the others. Tears welled in her eyes. "How am I supposed to–?"

Her eyes watered as Amaranth gripped her neck tighter. She gasped for air. Vines dripping with ichor slid along the walls until they reached her arms, pinning her. There was almost no train left, now. "Where is my beloved?!" Amaranth roared.

Luci's mind raced. If Razin Farhi was as important as she said, there was only one way his remains did not end up at the university. She went over Amaranth's story over and over in her head. Pain shot through her neck. There must be something. *The scorpion ruby!* "The – necro – polis –" she rasped, choking. The world was fading.

"What. Necropolis?" Amaranth pushed Luci against the glass so hard, she heard it begin to crack behind her.

Luci struggled for breath, clawing her fingers at Amaranth's hand. Finally, she croaked: "*Kasbah!*"

There was an eternal pause as the woman seemed to consider her claim. Then, finally, Amaranth released Luci from her grip. She slid down the glass and landed on her seat, coughing and sputtering for air. "Speak," her captor demanded.

"The necropolis," she panted, "behind the outer walls of the Kasbah Mosque. If his body was not at the university, it means somebody could tell who he was. His garb must have been completely decayed, but the Mozambique he wore, the one shaped like a scorpion's stinger – that would have remained around his neck. The expedition was working with a historian from Marrakesh. Which means an interested party in Marrakesh knew what that ruby meant and saw to it that Razin Farhi was buried in a tomb deserving of his station."

The swarming vines retracted, somehow slithering back into the blossom. Amaranth was just a woman again. For now. "You are going to take me there," she said. "You will guide me to my beloved, and finally, *finally*, we will be together again."

Tears streamed down Luci's cheeks. She nodded, frantic. The only escape Haresah's companions had from her schemes and desires was a merciless death. Would that be her only escape, too? Suddenly, her life felt fleeting and irrelevant. She had only ever been a bit player in someone else's game.

"Oh, cry not, little cub," Amaranth purred. "I am not done with you yet."

THE RED AND THE BLACK
Josh Reynolds

It was the red end of December and Trish Scarborough was in Venice. Rain mixed with snow sluiced down onto the canals like the arrows of the gods, and the city was making ready for the inevitable flooding. The sky was painted in the vibrant hues of dusk where it wasn't the color of old stones, promising greater storms on the horizon.

She hoped she'd be gone by then. The plan was to catch a fast boat to Istanbul, once things had been handled successfully here. If things were handled successfully. She pushed the thought aside. Worrying about failure was an invitation to sloppiness.

The Grand Canal stretched before her, chopped in half by the graceful arch of the Rialto. Water passed through Venice like blood through a body's veins. Knots of black gondolas bumped and shifted in the rain-tossed waters, the gondoliers calling out to one another in pugnacious jollity as they vied for fares or berths or both. But their cries fell silent as something new entered the canal. Curious, Scarborough slowed her pace.

A few moments later, a funeral gondola, highly decorated and blazing with lights and torches against the gray gloom of twilight, passed into view. It was followed by others similarly, if less elaborately, decorated. Something about the sight caught her attention and she paused, watching in respectful silence with the rest of the crowd.

A young woman lay in an enclosed bier atop the lead gondola, bound for some small island necropolis near the city. Priests and family members stood atop the gondola, faces lined with grief – all save one. A tall figure, clad in an archaic black cloak and tricorn hat, stood at the rear of the gondola, like a modern Charon, overseeing the dead woman's passage into the underworld. Scarborough frowned as she studied the eerie figure.

It was not the outdated costume that bothered her. Rather, her unease stemmed from the elaborate, vibrantly crimson Carnival mask they wore. The mask wasn't that much of a surprise. Traditionally, you could wear one between the feast of St Stephen's Day and midnight on Shrove Tuesday. But why to a funeral?

As the procession drew closer, she realized that the masked figure was scanning the fondamenta, as if in search of something or someone. She stepped back, seeking the thickest part of the crowd, and moved away as quickly as she could without drawing attention to herself. There was no guarantee it was her they were looking for, but why risk it?

Scarborough slipped off the fondamenta and down a

narrow calli, heading away from the Grand Canal and the city's main artery. She pulled her coat tight as water from an overhanging rood peppered the brim of her hat and splashed down her back. It was cold even through her coat, and she gritted her teeth against the sudden chilly pulse that ran through her. She was reminded of the old cliché about someone walking over a grave.

Not hers, of course. Her grave was thousands of miles away and decades in the future. A state funeral, she figured. Nothing too fancy; a few colleagues in attendance, some quiet homilies, then the soft patter of soil on a coffin lid. It was better than what some got, especially in her line of work. She pushed thoughts of mortality from her mind, and concentrated on her surroundings.

The city had always held some fascination for her, even as a girl. As a woman, that fascination had only increased tenfold. A good thing, for she visited at least three times a year. Though always for business, rather than pleasure. Then, business was pleasure, if you enjoyed your work. Which she very much did. It was why she had taken the job with the Cipher Bureau in the first place.

Scarborough thought of herself as a professional problem solver. She often joked to her few close acquaintances that she unraveled knots for a living. It was true, as far as that went. Ostensibly, she worked for a commercial code company. But the reality of her employment was far removed from the presentation.

The Cipher Bureau – or the Black Chamber, as some knew it – was America's cryptanalytic organization, responsible for the sanctity of the nation and the safety of its citizens, wherever they chose to make their home. And whatever sort of trouble they got into. Especially when it had bearing on national security.

Director Yardley had given her this assignment personally, pulling her off the Soviet business and sending her over the Alps, to untangle a new knot. This one was proving trickier than most. Less a tangle than a labyrinth, without any golden thread to mark her route – but still a minotaur to fight.

It had started with whispers. It always did. Someone somewhere knew something, and had told someone else what they knew. Word spread. Scraps of information, hidden in footnotes of books on architecture or history. Anecdotes buried in the biographies of Shelley and Byron. The illicit, unpublished writings of Baron Corvo. All concerning a set of keys and the people who desired them. What those keys unlocked, Scarborough didn't know and wasn't sure she wanted to. With regard to certain matters, ignorance was the best defense.

With the whispers came deaths. A scholar in Vienna, pushed from a window by a man wearing red gloves. A bookseller in Paris, drowned in the Seine. A famous industrialist and collector of occult relics who suffered a death by mysterious causes. A pair of archaeologists, crushed by a collapsing ruin in the Valley of the Sorcerers. A writer in Massachusetts, torn apart as if by a wild animal in his own hotel room. Whispers and deaths. Knots and tangles.

But untangle the knot and you had a line, stretching through the margins of history. A red line. It intersected with other lines; ley lines, bloodlines, lines of thought and inquiry... even storylines. Poe's Red Death; Red Riding Hood in the dark forest; Rose-red and the ungrateful dwarf; the red rider of the noonday, whom Vasilisa the Beautiful saw.

It was all strands of red, winding tight about the bones of the past. The Red Coterie was how Corvo had referred to them. Ibn Qudamah called them the Congress of the Keys. Whatever name they went by, they were trouble.

They were the reason she was in Venice, on the hunt for a book; a collection of notes, compiled by someone who'd followed the scarlet traces through histories and personal accounts. Those notes were the key to untangling the larger mystery – and right now, they were hidden somewhere in the city. She was certain of it.

But the Red Coterie knew about it as well, and they were closing in. She had the same feeling she'd had in Sevastopol, and in Bucharest before that. A feeling that always preceded trouble, in her experience. Like she'd stepped into a trap a half-second before it snapped shut.

A harsh voice cut into her thoughts. "*Mi scusi, signorina,*" it began, and a hand reached out of the shadows of a darkened doorway. Scarborough avoided the groping fingers deftly. She smelled cheap tobacco and even cheaper booze, but that didn't mean anything.

Her accoster stepped into the street as she hurried past. He was dressed like a sailor on leave, with a vivid carmine neckerchief wrapped about his throat. He cast aside a cigarette and started after her, calling out again. She ignored him, and made to keep going until someone stepped into her path. Another man, dressed like a laborer, in a faded cerise shirt beneath his smock and braces.

Red – they always wore red. That was the first thing she'd learned about them. The most important thing, perhaps. It made them easily identifiable. The man in the red shirt moved towards her, as if he were nothing more than a passerby. She hugged the wall of the passage, allowing him to brush past. He hesitated as he did so, half-turning as if to speak, but she was already hurrying away, leaving him no opportunity. There were too many people within earshot for them to try anything untoward.

They didn't follow her, but that didn't mean anything. There'd be more attempts before she was through, and more aggressive ones. She paused at the arch of a footbridge and pretended to light a cigarette. As she hunched forward, she darted a glance back the way she'd come. Her eyes narrowed as she spied a hint of movement, a flash of crimson – someone ducking down another side passage, perhaps. There was no telling how many people they had in Venice.

They'd been following her since Trieste. Trailing her as she trailed the book. She'd managed to stay a few steps ahead of them, but even so, it wouldn't pay to be too cocky about it. This bunch was older than most of the espionage networks in Europe – older, in fact, than most countries. Longevity was a skill all its own, and age brought wisdom, and often at a cost too horrible to contemplate.

Secret societies survived only by staying out of the light. But the invention of paper had inevitably led to the creation of the paper trail. You couldn't hide forever.

Clues hidden in apocryphal or banned texts, rumors and yarns – it all built to something, if you were smart enough to put it together. Solving puzzles like that was the whole reason the Black Chamber existed. Only some riddles resisted solutions. Hence all the crushed archaeologists and mauled writers and such.

Scarborough thought of red lines stretching down through history like blood dripping down the surface of a map. She shivered, straightened and kept walking. She turned her attentions inwards, to the map of the city she carried in her head. She had a good memory, better than most. It was one of the reasons she excelled at her job. Among other things, she'd memorized the layout of a dozen different cities, including Venice.

But maps only told some of the story of a place. They were sanitized depictions, accurate to the point of inaccuracy. They didn't show everything. In fact, they showed only what the mapmakers wanted you to see. To see everything, you had to walk the city yourself. You had to read the right books, and ask the right questions.

She found the entrance to the Calle Varisco a few minutes later. It was reputed to be the narrowest street in all of Venice, barely wide enough for one person to walk comfortably. She navigated the tight stretch of pavement, turning her body to squeeze through the passage more than once, searching the doors that lined it for the number she'd memorized earlier on the train from the mainland.

She found the door, and paused, senses straining against the muffling effects of the rain. Were they watching her, waiting to see if she went in? Impossible to tell. A familiar paranoia flitted at the edges of her awareness. What was the old joke? You weren't crazy, if they really were out to get you. She wished, not for the first time, that she were armed. But a woman with a firearm raised too many questions and drew too much attention.

Inside, steps wound upwards in a tightly scalloped ascent. The apartment she was after was on the third floor. She started up, taking the steps two at a time. Her heart was beating rapidly from equal parts excitement and unease. It was always like this, at the end. That was how she knew she was on the right track, even if evidence was lacking.

When she reached the apartment, she paused again. The lights on the landing flickered, probably due to the storm. Hazy shadows climbed the walls and cavorted silently. She felt as if she were being watched. Her eyes flicked to the other doors on the landing, but they were all shut. The air felt claggy and damp. She could smell the canals, even here.

She hesitated. If they really wanted to catch her, they'd have someone in the apartment already. She heard the door slam downstairs, and heard someone coming up. Another door opened somewhere on the floor below. Silence. She counted the seconds, listening to every creak. It felt as if the entire building were holding its breath along with her. Finally, she tried the door. Locked, of course.

She reached up and extracted a bobby pin from her hair. She had the door open after a few minutes of awkward finagling. She stepped inside and let it swing shut behind her. As an afterthought, she locked it, using a spare key she found in a bowl next to the door. If they wanted to come in, they'd have to either pick the lock, or bash the door down. Either way, it'd give her a chance to react.

The apartment was a gaudy emptiness of bright colors and tight corners. The only sign of personality was the expanse of news-clippings that covered the far wall. The clippings were in a dozen languages – French, English, Turkish... even Russian; all connected by lengths of dyed string and pins. She recognized the telltale signs of a hunt – obvious, even to the untrained eye. She'd employed such methods herself, on occasion when she needed to see things from a different angle.

The apartment belonged to the Cipher Bureau, though only a select few people knew that. It was one of a dozen safehouses scattered through this part of Europe. She prowled the square footage, noting the telltale signs of intrusion – scratches on a window frame, a scattering of dried mud, a cigarette butt deposited in the toilet bowl. They'd beaten her here, then, as she'd suspected. But they hadn't found what they were after, otherwise they wouldn't have bothered with the whole cat and mouse rigmarole.

She returned to the main room and the wall of clippings. They'd left them in place, but there were telltale smudges on some, spots where the ink had run. They'd tried, and failed, to make sense of them. Otherwise, they wouldn't have bothered following her.

She traced the strings without touching them, following the path between pins. It was easy, if you were familiar with the Newtonian mnemonic, *roygbiv* – red to orange to yellow to green to blue, and on to indigo and violet. After a few moments, she realized that red strings outnumbered the others. She smiled in satisfaction, and noted the careful placement of the pins. Each one pierced successive letters of certain words. First letter, second letter, third. A few numbers as well, at the end. Another cipher, and a simple one.

She found a scrap of paper and a nub of pencil and jotted down the cipher. At first glance, the jumble of letters and numerals meant nothing. But if you were familiar with the cipher, and the city, you soon realized it was a name. But not that of a person; rather, a street. One she was familiar with. That would be where the book was hidden.

Scarborough froze as a floorboard creaked. She waited, eyes on the bottom of the door, where a thin slash of light was visible. Something passed across it, momentarily blotting out the light. The handle turned – stopped. Someone was testing the lock. She frowned, more irritated than worried, and scanned the room, looking for something she could use. She spotted a letter opener and snatched it up. It was sharp, if not particularly well-balanced. Good enough.

She crossed to the door, moving as silently as possible, and pressed herself against the wall next to the door. She held the letter opener low. A quick strike was all she needed – just something to distract them, and slip past. But a moment later, they were gone, retreating back down the stairs. She waited for a ten-count and then went back into the main room. Had she fooled them, with the door? Maybe. Maybe they were satisfied that she hadn't gotten in. Or maybe they were waiting downstairs. There was only one way out, after all. They could afford to be patient.

Moving quickly now, she went to the window and levered it open. A canal stretched below. Not a big drop, but she didn't relish the thought of making the attempt. She looked back at the door. She could try to bluff her way out, pretend to be a resident out for an afternoon stroll – no. They knew what she looked like by now, and probably more besides. Only one thing for it. She needed a distraction. Something big.

Her gaze settled on the news clippings and she smiled. Quickly she peeled them off the walls and tossed them into the wastepaper basket, which was soon filled. Then she took the basket over to the door, pulled out her lighter and lit one of the scraps, before tossing it in to join the others. The fire would be small, unless something disastrous happened. At the last moment, she shut the window so that the smoke wouldn't be pulled outside.

As the fire grew, and smoke rose, she unlocked the door and stepped into the hall. She left the door open a crack, so that the smoke would readily escape into the building. Then, taking a deep breath, she shouted "*Fuoco,*" at the top of her lungs. Fire was the one alarm certain to get some attention in Venice. One good blaze could eat half the city, if it wasn't checked. She shouted again, banging on doors as she did so. "*Attenzione! Fuoco!*"

Soon enough, half the building was up and shouting for the other half. People were hurrying down the stairs, or frantically calling the local fire brigade. Scarborough didn't spend too long congratulating herself; instead, she seized the opportunity to merge with the human tide and let it carry her down the stairs and out the door.

As she went, she caught a flash of scarlet out of the corner of her eye – someone in a red coat. Maybe the one who'd followed her, maybe not. Regardless, she passed them by without being noticed, and hurried towards the far end of the claustrophobic passage. A shout from behind her nearly made her turn, but experience told her that would be a mistake. Instead, she increased her pace.

It was still raining, and the stones were slick with slush beneath her feet as she hurried down one calli and then the next, losing herself in the humble-jumble of Venice. Voices haunted her steps, echoing out of doorways or from behind her. Confusion reigned, as her imaginary fire spread. It wouldn't last long, but long enough to buy her the time she needed.

The edges of her vision were dotted by flashes of red among the nighttime crowds. Tricks of the light, or perhaps her paranoia acting up. But maybe something else. The sensation of being hunted wasn't a new one for her. Her first instinct was to get out of the city by whatever means were most expeditious, but that wasn't an option. Not until she'd gotten what she'd come for.

It took her nearly twenty minutes to find the place. Luckily, it was still open. Much of Venice shut down with the setting sun, but some places stayed open. This particular bookseller was one of those.

The *Libreria Leone Scarlatto* occupied a narrow street, away from the main drag. It was a small storefront, consisting of a lonely window and a wooden, iron-banded door with a doorknocker wrought in the shape of a lion's head. The doorknocker had been painted red at some point, but the paint had long since faded to a few errant chips of dull carmine around the lion's jaws, giving it the appearance of having just fed.

Scarborough studied the lion, and wondered if that was an omen. Not that she believed in such things. As far as the rest of the world was concerned, Americans only believed in death and taxes. But she'd seen enough of late to convince her that the world was a far stranger place than most knew. For every secret told, there were a hundred as yet unknown. And some of them were nasty indeed.

She took a breath and entered the lion's den. Immediately, she was struck by the smell of cigarette smoke and decaying paper. Heavy shelves bulwarked the entrance, and more occupied the immediate area around the front counter. Electric lighting cast a watery yellow glow over the shelves and patchwork carpeting.

A small man, balding and dressed in a stained red waistcoat, sat on a stool behind the counter. He was flicking through a ledger, muttering to himself. Books were piled up around him like the Alps and his merest twitch caused minor avalanches that he didn't seem to notice. Though the bell hung over the door had rung at her entrance, he didn't look up. Scarborough headed for the counter.

"*Mi scusi, sto cercando un libro,*" she said, haltingly, in guidebook Italian. She was fluent, but it gave her an advantage to pretend otherwise. The bookseller looked up from his ledger and then gave an exaggerated glance about him, cigarette hanging limply from nicotine-stained lips.

After an awkward moment, he blew a plume of smoke into the damp air and replied in heavily-accented English.

"Specificity is often necessary, when it comes to books. Do you have a title? An author? Even a color will do."

"Red."

"Title, author or color?" he asked, peering at her.

"Yes," she said.

The bookseller closed his ledger. He was silent for several moments. Then, he heaved himself off his stool and came around the counter. "This way," he said, a halo of cigarette smoke encircling his fraying scalp. "I remember seeing one yesterday. It might be the one you are after."

"It must be my lucky day," she said, with a smile.

He glanced at her. "Red books are the most interesting, I think. Red is a hungry color – it seizes the eye and the attentions of passersby. One cannot help but notice it."

"Is that so?"

"Red, red, red," the old bookseller continued. "The Egyptians colored their faces red for certain ceremonies. Roman generals painted their bodies red to celebrate the triumphal slaughter of victory. Here, in Venice, red was the color of wealth and power. Everywhere, red is the color of courage and sacrifice. Of blood spilled and that yet to be spilled." He glanced at her. "Did you know that Venice is the birthplace of the modern spy?"

"Is it?" Scarborough asked, politely. She had known that, in fact. It was one of the reasons Venice had so fascinated her as a child. "Parisians might argue the point."

He smiled. "You Englishmen too, eh?"

"I'm American," she corrected.

"Ah." The bookseller packed the exhalation with a lifetime's worth of scorn, pity and resignation. He gestured to a cramped labyrinth of shelves that crowded the rear of the store. Space was at a premium, and the shelves leaned against one another like drunks, threatening to spill their many burdens onto the damp Turkish carpet. The bookseller, small as he was, navigated the perilous literary canyons easily. Scarborough, somewhat taller, had to duck and squeeze to keep up.

As they passed through the shelves, she began to imagine that the store was somehow expanding around her. Her senses told her it was larger than its exterior promised; it extended back and back, into what seemed to be an infinity of rickety shelves and mildew smell. It was a trick of the space, she knew. Venetians made use of even the smallest nooks and crannies, lending a feeling of great size to small spaces.

The bookseller rounded a corner, vanished for a moment, then reappeared, gnome-like and smiling before her. "Here, I have found it I believe. A most curious volume. No title, no author. Simply a red cover." He paused, his smile slipping. His expression became uncertain. "I do not recall how it came to be here." He looked around, as if trying to find the answer among the stacks. "Which is odd, as I know where all of my books come from."

"How strange." Scarborough pulled the book off the shelf with her index finger. It wasn't large, or especially weighty. A folio volume. Discreet and tidy, with battered cover boards stained red, and its title and author faded to illegibility. She flipped through the book, noting that it was handwritten, rather than printed, like a private journal, and snapped it closed. "How much?"

There was no reply. She turned. The bookseller was gone. She smiled and hefted the book. The air felt different – colder. The trap was closing about her. She waited, book in one hand and the other in her pocket, on the letter opener. She didn't have to wait long. She heard the bell on the door ring, and the murmur of voices.

The thud of feet told her they'd split up. Circling her like sharks. She slid the book into her coat and cast about for the nearest exit. There would be a water door somewhere nearby. If she could get to it, and to the canal, maybe she could flag down a gondola.

A man appeared at the opposite end of the row. He began to shout, and she darted away, heading for the back. He pursued, but slowly, in no hurry. So did the others. She spotted the entrance to the water door, set between two shelves. She hauled at it, pleased to find it unlocked. A gust of damp air struck her full in the face. The water door itself sat at the bottom of a small set of slimy steps. She slammed the door behind her, and headed down the steps. It was dark, but she caught a glimpse of light past the water door.

The water door was locked, but it was also rotten. A few kicks and she had it open, revealing a small portico, extending away from the fondamenta to either side. There was even a gondola waiting – only it was already occupied.

A familiar figure in a vibrant red Carnival mask rose up out of the craft, flinging back the edge of his cloak. "Miss Scarborough," he said, a deep, mellifluous voice. "We meet at last. It is a pleasure." As he spoke, he gracefully disembarked and strode towards her. He carried an ornate, ruby-topped cane in one hand, and was dressed as if for a gala.

"You know my name," she said, utterly unsurprised. She glanced around, and saw that her pursuers were loitering in the doorway behind her, and on the fondamenta. No way out in either direction. As was to be expected.

"We know quite a bit about you, and your efforts on behalf of the so-called Cipher Bureau. For instance, we know about your recent escapades in Russia and that unpleasantness in Bucharest." He tapped his shoulder with his cane. "You are quite precocious."

She frowned. "Was that a compliment – or an insult?"

"Oh the former, I assure you. I am afraid you will not be making your boat to Constantinople. Take comfort that even if you had, we would have been waiting for you."

"I think they call it Istanbul now," she said.

He waved her comment aside, as if it were of no import. "You have led us quite the chase, but it is ended now."

She hiked a thumb over her shoulder, indicating the book store. "This place – it's yours, isn't it?"

"Venice is ours," he said. He gestured with his cane. "The world is not as simple as you might think, Miss Scarborough. The shadows deeper, the nights darker. There are things moving in the deep, and they are hungry. You should be thankful that we got to you first."

"And who is we?" she asked, already knowing the answer.

"We is me, and I am called *Il Cavaliere Cremisi*," he said, doffing his hat and bowing low. "That is to say, the Crimson Cavalier." She sensed the display of courtly grace was as much a mask as the one that hid his features. Silk, hiding steel.

"Evocative," she said.

"I have always thought so." He straightened and held his hat to his chest. "I am pleased to be the representative of a certain party in *La Dominante*." He indicated the book. "A party which is most interested in that book you hold."

"This book?" She held it up.

"That book."

"I bet you feel kind of dumb, hunh? It was under your nose the whole time." She couldn't help but grin. "All that running around after me, and you could have just walked in and taken it for yourself."

"It does not matter. Give it to me." He snapped his gloved fingers imperiously.

"No."

He paused, head tilted. "No?"

"You heard me."

"You have noticed, I trust, that you are somewhat at a disadvantage?" He swept his hat out, indicating the lurking presences all around. "You are surrounded. Caught fast in a trap. Surely, even American arrogance has its limits."

Scarborough looked around. "Acknowledgment and surrender are not the same thing. Why are you so interested in it?"

He paused. "What does it matter?"

"Humor me. You have me surrounded, after all."

He sighed, but she'd read him right. A man wearing that sort of outfit was incapable of resisting the opportunity to talk. "It is a danger to us, Miss Scarborough." The Cavalier tapped the ground with his cane. "A danger to all that we have accomplished thus far. What do you know about us?"

She considered lying, but decided against it. The truth was her ally here. "Not much. Hearsay, mostly. You're looking for certain … items of esoteric provenance. You call them keys, but they can be anything, including weapons and books. What we don't know is why."

"Because we are at war," he said, simply. "The keys are just that – objects which serve to open the way, or to close it. We stand at the threshold, Miss Scarborough, ever vigilant for any sign of our adversaries, who are legion. But they are clever, and they are ever in search of ways to undermine us and destroy us. That book is a weak point in our armor that they could exploit. It must be destroyed."

"I can see why you might think so," she said. "But I'm not one of your enemies. Neither is the Black Chamber."

"No. You are collateral damage." He sounded regretful, as he said it. "It is not your fault that you stumbled upon our secret. But that doesn't change what must happen."

"No, I suppose it doesn't." She paused. "Didn't you wonder where he'd gone?" she asked, tapping the book. "You searched the apartment. Looking for my contact here. The person who compiled this book on you. An empty apartment, clippings on the wall – didn't it strike you as curious?"

The Cavalier was silent. Scarborough nodded. "They were gone, obviously, and the book hidden. That was what the messages you intercepted – that we allowed you to intercept – implied." She tapped the book again. "You couldn't take the chance, could you? Someone slipping in, under your nose. Gathering all those secrets. Threatening everything your bunch has worked for, for centuries…"

"Longer," he said, softly. "We have crossed vast seas of time in pursuit of our goals. For far longer, I fancy, than you can conceive. The oldest city in your country is but an infant next to *La Serenissima*, who is herself counted a child among the great cities of this world. Cities older even than Rome itself."

"You'd be surprised as to the limits of my conception," Scarborough said. "The people I work for take the long view – positively antediluvian." She smiled. "That's why I'm here, after all. That's what all this was for."

The Cavalier twisted the top of his cane to reveal a slim blade. He drew it with a flourish and brandished it. "Enough. The book, *signora* – you can either hand it over, or I can take it from your dead hand. It is your choice."

Scarborough laughed. "Oh, have it, with my compliments." With that, she flicked the book towards him. Startled by the sudden movement, he made to slap the incoming missile aside with his sword, and gave her the opening she required. It was a simple thing to palm the letter opener and leap forward.

Even simpler, to press the sharp tip to his throat, just beneath the edge of his mask. He grunted, though whether in shock or admiration, she couldn't tell, and didn't care. The trap had been sprung. All that remained was to see which of them got out intact. "Tell your people to get back," she murmured. "I'd hate for there to be any accidents at this stage of the negotiations."

"Negotiations?" he asked, in a slightly strangled voice.

"What did you think this was? Now tell them to back off."

The Cavalier did as she bade, gesturing sharply with his hat. Slowly, the lurking figures receded into the shadows. Soon, only she and the Cavalier remained on the portico. "Good," she murmured. "Now we proceed as equals."

"The book…" he began.

Scarborough concentrated on keeping the hand holding the letter opener steady. "A fake. A very good fake. It took our best cryptographers a week to compile."

"It was never in the apartment, was it?"

"No. It's only been in that store for three days. Before that, it was in Padua." She allowed herself a small smile. "That's why you couldn't find it. It was never in the city, at least not when you were actively searching for it. Just as there never was anyone in that apartment. All this time, you've been searching for a ghost."

"Clever. But why the charade?"

"To draw you into the open."

He laughed softly. "You are an assassin, then. I warn you, I am but one man. Take me off the board, and another will replace me. This is a game you cannot win."

"We don't want to win. We just want to make you an offer." She paused. This was the most dangerous moment; the moment that made the difference between a knot unraveling and a knot tightening. She removed the blade from his throat and stepped back, conscious of the sword-cane still in his hand. He lifted it – hesitated – and sheathed it.

"An offer? What could you, or your masters, have to offer us?"

"An alliance. The Black Chamber and the Red Coterie."

"And what would this alliance of yours entail?"

"A sharing of information and resources. More perhaps, if needed." She shrugged. "We're problem solvers. And unless I miss my guess, your bunch has its share of problems, in need of solving."

He studied her for a moment, his gaze unreadable. "Why?"

She cleared her throat. "As you said, there are things moving in the deep, and they are hungry. Alone, we will surely be devoured. Together, well... maybe not." She looked up. The rain had ceased, and cold stars gleamed in the black overhead. "We know what's out there, waiting for us. And we've decided to deal ourselves in to this shadow war of yours."

"Some might call that foolhardy."

"Maybe." She hesitated. "But Benjamin Franklin once said, 'We must all hang together or surely we shall all hang separately.' I've been thinking about that a lot, these days." She swallowed. "I've seen them, fought them. I've even read their mail, once or twice. They have to be stopped. By whatever means necessary."

He was silent for a moment. Then, "There we are agreed."

"Figured we would be." She held out her hand. "How about we shake on it?"

He looked at her hand, and then at her. "This is Venice, Miss Scarborough. We do not shake hands." He took her hand, lifted the edge of his mask, bent and brushed his lips across her knuckles. "Nor do we hurry into alliances with foreign powers." He released her and stepped back. "But we are always open to the possibility of mutual profit. I will speak to my fellow Key-bearers, and the Congress will decide whether to accept your offer of alliance."

"And when will we have your answer?"

"At a time and in a place of our choosing," he said, as he stepped carefully onto the red gondola. He swept his cloak back, and picked up a pole.

"How will we know?" she called out.

"Do not worry," he said, looking back. "We will find you." Then, with a strong, sure thrust, he pushed the gondola away from the portico and began to swiftly pole away into the darkness of the city. Soon, she'd lost all sight of him.

"I bet you will," Scarborough murmured. She felt some satisfaction, as she always did, upon successful completion of a mission. She'd been sent to do a job, and she'd done it. For better or worse. She pushed her unease aside. There was a war coming. She could feel it. She wasn't sure who their enemies were, not yet. But she'd seen enough to know that they'd need all the help they could get. Even if that help took an unsettling form. Strange times made for strange bedfellows.

She pulled her coat tighter about herself. It had begun to rain again, and the night was cold. Whistling softly, she turned and started along the fondamenta.

Istanbul awaited, and she had a boat to catch.

CONTRIBUTORS

DAVID ANNANDALE is a lecturer at a Canadian university on subjects ranging from English literature to horror films and video games. He is the author of the *Marvel Untold* Doctor Doom trilogy, and many titles in the *New York Times*-bestselling *Horus Heresy* and *Warhammer 40,000* universe, and a co-host of the Hugo Award-nominated podcast Skiffy and Fanty.

davidannandale.com // twitter.com/david_annandale

DAVIDE MANA was born and raised in Turin, Italy, with brief stints in London, Bonn and Urbino, where he studied paleontology (with a specialization in marine plankton) and geology. He currently lives in the wine hills of southern Piedmont, where he is a writer, translator and game designer. In his spare time, he cooks and listens to music, photographs the local feral cats, and collects old books. He co-hosts a podcast about horror movies, called Paura & Delirio.

karavansara.live // twitter.com/davide_mana

JASON FISCHER is a writer who lives near Adelaide, South Australia. He has won the Colin Thiele Literature Scholarship, an Aurealis Award and the Writers of the Future Contest. In Jason's jack-of-all-trades writing career he has written comics, apps, television, short stories, novellas and novels. He plays a lot of *Dungeons & Dragons*, has a passion for godawful puns, and is known to sing karaoke until the small hours.

jasonfischer.com.au // twitter.com/jasonifischerio

CARRIE HARRIS is a geek of all trades and proud of it. She's an experienced author of tie-in fiction, former tabletop game executive and published game designer who lives in Utah.

carrieharrisbooks.com // twitter.com/carrharr

STEVEN PHILIP JONES has written over sixty novels, graphic novels, radio scripts and non-fiction books for adults and young adults. Steven's best known credits include the graphic novel series "H P Lovecraft Worlds," the horror-adventure comics series "Nightlinger," and the review text "The Clive Cussler Adventures: A Critical Review." A graduate of the University of Iowa, Steven majored in Journalism and Religion and was accepted into Iowa's prestigious Writers' Workshop MFA Program. A proud husband and father, Steven currently resides in northern Utah.

stevenphilipjones.com // twitter.com/stevenphilipjo1

LISA SMEDMAN is the author of more than twenty books, ranging from science fiction and fantasy novels to non-fiction histories of the Vancouver, the city where she lives. In 2004, one of her *Forgotten Realms* novels made the *New York Times* bestsellers list. She is also an accomplished game designer, having written dozens of adventures for the *Dungeons & Dragons* roleplaying game and other tabletop RPGs. She worked as a journalist for twenty-five years, and now makes her living teaching video game design at a local college.

lisasmedman.wixsite.com/author

JAMES FADELEY is a software engineer by day and a writer by night. While this sounds hectic, he has recently become a father and thus no longer sleeps. When not feeding his daughter, the milk vampire, he can be found researching topics for his next story. James is a huge fan of *Mansions of Madness* and both board and video games in general.

jamesfadeley.com // twitter.com/jamesfadeley

MJ NEWMAN is a writer and senior game developer with Fantasy Flight Games in Roseville, MN. She is the co-designer of *Arkham Horror: The Card Game*, and is an enthusiast of horror, fantasy, and romance. Her credentials include insomnia, existential dread, and jumping in fear whenever she sees a spider.

bewaretheblackcat.com // twitter.com/natsunoyoru

JOSH REYNOLDS is the author of over thirty novels and numerous short stories, including the wildly popular *Legend of the Five Rings, Arkham Horror, Warhammer: Age of Sigmar* and *Warhammer 40,000*. He grew up in South Carolina and now lives in Sheffield, UK.

joshuamreynolds.co.uk // twitter.com/jmreynolds

CHARLOTTE LLEWELYN-WELLS is a bibliophile who took a wrong turn in the wardrobe and ended up as an editor – luckily it was the best choice she ever made. She's a geek and fangirl with an addiction to unicorns, ice hockey and ice cream.

twitter.com/lottiellw